A tale of
Bone
&Steel
BOOK I

# LEGACY of BONES

## KIRK DOUGAL

Books by
**KIRK DOUGAL**

## A TALE OF BONE AND STEEL
*Legacy of Bones*
*Black Shadow Rising*
*Wings of the Storm*
*Joiner of Bones (forthcoming)*

## THE DOWLAND CASES
*Reset*
*Quest Call*
*Gemini Divided*
*The Beach (forthcoming)*

## THE FALLEN ANGELS
*Dreams of Ivory and Gold*
*Valleys of the Earth*
*The Ring of Solomon (forthcoming)*

## YOUNG ADULT
*Jacked*

I t was the eyes.

The black eyes threatened to steal his spirit, rip it from his body, and burn it to ash. That was when he should have turned down the gold, walked away from the job. He should have run when he had his first glimpse of the black eyes that emptied into a bottomless abyss. He had started running too late.

His lungs burned. His muscles ached. But he never slowed as he darted between trees, flowing from side to side so he never remained on one line of sight for long. He veered once more to the right but, this time, he stopped in the shade of a massive pine tree.

He tried to swallow, but pain shot down his throat instead. His head cocked to one side, he listened for the pounding of pursuers' steps, but all he heard was blood rushing through his ears. He took a deep breath and bit his lips against the scream that tried to escape. Fire had danced down his side, but now the pants slowed, and his racing heart did the same. His palm was wet when he wiped it across his face, but he was in control again, the terror of the attack fading. The man glanced around.

The ground he had run across continued a gentle rise, but increased in pitch as it moved into the foothills of the mountain range known as the Teeth. He grimaced as he stared. In the distance, the cone-shaped pine trees surrounding him thinned, growing sparser until they gave way to their smaller, twisted mountain cousins. Cover would not be as easy to find there.

The thought brought back memories of the men chasing him. He peered around the branches of his hiding place. The air rushed from his lungs as he watched a man dart across an opening and disappear behind a tree. A twig snapped farther to his right, and he felt the trap closing.

The young man ducked beneath the low-hanging boughs while panic clutched his body with icy fingers. He rolled until his back slammed against the trunk, the sap sticking to his blood-soaked shirt and trying to hold him close. Too late he remembered where the sword had cut through his coat. His fingers quickly told him the steel left a gash deep enough to hit bone, something that would be tough enough to heal out here in the wilderness if he could see the wound, even harder when he could not. The sweat on his forehead went cold at the thought.

Several pairs of boots stopped in view beneath the limbs, and he held his breath. It was only a matter of time now, waiting for them to duck down and drag him into the open to finish the killing.

The area fell quiet, shuffling feet and the occasional bird call the only noise. Then even that stopped as another pair walked into sight, their dark leather draining the sunlight of its warmth.

He knew who those boots belonged to, and he trembled as thoughts of the black eyes leaped into his mind. He imagined the heat behind them as they searched for some sign of where he had disappeared in the forest. The other boots moved away.

Low, guttural mumbling reached his ears. If fear had gripped his heart before, then blind terror clutched him now. He felt the search continuing for him in ways beyond sight, ways he did not understand and never wanted to know, but just as real as if the other man had knelt beneath the tree and stared him in the face. Blood-stained fingers grabbed his knife hilt so tightly his fingers turned white beneath their scarlet cover. The thought the blade may not have any effect against the searcher almost made him scream out in madness. He closed his eyes against his coming death, the black eyes racing after him in his thoughts, the abyss closing in on him.

When he awoke, night had fallen outside the tree. All the boots were gone, but he remained still, not believing they had left. After a while, he wriggled forward on his belly, each movement sending daggers of pain down his back. He stopped when he could stare out into the darkness.

He was alone. The young man stood, but nearly fell onto the pine needles, dizziness washing over his body and the world tilting beneath his feet. He breathed deep, ignoring his wound, and staggered toward the slope with his only thought to put as much distance between himself and the previous camp with the men he had been guiding. After a few steps, he bent over, hands on his knees, and emptied his stomach.

He continued walking until he stumbled from exhaustion as well as pain. Black dots swelled to the size of pools in his eyes and threatened to take away his sight. He glanced up at the moon, its pale color reminding him of the oblong boxes his employers had loaded into three high-wheeled carts. The leader had insisted on traveling cross country away from the mountainside, away from the roads onto the plains of Xenalia. He had wanted to argue, wanted to tell the man how much easier it would be to move through the city to the port and buy passage on a boat. But the man's black eyes flashed, and the large guards with the heavy-bladed swords had glared so he kept his mouth shut and led them onto the plains.

Fear kept his feet moving. Not only fear of the black-eyed man, but fear of never rising to his feet again if he fell. But eventually even that will to continue dwindled and flickered like a candle in the wind.

He stopped. Shoulder leaning against a boulder, he rubbed his eyes, chasing away the darkness with little points of light. But when he opened his eyes again, one of those points remained in the distance, dancing flames moving from side to side.

He never considered the fire might belong to the men who had tried to kill him. The light called to him like a mother to a child—urging, begging, and ordering to come near. He answered the call, shaking foot placed in front of shaking foot, stumbling until he lurched into the circle of light, falling into a group of sleeping men.

Shouts rang out, only to be answered with the ring of steel. Surprised sentries burst from their stations in the sparse trees, faces red with embarrassment, and leaped into defensive positions beside the men they were supposed to be protecting. He saw them all as shadows, fading from his sight. A sword leaped toward his chest.

aughter and voices echoed in the night, winding their way through the streets, moving around the few people walking in the semi-dark. The noise was a reminder of the people who had filled this part of the city earlier in the day as they shopped, filling their lives with the day-to-day routine the city had given them.

The figure on horseback paid no attention, angling the mount through an opening in the fence and under the sign crossing over his head. Only a bare orange hint remained in the distant sky, but the lamplighters were moving quickly down the line of posts, chasing away the night with pools of golden glow. The rider could have read the sign if he wanted, but he kept his head down, hat pulled low over his forehead, and never glanced up. He did not need to see the sign. He had known the words for the past eight years.

The rider halted the horse in the courtyard between buildings and stepped down from the saddle. A breath escaped his lips, the sigh deepening as he reached his arms over his head and then bent back.

"Trouble on the road?" The words came out of the shadows, rumbling over each other like rocks in a flow.

The rider whirled, arm outstretched with his palm facing out while his other hand jerked on the hilt of his sword. Half the steel was clear of the scabbard before he was done turning.

A figure stepped down from the porch lining the front of the house. Two steps forward its monstrous bulk reduced, shrinking to the size of a large man. A pipe bowl glowed hot as he drew in, and a wide face came into view, the bottom half covered by a black beard streaked with gray and trimmed beneath his chin. He chuckled.

"Jumpy as a recruit in his first fight. You making off with the barmaid's till, lad?"

The rider's shoulders slumped, his free arm falling to his side while the sword slid back into its scabbard.

"You startled me, Master Greenward. I didn't see you by the house." He stood straight, gathering his horse's reins, and began walking toward the barn at the back of the property. The other man fell into step beside him, towering a full head above.

"I'm no stray cat slinking through the alley, Gera," the larger man said. "It'd take a damn blind man not to see me. But you didn't answer my question. Three bells later than I expected and ready to attack a rat scampering across the barn floor. What happened?"

Gera handed Hamson Greenward, Sr., the reins and pulled back the barn door. Lantern light spilled into the yard and revealed his ripped coat, blood staining one side.

"Bloody hells!" the man said, reaching out with one hand.

"Are you hurt?"

Gera shook his head.

"It's not my blood."

Ham stared at him for a moment before leading the horse the rest of the way inside.

"Get in here and shut that door before Ella sees you. She'll skin me if she thinks you were hurt on this final trip."

Gera smiled, but quickly closed the barn door behind them. Mrs. Greenward had always treated him like a second son, but her temper was something not even her huge husband wanted to face. He turned and saw his master looking him up and down. The smile froze on Gera, however, when he noticed the concern in the lined forehead and pressed lips.

"Treblehorn's wagons were attacked on our return from Lebon." Gera yanked off his hat and slapped it across his leg. The noise made the mare jerk her head up. "We were barely out of sight of the city walls when they came running out of the trees, yelling and waving their weapons. I was happy to see that monk-and-sword banner flying when the Halon Watch came riding down the road."

"After?" Master Greenward asked. "You were attacked after you left Lebon?"

Gera nodded and turned to the saddlebags still strapped on the mare's back. He untied the nearest one and reached inside, pulling out a full purse. He bounced the bag on his palm, testing the weight, before tossing it to Greenward, the contents clinking when his master caught it.

"They didn't get anything from us except steel and blood," Gera said. "But Old Nick and one of the new guards paid for it with their lives."

Greenward rolled the purse in his wide palm, the clatter of coins filling the barn. After a few moments, he nodded and slipped it inside his jacket pocket.

"Two other merchant trains were attacked since you left," he said. "The bloody highwaymen are growing bolder." Greenward hesitated before gesturing toward Gera's left hand, the one that had been pointing toward him in the yard. "Did you need to..." The words faded away, question hanging unasked between them.

Gera shook his head.

"No. The robbers didn't really want to fight. We drove them off pretty quick. They only got Nick because he was closest to the tree line and was surprised."

"Okay," Greenward said, flipping the reins to Gera. "See to your horse, then come inside the house. Everybody's waiting."

◆ ◆ ◆

Gera walked across the yard, his arms laden with four small packages and two longer, heavier ones. He crossed the open area with a firm stride, but hesitated at the bottom porch step. His gaze dropped to the objects in his hands before he glanced up to the house again. Long moments passed while indecision fell over his face, its shadow darkening his cheeks. Finally, a great breath escaped between his lips, and his shoulders straightened. He stepped up to the porch and opened the house door.

Singing burst out with light, both washing over his body. The high-pitched voices of a woman and three girls mixed oddly with Greenward's booming bass tones. His master stood by the hearth, outlined by the fire's flames, waving his arms to lead the song. Drink sloshed over the side of his mug onto the floor, drawing giggles from the girls and a glare from the woman. As Gera kicked the door shut with his heel, a boy only a couple of years younger walked through a doorway from farther in the house. He carried a tray with a plateful of meats and cheeses, as well as a pitcher of ale.

"Thank the gods you're back, Gera," the boy said while he sat the platter on a low table. "Father was going to lead us through all the verses of 'And the King Fell Down' until you arrived."

"Yes, I heard, Bac," Gera said, fighting a growing grin. "All the dogs in Willshire are howling along in harmony outside right now."

Mock indignation spread across Master Greenward's rose-colored cheeks.

"Listen to me, you two little whelps." He paused to gulp down some more ale. "I could send you both out to the shop if you don't like the entertainment. There's plenty of work to be done out there since you've both done so bloody little the past few days."

"Ham!" the woman exclaimed. "I'll not have swearing inside my house!"

Master Greenward leaned forward and planted a quick kiss on his wife's forehead before he plopped into a nearby chair. The wooden frame groaned under the strain.

"What have you got, Gera?" Karin asked, the youngest of the Greenward children. Amlin and Erin leaned in closer as well, smiles spreading across their faces.

He smiled, but took his time laying all the packages on the table, purposely teasing the girls with his slow pace. They whispered back and forth between giggles, but none of them looked away from Gera. When he realized he could not make them wait any longer without being mean, he turned and held out three of the smaller items.

The girls ran to him and grabbed the presents. The two younger Greenwards immediately attacked the simple cloth wrappings but Amlin, the eldest, showed enough restraint to nod silently before turning her attention to the ribbon binding her gift.

Squeals caught Gera's attention, and he turned back to Erin and Karin. Both fingered matching silver rings in the shape of intertwining leaves. He laughed and nearly fell under their enthusiastic hugs. When the two girls finally let loose their lung-crushing embraces, they ran back and forth between their mother and father to show off their gifts. Ham quickly found the free vine in the rings that would allow them to be expanded as the girls grew older so they would never be too small. Gera blinked in surprise as the corner of his master's mouth tilted up when he continued his examination of the gifts.

"Thank you, Gera," Amlin said. Her voice had been soft and barely reached him, although her chair was only a few feet away. "It's the most beautiful thing I've ever been given."

Gera stared into the young woman's eyes, searching for something he hoped he would not find. His shoulders relaxed when he did not see the sadness or, worse yet, the accusation he had been worried he might see. Instead, her smile was wide and genuine. They nodded to each other at the same time, causing their grins to grow wider, happy that neither had been hurt by the way the night had played out. Gera finally glanced back at the rest of the group and caught the look passed from Ella to Ham once the parents noticed Amlin held a ring identical to her two younger siblings. He reached for the slightly larger package on the table and walked to Ella.

"Mrs. Greenward, I..." The words caught in his throat, and he stopped with a sigh. Gera gave up and handed her the gift without trying again.

Ella gave him a wink, squeezing his hand as she took the package. A moment later a giggle escaped her, and she began folding back the wrapping like her younger daughters, throwing out ridiculous guesses about what was inside. The act stopped, however, when the last bit folded back and revealed a stunning silver broach made to resemble roses and twisted vines. They appeared so real, despite the firelight reflecting off their metallic surfaces, she ran a finger over them as if to test if they were only real flowers painted.

"Gera! It's beautiful. Ham look at this work." She held the jewelry toward her husband.

"I told you she'd like it," Bac said, laughing over the sounds of his sisters begging to hold the pin. "You'd have thought he was making it for his own mother the way he slaved over the details, Father. It was the same with your present, too."

"Nothing wrong with taking pride in your craft, son," Ham said, turning the broach over with his thick fingers. "It's something it'd do you good to remember."

Gera turned away from the hurt spreading over his friend's face at the rebuke. Hamson Greenward, Jr.–Bacon, to his friends–continually reached for approval from his father, but never quite achieved it. Luckily, the behavior had not affected the boys' friendship through the years of Gera's apprenticeship with Ham.

"You may have known what everyone else was getting, Bac, but you don't know about your present." Gera laughed as he held out one of the larger gifts.

Bacon rose from his seat and walked close. Though two years younger, he was already a hand taller than Gera and would soon approach his father's height. He shook his head as he accepted the gift.

"I told you not to make me anything," he said. "You know it's not tradition to give something to the other apprentices."

"I know. Call it a present from brother to brother."

Bacon glanced sideways at Gera while he slipped the cloth off and let it drop to the floor. A moment later, his jaw threatened to do the same. He held an unstrung hunting bow, well worn, but still holding a deadly elegance in its curved lines.

"Gera," he said. "You can't give me this. It was your father's bow. It should stay in your family." Bac held it out.

"It's staying with my family." Gera paused before grinning again. "But don't make your mother mad at me by putting an arrow in your own foot."

The laugh between friends stopped when Ham's voice rode over the top of the noise.

"Apprentice Gera Staghorn." The words echoed with a formality that matched the look on Ham's face. "Is it your wish to be acknowledged as a Master Metalsmith?"

Bacon moved away as Gera turned to face his master. Though he had grown accustomed over the years to seeing the stern look Ham wore around customers and with the other nearby tradesmen, his knees trembled at the thought of years of training coming to this single point in time.

"Yes, Master Greenward."

"Then come forward and be judged."

Gera picked up the final package on the table and stepped forward. His footsteps were loud in the silence that had fallen over the others. He held his face in check, hoping to hide the emotions roiling just beneath its surface, but realizing he was probably failing miserably. His white-knuckled grip also gave away how important this moment was to him. He handed over the package with a bow of his head.

Ham's eyes widened when his practiced hands felt beneath the cloth. With a movement surprising in its dexterity, he twisted the knot open and pulled away the wrapping in the space of a breath.

All the Greenwards, with the exception of the grinning Bacon, gasped at the sight. Firelight danced along a sword blade nearly two paces long. No ripples of imperfection dimmed the surface, even down the fullers in the center of the blade. When Ham's gaze traveled up the weapon's entire length, past the guards and two-handed hilt, he gasped once more. A small replica of an anvil served as the pommel.

"Gera," Ella gasped. "It's..." She stopped when she noticed the glare from her husband.

Ham stared down the blade, even pulling it up to eye height, searching for a flaw. He abruptly dropped the tip and twirled the sword by his side with only one hand. The weapon flickered like a blade of light until he snapped it to a halt in front of his body with the tip pointed up.

"You created this in the shop?" he asked.

Gera shook his head.

"I was afraid you'd find it while I was working. I made it in the evenings at Thurl's."

Ham's eyebrows raised at the mention of his rival metal-smith's name.

"He wouldn't let that happen out of the kindness of his heart. Even if he's supposed to by the merchant's code. The cost must have been high." The comment hung between them, more question than statement.

"I worked a trade with him."

Ham stiffened, the sound of his gripping the leather hilt tighter making sweat pop out on Gera's forehead. After a few moments, his master nodded.

"Tomorrow, I'll go to the Council of Merchants and announce that I've accepted Little Tomm as my new apprentice. I'll also inform them," he hesitated for a moment before his shoulders relaxed, and he let the sword lower, "of you, Mastersmith Staghorn, and your passing of the final test."

The rest of the Greenward family rushed forward to congratulate Gera.

◆ ◆ ◆

Gera ran through a walled maze, first hedges, then wood, and finally stone. Fog drifted down the corridors and laid its touch on his sweat-drenched clothes, chilling him more than any real mist. His gaze darted from side to side in search of an opening to escape, but all he saw were barriers. He ran faster.

The wall fell away to his side, and Gera rounded a corner only to be brought up short by the sight of the Greenward house. The haze stopped before reaching the buildings as clearly as if someone had erected a giant glass pane to hold it back. The entire family stood on the porch and waved, beckoning him to join them, their mouths opening and shutting with silent shouts. He stumbled forward another step, wanting to climb the steps. But that was where he stopped. Gera stood straighter and felt his face go slack, emotion sluicing away.

This was not the first time he had come upon the scene. A few times, especially when he was younger, he had given in to his feelings and ran toward the Greenwards. But each time the fog had followed him, closing in until they were all surrounded in its clinging embrace. Even now, a few wisps crossed the invisible line and drifted into the clearing. He turned and ran farther down the passageway, the walls forming on each side of him again in the maze.

Bodies flew over Gera's head. Blacker than night, they swooped down between the barriers, diving closer on each pass. Cries rained upon him, not with sound, but beating him until he vibrated with each blow. He did not try to fight the creatures off. The one time he had attempted to before, sleep deserted him for the next three nights because of the nightmare that followed.

Gera ran. His feet pounded the unseen ground while the walls flew by, changing until they became a blur. The beast's cries changed as well. Now the screams held words, questions echoing through his body. Who are you? What do you want? What will you do? Yet, intertwined with all the others, one increased in volume until it became the only question still beating his body: Is this all there is?

Gera stumbled when he rounded another corner, and a new clearing appeared. He reached a trembling hand forward, eyes blinking in confusion. His family's cabin sat deserted in front of him, settled in the woodland scene. The maze ended here. In all the years this nightmare had haunted him, Gera always had a choice to continue or to stop, just like at the Greenward home. Tonight, however, there was no path leading off through the fog to the left. He stared at the cabin again and saw an opening on the far side.

But reaching the other passageway meant crossing the clearing.

Gera's foot rose up, almost of its own accord, and he stepped out of the haze. He glanced up when a shadow plummeted from unseen heights, black wings folded tight against its massive body. Cowering down, he threw his arms overhead in terror. Nearly on top of him, a roar beat down, contorting his body beneath the words crushing his mind.

*Is this all there is?*

Gera bolted up in the chair. His chest heaved, and he blinked before rubbing a hand across his face, palm coming away covered with sweat.

"What was that?" he mumbled, still not sure if he was awake.

"You said you wanted more," Ham said in between puffs on his pipe, "and I said I didn't think you needed more ale. But, you're your own man now." He pointed his stem to Gera's right. "Bac won't be joining you, though."

Gera turned and stared at his friend in the chair next to him. Bac sat curled up like a small child, knees somehow folded enough to allow him to sleep with his legs draped over the furniture's arm.

"He's not going to be able to move tomorrow if he sleeps like that all night," Gera said.

"He's not going to be worth a bucket of spit in the shop anyway. He'll howl every time a hammer strikes metal. I'll need to leave him in the front of the store taking orders from ladies." Ham shook his head, a frown turning his lips. "Let him sleep while we talk."

Gera's gaze fell to the floor between his feet.

"You want an answer."

"It's better if we talk about it tonight instead of over the breakfast table in the morning," Ham said. He rubbed a hand over his bearded chin, callouses rasping in the quiet. "You've already answered the first part with the ring, the three identical rings."

Gera sank lower in his chair.

"I can't marry Amlin, Master Greenward." He hesitated, waiting for the explosion he was certain would be unleashed. "She's as much my sister as Keely, maybe even more so because I've grown up with her for the past eight summers. It would feel...wrong." Gera glanced up at Ham. "Besides, she doesn't love me, either."

Ham turned to the hearth and nodded slowly.

"I thought as much. Ella must've known your answer for a while because she's been preparing me for it." He looked at Gera again. "I'm worried about what this means for my second offer."

Gera's thoughts returned to his dream, the dream he had survived for so long he no longer remembered when it had started. He knew he could be happy here with the Greenwards, just as they had made him happy since he arrived as an apprentice eight years earlier. But he knew, just as his dream had always told him, he had to discover if his life was someplace else. He had put off answering Ham's offer of partnership for several moon cycles, and now his time had run out.

"Master Greenward," he said, throat drying on the words. "I can never thank you and Mrs. Greenward enough for everything you've done for me. Bac, the girls. I can't imagine being anywhere else, but..."

Ham leaped to his feet, startling Gera into silence.

"But you've got your own damn path to follow. Is that it?"

Gera rose to his feet, hoping he would not be knocked down into the chair—or over it—very soon.

"Yes," he said. "I've got to find my own way."

Ham drew in a breath, chest thrust out and hands on his hips. He glared down at Gera for a long moment before the air escaped through tight lips.

"Spoken like a man," he said. "Fair enough." Ham paused to draw on his pipe, his gaze rising to the far wall. "You know, I was your age once, too, Gera. I had my own wanderings to see to when I thought I was old enough. My way was the army. I lived, and I saw death. I hope your path is clearer and less painful than mine." He glanced down again.

"I'd call my path anything but clear," Gera said with a snort.

"It never is when you're the one walking it. Where will you go?"

"Home, first. I haven't seen Keely for several summers. It feels like the right place to start."

"What about that brother of yours?"

Gera paused while an image of Dax rose in his thoughts.

"I'll have to see him, too, I guess."

Ham nodded.

"When I set out on my own, I thought I'd closed every door behind me. It was a long time, almost too long, before I realized that many of them were still unlocked, waiting my return." Ham waved his arm towards the front of the house. "That door's always open to you, Gera Staghorn."

Gera looked away, unwilling to let his master see his eyes glisten.

"My bed's calling," Ham said, his voice fading toward the

room he shared with Ella. "We'll talk in the morning before you leave."

Gera nodded. When he heard the door shut behind the other man, he sat down and stared into the glowing embers in the fireplace, wondering if his new path could cause him anymore pain than it had already.

era walked out of the house and stopped on the edge of the porch. He had known it would be difficult for him to say goodbye to the family, but not how hard it would be on them as well. All three girls eventually ran crying from the breakfast table. Bac sat silently in his chair, his gaze never moving from the untouched plate in front of him. Even Ella was quiet, her lie about catching a cold not fooling anyone about her sniffles.

Only Ham acted like himself. He wolfed down his breakfast like a starved man and barked at Bac to get into the shop before the day was wasted. Then the metalsmith walked out to catch the early morning news and gossip from the surrounding merchants, just as he did every day.

Gera glanced at the street as he crossed the yard to the barn behind the shop. He spotted Ham talking with a couple of the neighboring shop owners and a man seated on a four-wheeled cart. The driver was Sil Treblehorn, the merchant who owned the wagons Gera had traveled with to Lebon before they were attacked on the way home. Treblehorn was talking at a quick pace, his arms waving as he spoke. Suddenly, all four men turned and stared at Gera. He put his head down for the rest of the walk to the barn, aware of the sweat trickling down his neck.

The door opened easily under his hand, and Gera stepped into the semi-dark beyond. Thankfully, there was no need to return to his little room above the shop. He had laid his saddlebags and bedroll inside the door before going to eat his last meal with the Greenwards. He shook his head when he realized he did not remember lifting one forkful of food to his mouth. His stomach would regret that mistake before the morning grew old.

Gera led his bay gelding out of the stall and to the cross ties. Several moments passed with only the sound of the currycomb sweeping across the mount breaking the barn's silence. He turned to grab the saddle blanket and nearly jumped when he saw Bac standing beside him, the tack already in his arms.

"Bloody hell!" Gera said before laughing. "I didn't hear you come in, Bac."

"You were busy," the boy said, his words short and sharp, "and in a hurry."

Gera did not look his friend in the face while he settled first the blanket, and then the saddle onto the horse's back.

"Don't start this again," he said as he laced the cinch and then drew it tight. "You've known longer than anyone what my decision was."

"That doesn't mean I like it anymore today than when you first told me." Bacon stopped talking long enough to grab Gera by the arm and whirl him around. "Go find Father right now and tell him you've changed your mind. Tell him you want to stay and be his partner." His eyes narrowed to slits. "Unless you think that being trapped here as a metalsmith is beneath you."

"That's not it, and you know it!" Gera wrenched his arm out of his friend's hold. He took a deep breath and let it out slowly. This was no time to let his emotions run away with him. Besides, he did not want his last words to his best friend to be spoken in anger. Memories of the dream rose for a moment, peeking through the fog that followed him to the Greenward doorstep if he stayed. "I already regret my choice, but I've got to stick to the way I've chosen. For now, anyway."

"But what am I going to do without you here?" Accusation fled from Bac's voice, only to be replaced with the whining of a child. "It's bad enough being compared to someone here. Once you're gone..." His voice trailed off. "Maybe I think I'm the one who's trapped." Bac's shoulders slumped.

"They're your family," Gera said. "I'm sure everything will be fine. Before you know it, it'll be your turn to decide whether to leave or stay. I think your father might surprise you if you just talk to him and give him a chance. He probably understands more than you know." A small smile creased his lips. "But not unless you get back to the shop before he notices you're gone."

"I know, I know. Send word when you can and let me know what it's like out in the world." Bacon turned and walked to the barn door. He stopped and spoke over his shoulder without turning around. "Good luck with your own family."

Gera watched his friend leave and then returned his attention to the gelding. He hesitated when he tied down the saddlebags. They were heavier on one side because of the set of hammers and tools he had earned with Master Greenward. At least he would always have a trade to remember his time here.

This time he heard the barn door open, glancing up as Ham walked across the dirt floor with his usual flat-footed stomp, puffs of dust kicking up in his wake.

"Your Liberty Day will be half gone before you get out of here," he said, following the words with a laugh that sounded more like a bark. Gera glanced up and stared at his master. "Maybe you should stay another night," Ham continued. "Try for an earlier start tomorrow."

Gera watched the other man for a moment, looking for the hint of a lie, a reason to remain. All he noticed were Ham's eyes crinkled into lines at the corners.

"What's happened?" he asked.

"Sil told us it was you that saved the wagon train from more losses. His men told him you damn near drove off the thieves by yourself." Ham kicked his toe in the dirt. "Pretty impressive without using, you know." Red crept into his cheeks.

"Give yourself some credit, Master Greenward," Gera said. "You're the one who taught me how to use a sword." He walked to his bedroll and picked up the sword lying on top. Where the two-hander he made for Ham was long and beautiful, this weapon was short, thick, and wicked. Its pace-long blade showed scratches and nicks from plenty of use, but the edge appeared keen enough to slice parchment. He shoved the sword inside the worn scabbard and held it out. "Thank you for its use."

Ham waved his hand.

"Keep it. It served me well in the army. You can give it back whenever the need has passed." He pursed his lips. "That need may come sooner than you think. Treblehorn said he saw Crimson Guards outside the city walls with a wagon. Word is they're everywhere on the road."

Gera nodded and stared out at the sunshine.

"Staying one night won't be enough," he said after a few moments. "They're usually out for weeks at a time. I'll need to be careful when I'm on the main road."

"If you meet with a group of them Bloods on the road in the middle of nowhere, don't hold nothing back, Gera. Nothing."

He did not look at Ham.

"I won't."

"Good." Ham walked around the horse, checking the bridal, tugging at the cinch, and finally feeling the saddle. "Better let me take a look at those saddlebags. Looks like that one might slip."

Ham worked one of the leathers loose and opened a pocket. Gera could not see what he put inside, but the ring of coins tinkled in the air.

"Master…"

Ham shut him up with a raised palm.

"Fair is fair," he said. "I'll not have it said that Hamson Greenward used an apprentice for longer than called for by the tradesmen code without paying him." He pointed a sausage-sized finger at Gera's face. "Don't be afraid to punch Gassem in the nose for stealing a year of your life from you. And tell him the next time I hear he's lied about an apprentice's age, just to start him a year early, I'll look him up and do the same. You've more than earned that bit of coin in the last year. Now, get out of here, Mastersmith Staghorn, I've got work to do." Ham turned his back and stomped away before Gera could even thank him.

The young man slung his bedroll over the saddle and lashed it down before glancing around the barn one last time. Satisfied, he led his horse out into the sunshine. He mounted and gathered the reins, glancing up only when a wagon rattled to a stop in front of the shop. In it were Little Tomm, Ham's new apprentice, and his father.

Gera nodded to the youngster on the way by as he heeled the gelding into the street. He wondered if he had worn the same look of fear the day Gassem dropped him off at the Greenward's shop years earlier.

◆ ◆ ◆

Gera rode steadily to the northeast after leaving the outskirts of Willshire. A rider in need could travel the road to Milston in a little more than five days with enough fresh mounts. He would take closer to eight at the pace he chose, but the gelding would be almost as fresh when they arrived as when they left. He did not want to be stuck in Milston with a tired mount, if given a choice.

"Only the gods know what kind of greeting we're going to receive when we get home," he said as he stroked the bay's neck. "This might be a short visit."

Gera forced his mind onto other thoughts, and soon his worry melted into the ground around the horse's hooves. Meanwhile, outlying farms and fields grew farther apart until only the forest served as a border to the road.

He continued his leisurely pace, often smiling while he rode down a path of memories as real to his mind as the road beneath his horse. There was the clearing where he had taught Bacon to use his father's bow, losing more arrows at first than they found again. On farther was the area where Ham had taken the boys camping and taught them how to use the padded wooden swords they swung for lessons. Finally, he laughed out loud when he rode near the part of the woods where Bac had thought he was tracking a mule deer and stumbled upon a half-grown pack of tregboars. Luckily, they had not yet grown the hand-sized tusks they would eventually wear. Even so, Ella had been forced to throw away the shredded remains of Bacon's pants, and he had not sat comfortably for nearly a hand while the rest of the family roared at his accident.

Gera realized the memories were his means of saying good-bye, just like the party in the Greenward house the night before had been the family's way. He let the emotion roll over him, preparing him for what the next few days might bring.

The first day on the road passed without incident. Early in the afternoon on the second, Gera stopped at a stream crossing the road with a shallow ford. The gelding grazed while he munched on the last of the food Ella had prepared for him. With no inns open between Willshire and Milston, the rest of the way home he would eat highway bread, dried meat, and apples if he did not take the time to hunt.

Gera sat on the remains of a stone foundation while he ate and wondered what sort of a building had once sat there. As he rested, a feeling of peace rose from the crumbling ruins and enveloped him. His imagination wandered beneath the trees and built a story around the people who had lived in this area. He finally sighed and fed the apple core to his horse before preparing to leave. As he was stuffing the wrap back into his saddlebags, the sounds of riders approaching made him jerk around and face the road back toward Willshire. His skin went cold with the thought of who the riders might be.

"The last thing he says is to warn me about Blood patrols in the area," he muttered while grabbing the rest of his belongings off the ground, "and I'm riding around like a school boy on a family camping trip."

Gera risked one last glance to ensure he had everything, then led the bay into the forest across from the building's remains. After walking a short distance, he happened upon a dale and stopped. He turned and stared back toward the road before he nodded. Nimble fingers quickly repacked the rest of his things in the saddlebags, but curiosity had already squashed his better senses.

"Highwaymen or Bloods. I need to know who's on the road," he said, the words meant only for himself. "That's the only smart thing to do." Gera pulled some rope out of the packs and quickly tied a set of hobbles on the horse. "Be a good boy and eat some more grass while I'm gone. I'll only be a moment."

Gera knew he took a chance leaving the mount alone in the clearing. Though there was little chance of the horse being stolen this far from Willshire and off the road, the gelding would be easy prey with his forelegs tied.

Gera reassured himself as he returned through the trees. He would only be gone a few moments for a quick peek, and then he would be traveling on his way home again. But as he neared the road, his steps slowed to a gliding walk, working out what he expected to find.

*Travelers from the west will water their mounts before crossing the stream, using the shade on this side before moving on, the same as I did. They'll be looking forward, to the east, the sun falling behind their backs.*

Gera angled to the left. If he approached the riders from this side, keeping in the tree line, he would be able to see them from the rear with the sun's light helping to hide his shadow. He walked with a straight posture, moving from tree to tree, just like when his father and brothers had taught him years earlier how to hunt. If the riders remained on the road in the sunlight, he could count on them not being able to see very far into the shade beneath the trees. He concentrated on his movements, pausing at a leaf's whisper, stopping for several moments when a squirrel chattered above him. His father had been a great teacher, but it was his brother, Dax, who had been able to disappear in the trees, hiding from even the animals. His heart pounding in his chest, Gera wished for some of that ability right now.

He stopped about fifty paces west of where he had entered the tree line when he finally spotted movement on the road. Gliding to one side, he eased one eye around the tree trunk.

Gera's heart sank into his boots. Every one of the fifty or so soldiers milling around on the roadway was dressed entirely in red. Hauberks, gauntlets, clothes—even the leather wrapping on their sword hilts had been dyed. Only three patches of black interrupted the crimson on each man. Their insignia rank sat on each shoulder while the silhouette of raven on a branch watched from their left breast.

*Watching, always watching.*

Gera shuddered at the thought.

The men were from the Crimson Guard of the Sacara Institute. Formed decades before he was born as a non-aligned army with the purpose of watching over the well being of the school and its students, their reputation was not nearly as noble. Their real purpose made Gera want to dig a hole in the forest floor and disappear until they were gone.

Rough, mean-spirited laughter rang out from the soldiers and brought Gera's thoughts to the present. He watched a small knot of the men walk back to the main group from the direction of the fallen building. Gera wondered what they had found so humorous until he noticed some of them refastening their pants. He made a mental note to never sit on the stone wall again.

The Bloods parted enough for Gera to catch a glimpse of two wagon cages hitched to teams of draft horses. The interior canvas sides were rolled up so he could see they were still empty. He felt like losing his lunch at what those moving prisons meant for the children and families of Milston and other nearby villages.

Gera slowly crept away from the road and returned to his horse. On the way, he mouthed a silent prayer to the gods of the forest, thankful he was too old to take the test.

## CHAPTER 3

Sunshine poured through the branches and shined on the forest path, its rays warming the spring air with a promise of the summer yet to come. A rabbit appeared on the edge of the trail and hesitated, nose twitching. Clumps of winter fur clung to his coat and spoke of how recently the weather had finally turned fair this close to the mountains. Assured no predators lurked in the shadows, the rabbit took a small hop into the open and eagerly devoured the tender shoots on the path.

Suddenly, the animal's head shot up, blades hanging from its mouth and ears standing tall. Whiskers danced in jerking movements while his nose searched the breeze for the scent of what he had just heard. A moment later, he was gone, a flash of brown and white bounding into the safety of the underbrush, his tail the last thing to disappear from sight.

A handful of girls and an old hound walked into sight around a bend in the path. They ranged in age from the two pig-tailed girls skipping in front to the tall, almost-woman walking at the rear. Chatter and laughter shattered the stillness and drove off the rest of the timid creatures that did not possess a rabbit's keen hearing.

The group continued down the trail until the path widened at the edge of a meadow. By the end of summer, the lea would be a swaying green lake of tall grass. This early in the year, however, only the earliest of wild flowers rose above ankle height.

"Fill your baskets first. Then you'll have plenty of time to run around and play before we head back," said the young woman. The statement drew a chorus of whining before the girls spread out to pick blooms.

Keely's laughter tinkled in the air like a bell as she watched her young charges hurry to complete their duty. She was still young enough to remember whisking through her chores in order to play. Quick fingers pulled back long hair and tied it loosely at her neck, a black mane against her light-colored dress. She moved forward when she was ready, not like a cloistered city girl, but with the grace and assurance of someone accustomed to the uneven terrain of the outdoors.

The dog trailed close behind her for a while but, when it became apparent the girls would not be venturing into the woods for a hunt, he grew tired of wandering in the meadow. He found a spot near the center of the opening, made a few small circles, and dropped unceremoniously to the ground. A sigh escaped as he turned a half-roll to allow the sun to warm his belly.

"Tug, you poor old dog," Keely said between giggles at the Gassem family pet. "Have we worn you out already?" The question did not even warrant the opening of an eye from the canine.

Keely resumed her harvesting and quickly filled her basket

to the brim with a fragrant haul. She glanced at the other full bushels sitting on the ground near Tug. A quick look helped her decide they had picked enough flowers for Mrs. Reve. For as long as she could remember, the elderly woman had made traditional trains and headdresses for brides, weaving the stems into intricate patterns that made them appear to be a living cloth. But the days of her picking her own flowers had long since passed with her fading eyesight and unsteady steps. But now Mrs. Reve had asked Keely to bring her a supply for an upcoming ceremony. Convincing a few of the village's younger girls to help had been easy if the task meant leaving Milston for a little while after a long winter.

Keely glanced up when she heard the laughter from the other girls fall off, replaced by muffled squeals. It appeared three of them had become entangled while trying to dance. The resulting heap was a sight of arms and legs sticking out everywhere. Just as she was about to call out that it was time to head back to the village, foreboding floated across her thoughts like a dark cloud on a clear day.

The warning scream died in her throat as she leaped forward, a brown streak racing by her toward the girls. Tug flew along the ground with the precision of a deadly arrow, Keely following as fast as she could run in the long skirt, tongue stuck to the roof of her mouth. The dog let loose with a growl and jumped over the pile of girls. He landed on the far side, meeting a half-grown bear lumbering in from the tree line.

Screams cut through Tug's roar when the two animals met in a violent crash. Over and over they rolled in a tangled mesh of fur, fangs, and claws. Snarls mixed with the growls. Tug and the bear snapped at each other, trying to clamp their jaws around the other's windpipe in a killing strike.

Keely grabbed the nearest girl and threw her toward the center of the clearing before moving to the next. The girls appeared paralyzed by the life and death struggle just a few feet away. It took all her effort to get them moving away while they still had the chance.

The bear's savagery, probably half-starved after waking from its winter slumber, could be expected. The ferocity of the family dog shocked Keely, however. He waded into the fight with the larger predator without hesitation and, amazingly, held his own.

The clench finally broke. The two animals rolled away from each other, and Tug crouched to renew the attack. Despite his courage, he could not react in time. The bear used the opportunity to swipe with one large paw, tumbling the dog through the grass. Keely braced herself in front of the girls, their protector whining in the grass near her, and readied for the coming assault.

But the bear had seen enough. The combination of the dog and the screams convinced the poor animal he could find an easier, and quieter, meal someplace else. He roared one last time in the girls' direction, then rumbled back to the protection of the forest.

Keely sprinted to Tug's side. Her eyes opened wide at the sight of the claw marks across his ribs, peeling the skin down to the bone. Showing a burst of strength she did not know she possessed, she lifted the hound in her arms and staggered toward the path to Milston.

"Forget the flowers!" she yelled at the younger girls. "We're going back now!"

Tears filled the corners of her eyes while she walked, making it hard to see as she glanced back to look if the bear had reappeared. Her throat grew tight, and she sniffed to clear her nose. Keely's first instinct was to lie on the ground and cry, but she knew the rest of the group was counting on her to lead.

"Hold hands. Stay together in a group. A bear will only attack if you're off by yourself." She hoped none of them remembered they had all been together when the predator attacked the first time.

"Is he dead?" Sue was the next oldest of the girls and had dropped back to whisper the question. The others' stunned shock had quickly given way to sniffling and whimpering. The youngest had fallen all the way to openly crying, but they were all still moving toward Milston.

"No," Keely answered after a moment of inspection. "He's still breathing." She did not mention she felt each breath rasping with the heave of the dog's chest. Even more worrisome, Tug had not fought to be released from her hold since the initial lift.

Tears finally escaped down her own cheeks when she thought of the pet dying. When she had gone to live with the Gassems after her parents died, Tug had been little more than a pup and stayed with her many nights as she cried herself to sleep, especially after Gera was sent to his apprenticeship. Even the dog's name held precious memories for the household. When he was young, he had pulled on pants or skirts when he wanted to go for a walk. The tug was usually accompanied with a bark or whimper.

Keely lost herself in sorrow. Her love for the dog flowed through her, giving her arms strength to hold him close as she walked. Now, all she could do was wish over and over for him to feel better, to think of the day as a horrible dream that would melt away when she woke.

When her head cleared from the futile hopes, she noticed

the path widening and the forest beginning to thin. She spotted the top of the mill in the distance above the trees. The group was approaching Milston.

Keely let out a sigh of relief. Now that she was alert again, her back and legs ached from the strain of carrying the dog. She realized her previous thoughts had been a blessing. They had masked her from the exhaustion that danced along her muscles.

Tug's breaths grew quieter with each labored step. The rattling, liquid-filled gulps of air fell further apart. Sue waited until none of the other children were watching before quietly placing a hand over her own ribs. Keely nodded in reply to the unspoken questions, lips set in a pale line. Yes, Tug had probably broken his ribs in the fight.

"Damn my bloody legs," Keely hissed, causing Sue to jerk her head to the side.

Anger at her helplessness flowed through her thoughts. Why did Tug need to die? Nothing ever died at the Staghorn house when her mother had been alive. Fevers, sprains, childhood illnesses—none of them ever grew serious or lasted long once Kellin tended to the ailment. Of course, she had been unable to save herself from heartbreak when the news of Keely's father and brother's deaths reached her.

The young woman blew a soaked wisp from her face. The afternoon had grown unbelievably hot and sweat dripped from her nose and chin. Black dots swam in her eyes, as well, and her stomach boiled hot.

"Sue," she said once the group turned onto the road into Milston, "take the rest of the girls on ahead. Find Mr. Gassem and tell him what's happened."

Keely watched Sue herd the girls into a run. It was all she

could do to keep moving until they were far enough ahead to not look back before the pain and fatigue finally won the battle for her body. She staggered to the side of the road and collapsed against a tree with a groan, her legs only allowing her to slide halfway to the ground before wobbling knees gave out. Keely landed on the grass with a grunt. The spots in her eyes grew larger with each blink, dancing and diving until they covered her in black. As she slipped away, she remembered the time she had fell to the Harvest Sleep fever and lay in bed for a week with wild dreams to keep her company.

Keely surrendered to the black curtain surrounding her, wondering who was wiping her cheeks with a rough towel.

✦ ✦ ✦

Murmuring weaved in and around the images in Keely's thoughts while she dreamed. She flinched from the vivid pictures when they leaped forward and then receded slowly back into the shadows of her thoughts. War and famine passed before her eyes. Thousands of bodies lay on the ground, screaming for their own deaths. Great winged beasts dotted the sky while people scattered in terror beneath them.

More images flashed forward, but not all of them were filled with sorrow and pain. In one, a vast multitude sang and danced while they celebrated a birth, the mother standing beside a man holding the baby high. Another revealed a man with long black hair kneeling and receiving a crown. The good and the bad swayed and moved around each other in an intricate dance while she watched, appalled and fascinated at the same time.

Keely had just grown accustomed to the movement when

one bolted closer than the others. She gawked, gaze fixed on the scene. A woman walked out of an opening in the side of a massive mountain, her gown shimmering white in the sunshine against the dark stone. The figure stopped on the edge of a flat shelf, and seven black figures formed a semi-circle behind her. The woman stared out over thousands of people and received their shouts of adulation, rocking her in tribute.

She needed to be closer. Curiosity urged her to be near, then begged. The image floated toward her at the unspoken call. Keely wanted, no demanded, to see the face of this adored woman.

The figure grew larger and larger in her sight, but still she could not see the woman's face. A glimpse of a nose, a flash of skin on her cheek—all of it felt like only a drop of water to a man dying of thirst. At last, one white-clad arm rose up and moved the black hair out of the way.

Keely gasped at the face of her mother. Yet, even as she gaped in recognition, the vision changed. The face swirled, water rippling in a pond, and mixed together, swirling in a flat plane.

She tried to pull away from the faceless horror, but a stronger will held her in place. Another face rose up from the flesh, one she did not recognize, and just as quickly melted into the circling mass. Again and again, the faces rose, only to fall away. Finally, the swirling slowed, and another woman stared back at her.

Keely stumbled away from her own face.

The murmuring grew while the dream inched away. She reached out and tried to grasp it, needing answers to the sea of questions left in its wake. But the harder she lunged for the figure, the faster it flew from her unseen fingertips. Tiny pieces broke from the woman and dispersed until Keely stood alone in the darkness.

"She was probably just scared and saw what she expected to see," a woman said from the distance.

"It scared them all into seeing the same thing? You don't believe that damn story, do you, Martha?" Keely recognized George Gassem's voice as he questioned his wife. "Don't you realize what this means?" he continued. "For her? For me?"

Keely sat up and realized she was in her bed. A groan escaped as a vise pinched her temples and threatened to screw even tighter.

Martha crossed the room, her conversation with her husband abruptly finished. She sat on the edge of the bed and placed a hand on Keely's forehead. A satisfied smile swept over her face.

"You had us worried, child, but your fever's broken."

Keely opened her mouth, but only a rasping croak emerged. Martha handed her a glass of water from the nightstand, and she gulped it down.

"How long have I been asleep?" The curtains were pulled back, and she noticed it was dark outside the house.

"Since late this afternoon. When the men brought you back, you were delirious with fever. You just kept mumbling on and on in your sleep." Martha hesitated for a moment before continuing. "How do you feel now?"

"Tired. Very tired."

"Do you remember anything?" Martha glanced toward the door, but Mr. Gassem was gone.

Memories and emotion flooded back in a torrent. Keely buried her face in her hands.

"Oh, Martha. It was horrible."

Keely sobbed as the woman hugged her tight. Though the young woman kept too many memories of Kellin for anyone to replace her, Martha had become at least as loved as a favorite aunt.

"The bear charged out of the woods without any warning." She pulled away from the hug. "It was headed for the other girls. I felt so helpless...nothing I could...if Tug hadn't...you should've seen him, Martha. He ran right into that bear without even flinching. I just wish I could've carried him to town quicker. Is he..."

The click of nails on the floor interrupted Keely. A brown blur rushed through the open doorway and landed on the bed with a thump.

"Tug!" Keely exclaimed around the excited licking of the dog. She remembered the wet towel against her face and realized it must have been the pet's tongue.

"But how?" She glanced up at Martha. "I thought he was dying."

"Nobody knows how he lived," Martha said. They both jumped at the grunt from the doorway. Mr. Gassem had returned and stared at them for a moment before stomping away. "George has some ideas, but I think Tug wasn't hurt as bad as you thought." The woman finished with a smile that never reached her eyes.

Keely remembered the dog's labored breathing as she struggled to carry him home. She pushed the hound over on his side and examined where she had seen the claws had ripped hide off his ribs after the attack. Five red scars broke up his coat like furrows in a plowed field. But they were fully healed over, appearing like they had been there for at least a summer.

She glanced up again at her guardian. Martha stared at the far corner of the room and refused to return the look. Keely watched while one muscle twitched in the woman's cheek. She reached over and patted Martha on the arm and was horrified when the woman jumped at the touch.

"Martha, could you take Tug away, please? I'm sleepy again."

The woman nodded before she led the dog from the room, closing the door slowly behind her.

## CHAPTER 4

The Crimson Guard officer strode through the open gates of the compound, his long legs devouring chunks of ground despite his unhurried manner. A long red cape billowed behind him, held in place by a raven's head clasp at his throat. Troopers saluted as he crossed their paths, then hurriedly moved away before he gave them more than a cursory glance. No one wanted Lord High Commander Malich Gregol to notice them.

"Lieutenant!" he yelled at a passing junior officer. "Has Captain Randel returned from patrol?"

"Yes, my Lord. They returned a short time ago." The trooper stood straight, his eyes trying not to linger on the thin white scar blazing a path from the right ear to the corner of the mouth of his commanding officer. There were rumors about how the commander had received the scar, and from whom, but no one had been brave enough to ask.

"Tell him to report to my quarters immediately. Dismissed."

Gregol gave an indifferent gesture in answer to the young officer's salute. Nor did he wait to watch the man sprint across the parade grounds. Instead, he turned on his heel, entered the barracks, and began the walk to his room.

He ignored the hurried salutes and fleeing troopers while he pounded down the halls, his boot steps echoing off the walls. The scowl on his face, caused by the memories of his last inspection at the Greenville post, did not reflect how pleased he was with what he had seen here since he arrived. Of course, the angry stare added incentive to the troops' movements.

But his thoughts quickly moved on to more important items, nothing else breaking his concentration as he walked. So much depended on how well the plan worked here in Palamor. Many generations had sacrificed to make this moment possible for his people, and it all began at this garrison.

Gregol rounded the last corner and nearly plowed over an officer standing in the hallway.

"Come in, Captain," he said to his aide. "I just sent a trooper to search for you. I want to hear your report on the raids."

The commander walked into his room and crossed to the desk to check for messages. Finding none, Gregol settled onto a hard-backed chair, the wood creaking under his weight. During this time, Randel stood patiently at attention in the middle of the chamber.

"Report, Captain."

"Commander, after leaving Birse four days ago, the company crossed into Crandor west of Elarton. We changed into Palamoran army uniforms and completed a raid on a small village. We killed all the men and carried off a few of the women. Trackers will have no problem finding their bodies. As we left the village, we set several of the seed barns on fire. The crops in the fields have not grown enough to burn yet. The Crandori will have no choice but to think it was Palamoran soldiers who committed the attack."

Gregol studied his subordinate for a few moments, searching for some sign of pity for the farmers. He found none. A hint of a smile touched his lips.

"Seed barns? Nice touch. That'll drive those dirt eaters crazy." The smile faded. "They'll think it was the Palamorans, but will they do anything about it, Captain? By the Emperor! We've been killing the bloody cowards for nearly a cycle, and there's not been one sign of them fighting back. Not one!" He slammed his palm on the table, and the lamp on the corner teetered, but did not fall. "What'll it take to make them want revenge?"

"It's hard to start a war between two countries when one side refuses to fight, Commander."

Captain Randel's comment hung in the air and gave voice to Gregol's worst fear. Their thoughts were interrupted by a knock on the door.

"Come in," Gregol said after letting out a sigh.

The door opened and in walked the captain of the Birse garrison. From his seat, Gregol noticed a plainly dressed man, probably a merchant of some sort, standing in the hall and glancing back and forth with jerking movements.

"Yes, Captain. What is it?" After the past few days inspection, the commander was impressed with the troops' readiness. The officer should be proud of the job he had accomplished. The problem was the man knew he should be pleased and now his ego had grown to an almost insufferable size.

"Lord Commander," Captain Oswin replied with a salute,

his hand giving an extra flourish at the end. "There's a man here that I believe you should talk to. He's one of our loyal friends in Birse and gives us useful information from time to time." His grin dripped with honey as he cast a side glance at Randel. "I think you'll find what he has to say very interesting."

"All right, Captain. Show him in." Gregol's face remained blank, but his eyes shone with the promise of violence if this became a waste of time.

The townsman scurried into the room at Oswin's wave, his gaze still darting around like an animal waiting for the trap to spring. He fumbled to remove the soft formless hat, the current style of the Palamoran merchant class, and gave a quick bow.

"What do you have to tell me?" Gregol asked, the words clipped short and spit out of his mouth as if they were sour on his tongue. Like most military men, he detested the use of spies, but understood their usefulness.

"My Lord, I've been invited to a temple service," the man answered while his hat spun through clumsy fingers. "It's a service for a Draig temple."

Gregol's foot slipped off his knee and dropped to the floor. The sudden movement and noise caused the merchant to cower as if he expected to be struck. But he was not the only one to act. Randel's hand flew to his sword hilt at the mention of the name. Of all the men in the room, only Oswin remained calm. He wiped an imaginary piece of lint from his uniform sleeve.

"It's being held tonight, my Lord," the spy finished.

"Is it possible?" Randel asked, more to his commander than to the local man. "Or is it a trap to lure us into action?"

Gregol raised a single quivering finger from the chair arm, and his aide stopped the questions.

"Do you know where this...meeting...will be held?" A vein throbbed in Gregol's neck as he spoke. After the merchant eagerly bobbed his head, the officer continued with an even icier voice.

"Wait in the hall for Captain Oswin. You'll tell him exactly where this meeting is to take place. Make up an excuse if you need to, but don't go there yourself. Now leave."

The merchant bowed his head, relief flooding over his face with the end of the meeting. He backed into the hall, pulling the door shut as he left.

"How reliable is he, Oswin?" Gregol hated relying on someone else's assessment, especially the self-inflated captain, but he needed to know.

"He's always given us accurate information in the past, Commander, but he's never brought me anything this good before today."

Silence fell over the room as Gregol considered his options. Caution whispered in his ears like a lover trying to convince him to do something unwanted. However, the longer he thought about finding a group of Draig believers, the quieter the voice and the more his eyes brightened.

"Commander, should I ready the men for tonight?" Randel had been the man's aide for too long to not recognize the glint of anticipation in his eyes. He already knew what would happen tonight.

"Yes, Captain. Prepare the troops for action tonight." He paused, another thought leaping in his mind, and turned to the other officer. Gregol thought he saw a way to accomplish two goals in one night.

"Oswin, do you have Crandori uniforms ready to use?"

"Yes, Commander. We've prepared them for the raids on

this side of the border." He grinned again.

"Good. Captain Randel, you'll issue these uniforms to our men to be worn tonight. We'll use the same plan as before and change into them once we're outside Birse. Keep one large enough for me. I'll accompany Oswin while you stay here at the garrison. If this is a trap, you'll be responsible for reporting to Lord Ravenhurst. Dismissed."

◆ ◆ ◆

The sun glowed the faintest of oranges in the west as the trooper stared through the underbrush into the clearing. A little over two score of shadowy figures milled around in the deepening gloom in front of a low wooden structure. He stared and listened for a few moments before he backed slowly into the twilight beneath the trees. After a safe distance, he rose to his feet and walked back to a thin path.

He only traveled a short distance over the game trail before two hulking masses stepped from behind trunks. They did not issue a verbal challenge, but he noticed the moon's pale reflection on bare steel.

"Lead scout reporting to Lord Commander Gregol," he whispered. He continued to walk forward, his hands empty and held away from his body. It was doubtful the sentries could see him clearly in the darkness, and he did not want to be run through by his fellow soldiers.

"Pass." The two ebony shadows quickly melted into the surrounding forest.

The scout walked on in the hush of the night. Part of his mind replayed the scene in the clearing while the other half remained alert to his surroundings. The lives of his fellow soldiers might depend upon even the smallest detail in his memory.

A bridle's jingle caught his ear. He slowed and stared more intently into the murk. It was too easy to make mistakes between friend and foe in the darkness of unfamiliar territory. The scout took a handful more strides before another figure suddenly loomed in front of him. Only one man in their company could make a shadow that large.

"Lord Commander, they're gathered in a clearing about one hundred paces from the outer sentries. I don't believe it is a trap. There're only about fifty people and some of them are women and children."

"Light," Gregol ordered, his voice as soft as he could make it. Oswin brought forward a hooded lamp and opened a slit, releasing a single bar of illumination. "Show me the layout of the clearing," the commander continued.

The scout dropped to one knee and grasped a stick near his feet. Scratching quickly on the ground, he etched a rough outline of the vale he had watched. Three snaps followed, and the four pieces of the branch became the walls of the building. When the model was complete, the man glanced up at his commanding officer.

"The people were still standing in this area right here when I left, Commander. There appeared to be some sort of shallow hole or pit there, but I couldn't get close enough to see into it. Nothing else out of the ordinary. Otherwise, it could've been a woodland Temple of Light waiting for the Sentinel to begin the service."

Gregol ignored the reference to their own religion and examined the scout's rendition of the land for a few moments.

While he concentrated on his battle plan, he absentmindedly rubbed his left palm with his right thumb. The creaking of his leather gloves joined the night birds' songs.

"Trooper, you'll lead Captain Oswin around the clearing. Captain, set up defensive lines, here and here," Gregol said while tracing two lines into a wedge shape. "After I attack the front of the building, anyone trying to escape out the back will be your responsibility." He glanced up, his eyes burning with barely controlled hatred. "Remember, these animals belong to the Draig. Kill them all, or you'll answer to me."

"Yes, Lord Commander." Oswin grinned, his white teeth gleaming in the dark. "None of the dragon worshiping scum will get by us."

Gregol grunted and rose to his feet.

Whispered commands were given and repeated in hushed tones. Platoons gathered and started forward and soon reached the point where the outer sentries stood their post. The scout and Oswin left at an angle to loop around the clearing, troops trailing behind them.

Gregol watched them leave, counting slowly, his lips moving in silence. When he could not contain his excitement any longer, he moved his men forward again. More than once he glared into the dark in anger at stray noises from his men. A muffled grunt or the sound of a guardsman falling over the underbrush—the sounds screamed at him like bells sounding a warning for the Draig.

A less excited soldier would have realized it was impossible to move this many men through a strange forest in the dark without making some noise. Gregol had passed rational thought, however. His sword arm and fingers ached from the grip he held on the hilt. Blood coursed through his veins like a rampaging river, carrying the heat of his anger to every part of his body, returning to feed the flames of his heart anew.

*Twenty summers!*

It had been twenty summers since the last recorded time the Crimson Guard found a Draig congregation. Even then, the reports Gregol had read made the discovery sound like the followers had just been children playing with things that had gotten them killed. He did not relish telling Lord Ravenhurst the Draig were not gone, only in hiding.

The commander's thoughts turned back to the task at hand. He reached the tree line and peered around a trunk into the clearing. No longer pitch black, the meadow was lit by candles flickering through the open door of the building. An even larger glow rose from the pit the scout had described. Gregol watched in fascination while the remaining handful of worshipers walked across the light and then entered the structure. They chanted as they moved, mumbling in sing song, too soft for him to hear all the words. "Cleansed in fire" was a phrase that stood out, however.

A shiver traveled up his back, raising the hairs on his neck, as the last person moved inside the building. The door closed and, for a moment, silence enveloped the clearing. Then an un-dulating drone began in place of the chant, filling the area with soft, rhythmic sounds.

Gregol stepped out of the protection of the trees. He felt his troops moving with him, but his eyes never left the closed door on the church. The noise grew louder as he approached, draw-ing his lips down in response. Disgust roiled his stomach, and he almost bent over to retch. Two quick swallows stopped that need, but his skin still felt filthy, touched by the Draig mantra.

A red light at his feet finally dragged Gregol's attention away from the door. Embers glowed in the shallow pit beside him, heat rising from them in shimmering ripples. The legends were true.

"They were walking over that," a voice whispered from behind. "Bloody hell, I wonder if they were doing it barefoot, like the stories."

Gregol started to whip around at the voice, but suddenly stopped. The idea of seared flesh gave him an idea.

The commander grabbed the arm of the nearest guardsman and pulled him closer, jerking the trooper's helmet off.

"Grab six men and gather dead wood for a fire," he whispered, into the man's ear. "As much as you can carry. Send one man for oilskins from the horses."

The soldier straightened to attention when the orders were complete and then gathered the nearest men. They trotted off while Gregol's attention returned to the door.

He did not need to wait for long. The soldiers returned, their arms loaded with branches and fallen limbs. While they were stacking the wood against the door, the last man returned, two full skins in his hands. The rise and fall of the chanting masked the sounds of their preparation. A quick search revealed only windows on the rest of the walls.

The oil splashed in rhythm to the voices. As much of the temple as could be reached soon glistened with a layer of the liquid. The task almost complete, a grin spread over Gregol's face. At a different time, in a different place, he would have looked like a child about to get away with some small mischief.

The commander reached up and jerked off the green and gold Crandori officer blouse he wore. Ties hung limp in the still air as he wrapped it around the blade of his sword and doused the end with the last drops from an oilskin.

"Cleanse yourself in this, dragon spawn," he said through clenched teeth. He dipped the end into the hot coals and flames leaped up the improvised torch.

A half-dozen strides carried him to the drenched wood. Gregol stuffed his lit sword into the stack and watched the fire eat hungrily at the timber. The flames moved along the outer walls of the temple like a living being, at some points leaping forward, and at others creeping along as if hesitant to help with the deed. He stepped back as the temperature grew.

The worshipers' chants grew softer, wavering, then stopped.

"Watch the windows!" Gregol yelled, no longer concerned with quiet. "Don't let anyone slip away into the trees!"

Even as he finished the order, the door of the Draig temple flew open. An elderly man, his hair waving wildly in the heat, stared across the roaring blaze, his mouth open and eyes blinking. He wore a long vest, metallic threads in the cloth showing a winged beast in the fire's light. Gregol wondered if the man could see anything besides his outline and the flaming sword.

"Say hello to your dragonlord when you see him in hell!" the commander screamed. The priest slammed the door shut against the fire in reply.

Captain Oswin walked out of the darkness and saluted his wild-eyed leader.

"Commander, we saw the flames and feared you needed help." He paused while he glanced at the growing inferno, his smile skewed by the dancing light. "But you appear to have everything well in hand."

"I want the killings in Crandor and Palamor to increase," Gregol said, his chest heaving between breaths. "There must be open warfare between the two countries within a cycle, Captain, or you'll wish you were as lucky as those bloody damn fools in that building." He paused for a moment as part of the roof collapsed, crashing down and sending a shower of sparks skyward. "The sooner we have control, the sooner we can find out if there are anymore of these...things...around."

He stopped talking when the sounds of chanting began in the remains of the temple again. For a while, it resonated even louder than before the fire. Soon, however, screams punctuated the noise, and the troopers were forced to move even farther away from the building. The wailing abruptly ended when another large section of the temple collapsed inward, the flames welcoming the wall with a blast of heat.

Gregol remained still as the flames reached out, searching for more fuel. The wood now glowed like a smithy's furnace. Finally, the last section of the roof fell, sending another rush of air toward the stars, their pale light shimmering in the heat.

But that was not what made Gregol's skin go pale. Mixed with the wind was a screeching cry, rising and echoing off the trees before melting away in the distance.

eely left her bedroom and walked down the stairs to the kitchen. Motion in the yard caught her attention, and she paused on the landing to stare out the window. A smile crossed her face while she watched Tug wagging his tail in anticipation in the growing morning light. The grin melted, however, when she noticed the dog watched Mr. Gassem saddling a horse in front of the stable. Almost as if he felt the weight of her eyes, he turned and glanced toward the window.

She ducked behind the curtains. In the two days since the fight between Tug and the bear, Gassem had ignored her. His only acknowledgment of Keely was a nervous twitch he revealed the one time he walked past her open bedroom door and their eyes met. His actions did not bother her, however. She suddenly did not want to be near him as well.

Keely peeked around the curtain and saw the yard was now deserted. She continued down the stairs, the smile reforming as she went. Despite her protests, Martha had forced her to remain in bed the previous day. Keely had been secretly happy with the imposed leisure, her back and legs still throbbing with dull aches from carrying the dog. But she had never been one to just lie around. It was time to get back to work around the house, even if she moved a little gingerly.

"Good morning, Martha," she said as she breezed into the kitchen.

"Good morning. If you feel up to it, start on the boys' breakfasts. I want to finish cutting up these dried vegetables so I can boil them down for dinner."

Keely jumped into the chore. Martha had returned to her normal self, and the young woman was thrilled that maybe the rest of her life would return, too.

The room buzzed with activity. The two women performed an intricate weave of motion, the kind of action only accomplished by people accustomed to working side by side in close quarters over years. Soon, the odors drifting through the house accentuated the beauty of their dance. The smell also performed another duty, prompting the thumps of smaller feet on the hallway floor above and announcing the rising of the Gassem sons.

Keely retrieved a loaf of bread to make toast for the youngsters. When she reached for a knife to cut slices, Martha grasped at it at the same time. Their hands touched briefly, and pain flashed up the younger woman's arm.

"Yow!" Keely said, pulling back in shock. "Martha, why's your hand so hot?"

"Hot?" Martha asked. Her eyebrows arched. "My hand is fine." She punctuated the statement by clasping her hands together several times.

Keely paused and then forced a laugh.

"Maybe I'm more tired than I thought. I swear, it felt like you'd placed a hot poker against the back of my hand when we touched."

"Well, after the boys are fed, you can go lie down again."

The entrance of the three Gassem boys brought a halt to the conversation. The kitchen, which moments before had been a well-organized place of activity, dissolved into a whirlwind of energy. The accompanying noise only added to the chaos. Keely herded the two youngest children to the table while the oldest boy gathered plates from the cupboard. The usual grumbling about the breakfast food mingled with excited ramblings about friends and school. She smiled and nodded in all the right places, not that she was really listening. Keely was just happy life was back to normal.

A metallic crack pealed over the racket, and she whirled in time to see Martha lunging for the cooking pot. Still attached to the broken frame, the cast iron container tilted out from the hearth, threatening to spill onto the floor. The older woman reacted to save the food inside.

Martha's palms were spared the heat of the kettle by the towel in her hands. Her good fortune abandoned her after that, however. The pot's sudden stop forced some of the boiling broth over the rim, slopping onto her skin with the hiss of a snake. The sound could not drown out the woman's scream.

Keely saw red boils rising on Martha's skin as she ran across the room. After her initial shriek, the noise faded away, the woman biting her lips in pained silence, blood drizzling out and running down her chin. The two women lowered the pot to the floor together before Martha collapsed to her knees beside it.

The towel had attached itself to some of the rising skin, causing Keely's stomach to lurch when she examined the wounds. A gentle pull on the cloth made them burst as she tore it away. She glanced up when the oldest Gassem ran over to see if he could help.

"John," Keely said, "get me a bucket of cold water." She listened to whimpering rise from the two youngest children at the table. They would need to wait to be comforted.

"At least it's only my left hand," Martha said, her jaw clenched tight against the pain. "It could've been both. Dear gods, it feels like it's on fire."

Both women stopped examining the marks and glanced up at each other. One set of eyes was filled with awe, while the other reflected fear. Martha had injured the hand Keely thought felt hot earlier.

"Oh, gods," Martha whispered. "George was right." She twisted her head away and let her shoulders slump.

They jumped when the back door slammed open against its stop. Mr. Gassem rushed into the kitchen, his hair blown and wild. He glanced around the mess before returning his attention to his wife and Keely.

"They're here," he said. "The Crimson Guards are in Milston to test the children."

✦ ✦ ✦

Keely walked a few paces behind Mr. Gassem and his boys while they headed towards the village square. Too young to understand what was happening and happy school was canceled for the day, the children chattered as they moved, filling the air with questions their father ignored. Martha had decided to remain at the house, using her bandaged hand as an excuse. Keely did not understand why the woman refused to look at her as she left.

She would not admit it, but she was just as curious as the boys. Her mother was still alive, and her family was living in their forest home, the last time the Crimson Guard visited Milston, so she had never seen the testing ceremony. The rumors and townspeople gossip were enough, however.

The Crimson Guards were searching for sagias, people who could use saca. Keely had never known anyone use the power since everyone with the ability was taken to the Sacara Institute and never seen again. The official tale said the school trained the sagias to control their power and use it in a life of service. The people's stories were much more grim, including stories of murder and deceit.

Keely blinked when she realized they had reached the square. She stood near the edge of the crowd and stared at the center where Crimson Guards encircled some of the village's smaller children. Mr. Gassem continued on, pushing two of his boys ahead and dragging the youngest by the hand. Keely would have liked to be closer for a better view, but she was almost twice the age as the next child in the middle and was too old to be tested. She felt her heart skip a beat when two of the girls who helped her pick flowers were led into the circle.

"Line up, single file!" an officer yelled as he walked through the ring of guardsmen. "The quicker we get this done, the quicker we can get out of this backwater filth."

Some of the older kids helped the younger, suddenly scared, children into place. John Gassem held his youngest brother to his side, while the middle Gassem boy cried on the other side.

As soon as it was apparent the group was as organized as it was going to be, the officer waved at two troopers to approach. One of them handed him a thin piece of metal, bent in the center and resembling a collar. Both soldiers drew their swords and stepped behind the first child.

The leader reached into his belt with his free hand and withdrew a pouch. He worked a finger into the opening before letting the purse drop to the ground to reveal a gold necklace still in his hand. A large, milky white gem swung gently from the end. It was like no jewelry Keely had ever seen.

"Grab the jewel," the officer ordered the first child in line, "and leave it lay in your open palm." He yawned, letting everyone know just exactly how bored he was with this duty.

Shaking, hesitant hands reached up and let the setting rest on her hands. Anxious moments passed while the guardsmen stared at the gem. Keely thought she was the only one in the square still breathing as parents and children alike held their breath. Time slowed to a crawl while sweat took cycles, perhaps summers, to roll down a father's face. A mother prayed to every god she could remember while she stood on quivering legs.

"Nothing," the officer pronounced. "Next!"

The first child ran out of the circle to weeping, yet happy, parents while another family entered their time in purgatory. Over and over the routine continued while the group inside the ring dwindled.

After a couple score of exams, a brown-haired girl of eight or nine summers reached up to take her turn. The only noticeable reaction at first came from the child. Her eyes flew open, and her head tilted back so she stared at the sky, back bent at an angle.

Light flickered in the gem. Another quickly followed. Again.

Again. Again. Each burst of light came closer to the previous one until the gem held to a constant pale glow.

"Jen, no!" a woman screamed, as several people jumped into action.

The officer yanked on the gold chain, and the setting flew from the child's hand. It swung violently at the end of its leash, the dim light already extinguished, while his other hand shoved the blue metal at the girl's neck. It bent and conformed to her throat, the two ends meeting with a metallic click.

Jen's father ran forward, his roar echoing off the surrounding buildings. Dressed in simple farmer's clothes, he instead acted like a legendary warrior and rushed the guardsmen circle, bare hands reaching out to battle against steel. He beat the soldiers with his fists in despair, his initial challenge changing to a moan. Blow after blow rained down on his shoulders in return, finally driving him to his knees. Two of his sons rushed to his and their sister's aid, only to receive the same punishment for the attempt.

During the commotion, troopers led Jen, her body wracked with sobs, to the cage wagon on the edge of the village square and placed her inside. The two soldiers remained as sentries while the officer returned to the remaining children.

Keely gawked in horror at the punishment the guardsmen handed the girl's family. She also found herself glancing at the wagon and the lump on the floor that was the girl. She had never seen a sagia, never thought she would catch even a glimpse of one in her life. To her, saca was just a fairy tale and the Sacara Institute a place for bedtime stories when children were scared into behaving.

The commotion slowly faded. Eventually the guardsmen backed away and some of the other villagers edged forward and grabbed Jen's father and her brothers, dragging them back into the crowd. But the peaceful gathering had changed. Some of the other soldiers grasped steel in their hands now, gaze leaping around the crowd, searching for the next attack. The villagers' tone was also dark, punctuated by murmuring and angry glances. The entire area only waited for a spark to send it into a roaring inferno.

Child after child grabbed the gem, each eventually letting it go and running from the circle. Only a handful of them remained to be tested when Keely felt a shadow fall over her. She glanced over her shoulder and stared into a Crimson Guard's eyes.

"Need to test you, too," he said. "Get down there." He nudged her forward with a hand in her back.

Keely opened her mouth to speak, but shut it when the next shove was harder, forcing her into stepping forward or risk falling on her face. Several of the nearby villagers shook their heads, reaching out to stop her movement.

"She's past the age," an old woman said, gray hair twisting in the breeze. "Leave her alone." The woman received an elbow in the shoulder for the comment, knocking her back into the crowd.

Keely stumbled through the ring of soldiers, still not understanding what was happening. She turned to ask, but quickly understood why she had been chosen, despite her age.

George Gassem stood on the far side of the square, a Crimson Guard beside him, whispering into his ear.

The officer appeared in front of her, his gaze traveling down her body, lingering on her chest. After a moment, he turned to the soldier who had brought her forward.

"A fine choice, Belgius. But why in front of the town?" he asked.

"One of the villagers said to give her a try," the soldier answered with a shrug.

The officer nodded and held up the necklace.

"Grab the jewel," he said. "If you try to run, we'll kill you."

Keely raised a trembling hand, fingers closing over the milky white surface. Dazzling, blinding light flashed through her thoughts the moment her skin made contact, followed by a cavalcade of images, dancing in her mind on beautiful display. Beams of light shot between the fingers of her cupped hands, rivaling the sun in their brilliance.

The reaction of the guardsmen and townspeople was almost as spectacular. Silence fell over the crowd except for a couple of women who cried out and then fainted. The light sucked the air from the square, threatening to sear their lungs and turn them into pillars of ash, burned beneath its glare. An eternity passed before the officer, his face covered with sweat, jerked the gem from her hand. At least ten more lifetimes passed while he thrust a choker toward her neck. Only when it clicked shut did the air rush back into the area and time resume its march.

Keely sobbed as the light left her, blocked off by a towering wall in her mind. Desire shook her body. She reached out, trying to find a way around the barrier, but it was too strong to beat down, too big to avoid. Now that she knew it was there, losing the light was like having a limb cut off, the pain reminding her of what had been ripped away. She realized she was crying and opened her eyes, staring through her tears.

The officer and the other guardsmen were positioned in an arc, not looking at her, but facing the crowd. Tense moments passed, sunlight on steel glinting a warning. Slowly the officer straightened.

"No one's coming forward," he said to the soldier beside him. "I can't believe her family won't come to her aid."

The sergeant nodded, but never stopped glancing back and forth.

"Yes, sir. At least one of her parents must be a sagia for her to be this strong in saca."

"Keep a close watch," the officer said as he put his sword in its scabbard.

Keely watched him stare down at the gem as he turned to her, suddenly jerking it up to eye level. It twisted at the end of its chain, spinning with its own rhythm until he grabbed it with his other hand and stopped its movement.

"Gods," he whispered, his breath drawing short. He stared for a long time before he lowered the gem and placed it into the pouch again.

"Miss, step over to the wagon, please," he continued, his voice quiet.

Keely noticed the sergeant's head jerk around at the gentle request. She nodded and followed his gesture while he moved a step behind.

"Is there anything wrong, sir?" The sergeant stepped beside the officer as they reached the wagon.

"No. There's nothing wrong here. Disperse the crowd and send them home. There'll be no more testing today." He opened the wagon door and bowed his head slightly.

Keely felt blinded, the light still out of her reach. Her knees were weak, as well, while her head throbbed. With her thoughts screaming in warning, she walked up the two steps and into the cage.

"But, sir..."

Keely turned and watched the officer silence the sergeant with a single, wide-eyed glance.

"That's enough, sergeant," he said. "There'll be no more testing today!" Suddenly, he shook his head as if waking from a dream and stepped closer to the other man.

"She broke the eye in two, sergeant!" he continued, his voice cracking under the strain. "The only thing holding it together is the bloody damn setting."

igures darted from tree to tree, moving in the shadows with only the whisper of rustling underbrush to tell of their passing. The air hung thick, still and quiet without the birds singing, allowing the shapes to pass in silence.

A man dressed entirely in black paused at the front of the group and raised a closed fist. The motion behind him stopped immediately. He stared farther into the forest as the last of the afternoon sun broke through the leaves above and pasted a dappled pattern across his ebony skin. His hand inched toward the knife at his belt, the feeling in his stomach not allowing him to relax.

His diligence was rewarded. An armed man dressed in gray and black moved toward the hiding group, occasionally stopping to gaze at the forest surrounding him. The leader finally let out a breath before pulling his sword and waving it up and down a few times. The approaching man crouched when he noticed the motion, but then stood and quickly closed the gap.

"Lor' D'Alikar," he whispered as both men knelt at the base of a massive tree. "The Bakri are just ahead out of earshot. They're still traveling a few paces off the road and under the shade of the trees."

"Then why've you left your post, Ranger Banol?" The words rumbled through Balew D'Alikar's chest, deep enough to make the ground feel them.

"Quent found a small group of men on the road traveling toward the Bakri. There's no way they'll pass unnoticed."

Balew furrowed his forehead and concentrated on the ground by his feet. The mountain dwelling Bakri had attacked the surrounding peoples for centuries. Of course, in the legends, they did much worse than that.

"Ranger, can you and your brother warn the men before they reach the Bakri?"

"I doubt it, Lor' D'Alikar. That's why I came for you."

"Then we'll need to help them." Balew stood and faced the hidden troops. He waited only a moment before another man rose from behind a thicket of brambles and jogged forward.

"Ennis," Balew said to his lieutenant. "Some men are going to run into the Bakri on the road. The clutch will hurry forward to protect them. Send Dilane to me before you inform the rest of the troops."

"Yes, my Lord." The young man turned on his heel and waved his hands to the surrounding forest. Eight other figures quickly appeared from their hiding places and joined him. After a moment, a female warrior with long blonde hair left the group and joined the D'Alikar.

"Ranger Amathon reporting," she said, dipping her head.

"Dilane, go with Cristan to help his brother. He'll explain on the way." Balew hesitated for only a heartbeat before continuing. "Wait until after we attack the Bakri from the rear before you join the fight from the front. It's your decision how to do it best."

A grin split her face.

"Yes, Lord D'Alikar," she replied before gesturing to Cristan. They both ran off between the trees.

Ennis and the rest of the clutch of warriors walked to their commander and saluted. The lieutenant's eyes shined, and his hand remained on top of his sword hilt.

*How long did it take for me to lose that look of excitement for the coming battle? How many men had to die first?*

The questions raced through Balew's thoughts.

"Straight line spread with two-man formations," he said. "After I start the attack in the center, the two ends will curl in a closing fist. Questions?"

None of the fighters moved, their calm revealed in their silence. Ennis was the least experienced of Balew's clutch, only about six cycles. But all the rangers knew why he was second in command.

Balew trotted forward, and the group followed, stealth giving way to speed. They no longer attempted to scamper from shadow to shadow. They had an enemy to face.

Night fell under the ceiling of limbs and leaves, even though a hint of red remained on the horizon. Balew creased his forehead again as the black promised to overtake them. He was not afraid to fight in the dark, but no one was better at night battles than the Bakri. Living most of their lives in the bottomless caves of the surrounding mountains left them with the ability to see very well at night. He had successfully attacked them after dark before, but only when it was necessary, and he never looked forward to it.

Balew slowed his pace as he angled the rangers toward the road. It would do none of them any good to stumble blindly up the Bakri backs. If the Banol brothers were correct, the clutch should be nearing their enemy.

Each step dragged out as they inched forward. Balew's heart pounded in his chest. Blood coursed through his veins in rapid surges, and his muscles tingled with anticipation—anticipation that would keep him alive in battle.

"Bloody buckets," he muttered as he swiveled his head back and forth. "We should've found the cave slime by now."

"I don't hear any fighting," Ennis whispered from beside Balew's elbow. "Do you think they killed the men? Or are they waiting to ambush us?"

Movement caught Balew's attention before he could answer, and he slowed the rangers to a steady walk. A small clearing opened in the sea of trees, exposing figures milling around in the area. The sun had already blazed to its daily death behind the peaks of the Teeth, and now the D'Alikar and his clutch were completely immersed in the black of the eastern slope of the mountain range. The light from a small fire allowed them to watch the clearing activity.

The shorter, stockier Bakri removed backpacks and helped half a score of men unload what they held. The items were then repacked onto horses while rough laughter mixed easily with the banter of men. The scene could have taken place in any village marketplace.

Balew rubbed his chin while curiosity mingled with rage in his thoughts.

*Why would these men and the Bakri be trading? What was in the packs? Who were the men?*

Question after question tumbled through his mind, spinning over each other while he tried to find a connection between them. Faster they moved until they finally crashed in a roar of noise and confusion.

He watched the men prepare to leave the clearing, despite the late hour. They finished fixing loads to the pack horses and gathered lead ropes, their haste adding even more questions to the D'Alikar's list. As they filed back towards the road, one last figure stood on the edge of the forest, still talking to the Bakri leader. The conversation remained too low for Balew to hear from where he crouched in the shadows, however. After a few moments, they bowed and broke apart, the taller man walking off into the night.

Balew maintained his vigilance on the Bakri while they flopped down, lounging on the ground in small groups. He guessed they were resting before beginning the trek back to their underground homes in the mountains. While he watched, a new plan formed in his head.

The D'Alikar finally ripped his gaze from the clearing and swept the darkness surrounding him. He did not see any of his clutch but, within a few breaths, Ennis crept to his side.

"We'll wait until the other group is out of earshot, then we'll attack," he whispered into his lieutenant's ear. "Tell the troops to be ready to follow me into the clearing."

Ennis backed away silently. The moon rose into the sky above the trees, and its light rivaled the glow from the dying fire at the end of the meadow. The normal night woodland sounds floated on a cool breeze and wend their way around the low conversations of the Bakri. At a more innocent place and time, the figures could have been village boys out on a camping trip.

Balew shattered the serene setting with a roar that echoed into the night. He burst through the tree line, his black cloak flapping behind him like the wings of a demon. A moment later other parts of the forest erupted into motion as the clutch leaped out to aid their leader.

The Bakri were not defenseless foes, however. They jumped to their feet and brandished their own weapons, battle cries ringing into the night and echoing with the sounds of many more. The two sides clashed with the hatred of long enemies.

Clanging steel and screams of agony quickly replaced the shouts and filled the open area. Blood sprayed through the air like a warm mist, hilts growing slick in strong hands with no thought given to whether sweat or blood made them wet. Balew finished off one fighter and turned in time to see two more Bakri roll back into the clearing from the tree line. Dilane and the Banol twins followed them into the open area and quickly cut off their screams.

The D'Alikar did not have anymore time to observe his troops as another Bakri leaped toward his side. He swung his black blade down in time to save his hip from his opponent's steel while allowing his weight to pivot on the ball of his foot before lashing out with the other leg. He grimaced when he realized that only a few years earlier, he would have caught the smaller fighter in the head with his attack. The kick to the Bakri's chest, however, remained powerful enough to send his opponent flying backwards and off balance. Balew lunged and slashed downward even as his opponent fell. Blood flew from his sword as it continued on after contact.

The Bakri spewed curses at the D'Alikar even as his heart pumped blood out of the hole where his arm had once been attached. Ennis ended the noise by burying his weapon in the wounded fighter's back.

Silence settled over the clearing as the last of the screams died. The rangers, those who were still on their feet, remained motionless. Their eyes swept the area for more danger, but no movement continued in the trees or from the figures lying on the ground.

Balew counted the standing shadows and realized he still had all eleven members of his clutch. He would check on their wounds soon, but a relieved sigh escaped his lips.

"Ennis, two men to build up that fire and clear the area," he barked, the words clipped short and demanding action. "They may counterattack. Shieldmates, check for injuries." He knew from experience the rush of battle could sometimes keep fighters on their feet, masking the pain of wounds.

The lieutenant gave a few orders, and the group moved into action again. By the time the dead Bakri were stacked in a pile on the opposite side of the dale, the fire blazed as high as the nearest trees. Two rangers had also retrieved their horses and brought them into the light.

The flames reflected an eerie dance across Balew's body, shadows skipping along his dark skin while he rotated in a circle with his arms held out. Puckered scars reflected the light in contrast, some new and others so old he could not remember the battles where he received them. Ennis finished his examination of the D'Alikar and rubbed salve into the nick he found on the back of his leader's arm.

Balew stared around the flames at Dilane as she was inspected by another ranger. Her pale skin glowed in the light, yet she showed no hint of self-consciousness with her nudity in front of the other men. This was the life she had chosen, and she held only pride in the decision.

Seeing Dilane turned Balew's thoughts to his wife, Lizza. It had been almost four cycles since the last time he had seen her in the castle on Placado Island. He wondered how much longer it would be before he felt her warm embrace inside Netros Keep again.

"Dilane," he said while gesturing with his hand, "when you're finished, come talk to me."

Balew slipped a shirt over his head and was fastening his cloak around his shoulders when she approached. Dilane settled the faded gray and black tabard before she stopped in front of him and saluted. The embroidered black dragon on her left breast, threads frayed, stood out against the lighter field.

"Yes, Lord D'Alikar."

"What took you so long to attack from your position on the opposite side of the clearing, Ranger Amathon? Two Bakri almost escaped." Balew rose to his full height while he spoke, the flames lighting his dark eyes.

"We followed the men who left the clearing, Lord D'Alikar. I wanted to make sure they didn't double back. When I heard one of them mention Palamor and the Gap, we returned to help you." She stopped for a moment and smiled before continuing. "It was the longest I've ever heard those two brothers shut up. By the blizzards, I swear those two talk as much and say as little as any trade council I've ever sat through."

Balew ignored the barb at the Banol twins. He let the callused fingers of his right hand trail over his chin while his foot tapped a tempo in the grass.

"You're sure they're headed over the teeth into Palamor?" he asked. He waited until Dilane nodded before continuing. "Good job of thinking on your feet, Ranger. See to your duties."

She saluted and walked away, a lightness in her step. Even as she turned, Ennis approached from where he had been listening a few paces away. His eyes smoldered with heat rivaling the fire.

"I can't believe Palamorans would trade with Bakri," he said through clenched teeth. His hands closed over and over at his side until his knuckles remained white in the firelight.

"You can't let your birthplace cloud your thinking, Ennis. Once you take on the tools of the D'Alikar, you fight for all countries, not just your own. Besides, there are men, Palamoran and Grenomi alike, who would trade with demons if the price was right." He raised his right hand to stop the young man's further protests. "But I don't believe it, either. Your country has suffered as many attacks as any other from the Bakri. That's what has me so puzzled."

Both men turned and stared into the flames. Each struggled to find a solution to the question placed before them, tossing aside possible answers only to replace them with ones even less plausible. Balew finally shuffled his feet and sighed.

"This is more than we can figure out by ourselves. I meet with the other D'Alikars tomorrow night. Perhaps together we can find an answer. Until then, we follow those men."

## CHAPTER 7

Keely relaxed and let her body sway with the wagon's motion. She glanced down at Jen, the girl's head resting in her lap, and slowly caressed her hair. The terrified girl had alternately cried herself asleep and then awake since they had left Milston two days earlier. Exhaustion finally overcame the grief and cast Jen into a sound and unflinching slumber.

A particularly large rut in the road made the wagon lurch to one side. Keely could not stop her momentum before banging painfully into the bars of the cage.

"I'm sorry, Miss Staghorn," the Crimson Guard lieutenant said through the bars once his mount trotted closer to the wagon. "We're in a hurry, and this road isn't in the best shape."

"I understand," she said. She watched as he dropped back to his customary place behind the wagon. He had not let her out of his sight since they left the village.

Jen sat up with a groan and rubbed her eyes. Suddenly, her

mouth flew open, and her head jerked back and forth when she realized where she was riding. Keely thought she had the look of someone who was waking from a bad dream, only to discover the nightmare was real.

"I'm right here, Jen," she said with a small smile. "We're still on the road to Willshire with the Crimson Guard."

A lip stuck out in a pout but, for once, tears did not follow. "Aren't you scared?" Jen whispered.

"A little," Keely said, hoping her lie was believable. "Jen, did you know you could use saca?"

"No! This must be some kind of mistake, Keely. I can't walk on water or breathe fire. I'm no wizard or witch...or whatever they call me."

Keely laughed. The merry sound tinkled through the air like a fresh breeze.

"Is that what you think sagia can do?" She hesitated, suddenly realizing she also had no idea what a fully trained saca user could accomplish, either. She was relying on the same legends and old wives tales for information as the girl.

"I'll let you in on a secret, Jen, if you want me to." Keely waited until the younger girl nodded and moved closer. "You heard about the fight between the Gassem's dog and the bear?" She assumed the girl would know. That kind of news spread quickly in a small town. "I healed him. At least, I think I did. It all happened so quick, and I've never seen anything like that happen before. But the more I think about it, the more I believe that I healed Tug." She watched the other girl straighten, pulling away from her touch.

"You didn't know, either? But, you're so old."

Keely shrugged.

"I can't explain it. But these past two days...Jen, what if your mother or father were sick? Or your brothers? Wouldn't you want to help them if you could?"

Jen squinted, her face clouding over like storm clouds.

"I suppose so," she finally answered. "But what about all the stories about the Bloods...the Crimson Guards. They're supposed to be horrible. My nana and mother told me so."

"True," Keely said. "I heard the same bedtime stories growing up. But look at how they've treated us since the test. We've had plenty to eat, and they're always asking if we're comfortable, if we've got enough to eat and drink. I don't know. Maybe they're tricking us for some reason. Maybe the stories aren't true. All I know is that no one from Milston has been taken away to the Institute since before I was living with the Gassems. I can't even think of the name of the last person who was taken."

"But they beat my father and brothers!" The girl retaliated with another pout.

"Yes, they did. But they didn't kill them, and the law says they can do that for interfering in Sacara business."

The two rode in silence for a long time, Keely thinking about what had happened in the past few days, and Jen staring at the trees passing by their view. The shadows were long before the girl spoke again.

"What can we do when we're taught?" she asked.

"I don't know," Keely said. "But I can see things, sometimes. Not everyday things, either. And they come true. At least, one of them did. They're so real, it feels like I can just step out of myself and jump right into them." She paused again. "They're not all nice things, but if I know about them, then maybe I can find a way to change them."

Jen slowly nodded.

"If I really can use saca, I want to learn to fly," the girl whispered as she leaned forward. "I want to fly so I can drop eggs down on my brothers, and they wouldn't be able to catch me."

Both of them burst out laughing at the scene Jen painted in their imaginations. The Crimson Guards riding nearby all shook their heads in amazement. For his part, the lieutenant wondered if it was the first time the cages had ever heard laughter.

✦ ✦ ✦

Balew sat up in the darkness, pushing the blanket away from his face. A dusting of snow wafted down from the wool and joined its brethren on the ground. He lifted the choker in his hand and placed it around his neck again without even thinking about his actions. Only the dimmest of glows still rose from the dying fire near his feet yet, even by the pale light, he could tell he was alone.

"Strange," he mumbled while working the kinks out of his neck. "Where the bloody hells is Ennis instead of watching over me?"

He rose wearily to his feet, joints and muscles screaming protests at the movements. The last day had been hard on the old warrior. Balew and his clutch had trailed the men from the clearing and, true to Dilane's report, rode straight up the road toward the Gap. At this high of an altitude, spring had not yet gained a grip on the weather. Having grown up in the year-round warmth of Grenom, Balew had never been fond of cold weather, and it appeared his aging body liked it even less.

Of all the fighters in his clutch, only Dilane thrived in the cold. Of course, in the frozen wasteland of Faarene, these temperatures might have qualified as a warm snap. She had still been riding in short sleeves when the clutch stopped traveling for the night.

Ennis walked around the corner of the boulders and nearly dropped an armload of wood in surprise.

"Lord D'Alikar, I'm sorry. I didn't expect you to wake up from your meeting with the others so soon."

"As long as that is more wood for the fire, I forgive you."

Ennis nodded, and they spent the next few moments in silence. The lieutenant worked at rebuilding the fire while Balew draped the blanket over his shoulders. The older man finally stood and stamped his feet in the small depression in the rocks. It was not nearly deep enough to be called a cave, but he needed to make his blood start circulating again.

"Was there any news from the other four D'Alikars?" Ennis asked once the flames were climbing again.

"Kegan was as happy as a pig in slop. He and his clutch ran into a group of Bakri somewhere below us. They were outnumbered and surprised, but he waded into the fight like always. He fought them to a standstill before the Bakri ran back to their caves. At least the big bastard won't follow them underground anymore."

"How about Sanchere D'Alikar, my Lord? Is he still in the Galgoth mountains?"

"Yes, with a platoon of Xenalian soldiers. Sounds like a good thing, too. He said they've been finding larger and larger groups of Bakri."

Both men fell silent while they thought about what the news meant.

"Latham and Tagre are heading back into the southern ranges of the Teeth," Balew said after the silence had stretched to its breaking point. "They've been in Renrax getting supplies." He laughed softly. "Latham was furious because Tagre insisted on sleeping outside the city walls, even after one of the local lords invited them to stay in his halls."

"It sounds like Tagre D'Alikar still isn't happy unless he's underneath a tree someplace."

"Blood and ashes, you're right about that one, Ennis. And Latham would be happiest back in a palace with an army of servants to feed him his supper and bathe him after. They've got to be the strangest pair to hold those two swords in the history of the D'Alikars."

Ennis offered his waterskin to his commander. Balew swirled the liquid and felt chunks of ice inside before he took a drink and handed it back.

"Are we going to keep tracking the men tomorrow?" Ennis asked.

"Yes, I told my brothers we'd trail them into Palamor if we had to. We need to know the answers to this mystery." He slammed a palm on his knee. "Damn it to hell! Why would they meet with the Bakri?"

"The other D'Alikars had no answers?"

"None that we didn't think of ourselves." Balew glanced up from the flames and stared at his lieutenant. "The bones may have chosen us for this duty, but we're still just men. When it's your turn, you'll be given a great many gifts, but our brains, our ability to live and die, remains the same." He looked back at the fire. "With any luck, we'll reach the Gap by tomorrow night. At least we can stay at the Palamoran outpost there. I'm not like Tagre. At my age, I won't take offense to the offer of a fireplace and a bed."

Ennis stood.

"Well then, with your permission, Lord D'Alikar..."

"Sit down, lad, you can go to sleep in a moment. I swear you remind me more of my son every day. When Nabir was in the clutch, he would nap in the saddle if I let him." Balew lost himself in a memory for a few moments of adventures in the past. Finally, he shook his head.

"Dilane did well last night, Ennis," Balew continued. "She thought on her feet and made the right choices. When you become D'Alikar, I suggest you consider her for your lieutenant if the bones don't choose a second right away."

"Lord D'Alikar, you'll outlive me just as you have your previous seconds. You've many years of service still in front of you."

"Maybe, lad, maybe." A smile played at the corners of his mouth, but the steel in his eyes did not change as he listened to the faithful denials. "Get some rest. I'll stand watch the rest of the night while I think about the men some more. By this time tomorrow, you'll be back in your home kingdom."

irds flew into the air, startled from their roosts on the edge of the meadow. Gera rode from the shade of the game path and stopped in the afternoon sunshine. Almost three hands had passed since the young man watched the Bloods on the road to Milston. The forest route had doubled his travel time, but it had felt like the safest choice at the time for the rest of his journey.

Home. The scene in front of him no longer resembled the home from his dreams. A creek still babbled through the east end of the clearing, running past a corral missing planks and a barn badly in need of roof repairs. A log cabin sat in the middle like an uncharted island in the center of the Windward Sea. The yard surrounding it was strewn with limbs and weeds, creating a feeling of solitude and desertion.

Gera stared for several moments, searching for signs of life. Concern grew the longer he watched until he heeled the gelding to an old oak stump closer to the house. With one wary eye on the buildings, and his sword in his right hand, he dismounted and reached in between the jagged bits of wood reaching toward the sky. Cautious fingers probed for a moment before he pulled a small rock out of the depression. Relief washed over him at his father's old code. Dax had traveled to the mountains, one rock meant he planned on being gone for one hand, but that he intended to return. He sheathed his sword and stared at the house again.

"Blood and ashes," he said, not caring that his voice sounded like a trumpet in the quiet. "Mother would leave her grave and kill Dax if she saw our home now."

Gera placed his saddlebags and other belongings on the porch and went to work. First, he lashed some loose boards to the corral poles as a temporary fix and turned the gelding out with a bucket of water from the creek. Next, he checked the stalls in the barn and found at least some of them were still service-able. His mount's needs seen to for the present, he turned his attention to the cabin.

Much as he feared, the inside was as badly maintained as the exterior. Dirty pots and dishes sat all over the table while clothes lay in stinking piles on the bed and floor in his parents' old bedroom. With a few more muttered curses, he turned and walked to the main room again.

Gera flung open the board windows. Sunshine and fresh air poured into the house in a battle against the stench. He brought in an armload of firewood and soon had a blaze going in the hearth with a pot hanging over the flames. Several trips to the creek had the vessel full and approaching a boil. While he waited, he cleared the table, cringing when he discovered several empty bottles mixed in with the dirty dishes. The remains of brown liquid in the bottoms made his head spin with just a quick sniff. Gera dumped them outside before placing the bottles in a flat tub with the rest of the dirty plates and pans. By then, the water was ready, and he filled the vat so everything could soak.

Gera splashed more of the water on the floor, leaving streaks of dirt and mud in its wake. Sweat dripped from his face while he scrubbed, bruises forming on his knees and his feet falling asleep from crawling around. When he thought the floor was clean enough to pass inspection from his mother or Ella, Gera moved to the furniture. The simple wood pieces soon shined from the layer of fresh water on their surfaces.

More trips to the creek replenished the water in the pot, but he kept one bucket of cold water to rinse the dishes. Until now, Gera's entire focus had been on the duties at hand. A part of his mind wandered now, however, as he scraped old food from the plates. He remembered his days as a little boy when it was his turn to help his mother with the household chores. Dax and Ryne were older and often went off with their father on hunts or outdoor work. But with Keely still too young to be much help, he was the one left behind most of the time. The two of them had drawn close, later with his sister as well, but the division of work left him feeling as if he did not know his father and older brothers as well. Echoes of Kellin's laughter rang off the walls in his memories and, for a while, tears joined the sweat rolling down his cheeks.

By the time Gera had the cabin back into a livable condition, even for a pair of bachelors, dusk had fallen. With a glance toward the woods, he moved the gelding inside the barn before predators came out for the night. The last golden fingers of the sun disappeared below the tops of the trees as he walked out of the barn, and he stood still for a moment, taking in the sight and breathing deep. But just as quickly, his skin prickled, and the hairs rose on the back of his neck. He imagined eyes on him, and he could not feel if they were friendly. After a moment, he frowned.

"I've lived in a city for too long," he mumbled. "I'm in the Westwood after dark, and I'm not wearing a sword or even a knife." His father's voice chastised him, reminding him that a cautious woodsman was a live woodsman.

Gera made sure the latches were locked in place on the barn before walking to the cabin. His stride was long and firm, but his knees trembled with each step. Discounting bears and wolves that might be hunting, there were other predators, even more dangerous to an unarmed person, who roamed this close to the Teeth. Visions of his dreams and the flying shadows floated through his thoughts, and his gaze spent as much time on the sky as the surrounding forest.

Nothing happened, however, and soon the cabin door closed behind him. A long breath whisked between his lips followed by a laugh. Gera was still chuckling while he pulled the windows shut. He did not know which was louder, the sounds of the rusty hinges or his stomach grumbling. What little bit of odor the fresh air and his cleaning had not killed in the cabin was quickly overrun by the smell of wild turkey sizzling over the fire. It was the last of the game Gera had snared the day before and tasted like a feast with some stale bread he found in the cupboard and spring potatoes that were still sprouting wild in what had been his mother's garden.

Relief turned to contentment when he leaned back in his chair, letting his arms stretch out wide before folding in to rest on his full belly. He had barely slept the night before, knowing he would reach his home today and see his brother again. But now, relaxed and with a day to adjust to returning to where he was born, his stomach no longer fluttered with thoughts of seeing Dax. He closed his eyes for a moment and sighed.

When he opened them again, the first things he saw were the dirty dishes on the table. He stood and stacked the plate and pan before taking them to a pail of water. They were quickly cleaned, and he bent over to grab his cup.

His hand wavered and froze for a heartbeat before he continued to grab the clay mug. Out of the corner of his eye, Gera watched the candle on the table flicker, moving in the same breeze that caressed his cheek. He risked a glance at his sword leaning against the wall on the far side of the table.

Danger screamed in his ear and echoed in his mind. His heart pounded his ribs, threatening to burst. The partially open bedroom door was only two paces from his back. He knew he would never make it to the sword and turn in time to defend an attack, especially if he waited to react.

The cup shattered on the floor when Gera took a quick step to the left, feigning a rush around the end of the table. Instead, he flung himself to the right, diving across the top. He wanted to land on his shoulder on the planks and carry enough momentum to roll over to the other side. From there, he would need only one lunging step to his sword. With the table between him and whoever had climbed in through the bedroom window, he might have a chance.

Gera's tuck and roll never happened. Even as he launched himself, he felt someone else moving even faster. Something hard struck him across the back of his legs, and he lost body position in the air. He landed on the table, squarely on his chest, and the breath rushed from his lungs in an explosive whoosh. Terror gripped his thoughts.

A door opened in his mind, an opening he had only seen a handful of times before in his life. A ball of brilliant light raced into his thoughts and leaped to the rest of his body, gaining power as it flew. Time slowed, crawling so he could see the air tremor as it passed. The attacker's heartbeat pounded in Gera's ears, adding to the rhythm of his own. Beneath his sweating palms, every grain in the wood sang of a life in the forest where the world consisted of sunshine, rain, and wind.

Gera opened his eyes. Every nick and scratch in Ham's sword pulled into view, the weapon filling his vision. Without thinking, he raised his hand and reached.

The sword flew hilt first into his palm in the blink of an eye.

Rage escaped Gera in a scream, echoing off the cabin walls. He swept the blade behind him in a blind arc, the ugly blade striking something but then continuing on. The momentum of the swing allowed him to flip onto his back.

Standing above Gera was an older man dressed in the dirty greens and browns of a hunter. He was slender and at least a hand shorter, but that did not explain the haggard expression and pinched cheeks. The attacker had the appearance of someone who had witnessed more than his share of a hard life and did not know how much more he cared to see. The man was tired, weary of just being alive. Yet, there was no mistaking the deep brown hair, green eyes, and tanned skin. The attacker was his brother, Dax.

The light evaporated inside Gera, and the door in his mind slammed shut again, so tight he could not even see the outline. The anger was replaced with an icy ball that settled in the pit of his stomach, and he shuddered when he noticed the rest of his brother. The remains of an ax handle sat in Dax's hands, the white-knuckled fingers barely above the point where the sword had cleaved the wood into two pieces.

"I guess that'll be enough surprises for one night," Dax said before tossing the stub into the fireplace.

✦ ✦ ✦

"You've filled out since the last time I saw you in Willshire," Dax said as he turned from the cupboard. He cradled a full bottle of the foul-smelling liquor in his arms. "I wasn't sure it was you when I came in through the window."

"I guess a guy tends to grow up a little when you've only seen him twice in eight years." Gera said. His cheeks bloomed red when he noticed the wince the words produced in his brother. "You know what I've been doing since then. How's life been around here?"

Dax shrugged.

"About like life has always been in the shadow of the Teeth. I pick up some guide work and run trap lines for fur. A couple of years ago they had a disease run through the cow herds around Milston so there was a big demand for deer and other meat. I only need enough money to buy the things I can't kill or grow out here."

"You're not growing much by the looks of the garden."

Dax continued as if he had not heard Gera's comment.

"What money I've got left over, I usually give to Gassem for taking care of Keely. You been staying there the last few days?" He stared at the wall, looking through it to sights that were beyond anyone else. "She looks so much like mother now."

"I haven't seen her yet," Gera answered. His brother's vacant stare made his skin crawl, so he glanced at the tabletop. "I left the road outside of Willshire because a company of Crimson Guards were traveling on it. I came through the forest from the southwest."

"Makes sense," Dax said, nodding his head but still looking away. "You know, with...best to stay away from the Bloods as much as you can."

"Dax," Gera said after coughing to clear his throat. His tongue was suddenly dry, but this talk was one of the reasons why he had left the Greenwards and returned home. "That time in the shop, I said some things..."

Dax waved his hand and then gulped down more liquid from the bottle. Some of the brown juice dribbled from the corner of his mouth, and he rubbed it away with the back of his hand.

"Bah, that was a long time ago, Gera. I never blamed you for what you said. The gods know I've heard a lot worse from others around here. I couldn't expect to take care of you and Keely when I couldn't even watch out for myself." Dax hesitated, his voice dropping to a whisper that Gera suspected was meant only for himself. "Maybe that's all I ever *could* do."

Gera sat across the table from his brother and decided it was best to act as if he had not heard the last comment. It had taken him several years of growing up before he realized how badly he must have hurt Dax that day in the Greenward shop. After all, he had just lost his parents as well.

"Anyway," Gera said, "I'm sorry about what I said. I wasn't there when Father and Ryne died. Maybe if you told me..."

Scratching at the cabin door interrupted Gera.

"That'll be my roommate," Dax said, talking over the top of his brother. "Don't get too excited when you see him."

His brother stood and crossed the room to the door, taking another drink from the bottle as he went. He unbolted the latch and stepped to the side with a childlike, theatrical flourish.

Gera felt his chest go tight as a dyr padded into the light. At least, he thought the animal was a dyr, but part of him had always assumed they were imaginary beasts from bedtime stories and adventure tales.

"It's...it's a...," he stuttered.

"A dyr," Dax finished before taking another drink.

Gera stared at the animal. Twice as large as the biggest pucat he had ever seen, the dyr was the basic shape of a large predator cat, only with his head reaching to Gera's chest and weighing at least two hundred-fifty pounds. But that was where the normal comparisons stopped. Moss-colored eyes sat above a coat that was without fur, instead appearing to be more like supple leather. Also, when the beast trotted into the cabin, he had been the pitch black of a moonless night. Now, after only a few moments inside, the coat matched the light brown hue of the inner logs.

Gera rose slowly to his feet as the animal approached, uncomfortable in looking up at the bared teeth. Voices echoed in his head as if a crowd of people tried to shout from far off and memories of the nightmare and swooping black shapes suddenly flashed before his eyes. His head spun and black spots appeared in his vision. Gera finally put a hand on the table to steady himself so he would not fall over.

"Don't make any sudden moves until he gets used to you," Dax said. "You're the first person I've showed him to since I found him as a cub. I don't know exactly how he'll..." Dax stopped in mid-sentence when the dyr continued to close the gap to Gera. "Hey, this was a bad idea. Let me get between you two. He won't hurt me."

Gera raised his hand without breaking eye contact with the animal. Voices still sang their undecipherable messages, but at least the images had disappeared.

"Hot," he said, his voice cracking. "It's just so damn hot." Gera shook his head. "Stay where you are, Dax. Everything will be fine."

The beast padded to a stop less than a pace away from Gera. The dyr leaned in close, sniffing deep, the breath rustling like wind blowing through a deep canyon. Abruptly, the animal rose to its full height and yawned in his face.

"What's his name?" Gera asked, ignoring the stench of whatever fresh meat the animal had eaten for supper.

"Nava."

Gera glanced at his brother before returning his attention to the dyr.

"From the stories Father told us at bedtime when we were kids?"

"Yeah. It was the first thing that came to mind when I found him."

Gera nodded, remembering the story. A little boy had become lost in the forest while hunting. As night fell, he became frightened and began to cry, eventually praying to the god of the trees to help him find his way home. The forest god heard his pleas and took pity on the child, sending the spirit of a great warrior to be his friend and protector. They had many exciting adventures together before the boy finally returned to his parents. The warrior's name was Nava, which meant "wind."

"Thank you, Nava," Gera said as he reached up and touched the dyr on the nose. Both of them quivered at the contact. Another wave of dizziness swept over him and, for a heartbeat, the outline of the door appeared in his mind again. "I'm going to go lie down now. I can't seem to keep my eyes open." He stumbled away, dragging each foot across the floor.

Gera heard Dax mumble as he moved away.

"Blood, ashes, the whole damn bucket. I need another drink."

ax stood in front of Ham, his head only coming to the mastersmith's chest, not that the size difference mattered as the bigger man backed away from Gera's wild-eyed brother. The apprentice listened in horror at his brother's curse-laden rant, Dax's words slurring together as he spoke, and spit flying from his lips in his rage.

"I didn't know he was too young to be an apprentice!" Ham said during a lull in the tirade, putting his hands up in protest. "Gassem lied to me about his age. I'll go to the Merchant Council and renounce his apprenticeship immediately..."

He never had a chance to finish. Gera leaped forward, his face red.

"No!" he screamed, startling the two older men into silence. "Why would I want to go with you?" He stepped in front of his brother, their bodies nearly touching, his head tilted back to look him in the eye. "Bloody hell if I'll go with you! Why would I trust someone who was too much of a coward to protect Father and Ryne in battle? Did you run away and hide, Dax? Is that why you're still alive and everyone else in your group is dead? Is that why you were the only one to come back?"

An eerie light shone in Dax's eyes. His fist flashed up and struck at Gera's head with the speed of a striking snake. But even as the knuckles touched the boy's chin, the boy flew into action.

The door in his mind burst open for the first time, light and flame leaping down his body and into his arm. Gera's hand shot up, racing his brother's fist and time, and brushed Dax's chest.

The air convulsed around the brothers, then rushed out like a summer gale. Just as the hot blast reached Ham, Dax screamed and flew backward through the air. He struck the wall of the shop a few feet off the ground and slid down with a thump.

Gera bolted up in bed, head jerking from side to side in surprise. Nava lay in the open doorway of the bedroom, his tailing flicking back and forth in rhythm. A few more moments passed before Gera's chest stopped beating against his ribs and his breathing slowed. The dream was a memory he had not thought about for years, but it was understandable why it had reappeared after meeting with Dax again. Almost eight years had passed since that afternoon, but the pain was fresh in his thoughts now. A shake of his head and he slipped out of bed, dressing in a hurry with the hope the day's activities would chase away the memories.

Nava stood and stretched before silently padding to the door. Gera glanced at the table on the way by and shook his head in frustration at the sight of the empty liquor bottle. Dax must have been awake for quite a while after he collapsed in bed.

Gera opened the door and watched the dyr streak across the clearing, spooking a flock of birds from the unkempt yard as he went. He hesitated before only strapping on a large hunting knife. With what he wanted to accomplish today, the sword would be too cumbersome.

The gelding neighed as Gera entered the barn. The trip's pace from Willshire had not been harsh, so the bay appeared ready for travel if needed. The mount remained calm as he munched on some of the last old hay left in the loft. Several fresh gouges in the stall's walls spoke of a more interesting night, however.

He checked the horse's hooves for damage before pulling out a currycomb and going to work on the bay's coat. After finishing, Gera led him outside and turned him into the corral. Nava caused a few tense moments when he padded around the corner of the barn and approached the fence. The gelding neighed, a fear-filled trumpet, before rearing and then pawing the ground with a front hoof. He snorted, and his eyes went wide with white showing all around, but the warning was ignored. The dyr leaped over the top rail with ease, landing with little more than a puff of dust, and then walked closer.

The two animals froze a few paces apart, each staring into each other's eyes. Gera watched, realizing there was nothing he could do to stop an attack, while he hoped he would not be walking for the foreseeable future. After a few more moments, Nava glanced over his shoulder at the anxious horse owner, and then loped to the far end and jumped out of the corral to enter the woods. Gera was not sure what had happened between the two animals, but the next time Nava made an appearance, the horse never raised his head from grazing.

Gera dived into the day's labor, eager to lose himself in work for a while after all the tension of the previous night. He started by gathering dead limbs in the clearing and making a large pile. Just as he finished, Dax emerged from the cabin. His pale face and dark-circled eyes did not give Gera much hope, but he bit off the comments on the tip of his tongue and instead held up an ax and a scythe without a word.

Dax stared at the two implements before choosing the ax, a thin smile creasing his face. Gera suspected his brother thought it would be better to be his own tormentor as long as his head needed to suffer the sounds of chopping firewood.

Gera took the scythe to the far side of the meadow and stopped near a small pyramid of stones. He stared silently at his mother's grave, the grass and weeds waving gently in the shallow depression. The silence surrounding him was a deafening roar. When he glanced over his shoulder in Dax's direction, he was certain he caught his brother quickly looking away. Gera turned forward, and the scythe flashed in an arc. A swath of grass fell flat to the ground. A breath later the ax biting into wood was the answering call.

Gera kept up his attack on the untended yard and soon fell into a rhythm. Taking care of the area was done for practical purposes, as well as for neatness. Their father had taught his sons that a clean, wide-open area was what soldiers called a kill zone. With the yard well kept, it would be virtually impossible for a person or animal to approach the cabin unseen. Plus, it would allow someone with a bow and full quiver to unleash several arrows before an enemy reached a hiding place.

The brothers stopped briefly to eat a lunch of dried venison and apples while sitting in the porch's shade. This time also passed in silence, each Staghorn lost in his own thoughts. Gera was happy, however, their working together feeling natural and right. But he nearly broke out in laughter when he offered Dax some water to drink. The squinting eyes and wrinkled nose on his brother made him wonder if he had offered poisoned wine by mistake. Dax accepted the pitcher after a glance at the rest of the wood still to be chopped.

They maintained their pace until late in the afternoon. Gera's hands were beginning to ache from holding the strange tool, but he was glad for the muscles he built up in all the years of swinging a hammer at the Greenward shop. Even so, blisters were rising in places where calluses did not sit. He was examining his fingers when Nava suddenly broke through the tree line and streaked like an arrow across the clearing, sliding to a stop a few feet away. The last ring of metal on wood was still echoing in the air when Dax also halted his work at the abrupt entrance.

Silence fell over the area until the faint sounds of a galloping horse escaped the trail from the woods. Dax whirled and, without saying a word, placed one hand behind the other in front of his body. Gera nodded at his father's old hunting signal and sprinted into the tree line.

The young man gripped the scythe tighter, glancing to the side when Nava passed him. He ran as quickly as he could, dodging around trunks and underbrush, loping in a semi-circle towards the Milston path. With any luck, he would be behind the horse and rider when they entered the clearing.

Gera slowed his pace as he neared the trail. A large elm tree offered shelter and a good position to see the rider as they passed, so he stopped in the shade of its trunk. He closed his eyes for a moment, trying to slow his racing heart, but still holding his concentration on the approaching hoof beats.

The rider thundered by his hiding spot, never slowing his pace or glancing away from the trail. From Gera's glimpses through the trees, the traveler appeared to be a boy of about fifteen summers and dressed like a villager from Milston. Judging by the lather flying from his mount, the lad must have been riding hard for quite some time.

Gera started to slip out onto the road to follow the rider, but froze when a rumbling growl reached his ears. He had been concentrating so hard on the rider, he had forgotten about Nava. The dyr's coat had changed color to the surrounding tree bark and would have gone unnoticed if not for the warning and exposed fangs. The predator still faced down the route from where the horse and rider had appeared.

*Someone's either trailing the rider, or the boy's just the spring to get Dax in the open for the trap.*

He had no idea why someone would want to harm his brother, but he had to admit he did not know everything Dax had been up to lately.

Gera kept silent watch, waiting with his hand on the dyr's shoulder. He realized the boy must be in the clearing by now, but Dax would need to handle him on his own. A few more moments passed before three riders appeared on the shadowed path. Their long-limbed horses moved easily at a ground-eating gallop. The mounts barely earned a first glance from Gera, however, as he was too busy staring at the familiar red uniforms on the men.

The Crimson Guards rode by Gera for another fifteen or twenty paces before they halted and swung down from the saddles. From where they stood, they could see the opening in the trees to the clearing, although the cabin would still have been hidden. After a couple of quick, whispered orders from one, all three walked slowly toward the sunlight. One of them readied an arrow as they moved.

A breath stuck in Gera's throat. They could shoot from the

safety of the trees, and Dax would never know he was being fired upon until it was too late.

Gera worked his way from tree to tree in pursuit of the Bloods. Fortunately, they were not moving very fast because of their desire to remain quiet. Even so, Gera did not think he would reach them in time to stop a hurried shot. Worry for his brother made him angle to the left, picking up speed as he approached the path, desperate to gain more ground in the open.

He had closed about half the distance to the rear soldier when bad luck reared its head. A stray breeze wafted down the path toward the men and their mounts. The horses immediately snorted loudly, and one of them finally screamed.

Gera glanced to his side, but Nava was gone. He did not know when the dyr had left, but the animal was carrying out his own hunt.

The last guardsman turned to see what caused his horse to spook and stared straight into Gera's eyes. With a bloodcurdling cry, he dropped the reins and charged headlong towards the young man.

Gera stood his ground. He had faced bears and wolves by the time he was ten summers old and had been riding guard for Ham and other merchants for more than a year. He would not cow down or beg for mercy when faced with a man carrying a sword. Given a choice, however, he would have liked to hold more than a grass cutter when it happened.

Gera was vaguely aware of the forest leaping to life beside the second guardsman. Nava growled, savage and full of hate, as he attacked, teeth snapping loudly enough to echo in the forest. But Gera did not have time to watch the fight. Instead, he patiently waited in the center of the road for the charging soldier. Calm floated through his thoughts while cracks of light appeared around the door in his mind.

The guardsman began his strike with another shout. Gera feinted to the right before dropping to a knee and rolling left. A low whoosh swept past his ear as the experienced soldier almost adjusted his swing enough to score a hit. Yet, all the blade cut was air and a lock of black hair. Gera was already swinging the scythe upward in an angled arc when he completed his roll, the blade of the farming tool striking home below the left arm of his foe. With a sharper edge, the blow might have caused a mortal wound. However, the scythe was designed for mowing down grass and wheat, not cutting through a ringed shirt. Though three of the Crimson Guard's ribs broke with an audible crack, his opponent was still very much alive.

The guardsman recovered and struck down with a gasp of pain, cracking the handle in Gera's hands and knocking it to the ground. With one hand holding only a few inches of the wooden grip, he scrambled backward, searching his belt for his hunting knife with the other. The Blood sucked in a wet breath and held his left arm close to his side. A trickle of crimson appeared at the corner of his mouth, and he coughed, blood spraying in the air. With a final scream in a language Gera had never heard before, the soldier raised his sword to deliver a killing blow.

Heat exploded in Gera's chest, and the door flew open in his thoughts, flooding his insides with light. His left arm flew forward, releasing the handle fragment. Gera's eyes remained locked on the other soldier's face as the wood left his fingertips, his thoughts pushing outward.

Wind whipped the Blood's hair, and then his throat was thrust into view, his head snapping back. The sword bounced on the ground while the guardsman fell backward, almost floating to the ground in Gera's slowing view, and crumpled beside his weapon.

Time rushed back into sync and suddenly another being raced along with the light and heat in Gera's body. He tried to grab hold of the second power for a moment, but then lost control, thrown to one side.

Gera stumbled to his feet and stared down at the guardsmen. He knew the handle had left his hand, but he could not remember the feeling of throwing it. But there it was, buried in the soldier's forehead, a pool of blood already forming on the ground around the top of his skull where the tip had emerged.

He had no time to relish the victory, however. Weakness swept through his muscles now that the light was gone and threatened to turn his legs into water. He dropped to one knee and continued onto his side as a giant bee droned by overhead. Fear of the Crimson Guards gave him enough strength to raise his head in time to watch the last soldier's throat explode toward him in a scarlet spray. When the man collapsed forward, he saw Dax's silhouette in the clearing opening, still in the follow through of firing the arrow at the guardsman.

Silence filled the air as the forest held its breath, waiting for more death. After a few moments, Dax ran to Gera's side.

"Are you hurt?" he asked, his face pale and sweating. "Was I too late again?"

"I'm fine," Gera said in between gasps for breath. He tried not to think about what his brother meant by *again*. "Your last shot came just in time."

"Bloody hell, Gera!" Dax exclaimed, spit flying from his lips. "I'd have killed him sooner, but I was trying to get a shot at the first one attacking you. I thought you was dead, sure as rain. Taking on a Blood with a sword and all you had was a damn scythe! I never even saw your arm move forward when you jammed the handle into his head."

Gera glanced away, realizing Dax had been far enough away to not see exactly how he killed the first soldier.

"It all happened pretty fast," he said with a shrug. His thoughts turned to the heat and light, and his struggle to control it. He also remembered the beauty in his fingertips as the wood left his hand. He shook his head. "Did you need to kill the rider, too?"

"No, but we better get back to him. It's just a village boy with a message for me. All I got out of him before I ran to you was that he heard someone following him on the road and got scared. I don't think he knew it was Bloods."

Dax helped Gera to his feet and both brothers walked toward what was left of the soldier Nava attacked. The body appeared to have been hacked to pieces by a handful of swordsmen. The dyr abruptly appeared from the woods and loped to their sides.

Dax gave the animal a quick inspection.

"Not even a scratch," he said with a smile and a nod. "Let's gather up the rest of these weapons and go see what our visitor has to tell us. I told him to wait inside the cabin until I returned."

The sunshine in the clearing heated Dax's anger again, and he turned on Gera as they walked.

"You know that jumping three Bloods by yourself goes past courage to flaming stupidity!" he said. "At what point in your life did you think you became a master armsman?"

"I had to do something." Gera's voice was calmer, but held just as much heat as his brother's words. "You didn't know how many men were following the boy up the road. And they had a bow. Besides, I wasn't alone. Nava was there with me." He rubbed the dyr behind the ears and was rewarded with a blood-covered palm. "With his help, I was hoping to slow them down enough to give you a chance."

"Give me a chance? You were making it up as you went along. Like some damn game."

Gera shrugged.

"A game we won."

Dax threw his hands in the air and blew out a breath before opening the cabin door. A boy rose from his seat at the table when they entered. He started to speak, but all that came out were odd squeaks and gasps while his face faded pale. He stumbled backward, one hand fluttering up to point.

Gera turned to ask Dax what he had done to the boy to frighten him so much when he caught a glimpse of Nava out of the corner of his eye. The dyr was an imposing sight at any time, but even more so now. From his nose to his chest and down onto his legs, the animal was covered in guardsman blood. Gera also spotted a few bits of flesh mixed in as well.

"Dax, maybe Nava should wait outside while we talk to our guest."

"Yeah, you're probably right. His damn tongue will never move if it's stuck to the roof of his mouth. Go on to the creek, Nava. Drink some water and wash some of that blood off your body."

Nava turned to Gera. The beast appeared to be waiting for some signal, so the young man nodded his head, and the dyr left.

"Wh...wha...what was that?" the boy whispered once the cabin door was shut with Nava on the other side.

"That's one of the reasons why you never come here unless you're invited, boy," Dax said. "Now what was so hellfire important that you damn near killed yourself and your horse to tell me? I don't even know who you are."

"I'm sorry, sir," the boy said, the words tumbling out in a rush. "I'm Clark. My father is the miller in town. He sent me because they're still watching Mr. Gassem. I don't know why they're still in Milston. Nobody does. Fa says they've never stayed for more than a couple of days before now, but it's hard to know because it's been so long since they've been there. He said they act like they're waiting on someone."

Gera felt a ball of ice form in his stomach. He wanted to throw up what was left of his lunch, his thoughts already leaping down the path where he believed Clark was leading them.

"Who's waiting? What're you talking about, you mumbling idiot?" Dax asked. His patience ran even thinner with the boy's rambling.

"The Crimson Guards, sir. They've taken your sister, Keely, and another girl. They failed the test."

The ice in Gera's stomach exploded into a million cutting shards.

✦ ✦ ✦

An hour after the battle with the guardsmen, Gera, Dax, and Clark were galloping down the trail toward Milston, with Nava out in front. It had been a busy time for all concerned. The brothers had dragged the bodies of the dead soldiers deep into the woods before stripping off their clothes and leaving them for the forest scavengers. Gera quickly buried their belongings while Dax sorted through their armor and weapons. It took some coaxing from Gera, and sharp words from Dax, before Clark entered the woods where he thought Nava was lurking in wait. By the time the siblings made it back to the cabin, the somewhat less terrified boy had recovered enough to round up the guardsmen mounts and put them in the corral.

While Dax and Gera packed saddlebags with enough clothes and provisions for a few days, Clark explained what had happened in Milston. Gera became so engrossed in the boy's story, he did not comment when he noticed Dax packing several bottles of the dark liquor into a bag with rags to keep them from breaking.

"The Crimson Guards rode into Milston shortly after dawn," the boy said, slowly picking up speed as he became more excited. "It took a little time for them to get everybody together in the town square but soon enough, all the kids were in a circle." He sat a little straighter in his chair. "They didn't test me because I'm too old." He slouched again when Dax glared at him. "Anyway, the leader came out and announced that they all had to take a turn holding a necklace. And they did. For a long time, nothing happened. Each kid grabbed the necklace, and then the guardsmen let them walk out of the ring.

"About halfway through all of 'em, a farmer's daughter grabbed the jewel in the necklace. I couldn't see what happened from where I was standing, but all the sudden, her mother is screaming, and her father is running toward the circle. The Crimson Guard beat him all to...they beat him up real bad. Then they tore into two of his sons that went to help, too. They're still alive, but they're busted up real good. They threw the little girl into the wagon and started testing again."

Gera closed his eyes, remembering the sight of the cages built on top of the wagons.

"There wasn't more than a handful of kids left to test when one of the guardsmen dragged your sister down into the circle," Clark said, his eyebrows dipping together. "I don't know why they did it. She's older than me and was the oldest in the circle by at least six or seven summers. Anyway, Keely grabbed the necklace and bam! It was like someone threw a lantern into a pitch-black room. She looked like she was holding the sun in her hands, it was so bright. Then, just that quick, the light went out. The Crimson Guards stood around for a little bit, and then walked her over to the wagon, and she got in."

Gera and Dax looked at each other. Gera glanced away first, staring at the hearth.

"What happened after that?" Dax asked. The words cracked as he spoke.

"The leader came back to the circle, but something was wrong. He and a couple of the other guardsmen looked at the necklace for a little bit, and they talked. Then they called off the testing even though there were some other kids still in the circle and sent everyone back to their homes."

"The stone," Gera said. "Was the stone broken in two?" He felt Dax's gaze on the side of his face, but he ignored it.

"No, Master Gera," Clark said after thinking for a moment. "Not that I could see. But no one ever did figure out what they talked about or why they just stopped the testing like that."

"Go on, finish your story," Dax said. "Get to why you're here with Bloods on your trail."

Clark swallowed and nodded.

"The Crimson Guard put the Gassem's and Markem's houses

under watch and left soldiers at the roads on the edge of town. The wagon left with your sister and the Markem girl the next morning. They wouldn't let anyone else leave Milston for the next few days. Until this morning," Clark continued, "then it was like they didn't care who went where or why."

Dax snorted in disgust.

"Well, I guess it wasn't a trap or anything."

"Yes, but if Clark hadn't risked coming here today, they might have even more of a head start on us," Gera said, smiling at the boy. "For that, I'm grateful he did."

His brother grunted again, but did not say anything.

◆ ◆ ◆

Twilight came and left while full darkness settled on the path. A few hours of nearly conversationless riding after Clark finished his story had the trio nearing Milston. The forest soon fell back, letting the narrow trail widen into a road, and allowed pale moonlight to filter down on the silent group. Clearings sporadically appeared at the sides, often containing farmhouses. Eventually the tree line gave up the battle and surrendered completely to farm land.

Dax angled his Crimson Guard mount off the road and circled to the southwest. After skirting around the outlying homes for another few miles, he called a halt to their ride just south of the road leading to Willshire.

"I'll go into town with Clark," Dax said, his figure only a dark shadow to the others. "It's best to see if anything else has happened here before we go after Keely."

"You're right," Gera said, "but not about you going into

Milston. I'll go with Clark."

"Like bloody hell. Why you?"

Gera heeled his gelding closer.

"If I get caught, I can explain why I'd be riding into town from Willshire. What excuse would you use?" He paused for a breath. "It's you they're waiting on, Dax. You're the brother that still lives here."

"But what happens if the Bloods find you?" Dax said, dropping his voice to a whisper. "What if they force you to take the test? You know your treatment isn't going to be any better than Keely's. Maybe worse, if you believe some of the stories."

"I'm betting they can't use that amulet anymore." Gera stared in the direction of the black spot that was Clark. He leaned closer to his brother, not wanting to say too much in front of the boy. "That's why they stopped the testing before all the children were checked. The gem's broken. But even if it's not, I'm willing to take the chance for our sister. Call for Nava after I'm gone. We'll leave for Willshire as soon as I get back."

Only the stars and the moon heard Dax's mumbled curses as Gera and Clark turned their horses toward Milston.

◆ ◆ ◆

Gera and Clark rode into town at a walk. It was not late enough that entering town would normally arouse suspicion, but the streets were eerily deserted. The reason became apparent at the first crossing. A mounted squad of Crimson Guards rode down the opposing street at a trot. Some of them glanced down the road toward the pair, but no one offered a challenge.

"We must be out of the lamplight," Gera whispered. "We

can't trust on that luck again and there are bound to be more patrols. Can you get us to your house without being seen?"

"Yes," Clark answered. "We can go through alleys and between houses."

The remainder of the ride was as stressful as any time in Gera's life. Clark, however, appeared more relaxed in the familiar setting. Gera wondered if the boy understood how much danger they were in at the moment and what would happen if they were caught. His own mouth was dry, and his heart pounded at the thought. Despite a couple more close calls, the pair soon reached the Miller house without incident.

Clark led Gera to the back of the home where they tied their horses. A dim light shone through the kitchen window and promised that someone was still awake inside. But when the pair opened the back door, Mr. Miller and two men jumped in surprise from their seats at the kitchen table.

"Fire and ashes, Clark!" the elder Miller exclaimed. "You scared ten summers off my life. Would that no account drunk not even let you stay the night rather than make you ride back in the dark?" He paused when he suddenly noticed Gera standing in the doorway behind his son. "But who's this sneaking around behind you?" The man reached for the carving knife on the table, but froze when his gaze fell to the sword strapped around the outside of Gera's cloak. The other two men turned white.

"Fa, this is..." Clark began.

"Just a stranger who wanted to make sure your boy made it home, Mr. Miller," Gera said, glancing at the two men he did not know. "I'll leave you alone to entertain your visitors."

Sudden recognition flashed across the miller's face, and he smiled.

"That won't be necessary, Gera Staghorn. Kindly forgive a person who didn't see the man that a boy had become. Ashes, lad, it's been a long time, but I can still see the look of your mother in you. Ah, but here I am rambling on when I should be consoling you in your time of trouble. Has Clark had a chance to tell you what all's happened?"

"Yes, he has. I wanted to thank you for sending him with the message. I know what a risk you've taken by associating yourself with my family."

"Nonsense. There'll be no thanks asked for and none accepted in this matter. Shut the door, sit down here at the table, and have a drink with us. I owed your father my life several times over from the war. As did many of the men in Milston. I'm just ashamed I stood by and did nothing when those damn Bloods took your sister. And I'm not the only one who feels that way, too."

"You got that right, Ben," said the man beside him at the table.

Gera stared at the floorboards by his feet.

"I'll not ask anyone to sacrifice themselves. It's a family matter, and we'll see to it. But I can't stay long. I was hoping to visit the Gassems tonight, as well, before I left town. I thought they might have some more information."

"Burn my eyes, son," Ben said while one of the other men grunted. "Don't do that. The Crimson Guards have their house under guard. Same as the Markems. You'll never make it within a hundred paces of the front door."

"You won't want to be visiting them unless you're going to use that blade," one man said before grunting again. "Gassem's the one who turned in your sister to the Bloods."

Gera's blood froze, and he grabbed the back of the chair in

front of him to keep from falling.

"We don't know that, Rob," Ben said. "Not for a fact."

"Close enough for me. We all saw Gassem talking to that guardsman before he grabbed the girl and took her down to be tested. She was five summers too old to be in that circle, and you know it."

Clark's father nodded.

"I suppose it's true," he said. "Now it sounds like a patrol came up missing this afternoon, and the guardsmen have become even more skittish since then."

"They must have been the ones who followed me to your house," Clark said.

"You were followed? I'm going to put you back into short pants, you fool. I'm sorry, Gera, but he's spent too much of his life in the mill or neglecting his duties and playing Talbreath. It's addled his brain. Did they cause you much trouble?"

"A little," Gera said, "but they won't be bothering anyone else again." The words hung in the room, and the other three men blinked in surprise. "Just the same, it may not be a bad idea for Clark to ride with us as far as Willshire. He can stay at Master Greenward's house for a few days until the rest of the Crimson Guard leave Milston. Maybe we can make it look like a business trip and have him bring back some metal goods. That should throw any suspicion from your family."

"What you say makes sense, Gera," Rob said, followed by a grunt. "It might not be a bad idea to get the boy away from here for a while, Ben."

The elder Miller rubbed the back of his neck before slowly nodding.

"Yes, I know you're both right. But I don't want to need to

be the one to tell his mother about it. She's your sister, Rob. You know what she's going to say." Ben glanced up at Gera. "I trust you to see Clark to Willshire safely."

Gera felt a line of sweat form on his lip. He had never been responsible for anyone else before.

"I'll see he makes it."

Ben nodded.

"There's something else you need to know before you leave. Something's changed with the guardsmen. Over the years, we've all seen them come in, do their test, and rough up a few towns-people before going away for a few years. It's been that way since I was walking around in bare feet. But this group, they're waiting for someone, or something to happen. I don't know how, or even why, but the rules have changed, and I'm afraid what that means for a lot of people."

The older man abruptly dropped his gaze to the table and rubbed his hands together. Red crept into his cheeks and revealed a lot more about his inner fears than any words he could have spoken. After he regained his composure, he stared Gera in the eye again.

"Now look. You two be careful traveling to Willshire alone. Don't trust anyone along the road unless you know them. Maybe not even then."

"Oh, we won't be alone," Clark said, his excitement at the adventure spreading over his face. "Master Dax is waiting with extra horses outside of town."

"All hells," his father said. "Now I *am* worried. This is a hard thing to say to your face about flesh and blood, Gera, but damn it. Don't rely on him. After what happened to your father and brother, you of all people shouldn't be trusting Dax."

"That reminds me of something I'd like to ask you, Mr. Miller," Gera said.

While Clark and his uncle Rob packed clothes and food into a bag, Gera and Ben spoke quietly in one corner of the kitchen. After a short conversation in whispers, carried mostly by the older man, a white-faced Gera gathered up Clark and left Milston. He stopped on the edge of town and glanced back into the darkness, wondering if he would ever see it again.

## CHAPTER 10

The next few days were a blur for the trio as they traveled to Willshire. By rotating between the extra mounts they took from the dead guardsmen, they made much better time than normal. Eventually, however, the pace began to take its toll on beast and humans alike. Clark grew so tired, he forgot to tremble with fear every time Nava walked by him. Gera's back and legs ached from constantly being in the saddle. The dark circles on Dax's face expanded until they looked like half-healed black eyes. Even the seemingly inexhaustible dyr began to lie down during brief rest stops to change horses.

"I'd go faster if I thought I could push us some more," Dax confided to Gera during one such break. "But if one of the horses breaks down, we could be in real trouble. Bah! Maybe I'm just stalling because I don't know what we're going to do when we catch the wagon."

Gera was stunned by Dax's honesty, wondering how much

of his brother's opening up was just exhaustion. But he kept his mouth shut. Memories of his whispered conversation with Mr. Miller also clouded his thoughts.

The group pushed on at breakneck speed, rising with the sun and remaining in the saddle until well after its light faded in the west. With every stride, however, questions hung over Gera's head like an executioner's ax. Was Keely uninjured? Was she still alive? Do all captives go directly to the Sacara Institute? What really happened to them once they arrived at the school?

All these questions, and many more, tumbled through his thoughts in rhythm with the hooves beneath their mounts. The answers he imagined became increasingly frightening with every galloping stride.

On the fourth day, the inevitable finally happened, just as Dax had feared. As dusk approached, the trio were making a last push to cover a few more miles before it became too dark to see the road clearly. A bird, likely spooked by the thundering hooves, flushed from the undergrowth in the face of Clark's horse. When the startled mount shied to the left, Clark reacted slowly and flew from the saddle.

Gera brought his gelding and the extra horses to a stop before trotting back to where the boy lay in the roadway. Dax continued in pursuit after the spooked mare while Gera dismounted and helped a struggling Clark to sit. The boy was biting his lip and wincing every time he moved.

"Slow down and let me look at you before you try to get up," Gera said. "I've taken a tumble or two off of horses, and I can guess what that one felt like."

"I'll be fine," Clark said, his teeth still clenched tight. "I just need to catch my breath. I won't slow you and your brother down on your trip, Master Gera."

"Yes, I know. Now, just humor an old nursemaid then." He hoped his smile hid the worry dancing through his thoughts.

He spent the next several moments running his hands over Clark. Some touches brought more winces, while others drew muffled yelps. By the time Dax rode out of the deepening darkness, he had finished his impromptu examination.

"How bad is it?" Dax asked, only staring at Gera as if Clark could not hear what he asked.

Gera glared before replying.

"He's got some bruised ribs, a jammed shoulder, a nasty knot on his head, and a bunch of minor cuts. At least there aren't any broken bones. He should be able to ride in the morning, but I doubt it'll be with any speed. How's his horse?"

"Looks like they'll be moving at the same pace," Dax said. "The mare's foreleg isn't broken, but she's already starting to favor it. We won't be able to tell if there's any heat or swelling in the leg until she cools down from the ride. You walk the horses out, and then make camp while I scout the area."

Dax disappeared into the surrounding woods, and Gera got to work while Clark sat on the ground, leaning awkwardly against a tree. Before long, the horses grazed on a picket line along the roadway, and a campfire burned bright in the deepening twilight. Gera had just started rummaging through the saddlebags when, out of the corner of his eye, he noticed Nava raise his head and peer into the darkness. Without another thought, Gera stepped out of the firelight and blended into the black beneath the trees. Before moving any farther, he noted the breeze direction and where the dyr stared.

The young man circled out and approached the campsite

from a different bearing. As he neared the edge of the trees again, he saw Clark still dozing beside the fire, oblivious to his leaving. He also noticed Nava was no longer within the circle of light. Suddenly, like an arrow striking an unsuspecting deer, a single clear thought leaped into Gera's mind.

*Left!*

Gera dropped to one knee and reached back for the shadow rushing toward him. His abrupt movement caught the ambusher by surprise, widespread arms catching nothing but air. Gera allowed the figure's momentum to carry them up and over his head, pushing them forward and to the side, before tumbling into the firelight. Clark jerked awake when Dax rolled to a stop near his feet.

"You think I'd learn my lesson by now," Dax mumbled as he rose to a knee, brushing dirt off his clothes. "Well, come on out and get your gloating done," he continued, this time at a normal level.

Gera walked into the opening, forehead furrowed as he thought about the warning. He turned and searched in the direction from where he felt it arrived. A moment later, Nava trotted out of the forest a few paces away, the light revealing his black coat.

"What happened?" Clark asked. His eyes were wide open as his head jerked from side to side, searching the trees for a thousand imagined enemies. "Is it the Crimson Guard?"

"No," Gera said as his brother stomped over to the saddle-bags. "Dax was testing me to see how alert I was."

"Oh. You must be very proud of Master Gera," Clark said in Dax's direction. "He found you right away." The boy glanced up again when Dax went into a coughing fit, spitting out some of the brown liquor from his waterskin.

The group ate in silence. Clark tried a couple of times to start a conversation, but each time was thwarted by the distracted Gera and brooding Dax. Eventually, he sighed and gave up.

Dax had located wild herbs for Clark during his scouting excursion. After the meal was over, he crushed some into small pieces and mixed them with some of the liquor he had in the saddlebags. It took name calling and several threats before the boy gagged down the entire mixture. In a short time, however, Clark was asleep on the ground. Gera listened to his soft snoring while cleaning up the campfire area.

The moon was well above the tree when Dax left the light to find a position for first watch. When his duties were completed, Gera checked on the horses and the picket line. Clark's mare had some heat in her foreleg, but was placing pressure on it as she moved. He used the rest of the herbs to make a poultice before climbing under his blanket with a sigh.

He stared at the stars for a while, his mind churning through everything that had happened over the past few days, and what they were going to do next. What would happen when they found the Crimson Guards? How could they free Keely and keep Clark safe at the same time, especially since he was now injured? Was what the miller told him the real story of his father and brother's deaths? The list of questions grew longer but none of them offered any answers.

The list ground to a halt when a final question was asked: Where had that warning come from in the forest?

Gera's chin bounced against his chest, his thoughts finally succumbing to his exhaustion.

he moon was low behind the trees when Gera's eyes snapped open, his hand gripping tighter on the sword hilt beside him. He stared at the dark shape leaning over him.

"Come with me," Dax whispered.

Gera strapped on his sword as he followed Dax into the trees. His ears strained to hear hints of an approaching enemy. All he heard, however, were the normal night sounds he had grown up with at his parents' cabin and the blood rushing through his ears.

"No, there's no one around." Dax chuckled as he spoke. "I wanted to talk to you without a chance of the boy overhearing what was said."

"Damn you to hells, Dax! You could've let me know we weren't in any danger."

"No," Dax said, the grin melting, and his gaze boring into Gera's eyes. "We're in danger and probably will be for a long time. You need to stay on edge for what's approaching us. The Bloods aren't going to give up Keely without a fight, and I don't know how far we'll need to run after she's free. Maybe to the other side of the Teeth, maybe for the rest of our lives. You can't let your guard down for a heartbeat, or I'll be burying another brother."

Gera returned the stare. In the dim starlight, his brother's face was an odd mixture of light and shadows. He shivered when he realized Dax looked like a living skull, pale skin stretched tight over bone.

"You make it sound like you won't be around to keep reminding me," he grumbled after hesitating for another moment.

"I might not. I'm leaving for Willshire before dawn. It'll take you at least two days to reach the city at the pace the boy is going to be able to travel. If I ride hard, I can be there by late tomorrow afternoon. That'll give me at least a full day to snoop around the city for information about Keely before you get there."

"You're not going ahead without me," Gera said. "Clark can follow along at his own pace. He'll be fi..."

"No!" Dax interrupted, the word ringing off the trees. "You can't leave a wounded man behind to fend for himself. Besides, you told me you vouched to his family for his safety. Your word needs to mean something or you're no man."

Gera's thoughts flew back to his conversation with Ben Miller as he listened to his brother's labored breathing. Judging from Dax's reaction, more of the story might be true than he cared to believe.

"It does, I mean, I know." He kicked at the ground before continuing. "Where do you want to meet once I make it to Willshire?"

"Go to the Greenwards' house. I'll meet you there in two days. If I need to leave before you arrive, I'll leave word with them about which direction I've gone. Hopefully, the Bloods will stay at the Willshire garrison for a few days while we make a plan to get Keely back. Do you think the Greenwards will let us meet there? It might mean trouble for them if anyone ever found out."

Gera nodded, hopeful the night hid his emotion at being left behind. He hated to slow down the pursuit of his sister, not to mention his nervousness at letting Dax go on alone, but he had given his word to watch over Clark. So far, he had done a poor job of it.

"Master Greenward will be mad, but Ella will insist. I'm sure they'll even watch over Clark after we leave." He turned away. "I'll take the next watch."

"Gera, wait."

He stopped moving at his brother's words.

"There's something that's been bothering me for a few days," Dax continued, pausing on each word as if they hurt to be said. "When the boy told us the story of Keely's testing, you asked if the stone had broken in two. Have you heard stories about that happening before? What does it mean?"

It was Gera's turn to pause before answering. Telling Dax would bring back memories buried deep, deep enough he had never wanted them to see the light of day again. But now, with everything that was going on, they needed to be brought out. Besides, Dax needed to know.

"I'd been at the Greenwards for a little more than a year, a few months after your visit." He paused, remembering how that meeting had gone, before rushing on with the rest. "A group of Crimson Guards rode into the shop yard, yelling and ordering and demanding. They were ready to leave on a testing trip but the necklace that held their gem was broken. They demanded

Master Greenward stop his work and fix it immediately."

Dax let out a soft laugh.

"I'll bet that big bastard doesn't take being ordered around very well."

"No, but he and the captain and myself walked through the barn on the way to the smithy behind the shop. Master Greenward told me to run ahead to stoke up the fire. Later, I understood he was trying to get me away from the guardsmen. See, he suspected what I was after your visit. Anyway, before I could leave, the captain shoved the necklace into my hand." Gera stopped, the memory brilliant in his mind. "I...I can barely describe it, Dax. As soon as the stone settled onto my palm, light blazed through me, beautiful, never-ending light. Pain followed, and I felt the world crushing down on top of me. It was like nothing you could ever imagine, Dax. Beauty and ugliness. Life and death. Good and evil. It all swirled together in one display of white light."

Gera stopped and let out a sigh.

"I opened my eyes in time to see light pouring out of the jewel, probably like Clark described. Thunder cracked through the barn, and the setting fell out of my hand in two pieces, bouncing in the dirt by my feet. The captain was so shocked, he tried to call for help, draw his sword, and charge all at the same time. But the light hadn't left me. That was only the second time I ever felt saca, and it surged through me. I grabbed a horseshoe that was hanging on the post beside me and threw it towards the captain. It leaped out of my hand like it had a mind of its own and dove straight towards his head."

Gera closed his eyes, shaking his head at this part.

"It crushed the side of his helmet and drove it into his skull.

Blood and brains sprayed everywhere. Master Greenward told me later that the guardsman was killed instantly. I don't know. All I remember is that I fell into a black hole and slept for two days."

"Why didn't they drag you away to Sacara?" Dax asked.

"Master Greenward dragged the body over by a horse stall and put the broken pieces of the stone underneath his body. Then he began yelling for help. What else were the other guardsmen going to believe when they rushed into the barn? For the love of the gods, there was a perfect imprint of a horseshoe in the side of his helmet. The horse was blamed for the captain dying. That was when I really understood what I could do. After I...after I threw you against the barn wall," Gera glanced away from his brother and stared into the night, "Master Greenward never spoke of what happened. But after this second time, he told me that we had to find a way for me to defend myself in a less dangerous way. So, he taught me how to use a sword like he learned when he was in the Moramet army. I was able to control the light and never used it again until the other night in the cabin."

An owl hooted, and the brothers stared in the direction of the sound.

"I asked if Keely had broken the setting because, if she's as powerful as I seem to be, it may change our plans on helping her escape," Gera said. "If she knows what she can do, she may be able to help in the escape, or even get away before we reach them."

Dax shook his head.

"Maybe, but it doesn't sound like she broke the stone, so we can't count on anything from her. Let's stick with the plan we've made and find a way to grab her. I'm going to get some sleep before I ride on ahead. Goodnight, brother." Dax started to walk away before he stopped. He did not turn around as he spoke. "Thank you for coming back to the cabin, Gera. I know you didn't need to, even if you wanted to visit Keely." His shadowy figure moved farther into the darkness.

Gera nodded slowly before turning to find a good spot to watch over the camp.

era considered the next three days the longest he had endured in his life. On the morning Dax left, it became apparent less than a bell into their ride that Clark would not be able to bear much of a pace. Every stride his Crimson Guard horse took above a walk caused him to wince or groan. The boy was in pain, but he did not complain. Only an opportune glance from Gera caught Clark biting his lip to keep from crying out, his eyes clamped shut.

Heat bloomed on Gera's cheeks at not noticing his charge's discomfort earlier, and he reined in his gelding, slowing to a steady walk. He paid more attention to Clark from then on, even though his thoughts leaped down the road in front of them, rushing to catch up with his brother and sister.

Since a walk was the best they could manage, Gera did what he could to lengthen their day. They ate their meals in the saddle. They climbed onto the horses before sunup and ended the ride well after full night had fallen. The only times they dismounted were to water the mounts and heed the call of nature. Gera felt the tedium gnawing at his nerves like a dog munching on a bone, wearing them away and threatening to snap each one in two.

The excitement of the adventure had worn off for Clark, as well. The boy withdrew into his own thoughts, no longer attempting to start conversations or gawk around at his new surroundings. A sour mood descended over the two riders and hung around them like a fog over a marsh, clinging to their skin.

By the end of the second day, Gera's worry-filled, personal darkness had almost devoured him. But as he rode, a nagging concern buzzed in his thoughts, dragging him away from the troubles about his family. He battled against the emotions until he blinked, seeing the world around them with new eyes. The sword slid smoothly from his scabbard as his gaze swept the early evening gloom. Only the steady plop of the horses' hooves broke the silence of the roadway.

Gera reined in the gelding and dismounted, his scan of the shadows never faltering. The worry and fear sluiced away a few moments later, however, when he spotted the blacker-than-night spot beneath a nearby tree.

"Come on out, Nava," he said between laughs. "You can't hide in the dark while baring those big white fangs of yours."

The dyr rose and walked into the roadway before beginning an overzealous display of grooming himself. His body actions screamed of his intentions to be caught.

The spell of despair broken, the remainder of the trip was more enjoyable, even if the next day moved just as slowly. Gera and Clark talked that night about everything from family to what Clark wanted to do with his life. There was even good-natured banter about beating each other in a game of Talbreath, a strategy game in which Clark declared himself an expert.

Gera was envious of his younger companion. Clark's self-assured desire to work alongside his father in the mill and eventually take over was so much more defined than what he had planned for himself. Of course, "seeing a bit of the world first" was not out of the question, although at this point in the boy's life, getting as far as Willshire was expanding his world quite a bit.

The next morning, the countryside changed as they continued their journey. Outlying farms and cabins appeared along the road and soon forced the forest into a retreat. Like most of the Milston villagers, Clark had never been more than a day or two ride away from the town in their lives. He badgered Gera with questions about Willshire and the people who lived there. The older boy smiled when he thought about Clark if he ever made it down to the river docks and had a chance to listen to some of the tales the old boatman told of their adventures. Gera was certain Mrs. Miller would not approve of that education for her son.

The two riders held back on the edge of town in a small grove until dusk. The lighter mood had not dulled Gera's wariness, and he wanted to enter Willshire as inconspicuously as possible. The two riders would not have drawn anyone's special notice, but talk of a dyr entering the city with them would race through the neighborhoods like wild fire and probably draw the city watch's notice.

The sun was a distant memory when they left their hiding spot and rode into Willshire. Gera led them down a dizzying maze of side streets and alleys, preferring the stench of refuse and sewage to the possibility of being noticed. Nava's coat turned black in the shadows again as he padded silently between the horses as they moved. Even so, Gera gratefully veered off the street and beneath the Greenward shop sign when they reached his old home. To his mind, he felt as if he had been away for a hundred summers.

He dismounted with a stretch and groan. The sounds should have come from someone three times his age.

"I've done more riding in the past three hands than I have in five summers," he said, a sigh replacing the groan. "I've got the bruises to prove it."

Clark climbed down from his saddle with a sharp intake of breath.

"I think I'll manage to live through my ribs and bruises, but I'd fight Nava for a good hot meal right now."

"That's one thing you won't need to worry about around the Greenward household," Gera said, shaking his head at how easily the boy had made a joke about the dyr after being terrified of the beast only a few days earlier. "I better let them know we're here before I bed down the horses."

Gera walked across the dark dooryard to the porch, before he hesitated. Something was wrong, but he could not place his finger on the issue. He placed a foot on the bottom step, the one he had learned to avoid years before, and its creaking rose above the surrounding town noise. The house door flew open and light flooded into the yard, blinding Gera. It struck him too late that what had been out of place was the lack of light, blocked by the tightly shuttered windows. He threw an arm up, trying to shade his eyes.

"Gera," Ham hissed, "come inside before you're seen."

Gera turned to the darkness and called softly to Clark. Almost as an afterthought, he whistled for Nava as well. The young man waited on the step, searching the street for anyone who might have followed them. Lessons from his father and Ham echoed in his thoughts, his silhouette outlined in the door's light being a perfect target for an archer, but he ignored them.

He bounded up the stairs and followed his two companions through the doorway into the Greenward home. After bolting the door shut, he turned to stare at the room he had seen countless times over the past eight summers. But that did not stop the laugh bubbling out of his mouth.

Clark stood a few paces away, trying very hard to appear as if Ham's physical presence was not imposing. That was not an unusual sight. Gera had seen men much older and more worldly with the same expression on their faces. The amusing sight was Ham. The mastersmith was gazing at Nava with a mixture of childlike wonder and knee-shaking fear.

A stifled scream and the clatter of dishes on the floor ripped his attention to the other side of the room. In the doorway to the kitchen stood Ella, pale and shaking. Erin peeked over her mother's shoulder with eyes showing white all the way around the brown centers. Both women were staring eye to eye with Nava who stood motionless in the center of the room.

They were suddenly thrust to one side as Bacon burst between them, the firewood ax brandished above his head. Ashen and sweaty from terror, he threw himself at the dyr to protect his family.

Gera raised his right arm and the warmth spread throughout his body. Although he was several paces away, he felt the weight of the ax in his hand. The grip of the wooden handle, smooth after years of use, caressed his fingertips, and the keen edge of the blade leaped into his sight. Bacon's breathing echoed in his ears with the roar of a tornado. Even with all these things assaulting his senses, Gera felt another presence, just out of his understanding.

"Nava, hold!" he shouted.

Time and reality slammed into Gera with the force of an unexpected body blow, yet the warmth still survived, a ball centered in his chest. His knees wobbled from the change, but he remained on his feet. Bacon still stood, a pace in front of his mother, his face red from struggling to attack the dyr.

The ax flew across the room, and the handle settled gently into Gera's hand. A breath later, Bacon stumbled forward, the invisible wall holding him back suddenly removed. Two steps brought him face to face with the calmest being in the room—Nava.

The dyr opened his snout to the point it appeared it would snap and yawned directly into Bacon's face. Nava then turned and padded over to the fireplace where he flopped down and began cleaning himself.

"Ashes and blood on a..." Bacon exclaimed.

He never finished his colorful sentiment. In the blink of an eye, Ella untied her apron with one hand and snapped it forward with the other. It cracked like a linen bullwhip on her son's ear.

"I'll not allow such talk in this house, no matter how big you've grown," Ella said over Bacon's howl of surprise. "Or the circumstances," she finished in a mumble that was probably meant only for herself.

"Boy, go outside and bed down Gera's horses in the barn," Ham said. "That'll give us a chance to talk alone for a bit before he eats."

"I'll help you," Clark said. He obviously did not feel that "alone" included him, and he was not about to ask the mastersmith about it.

"Show Bac the mare's foreleg, Clark," Gera said as he leaned the ax against the wall, "and look for the last of the poultice in the saddlebags. Just wet it down with some warm water, and she'll be fine." The two boys walked out the door into the night.

"Erin, pick up the dishes and get some water on the fire for those boys." Ella turned to Gera. "Have you and your friend eaten yet?"

"Just what we could while we were in the saddle," Gera answered with a shake of his head. "I'm afraid I haven't taken very good care of Clark in my hurry to get here. He needs to eat some good food or his injuries won't heal right."

"Send them straight to the kitchen, if they come back in this way, and I'll have food on the table. Don't keep him too long, Ham. I'm sure he could put a bite or two into his own stomach." Ella stared at Gera, starting to raise her hand as if she meant to touch his cheek, but then she whirled and herded Erin through the doorway and into the kitchen.

During this time, Ham had moved cautiously by Nava and stared down at the now purring dyr. Gera crossed the room and stood beside his former master. Though it was a warm spring night, a good-sized blaze burned in the hearth. The heat did not chase the chill from Gera's thoughts, however. He was afraid to hear what Ham would not say in front of his family.

"A dyr sleeping by my fire," Ham muttered. "The size is right, the muzzle, heh, even his coat has changed gray to match the stones. How in bloody buckets does someone manage to get a dyr as a pet?" Turning to Gera, his voice returned to normal. "Your brother has a wicked sense of humor, son. All he told me was that you'd have a couple of visitors with you and one wouldn't take any guff."

"Nava's not a pet, Master Greenward. He's more like a companion, a friend, than a wild animal."

"I thought the damn things were just from myths and children's stories. If they ever really lived, I thought they must have died out a thousand years ago, like the dragons." Shaking his head, Ham continued. "Your brother was here the night before last. He told us about Keely. I'm sorry, Gera, although I probably should have guessed, knowing what I've seen you do."

Gera stared at the flames.

"Is there any chance she might be able to escape on her own?" Ham continued. "I mean, some of the things I've seen you do, if she can..."

"I don't know if she can help or not," Gera interrupted before slapping his palm against his leg. "I don't have much control over my own saca." The words caught in his throat as he remembered the way he held the heat and light in his body after he took the ax away from Bacon. Even now, he could feel the door in his mind, barely containing the light behind it. "It sounds like she might be as strong as I am, so maybe." He quickly recounted the story of his sister's testing.

"We hoped to be here last night," Gera finished, "but Clark couldn't ride any faster after his fall. Is Dax out in the barn or the shop? We need to plan our next moves."

Ham sucked in a deep breath.

"He's gone. But he gave me a message for you, though it gives me no pleasure to tell you all of it. It appears Keely was taken directly to the garrison, but he had trouble tracking her from there. Your brother did learn that two groups of guardsmen left Willshire the morning he arrived. One was headed west, toward Tralain."

"The Sacara Institute."

Ham shrugged.

"Probably. Perhaps. At least that's what Dax thought. He felt Keely was probably in that convoy."

Gera nodded.

"All right. I'll leave first thing in the morning."

"Whoa, boy! You haven't heard everything yet. Don't try to leap the whole flaming creek when there's a rock path across. Another group left Willshire at the same time. They were headed north, up river."

Silence settled over the two men so Nava's rumbling purr was the only sound in the room.

"When did Dax leave?" Gera finally asked.

"He slept in the barn that night and was gone before I woke up. Refused to sleep in a proper bed. Probably some damned nonsense about what happened a few years ago. Anyway, he was going to trail the group toward Tralain." Ham paused before starting again. "Before he left, he made me vow to do my best to get you to follow the group to the north."

Ham held up his hand when Gera started to protest. He also knit his eyebrows together in the stare he used when he would not put up with anymore silliness from apprentices.

"Now, listen here before you go spouting off. We both know your sister was most likely in the first group, there's no denying that fact. But there's always the possibility that we're all wrong. The obvious choice could have been a decoy, and they sent her around in a circle with the other group. But more than that, we also agreed on the second reason you should go that way. Your being who you are and what you can do means you should stay as far away as possible from that school. If not for yourself, think about your sister. We don't know what fully-trained sagias can do. All we have are bedtime stories and legends to go by. What if they can sense your ability somehow? You could get everyone captured or killed before you ever made it close enough to see Keely."

Gera turned away and paced the floor, his steps landing in a hard patter. Keely was his sister, and he had already lost so many of his family. How could he not go help with her rescue? His emotions rose and ebbed, running wild through his thoughts. Anger, despair, a thirst for revenge—they all burned his heart like a brand, each one leaving its own mark.

After a while, his pacing slowed, and his circles grew smaller. Some of Dax and Ham's reasons made sense. To his credit, his old master remained quiet during his internal battle, not attempting to persuade him any longer. Gera eventually wore down and stopped beside the mastersmith again.

"So, what did Dax want me to do? Just track the Bloods and do nothing?"

"No," Ham said without looking away from the hearth. "He wanted you to follow and harass them in any way that you could. If your sister is in the group, try to get her out, if you think you can. Once you find her, or can't do anymore damage to the Crimson Guards, he wanted you to go to a village in northwest Moramet called Nason. Once you're there, look up a man named Legin Barlow. He was a friend of your father. If Dax finds Keely in his group, that's where he'll take her."

"I didn't think I'd ever be going to Milston again," Gera said with a shrug. "It'll never be safe for any of us there again."

"No, it's not," Ham said. He shuffled his feet for a moment and when he glanced up, he did not look at Gera. "It's not safe here, either. If it was just me, or even Bacon, it wouldn't be a problem. But it'll be too dangerous for Ella and the girls to have any contact with you once you've started fighting the Guard. You can't come back here again after tonight. The name of Staghorn will be a dangerous word to say. I'm sorry, but that's the way it is."

The world crashed around Gera's feet. It was as if he was losing his home all over again, just like when his parents died.

"One more thing. I've got something to tell you, and it won't be easy to hear. I guess I can even understand why your brother didn't tell you himself. Ella and I were the only two to hear this, and we'll never say a word to anyone." Ham finally turned to Gera and stared him in the face. "Dax wanted you to know the Crimson Guards had also taken your mother when she was younger. Your father rescued her along with several other children. That's how they met."

The ground lurched beneath Gera's feet. Sweat beaded on his forehead while he considered what this news meant.

"I guess there's no doubt where I got my ability to use saca," he said. The thin-lipped smile he wore held no humor.

"Your parents kept this from you and your sister because you were still too young to understand when they died." Ham placed a hand on Gera's shoulder. "Dax kept it from you, well, for obvious reasons. Looking back now, that was one of the reasons he wanted to take you away from Willshire and away from the garrison when you were young. It would have been easier to hide a sagia in a cabin in the mountains than a few streets away from the Crimson Guards. But that's why he wanted you to know about your mother. If your sister's not in the northern group, he wanted you to harass them to the point that no other families would need to go through what's happening to you."

"I can't take Clark with me. I promised his family I'd see to his safety."

"Don't worry about Clark," Ella said as she walked into the

room. She glanced at the glare on her husband's face, but kept walking until she had a hand on Gera's arm. "He can stay with us until it's safe to return to his home."

"Safe," Gera said, thoughts turning over in his head. "You were expecting trouble when we arrived tonight. The windows are shuttered, and Bac was armed." He whirled, stopping when he saw the sword he made leaning on the door frame. "Your sword is unsheathed by the door. What's happened?"

Ham and Ella glanced at each other before the mastersmith answered.

"Not long after your sister arrived at the garrison, the Crimson Guards became even more pushy than normal. They arrested a few people for supposedly speaking out against Sacara. Then a few came by here asking questions about you."

"Damn it! What've we done?" Gera moaned. "Dax and I've managed to drag two different families into our personal mess."

"That's enough of that talk!" Ella snapped. She jerked him around and grabbed both of his arms at the elbows. He expected her to shake some sense into him like he was still a little boy. "Your troubles are our troubles because you're family. It may not be blood, but the bond is through choice, and all the stronger because of it. Now," she continued after she released him, "that's all that will be said on that subject. Come on out to the kitchen and grab something to eat. Bacon and Clark have already started, and you'd better hurry because I don't think there's a bottom to either of those two's stomachs."

Gera trailed behind Ella but stopped in the kitchen doorway. Ham had not followed and was still standing by the hearth, staring into the flames.

ax lowered his head and quickly turned to stare into a store window. A handful of Crimson Guards passed behind him on the busy street, their banter filling the air around them. It was only after he watched their reflections walk out of sight that he noticed the store was a dress shop. A seamstress looked at him over a display.

Panic ran through his thoughts when the woman leaned forward and stared in the direction the guardsmen had walked. Dax prayed she would not scream or raise an alarm. He was about to bolt across the street when the shopkeeper glanced back at him. She gave a small wave of her hand and nodded slightly.

Dax was shocked by the stranger's willingness to help. He glanced down the street and was relieved to see the Bloods were indeed out of sight. He turned back to smile his thanks, but the woman had already returned to hemming a dress. He suspected no amount of pounding on the window would force her to look up again.

That was the way things had gone for Dax in Charlser. What little help or information he was able to glean from the area was quickly followed by a demand to leave.

*I don't care. These fools are happy to shut their eyes and live on top of each other forever.*

He had discovered what he needed to know anyway. The group of Bloods transporting Keely had not stopped in Charlser. They continued to the west, farther into Galadon and closer to the Sacara Institute. Luckily, the information had only cost him a kick in the ribs and being the target of curse words. Some pride was a small price to pay for his sister's rescue.

Dax did not regret the lie he left behind at the Greenwards' for his brother, either. He had known before crossing the Pennick River which group of Crimson Guards transported Keely. The big metalsmith acted as if he had seen right through the story, but Dax suspected Ham did not want Gera to go near Sacara, either. If the Institute discovered his brother could use saca, there would be plenty of questions for the man who had him as an apprentice for eight summers.

*Nava might even be able to help him run off some Bloods' horses without getting caught.*

Dax walked into the barn where he had left his horses while searching for news. After saddling his mounts, he paid his stabling bill and led them outside. The late afternoon sun barely peeked a yellow sliver above the nearby city walls, but he did not want to wait for the morning. Even though the hustle and bustle of Charlser's business district was less here, he still felt trampled and confined.

Traffic flowed steadily through the city gates. Dax matched the pace of the outgoing crowd, blending in as just one of many in the line. He let out an audible sigh, however, after he passed through the opening in the stone wall. Sighting a break in the throng, he led his mounts to the side of the road to let down his stirrups.

Dax was about to step into the saddle when he glanced over the back of his horse. A few more paces up the road, a half a score of beggars stood in a loose group, pleading with the passing crowd. The woodsman could not remember seeing any of their kind wandering the immaculate streets he had just left and wondered if the city watch would not let them inside the walls.

"Out of sight, out of mind," he whispered.

One of the men caught Dax's gaze. The beggar walked haltingly toward him and gave a better view of himself in the fading light. Filthy clothes, too dirty to reveal their true color, hung from bony shoulders. The man no longer stood completely erect as he raised a shaking hand, his back a hunched over mess. His lips cracked open in a toothless grin or grimace, Dax could not tell which it was meant to be.

"Uh coin fo' uh po' mun?" the beggar mumbled.

The man flinched and threw up his arms to protect himself when Dax swung into the saddle. The woodsman reached beneath his cloak and pulled a copper coin from his belt. The last rays of sunshine glinted off its dull surface, and the other man's eyes opened in anticipation.

Dax could not rip his gaze away from those sunken orbs as he flicked the money through the air. Red-lined maps ran through where only white should have been visible. Black, puffy bags hung beneath them like heavy purses from a belt. Yet, it was the returned stare, as if the beggar was looking at something far off that only he could see, which shook Dax to his boots.

"Uh drag'uns blessin' on ya," the man said in thanks as his hands stopped twitching long enough to catch the coin. Sour body odor and cheap alcohol mixed together in a fetid stench, wafting off the man and making even the horses toss their heads.

Dax did not answer as he heeled his mount down the road. It was his turn to offer a little help and then demand to be left alone.

His horse had only gone a few strides before a ruckus made him stop and turn. He watched in horror as the beggar he had given the copper to fell to the ground, beaten and kicked by three of the other men. One of the trio stomped on the man's wrist and the coin fell into the dirt where others also joined in on the free-for-all. Soon, a dozen men were punching and kicking in search of the single coin.

Dax closed his eyes and turned away.

◆ ◆ ◆

Dax rode steadily for several hours before stopping for the night. A few hours sleep would be a blessing before the hard ride he planned for the next day. He had passed several inns since leaving Charlser, but his money supply was limited, and he did not know how long he would be on the road. The coin to the beggar was something he might live to regret, in more ways than one.

The moon poised high in the sky and allowed its pale glow to help him see to loose-tie his horses so they could graze during the night. He decided against a fire and settled in next to a tree, using it for support. His supper consisted of traveler bread and dried meat, courtesy of Mrs. Greenward. Dax nibbled the food for a while as he stared at the stars winking in the black curtain above his head.

He eventually pulled a bottle of the dark drink from a saddle-bag and took a long swallow. Boiling heat tumbled down his throat, into his stomach, and exploded in a cascade of fire through the rest of his body. Dax welcomed the familiar numb feeling. He downed nearly half the bottle with his next tilt. Dark haze floated aimlessly through his thoughts until his mind wandered in a dense fog.

It did not take long for restless sleep to settle over him like an ill-fitting shirt. He hovered in the mist for a second or an eternity, his mind no longer cared. As the initial effects of the liquid leveled off, dreams flapped at the fog in an effort to part it and be seen.

A figure sprinted into sight. It was the beggar from the Charlser wall. Dax tried to avoid him, will himself farther away from the man in his mind. No matter how hard he fought, however, the man drew closer.

"Don't fight it," the beggar said clearly, despite his lips being out of sync with the words. "You're one of us, my brother."

Dax felt his stomach roil just watching the man. The beggar moved with a jerking motion as if the woodsman was blinking his eyes for varying bits of time and missing part of the action. Suddenly the man leaped close, twitching arms thrusting a mirror in front of Dax's face.

He stared at his reflection, mouth dropping open in horror. Bile rose in his throat and raced to beat the scream out of his mouth. Dax gazed back at himself with the same red-laced, dead-eyed stare the beggar had shown to him earlier in the evening.

Terror finally gave Dax the strength to break away from the man. He ran straight into the fog bank, blind and alone in his revulsion. After a while he tripped and fell heavily to the ground.

The swirling gray mass parted, and he raised his head, painfully stretching to look around.

Dax was on his belly at the top of a rise. In the shallow valley before him, two men lay on their backs, tied to stakes in the ground. Blood darkened their shirts to a burgundy sheen. The two prisoners weakly raised their heads and glanced around. Dax ripped out two handfuls of sod when he recognized his brother, Ryne, and his father.

A scream of rage and despair died in his throat when he suddenly noticed the crowd of gray-cloaked bodies dancing around his family. He would have sworn they were not there a moment earlier. Faster and faster they twirled and leaped until Dax felt dizzy just watching their movements.

With one final stamp of their feet, the group stopped in unison. Silence wrapped the air in its embrace, pressing down on Dax and making it difficult to breath. One cloaked figure, taller than all the rest, stepped in front of his father and Ryne. In his hands was a great bow, nearly as tall as himself.

Tears ran down Dax's face in streams as he watched an arrow be set, drawn, and fired into his father's chest. The wet thump did not mask the explosion of air from Tyre as the missile drove home. The scene was quickly repeated with Ryne.

"Noooooo!" Dax screamed as the pressure finally relented on his chest. He stood up on shaking legs and continued staring into the valley.

Every gray figure turned to face the intrusion. After a long moment, the one with the bow in his hand reached up and pulled down his hood.

"Come join us in our fun, brother," the beggar said, his blood-shot eyes glistening with excitement. "You can shoot, too."

Dax glanced down at his hands and realized the sod was gone, replaced by a bow in a white-knuckled grip.

"We're your family now."

Dax sat up in the cool predawn air. His chest heaved and sweat-drenched hair lay plastered in clumps against his head. It took several long moments for his mind to convince him the nightmare was over. Shivering racked his body and chills ran up and down his skin.

The nearly empty bottle was to his lips before he even realized his arm was moving. A vision of the beggar flashed out of the semi-dark and dashed through his mind. Dax snarled and heaved the bottle as far as he could throw it. The tinkle of shattering glass was still echoing when he began digging frantically through the saddlebags.

Crash! Crash! Crash!

Three impacts followed in rapid succession as more of the dark liquor joined its brethren to soak into the ground. As the last of the noise resounded in his ears, Dax stopped. The final bottle he had packed was in his hand, raised above his head and ready to be smashed. His skin went cold as comprehension settled over his thoughts.

He sank to the ground with a moan, cradling the remaining bottle like a mother with her newborn child. His sobs filled the air with heart-wrenching ache and threatened to make the nearby trees weep in reply. On and on he cried until at last the sun threw a fiery finger above the horizon.

Dax raised his head and stared through red-streaked eyes in the direction of Keely and her captors.

era left Willshire before the sun flamed into the eastern sky. Even the dangerous purpose of his journey did not detract from the beauty of the sunrise for the young man. As he watched, the night grudgingly gave way to shooting streaks of orange and yellow until finally surrendering, defeated by the light of a new day.

"Well, Nava," Gera said as he heeled the gelding into a trot. "Let's hope all our mornings can start on such a brilliant note."

For a while, the pair traveled down a deserted road, beating even the merchant wagons out of the city. As traffic increased, Nava ran off into the surrounding tree lines or underbrush with more frequency to escape notice. Gera stopped the travelers he met coming from the north to ask for news. He tried to steer the brief conversations towards information on the Crimson Guards and their movements, but sometimes the strangers would only talk about their own interests. Though he did not learn as much as he would have liked about the guardsmen, he did hear other, unexpected news.

"Bakri," spat an old merchant while his horses watered at the river during the heat of the day. "My woman's no-good brother makes the drive for me between Wapak and Nason. He comes crying back after his last trip and says that all the people in Nason will talk about are some raids made by Bakri on the outlying farms. Now he says he won't go back again until he's sure they've been driven back to their holes in the mountains. Bah! We haven't seen so much as a hair off a Bakri's ass in eight summers! More likely he just wants to make the run to Willshire so he's farther away from that ugly wife and handful of brats of his."

"It's those bloody fish eaters from Palamor!" a Crandori merchant guard said as his convoy rested alongside the road. "They've scorched farm ground up by the border. King Ashford sent troops to set them right, though. They'll all be laying down with soil in their mouths soon enough. No one gets away with the desecration of the mother land in Crandor."

Gera heard different versions of both of these stories, plus some local gossip, but the meaning was the same in all of them. He was riding into an area of unrest, but no one knew for certain who was fighting or why.

"You know, Nava," Gera said one night as they bedded down for the evening. "An adventure sounds exciting when you're bent over a piece of work that needs to be finished by the next day, but I think before this is over, I'll be wishing I was back at Master Greenward's shop repairing a pot or making a pin."

Nevertheless, the first few days on the road north passed uneventfully for the two companions. The first lucky break came to Gera at dusk at the ferry crossing to the Crandori town of Bagdon.

"Sure enough, I've seen too many of those damnable Crimson Guards for one lifetime," grumbled the ferryman with a shake of his head. "They don't pay to cross like honest folk because they're always moving about on *official* Sacara Institute business. The only business they're taking care of is below their belts! All hells! They can take my ashes if anyone thinks all they do is serve the people." He finished by spitting on the ground.

"Have you ferried any across in the last few days?" Gera asked, glancing around the area as if he did not really care about the answer.

The ferryman watched the young man out of the corner of his eye. Gera felt the man's gaze searching him, looking for answers to unspoken questions. He was afraid what the boatman saw was a nervous young man trying to act disinterested while attempting to hide a sword beneath his cloak. Gera was correct.

"Look at me," the ferryman demanded.

Gera's muscles tensed as he pivoted on his heels. His hand flew to the sword hilt while he stared back at the old man, the tobacco-stained chin in contrast with the man's steely gaze. After several long moments of sizing each other up, the ferryman's stare softened.

"Girlfriend?" he asked, lowering his voice as he stepped closer.

Gera slumped, his shoulders going slack.

"Sister. But I don't know how far I'll get if I can't keep my intentions to myself any better than this." He shook his head as he spoke.

"Humph! Don't go by me, lad. It's my business to know people and how they're going to act. Otherwise, they'd have found my body years ago, floating down the river or the birds breaking fast on my eyes. You'd have fooled most people, sure enough."

"Have you seen any Crimson Guards lately?"

"First thing this morning. I took forty-five men, mounts, and supplies over to Bagdon. It took three trips," the ferryman answered. "They was talking about being dispatched to Greenville. That's the bad news. The worse news is that about eight score of guardsmen stayed on this side of the river and kept riding to the north."

Gera glanced in both directions as if he could still see the Bloods from several hours earlier.

"Did either group have any of those rolling cages with them? Were you able to see if they had any prisoners?"

"None. No cages and no prisoners. At least, none that I could tell."

Rage bloomed inside Gera's emotions and spread heat throughout his body. Now he understood why he had not been able to catch up with a group pulling a wagon. Dax had to have known Keely was not in this group of Crimson Guards if there was no cage. His first instinct was to ride like a demon back to Willshire and try to pick up his brother's trail. Common sense, however, quickly regained control of his thoughts. He realized there was no way he could overtake them before they made it to the Sacara Institute now. His only option, and Keely's hope for freedom, lay in Dax's hands now. The memories of his talk with Ben Miller made him shudder.

*I've got to believe in him. But if he fails, he'll answer to me. I swear it.*

Gera did have one objective he could accomplish with this trip to the north. If Dax wanted him to play havoc with the guardsmen, chaos would reign. He would try to make it so these Bloods would never bother any other families again.

"Lord Ferryman," Gera said, half a grin tilting the corner of his mouth. "It appears I've business in Crandor."

"You got stones, lad," the old man said with a wink. "That's sure enough. But what good are you going to do your sister, getting yourself killed out here all by yourself?"

Gera glanced around in the twilight, the ferry lanterns revealing that no one else was nearby. He whistled once.

Nava rose from where he was lying near some crates, his coat blending in with the worn wood sides. He trotted past the two men and onto the ferry.

"I won't be alone," Gera said.

He was certain the white-haired old man set a record for the amount of time it took to cross the Pennick River.

◆ ◆ ◆

The two guards at the top of the dais snapped to attention when Commander Gregol walked into the otherwise deserted amphitheater. The sounds of his steps echoed in the emptiness as he crossed the room, the reverberations growing in volume the closer he approached the elevated platform. He had heard visitors to the Sacara Institute whisper in awe at the power of saca that allowed a person to speak in his normal voice from the cathedra and be heard clearly at the rear of the chamber. But Gregol knew this was no spell. The Hall of One Voice worked through a combination of gold-veined white marble on the floors, walls and ceilings, and a simple acoustical design. The approaching walls and ceiling near the dais also gave the impression of the speaker being much larger than in real life. All of it mattered. Anything that helped reinforce the public's view of the Sacara

Institute and sagias being all-powerful worked in their favor.

Gregol swept through the doorway at the rear of the dais and stepped into the room behind it. If visitors were allowed here, they would have been awed by the lavish trappings of a private library. Silks, decorative carpets, bejeweled and gilded furniture, even a colored glass mosaic of a dragon's head inserted into the center of the vast window at the opposite end of the room spoke volumes of the amount of gold used to decorate this sanctuary. Gregol walked toward the man reclining on a divan and saluted with one hand to his chest and a quick bow of his head.

"Lord Ravenhurst," he said. "I have a report."

"Chara," the man said to a young woman dressed in orange robes working over stacks of papers at the desk. "Bring the commander and I a pitcher of spiced wine and then go to your afternoon lessons."

The delay gave Gregol the opportunity to notice the further deterioration of his master since the last time he had seen him more than a moon cycle ago. Frankly, it was not as bad as he feared it would be. The frail body and pale skin relaxing on the couch had once belonged to a slim, athletic man who stood a hand shorter than the soldier. The black cropped hair and flawless features made it easy to believe this man would be drawing looks from ladies even as he wasted away to nothing. But it was Ravenhurst's eyes that always drew Gregol's attention, narrow slits that hid almost all the white, revealing only the bottomless black in the center. There was very little he had encountered that would make Gregol feel fear. Adal Ravenhurst's eyes were one of those things.

The commander removed his gloves and absentmindedly rubbed a scar on his left palm while he waited. It was the remnant of a wound where a spike had been driven through the soldier's hand long ago. After a few moments, he watched his master dip his head and stare at the papers in his lap. Gregol felt his impatience, and he was sure it showed, Ravenhurst making him wait to get the emotion under control.

The student fulfilled her task, bowed to Ravenhurst, and then closed the door on her way out of the room.

"Pour the wine, Commander," the master said. "Then tell me how our plans are proceeding in the north."

Gregol filled a silver goblet and offered it to Ravenhurst.

"The plan is moving ahead as you designed, Lord Ravenhurst," Gregol said while pouring himself a glass. "After two Crandori villages were destroyed with no effect, seeds were burned in the storage barns with obvious trails leading into Palamor. Two Palamoran villages were also destroyed and Crandori weapons and armor left behind as evidence of the raiders. This was accomplished with an acceptable loss of troops."

He slammed the goblet down on the table and then whirled toward Ravenhurst.

"But there shouldn't have been any bloody losses!" Gregol continued, rage flaring in his voice. "Most of the men have been in this gods forsaken country too long and have grown as soft as the local whores. Seeing a hundred of their own nailed to Cleansing Trees would put them back in the right frame of mind!" His hands moved together, and he began rubbing his palm again.

"What's the mood along the border?" Ravenhurst asked as he picked at an imaginary piece of lint on his pants.

"There've been skirmishes along the border between the villagers and patrols," Gregol answered once he had regained some composure. "But no outright battles between military forces. All it will take is for two groups of soldiers to find each other at the wrong time or wrong place, and there'll be a full-scale war. I left orders for that event to happen."

"Good, Commander. Step up the operation in the south between Spirache and Lebesh, as well. I want merchant ships flying both flags to be burning on the water within the week."

"I'll leave first thing in the morning for the garrison at Ponte. Master, there was another incident..." Gregol stopped when a knock sounded at the library door.

"Enter," Ravenhurst said.

A boy dressed in the all-black livery of the bird loft walked in and gawked in amazement while his gaze wandered over the splendors of the room.

"Yes, boy," Gregol said, his impatience returning. He walked over and towered over the youth.

"A message just arrived for Master Ravenhurst," the boy said while holding up an unopened bird tube. "It's sealed with black wax instead of red."

Gregol snatched the container from the boy and shoved him roughly at the doorway. The birder barely slowed down enough to close the door as he bolted from the room. Neither man paid him any attention, however. Instead, the commander walked to his master, sweat popping on his face. Ravenhurst rose slowly to his feet, leaning against the divan for support, and grasped the message tube with trembling fingers.

The seal cracked as he twisted the end, bits of black wax falling to the carpet as he tilted it up, and a rolled paper dropped into his other hand. The commander watched as greedy eyes devoured the short letter, leaping from word to word. Ravenhurst ran his tongue over his upper lip as he reread the note, and then read it a third time, searching for any unwritten meanings between the lines. Gregol had been forgotten so thoroughly, he could have been just another piece of artwork in the room. The master paced back and forth with a spring in his step that denied his frail body. He stared at the walls as he moved, but his sight was far removed from Sacara. While he walked, he softly mumbled a chant in a guttural, singsong language.

He abruptly stopped and collapsed onto the arm of an ornately decorated chair. His chest heaved from the exertion, and a thin sheen of perspiration glistened on his forehead when he raised his head to stare at the anxiously waiting commander. A smile spread over his face.

"They've found one," he half-whispered in between gasps for air.

Gregol's eyes shined with excitement, and his body shook.

"Who is she? Where did they find her?" he finally managed to ask.

"They found her in a small village in eastern Moramet," Adal replied as he slid down into a proper seat on the chair. "She cracked the eye all the way through. The captain of the Willshire garrison said the setting was the only thing holding the eye together."

"Does the message say when she'll arrive at Sacara, Lord Ravenhurst?"

"The bird was sent from Willshire, on the Pennick River, seven days ago. With good travel, they should reach the wall in four or five more days." The smile washed away, replaced by a scowl as he glanced down at the message again. "How well do you know Captain Ursel, Commander?"

Gregol rifled through his memories of the officers stationed in Moramet.

"Not especially well, my Lord. Ursel rose through the ranks with no exceptional notice, good or bad. I've no memory of ever meeting him, but what I remember of his reports are always precise and to the point. Does he say something else, my Lord?"

"It's what he doesn't say that troubles me. He mentions a patrol sent to the child's home did not return. They only found this out because a bird was dispatched to Willshire after part of the detachment had left with the girl. There's no reference to trouble, however, either in the village or on the road. He did leave immediately as soon as she reached Willshire."

It was Commander Gregol's turn to wear a path in the expensive rugs. He spent the next few moments delving into his memory for every report, every message, every rumor he had ever received from the captain, then applied it to the facts he had in hand now. He stopped his pacing in front of his master.

"My Lord, I believe Captain Ursel expects trouble. Eastern Moramet is still largely wilderness. No mention of trouble in the village leads me to believe she's from a family that lives outside of town, perhaps even in the foothills of the Teeth. That goes with not finding the bodies of the lost patrol. He left even though he had not searched out a Chosen's family and had them all retested. No officer who had risen through the ranks would take the chance of not completing his duties unless he was concerned about getting a possible Matra safely to Sacara." He paused before asking a question. "Does he say how many men he was bringing with her, my Lord?"

Another smile twitched the corners of Adal's mouth.

"One hundred and eighty men."

"A full company of soldiers? I believe I'm right. Somewhere along the road, and from someone unnamed, Ursel expects trouble."

Ravenhurst leaned back in the chair and stroked his chin.

"You've come a long way since I first saw you in the fighting pits at Reesha, Commander." His brow furrowed, and he glanced away, staring at the far wall. "Only three times have Chosen been liberated from the Crimson Guard. The first was a boy in the early days of the trial, and he did it himself. He used his saca before the necklace could be placed on him. He was strong enough in the power to kill one soldier and wound two more before he was killed by an arrow."

"The first lesson of why we test with two guards standing behind the child with bare steel," Gregol said, his face covered with puzzlement at the reminder of the testing procedures.

The master nodded.

"The second time a Chosen escaped, a squad in northern Palamor was ambushed after they discovered six Chosen in one village near the mountains. One guardsman survived the attack and returned with reinforcements. They burned the village and killed all the townspeople they could find."

"This is the second lesson of why we have at least a platoon present when testing," Gregol said. He paused. "But I don't understand, my Lord. You said there were three times, and I've never heard of another escape."

"Now let me tell you the reason why we send a bird with the black wax and transport a Chosen who might be the Matra by themselves." Adal took several deep breaths and turned to Gregol.

"Almost forty summers ago, before you were born, but soon after the drafts began, a squad was traveling through the south of Halon with twelve Chosen in a cage. In one night, a lone man killed the entire squad with the ease of a tomcat destroying a mouse. When we finally received a report about it, I went myself to investigate by performing a seeing. However, since we hadn't known they were coming to Sacara, too much time had passed. The essence was almost completely gone. The man appeared to me as only an elusive shadow, but his work was a thing of beauty. You would have admired it, Commander. Eleven dead soldiers and only the last two had enough warning to draw steel." He tilted his head. "I even thought it might be a Crimson Guard because there was something familiar about his presence, but I never had enough of his feeling to track him."

Gregol opened his mouth, but closed it when Adal raised his hand, signaling for him to remain silent.

"Later on, it was discovered that the eye had been cracked by one of the Chosen who escaped," Adal continued, his voice rasping over the words. "It was a small crack, and she very well may not have had the power to become the Matra, but a proper breeding might have led us to the end. A chance we'd been waiting on for over nine hundred years was lost to us."

He buried his face in his hands, his body shaking with emotion.

"And me. Lost to me."

The whisper had been so quiet, Gregol was certain the words were meant only for his master.

Ravenhurst abruptly leaped to his feet and flung his hand out toward the tapestry on the opposite wall. A scream of pure rage poured from the depths of whatever soul he kept hidden and blue-green flames bolted from his fingertips at the weaving. The fire immediately began devouring the work.

The frail man collapsed into the chair again while Gregol braved the heat to dump the bowl of water cooling the wine onto the fire. Steam escaped into the air like a crowd of hissing snakes.

The majority of the flames were doused, but the commander knew from experience that given a small chance, a sagia's fire would re-ignite into a raging blaze again. He rolled the smoldering cloth into a cylinder and heaved the mass over one shoulder. He crossed the room, urgency revealed in each long stride, and flung his burden out one of the large windows flanking the dragon head glass. The once beautiful piece of art burst into flames as it fell into the surf below the school. Gregol left the window open to help cleanse the room of the smoke and walked to Master Ravenhurst. The man glanced up as he approached.

"Go to Captain Ursel and ensure that nothing happens to the Chosen he is transporting. Take a company at dawn. The instant you find them, I want you to send me a message." He paused for a few moments. "My replenishing ceremony is in three nights on the Sickle Moon or I would go myself, Commander. Brief one of your aides on what I want done in Lebesh and Spirache and have him report directly to me when he has accomplished his mission. Captain Trana will do fine."

"Yes, my Lord," Gregol said, every word clipped short. "But there's one more thing I need to tell you about before I go. We found a Draig temple with a group of worshipers outside of Birse." He quickly told the tale of killing the congregation and razing the building.

Ravenhurst's body stiffened, and his eyes burned with hatred until the commander was afraid he would need to dispose of another burning object. His master was able to control his emotions this time, however. When the story was finished, Gregol watched the man sit still while his lips moved in silent curses.

"We were obviously wrong in assuming we'd wiped that blasphemy from the lands," Ravenhurst said when he recovered his voice. "You were correct, of course, in your response. Once we've begun our moves in the open, we'll need to search out the Draig again. We might even be able to place the blame on them for some of the troubles. For now, we must see to the other duties."

Commander Gregol saluted and turned on his heels to leave the library. He was reaching for the door handle when his master's voice stopped him again.

"One more thing, Commander," Adal said, his voice level and calm again. "Have construction started on two hundred Cleansing Trees in the barracks quad. I believe you're correct. With what we've begun, the men must truly remember who we are."

era felt a renewed purpose in his quest as he and Nava pushed on through the darkness. Weariness sluiced from his body like a river over a waterfall as they traveled, and his mind whirled with ideas on how to delay the Crimson Guards. However, eventually even this burst of energy and resolve was not enough to sustain him past physical exhaustion. Just before dawn, Gera lay down to rest beneath the branches of a half-dozen trees a small distance from the road.

The sun had made about half its morning journey through the sky when he awoke with a start. A second growl from Nava brought the rest of his attention forward. Gera noticed five men had dismounted at the road and were walking towards him.

"Nava." Gera whispered in the direction of the growl. "Stay out of sight, but circle them if you can. Let's see if they mean us any harm." He grimaced when he realized he had fallen into the habit of addressing the dyr as if he was a person.

As the men approached, Gera noticed they were all dressed as soldiers, complete with ring mail, tabard, and carrying a bill. The covering was springtime green with a gold sheaf of wheat and a scythe stitched into the material. From his days at Ham's shop, he recognized the sigil as part of the Crandori Royal banner.

Gera rose to his feet, but made no move toward his sword as the soldiers dispersed into a semi-circle, a few paces away. The thrusting spikes and cutting blades on the ends of the bills shined brightly in the morning sunlight, the polearms effective weapons for infantry to use against cavalry and, in this case, to keep unmounted men at bay. All the men were shorter than Gera, while curly brown hair peeked out from under helmets and brown eyes studied him from head to toe. He searched his memory for anything the merchants at the Greenwards' shop might have mentioned about the customs of Crandor.

"Hail, good stranger," said the soldier in the middle. "May your ground bring you happiness until the harvest."

The greeting reminded Gera that the Crandori economy was based upon agriculture. There were even rumors their love of their land was also the basis for a religion. It was a common traveler's tale that said a Crandori man would shrug off an insult to his wife or mother, but would knife you for spitting on his land.

"Hail, good soldier," Gera said, letting a smile spread over his lips. "I'm not from Crandor, so I'm afraid I don't know the proper answer to your greeting."

"Where do you call home?"

"A small village at the foot of the Teeth in Moramet is where I was born. But I haven't been there for years. I just finished my apprenticeship in Willshire, downstream from Bagdon."

At this point, the soldiers visibly relaxed but did not move any closer.

"What's your business in Crandor? I'd think you would've headed straight for home after finally gaining your freedom."

Gera decided to move forward with the cover story he had created for these kinds of events after hearing Clark talk about his future.

"I decided to see a little bit of the world before I went home and settled down to a family life." He shrugged. "I may not have time to do it later."

The comment brought a chorus of laughs from the amused soldiers. The leader turned to the two men on his left and waved them back to their horses on the road.

"Well, either you're a lot smarter than the rest of us put together," the leader said with a twinkle in his eye, "or you've gotten better advice than I ever received. Your safest road, however, isn't to the north. There's a war brewing, and it's liable to cut short your adventure, if not your life, if you go that way. Safe passage, lad." With that, he and the remaining soldiers turned to their mounts.

Gera watched as they trudged back to the road and climbed into their saddles. Before they rode away, their leader wheeled his horse toward Gera.

"Your answer," the man yelled across the distance, "is, 'until the next planting.'" The soldiers then heeled their horses into a trot toward the south. Gera raised his arm in thanks.

"This really would be a nice trip," he said to Nava after the dyr padded up to stand beside him, "if it wasn't for the reason why."

With a sigh and a shake of his head, Gera began to break camp.

arly the next morning, Gera found a camp where the Crimson Guards spent the previous evening. He counted the number of cold campfires and turned a forgotten red uniform blouse over in his hand.

"I guess tonight is the night, Nava," he said as he glanced around. He wondered why the guardsmen had not stayed at the inn he had passed down the road, but finally decided they must not have had room for the troops.

The rest of the day, Gera fought an internal battle while he pushed forward. Now that the time for action was near, doubts about what he was about to do crept into his thoughts. When he was growing up at the Greenwards' house, he had been in his share of fights with other boys. He fought off the highwaymen when they attacked on the road and gutted Old Nick, and he had killed the guardsmen when they followed Clark to the cabin.

But what he was doing now was stalking men as if they were prey. It was not a pleasant emotion that gnawed at his conscience as he rode. Nava appeared to sense his uneasiness and stayed closer throughout the day than he had at any other point of their travels.

Just before dark, Gera made some final preparations for the evening he expected. He mustered the memory of every tale he heard about this style of fighting. Most of what he could remember were tidbits overheard from when his father taught Ryne and Dax before they all went off to fight in the Bakri War. The rest were scraps of tales from men in Milston who had either fought against the Bakri, or mercenaries who came to the Greenward shop for repairs. For his part, Ham rarely talked about his days in the Moramet army. Gera trusted what he had learned from his father, but he suspected much of the rest were just stories or exaggerations.

He tore strips of cloth from an old shirt and wrapped the metal pieces on the gelding's bridle so they would not jingle when he moved. Next, he put on his remaining two shirts with the darkest one on the outside. They would keep him warm in the cool spring air at night without the bulkiness of his cloak. Finally, he spread mud on his forehead, cheekbones, nose, and jaw. Although the moon would not throw much light tonight, this would help to break up the pattern of his face in what little glow was present.

After riding until well after nightfall, Gera finally spotted a fire in the distance. Believing he was close to his destination, he became even more nervous, his hands twitching the reins. In his excited state and his unfamiliarity with the flatness of the Crandori land, he underestimated the distance to the guardsmen campsite. On and on he rode, each stride by the gelding seeming to push the light away rather than draw it closer. The anxiety grew in Gera with the passing time.

At last he decided he was close enough to dismount and walk in on foot. Gera led the gelding to a stand of trees a long bow shot from the road. He then pulled a set of rope hobbles out of the saddlebags and placed them on the horse's front legs. The mount might wander a little while he was gone, but Gera did not want to tie the animal to a tree in case he did not return from the evening's adventure.

Gera and Nava crept quietly through the fields and approached the camp from the west. There was very little movement within the five circles of campfire light. The dyr's black coat was enough to hide him, but Gera lowered himself to his stomach and crawled along the ground, searching for the outer sentries as he inched his way forward.

His heart beat against his ribs. Sweat soaked through both shirts and made mud from the dirt clinging to the cloth. An image of Keely dragged away, and then thrown into a cage, was the only thing that kept him moving forward, giving him enough resolve to continue.

A thump to his left was followed by a low, quiet growl. Nava had struck first blood.

A sentry appeared out of the darkness from Gera's right, walking cautiously towards the sounds with his sword already drawn. He passed less than a pace from the prone young man, his attention on the night in front of him.

All doubts flew from Gera's mind, the internal struggle fading to a distant memory. He leaped to his feet the moment the Crimson Guard walked by his position. The wicked short sword split the air with all the force and fury he could summon. The blade sliced between the helmet and the mail on the sentry and then stopped with an elbow-rattling crunch.

The hilt slipped from his hands as the sentry collapsed to the ground. The sword was embedded deep into the man's neck, burying itself into bone when it cut through the man's spine. It took a few stressful seconds before he was able to wiggle the weapon out of his victim, finally succeeding when he put a foot in the man's back and pulled it free.

Gera doubled over and crept towards the area where he last heard Nava. After a half a score of paces, he stumbled and nearly fell over the dyr's kill. A quick examination revealed the man was indeed dead, his fingers finding only mangled flesh where the guardsman's throat should have sat. Like a pucat, Nava must have latched onto the sentry's throat and rode the man to the ground, laying on top until the soldier either died from a loss of blood or lack of air. In either case, it had been a violent, bloody death.

Once more, Gera moved through the night. After he traveled farther than the gap between the two dead sentries, he decided he must have wandered off the guard line postings. Even as he turned toward the campfires to adjust his circle inward, his mind rang.

"Two," the voice said, directly in front of him.

Gera felt it was the same presence he felt when Dax tried to surprise him on the road to Willshire, only now the voice was familiar. Improbable as it sounded, Nava was the only being around who would want to keep him safe.

He had no time to wonder how the warning was happening. Trusting to his belief, but still wondering if events had caused him to slip toward madness, Gera crept forward another twenty paces. He stopped when he heard two sentries talking to each other, their voices soft. A pool of pitch black to his right suddenly leaped up, transforming into Nava.

The dyr reached the near guard on his first jump. Fangs snapped together on the back of the man's neck, spine crunching, and they both fell to the ground with a thud. Nava shook his head violently back and forth, the air filling with the sharp sounds of breaking bones.

Gera was already moving for the second sentry by the time Nava and his prey rolled to a stop. His breath caught in his throat when he realized the remaining soldier already had his heavy-bladed sword in his hands. The shocked Crimson Guard quickly recovered and raised the weapon above his head to strike. As the blade dove downward, Gera thrust his own sword forward, aided by the momentum of his rush.

The point penetrated the mail on the guard's side and bit into a rib. The wounded man's off-balance stroke passed wildly to one side of Nava, scraping through the dirt instead of the dyr. Although the sentry was badly wounded, the blow had not killed him.

The power of Gera's charge and strike pushed the man out of reach. The trooper wheezed as he drew a breath, turning toward the camp to sound the alarm, even as he snapped his sword up into a defensive position.

Saca flowed through Gera, heat and light mixing together as it filled his body. This time was different, however. He had called to the power, throwing open the door in his mind, and it had answered. Without hesitation, he raised his empty left hand, palm toward the sentry, and pushed with his mind. Somewhere deep inside his body, the floodgate burst and saca rushed out.

The air filled with mist as the guardsman flew backward into the night. Gera moved forward to make sure the man was dead.

He found the body nearly five paces down the path from

where the man had left his feet. The nasal guard on the trooper's helmet pointed straight back, and most of the jaw and throat were missing from the corpse. Blood still pumped through the opening, spurting its warm liquid, the heart not yet realizing the guardsman would never draw another breath.

After a few anxious moments, Gera staggered to his feet. Nava padded to his side, and he leaned heavily on the dyr while they circled back to where they left the gelding. Luckily, the horse had not wandered far underneath the trees. Gera removed the hobbles and sighed, leaning against the mount before stepping into the saddle.

*A fight you can walk away from when it's over is a fight you've won.*

His father's words tumbled through his thoughts. Gera wondered what Tyre would have thought about how he killed the men tonight.

He rode back to the road and then heeled the gelding into a trot. His head spun with the realization of how much his life changed the day Keely had been abducted by the Crimson Guard. For a moment, he wondered if he would still recognize himself when this adventure was done.

## CHAPTER 17

The man strode down the gangplank, the heels on his boots striking sharp on the wood above the dock's din. Even in the mid-afternoon heat, he wore a calf-length black cloak, fastened at the throat, with the silk embroidered hood drawn low over his head. He moved like one of the ocean-born breezes through the flurry of activity, avoiding the workmen and the laden boxes with the grace of a Spirache hat dancer, despite his size.

He did not glance left or right, keeping his head tilted so the cowl's shadow hid his face. If asked later, no one on the dock could have said what he looked like as he maneuvered through the unintended obstacle course. Not that anyone dared move close enough to attempt a peek, however. His posture and stride told anyone with wits that this man did not want to be bothered.

The sounds altered as his boots left the wooden dock and stepped onto the gravel-lined street. A Crimson Guard detail, standing at post beside a waiting coach, snapped to attention as the figure neared. The officer opened the door, emblazoned with the black raven on a field of red of the Sacara Institute, and straightened to salute with his fist to his chest. Navy and red silk flashed through the cloak's slit as the man climbed in and sat down on the plush seat. He sighed with the self-important boredom that only someone accustomed to having his every whim carried out could muster.

"Drive on," he said, a rich baritone drifting from the depths of the shadow.

The escort detail assembled and led the way into the street traffic, the coach traveling in the middle of the group. None of the local citizens paid attention to the entourage, however. Diplomats and royals visited Sacara from other kingdoms on a regular basis. As long as the pomp did not interfere with their daily business, they moved quietly to one side to allow the guardsmen and carriage to pass without protest. Only the other visitors gawked and whispered behind their hands, wondering if they watched a concealed lady or a king pass by.

The group wound slowly through the streets, making their way up the climbing boulevard, until they finally passed through the gates of the Institute. Here, at last, the passenger swiveled his head back and forth to survey the complex. He stared for several moments at some construction in front of the guardsmen barracks, even turning in his seat a little to keep the men in sight longer. A rumbling chuckle startled the nearby outriders as they moved out of view of the works. But even then, he still did not throw back the hood or reveal himself to the students, workers, and staring petitioners on each side of the street.

The group stopped in front of the main building on the campus. Master Ravenhurst waited at the bottom of the stairs, thin and unsteady, with two Crimson Guards standing within an arm's reach. A breeze circled through the courtyard and ruffled the red and black robe draped over his emaciated shoulders, stirring black hair away from his neck. For just a moment, it gave the impression of the ebony wings of his namesake bird, threatening to carry him over the walls and out to sea.

Neither man offered a greeting as the new arrival climbed down from the carriage. Instead, they turned in silence and walked together up the long flight of steps toward the mammoth double doors that towered over the courtyard. The steps had been carved from the sea cliff rock when the Institute was built hundreds of years earlier. At one time, they had been an inspiring display of stonework, but over the years the harsh coast elements wore the beautiful designs in each riser smooth. Now they were so bald that on rainy days only the most adventurous or desperate students and petitioners braved their heights. More than one sagia or lord had found themselves in a bruised pile at the bottom of the steps after a tumble down the "Sacara Chute."

Both men made it to the top without incident on this day, though Ravenhurst was breathing heavily and sweating by the time they crested the last riser. The ironwood doors, covered with beaten copper and intricate carvings, already stood open, welcoming them into the formal foyer.

Adal stopped his halting steps once he reached the cooler sanctuary. He wavered for a moment like a sapling blown by storm winds, gasping like a fish on land for more air. Even so, his eyes snapped open, and he glared when the guards grasped his arms for support. Rage turning his pale cheeks purple, he waved them away and walked forward, his back ramrod straight and a renewed purpose in his stride. Another soft chuckle drifted from beneath the cowl, but the other figure followed along.

Ravenhurst made it all the way to the Hall of One Voice before his resolve finally crumbled beneath the weight of his ailing body. This time there was no fight as the guardsmen gently supported him by the elbows, the rest of his progress made more by being carried than under his own strength. The soldiers helped their master into the library before they stopped, lowering his body onto the divan, then silently bowing and exiting the room. Through Adal's entire ordeal, the tall guest had not said a word or offered a helping hand.

A student appeared, carrying chilled wine for the men. She filled two goblets with the golden liquid, serving one first to the visitor, and then offering one to her master. Ravenhurst still lay on the couch, spots of perspiration soaking through his clothing and leaving dark splotches on the silk. He shook his head to the young woman, saving his breath. Placing the goblet on the nearby table, she left the library, closing the door behind her as she left.

At long last, the guest pulled back the hood to reveal a handsome man with long, black hair tied loosely at his neck. A tight-lipped smirk danced along his mouth despite his humorless eyes. Only his complexion, the bright red skin of a painfully sunburned child, detracted from his looks.

"Do you think you'll even live to see your replenishment ceremony tomorrow night?" he asked, disgust enveloping his words in a cloud. The man removed his cloak and tossed it casually across the back of his chair before sitting across from Ravenhurst and sipping the wine.

"You and the others better hope that I do," Adal replied. He grimaced as he settled himself into a more comfortable position. "Otherwise, all these many years will have been wasted for nothing, Bacba."

The quiet words brought a fleeting look of pain to the newcomer's face before the composed mask dropped again.

"I thought your lapdog—Gregol, is it?—never left your side. What bone have you got him off retrieving now?" Bacba asked. The casual lifting of the wine glass dismissed the previous comment as irrelevant, but the deep draft and swallows told a different story.

At the mention of the commander, Ravenhurst sat straighter, one corner of his mouth twitching upward. He realized how close he had hit to home with his barb and wondered what the other man would say if he discovered what Commander Gregol was doing.

"How goes the rest of the restorations?" Adal asked, playing his own false disinterest, as well. "Have there been any problems with the last of us?"

"No, no problems at all." Bacba paused, his gaze sweeping over Ravenhurst. "Aphrun was the last," he continued. "She was raised with only a little difficulty right before Zerene, Melse, and I left the homeland to come to this Light forsaken place. They were in the process of fashioning a mask for her to wear the day we departed. It still remains to be seen how soon after a replenishment she will need to wear it to be able to move freely among the people without frightening children or the weak of stomach. If her ceremony was any indication, I wager she'll want it almost all the time. It's no secret she was by far the worst off of any of us that cursed day. Her screams...the pain still echoes in my ears."

"That will be difficult for her to accept," Adal said. His

words were quiet, and he glanced away. "She was very proud of her appearance. And the others?"

"Napol still can't hear a lion roar in his ears without using his saca. If possible, his injuries have made him even more paranoid, the whispers behind his back are real now, even if they're shouts." Bacba stopped for another drink. "Shibta will need to wear a mask as well, but not nearly as long as Aphrun." Glancing down at the scarlet skin on the back of his hands, his face twisted into a sneer. "Damn that slug! Will his blighted breath never stop burning?"

Adal leaned forward slowly, grasped the wine goblet, and raised it to his lips to hide the smile he could no longer control. He might feel sorry for the others, but his grin grew even wider when he thought about the constant pain his guest must be in at every moment. He brought his emotions under control before he spoke again.

"Our prayers may be answered sooner than we ever hoped," he said as he sat down his wine.

Bacba ripped his gaze from his hands and looked up, anger flashing in his eyes, and his mouth flying open. The retort died in his throat. Adal watched him out of the corner of his eyes. He could almost see the gears turning in the other man's head, thinking through everything he had seen on the way to Sacara. Suddenly, the man's eyes opened wide.

"You've found her? You've found the Matra?" he asked, the words floating on breathy puffs. Bacba leaned forward, and the goblet fell to the floor, forgotten as he placed shaking elbows on his knees for support. Only the thick carpet saved the crystal from shattering while the last few dregs of wine splashed onto his gleaming boots.

"The girl hasn't been tested at Sacara yet," Adal said, patting the air with a claw of a hand. "But the captain at the local garrison swears she cracked the eye in two. Besides, you know I don't dare put her to the trial without at least three of us and some of our underground friends present."

"I'll send a messenger to the ships at once for Zerene and Melse," Bacba said while rising to his feet. "But first, can I see her?"

Adal knew the unasked question was if it was *safe* to see her.

"No," he answered, shaking his head. "She hasn't arrived at the Institute yet. You asked about Commander Gregol when you arrived. He's not here because I sent him to meet the company she is with so he can escort her safely."

Bacba stepped closer to the couch, looming over Ravenhurst, his face turning from red to scarlet.

"You let your pet take on this responsibility!" His tenuous grip on his emotions slipped with the shout.

"Look at me!" Ravenhurst struggled to sit up. "I probably wouldn't have survived the journey, and where would that leave you and the others? Where would that leave the Emperor? None of us knows what will happen to him if one of the seven dies before the ritual."

The two men stared at each other, the silence stretching out and threatening to snap. Though neither man moved physically, the battle of wills released the same energy a warrior felt on the battlefield in the moment before the first blow landed.

*Our time is coming. Soon you will understand why the Emperor chose me for this duty, and I'll wet the ground with your blood.*

Adal relaxed at the thought. With a sigh, he reached for his wine and leaned back again.

Bacba continued to glare at Ravenhurst for a few moments before a breath escaped his lips.

"You're correct," he said. "Our only duty is to the Emperor. When will she arrive?"

"In less than two hands, she should be safely within Sacara's walls," Adal said. "Once she's here, I'll make her comfortable until the others arrive from home."

"That could be a cycle from now." Bacba cut his words short, leaving them with an edge.

"We've waited a long time already. What's a few more hands before we know if she's the one?" Adal smiled. "Besides, *you* must have control of Xenon and the mountain if she's to fulfill her duty as Matra. We will follow as soon as she proves herself to be the favored Chosen, and she's at an age to fulfill her part. That might take a few years, but we need the kingdoms to be prepared."

Bacba paced the room, his legs stretching out and chewing up the distance. Every time he passed beneath the dragon head in the glass, he lowered his head, ducking away from a blow only he could feel. Ravenhurst watched silently as the circles grew smaller, each stride shorter than the last. Finally, Bacba came to a halt in front of a painting depicting a battle, ranks of soldiers dying at the base of an impenetrable wall. His breathing slowed.

"I noticed what appeared to be Cleansing Trees being built in the guardsmen's quad on my way here," he said.

"That's correct," Adal answered. "Commander Gregol believed it would be best to remind the men what was expected of them."

"Really?" Bacba said as he turned, an eyebrow arched high. "Perhaps he does have some uses after all. Melse will be sorry he missed the little lesson. Of course, the remains will still be on display for him to relish." He walked across the room and stood before Ravenhurst again. "I'm afraid I'm too tired after my journey to continue this delightful conversation. I must be rested for your replenishment ceremony tomorrow night. We wouldn't want anything bad to happen to you *before* our task is complete."

Adal nodded, lips curling into a grin.

"I look forward to the day when it is done," he said, answering the thinly veiled threat with one of his own. "Until then, I'll have someone show you to your place."

## CHAPTER 18

The Farmer's Sickle was the last phase of the moon before it began to fill out again to its fullest. The barest amount of moonlight shone from the sliver hanging in the dark sky, even the stars choosing to stay away this evening. The night fell so dark that a sparse stand of trees outside the town threw inky shadows on the ground. Dax sat in one of these black pools.

He remained a motionless figure only five paces from a Crimson Guard on the outer watch line. His gaze swept the area, studying the troops, just as he had every night since catching up to the company west of Charlser.

It had taken ten days of living in the saddle, ten days of trailing the soldiers during the day, and testing their defenses at night. During the entire time, Dax had only caught one brief glimpse of Keely. On the second night, he had hidden at just the correct angle to see her descend from the covered cage and enter a tent. But that one quick flash had kept him on his feet with little rest, waiting for the opportunity to steal her away. So far, the moment had eluded him.

That dilemma puzzled Dax. Yes, the group was of company strength, counting nine score of men, but it was not the number that had him shaking his head late at night. The little experience he had in the past with the Crimson Guard revealed the officers to be lenient about letting the soldiers have their way with nearby townspeople, carousing with the women, fighting with the men, and generally taking whatever they could carry. But this captain had not allowed his men to enter the villages they passed, even when they camped within a stone's throw of a small town as they did tonight.

Their guard duty was just as strange. A full squad stood guard on Keely's tent each evening. Four more squads walked posts on the outer perimeter of the camp. This group of five rotated with two other five-squad crews for three separate watches during the night. The rotation kept the sentries at maximum alertness, not allowing Dax to sneak into camp when they grew tired or sloppy. Even more confusing, Keely appeared to be the only prisoner in the camp, making the number of guards feel excessive. He knew there must be some significance to the amount of watchfulness, but he had never seen anything like it before.

The only good fortune he stumbled across so far was the pace of the journey. A company could not travel as fast as a squad or platoon, even with the discipline of this group of Crimson Guards. It had taken two or three days longer to cross Galadon than he expected. But this small amount of luck was about to desert him. Sometime late the next afternoon, the company would reach the Wall of Purley and cross into Tralain. Once inside that immense barrier, as tall as five men and stretching from border to border, he doubted he would ever be able to escape with Keely, even if he did manage to break her free.

If he was going to make an attempt at a rescue, tonight was the night.

Dax dozed lightly in the shadows as the first watch gave way to the second. With his cloak wrapped around his legs and hood pulled down, he was just another spot of black in a dark night. He decided that unless a sentry stumbled over him, he was safe even this close to the camp.

Near the end of the second watch, that bad luck nearly occurred. Two guardsmen walked into the trees to relieve themselves and, as one unbuttoned his pants, the ebony heap beside him erupted into silent motion. The man opened his mouth to scream for help, but no sound flew out. Warm liquid already blazed a path down his chest, his throat cut so deeply he could not speak. The man grabbed his neck as he sank to his knees, life flowing between his fingers.

As the first soldier settled to the ground, Dax approached the tree of the second. The man finished his call of nature at the same time a knife plunged into the base of his neck. The spinal cord severed, Dax held his hand over the guardsman's mouth while they both eased to the grass. He knelt on the man's neck and watched the surrounding area for an alarm as the sentry suffocated beneath him.

*That's the diversion I need.*

Dax moved away from the two bodies, settling at the far end of this side of the camp's watch. Although he crouched in the shadows, he rested on the balls of his feet, legs coiled underneath himself like twin springs ready to be released. He drew in a slow breath and waited.

Long moments passed before the squad's sergeant noticed the two men had not returned to their posts. He cursed and gathered two more soldiers. Together, the trio walked into the tree line to search for his missing men, the sergeant still muttering a string of curses. The remaining six men spread their watch areas to span the entire northern line of the camp.

Dax slinked across the ground on his stomach while his head swiveled back and forth. He chose a point in the middle of two of the dispersed sentries. With the dark night, and the increased gap between the soldiers, he hoped to enter the camp undetected. In a few moments, he breathed a sigh of relief as he wriggled into the shadow of a troop tent. A sleeve wiped across his face came back covered in sweat and mud.

*And that was the easy part.*

Dax peered around the corner of the tent and watched where Keely was being held prisoner. A guard stood at each corner with a sentry posted at the middle of the solid canvas wall. From previous nights, he knew guardsmen also stood on either side of the tent flaps. That left two men unaccounted for and probably posted inside with his sister.

He shook his head, trying to erase the thoughts of what the soldiers might be doing to Keely inside the tent. He succeeded, only to find his anger replaced with despair at failing his family again.

*Again!*

The thought screamed in his mind, echoing until he was sure the voice escaped his head, and the nearby troops heard the cry.

*No! It wasn't my fault! I was doing my duty!*

Duty, duty, duty. The word sounded over and over. Forcing his eyes open, he concentrated on finding a solution to freeing Keely.

The first voice quieted and another, familiar voice replaced it. He strained to catch the words until they were loud enough to hear clearly.

"The way to go unseen, is to give the enemy what they expect to see."

Tears filled the corners of Dax's eyes at the memory of his father's voice.

He dropped to his belly again and slowly lifted the side panel of the troop tent a hand's breadth and peered into the gloom. Just inside the semi-darkness, he saw what he needed. Holding his breath as he reached inside, he inched a Crimson Guard cloak into the night. Dax reminded himself to take his time, even though his heart raced, knowing the two dead sentries would be found at any moment.

Sweat dripped into his eyes as he let the tent panel drop. The too large cloak flew around his shoulders, and he flipped the hood over his head. With a last deep breath, the woodsman began walking towards the back of Keely's prison.

An alarm cry rose from the outer watch line. Tent flaps flew open and well-trained guardsmen, in various stages of dress, poured into the night. Orders were shouted over the noise but soon, everyone was rushing to their posts. Dax jogged the rest of the way to Keely's tent, fumbling with his stolen cloak as if he was still dressing. Every ounce of his attention searched for an opportunity, however. Only a few paces from the lone sentry at the back of the tent, Dax glanced to check the corner postings. One guard had disappeared, and the other peered intently toward the tree line before walking in that direction.

*This time I won't fail. Not this time.*

He took one step past the sentry then whirled in a reverse

pivot. The cloak sailed up into the face of the guard, hiding the knife in Dax's hand. The blade struck the man at the base of the nose with enough force to knock his helmet off. Dax caught the sentry and eased his convulsing body to the ground. He wasted a moment attempting to withdraw his knife, but the blade was lodged in the dying man's skull, the hilt slick with blood. Without another thought, he drew a third dagger from a boot sheath and rolled beneath the tent panel.

The world spun at a blinding speed, but Dax felt half a step faster. In the middle of what should have been a terrifying situation, he felt alive, perhaps more than he had been in years. Blood raced through his veins with the speed of a diving falcon. Air rushed into his nose and filled his lungs to bursting. His heart sang, and the song was as beautiful as it was deadly. He could die with his next breath, but he would burst to life again. He was alive!

Dax rolled to one knee and threw a knife. It struck home with a dull thump into the back of the guardsman standing three paces away in the middle of the tent. The man staggered forward and groaned. Though it was a solid hit, Dax knew it would not kill the man before he cried out. He leaped forward, drawing his sword while still in the air, and swinging before his feet hit the ground again.

The blade gouged deep into the soldier's neck and stuck fast. The abrupt jolt pulled Dax off balance, and the two men fell in a jumbled heap.

Dax whirled to his feet, fanning the cloak wide to hide his body. His gaze raced from the body at his feet and swept the rest of the tent for movement. Nothing stirred in the dim light as he desperately searched for the next attack.

His sight reached the far corner. Shadows and light tricked his eyes, and he gasped as he stared at his mother standing in the crook. But when the woman moved forward, the vision melted into Keely.

"Dax," she whispered. "Is that you?"

"Yes," he said as he recovered enough to bend down and retrieve his sword and knife. "Can you travel? Are you hurt?" He grimaced with the last question, rumors of how the Bloods treated the captured making him unsure if he wanted to know the answer.

"No, no. I'm fine. My god, Dax. What have you done?"

Dax understood the fear and shock in his sister's trembling voice. She had been ripped from her home and just watched her brother kill another man. But there was still a long way to go before they were safe enough for him to comfort her. He answered with as much confidence as he could muster.

"It's time I got you out of here. Put on this Blood's cloak. We'll go back out under the tent the same way I came in. Once we get outside, we'll just have a quick walk to get past a few sentries, and then we'll be on our way." He hoped the confusion in camp lasted that long. "Ready?"

Keely nodded, then stared down at the dead guardsman by her feet. Her white cheeks grew even paler.

"Dax, I didn't think anyone...I didn't know..."

Boots pounded past the tent flap as more guardsmen ran to their posts. Dax decided it was time to shock his sister into action.

"You can make it, Keely," he interrupted. "We both can. But we've got to move now. What do you think they're going to do once they find a dead man in your tent? To you? To me? We've got to leave now before more of them come back." He smiled as he tossed the cloak around her shoulders and fastened it over an unadorned, metal collar. "Let's go."

Dax rolled out into the night. Luckily, the dead guard had not been discovered in the shadow of the tent. A moment passed while he waited for his sister to join him. He started to stick his head back under the panel when Keely crawled into view. Her face was lighter than the sliver of moon overhead, but her eyes were unblinking. She nodded and pulled the hood over her head. He grabbed her elbow and pulled her into motion.

Within a few moments, Dax escorted Keely past the last of the troop tents on the eastern side of camp. As they neared the outer sentries, he turned and growled at Keely.

"Probably just a bloody damn drill," he said loudly enough to be heard by the nearest guardsman. "The gods know we haven't had any real excitement in a while."

The nearby sentry nodded in agreement as he let the two figures pass without a challenge.

◆ ◆ ◆

The silent procession moved along the cliff top, the surf pounding the rocks below with the rhythmic beating of a tom stick against a Balami war drum. Though exceedingly dangerous, foolhardy even, the five figures walked the life-threatening path without the benefit of a single lantern or torch. The group could not risk being spotted from the Sacara Institute walls, even as unlikely as that possibility appeared at this late hour. The thin light of the Sickle Moon would be all the illumination this small band of robed figures would use to light their way.

The path, though to call it more than an oddly placed game

trail would be an exaggeration, meandered near the cliff's edge. It never drifted more than a few paces away from the drop, and often snaked alongside, making the walkers feel as if they were hanging over the side. The short figure in front, however, walked with the confident stride of someone pacing down a flagstone street in the noontime sun.

When the lights from Sacara shined no brighter than fireflies in the distance, the trail abruptly veered left and appeared to disappear over the side of the bluff. But it continued, comprised of crude steps cut into the rock face. The figures proceeded on the steady descent until the path ended on a ledge about fifty paces from the top of the cliff. A yawning fissure, blacker than even this nearly lightless night, opened along the back of the shelf. Smoke drifted out, the remnants of burning wood, before sweeping away on the sea breeze. The figures entered the opening.

The group stepped into what appeared to have once been a natural formation before it had been transformed long ago. The twisting passageway roughly followed the wanderings of nature's course, cut into the rock from the freezing and thawing of water. In fact, the turns were a cleverly designed series of blinds that allowed no light to enter or leave from the inner caves. That it still performed as a flue was an additional architectural marvel.

The corridor expanded until it fed into a cave so large that five braziers did not illuminate the far walls or ceiling. Hollow footsteps intermingled with the monotone chanting of the thirteen red-robed sagias already in the room. The two newcomers also dressed in scarlet quickly joined their brethren, the assembly continuing their intonation as they split into five equal groups of three around the small blazes.

The two taller entrants threw back their hoods and stared

silently at the smallest member of their group. He also pulled down the gray wool covering his head before walking beyond the circle of light.

Ravenhurst noticed Bacba's shake of his head, disdain sitting in the sneer on his lips, as their Bakri guide left them to fulfill the rest of his duties. Though Adal found the presence of the hairy, underground dwelling people distasteful as well, they had an important function to perform during the ritual.

He suddenly wavered and nearly collapsed, a wave of nausea racing through his body and threatening to turn his muscles to water. He was glad he had not eaten today. Two hands gripped his atrophied arms, fingers digging into his flesh and forcing tears into his eyes. It galled him to accept help from Bacba but, despite their mutual hatred of each other, replenishment ceremonies bound them together as brothers with a shared need.

Ravenhurst called upon hidden reserves and straightened to stand on his own as four more figures entered the light from deeper within the cave. The Bakri leader, whose name Adal had never bothered to learn, and two more of his race led a young woman dressed in the orange robe of a third level Sacara student to the middle of the chanting trios.

The group stopped beside the only piece of furniture in the ceremonial grotto. Flames danced in the polished shine of the waist high platform, carved from a single piece of obsidian. Not a scratch marred its smooth, perfect surfaces. Yet, as Adal stared at the rock glass, he thought he could see writhing images trapped within its inky depths, screaming silently for release into the world. He imagined the movement was a trick of the wavering light, but he had been using the dais for too long to not suspect more of the shadows.

Ravenhurst's gaze wandered to the Bakri, and he gagged. The short men had shed the robes they were forced to wear above ground to conceal their identities. Now they simply had on the knee-length pants and sleeveless vests they normally wore in their mountain homes. Thick hair covered their stocky bodies, except on the bottom of their feet, hands, and, strangely enough, faces. From a distance, more than one person had made the mistake of thinking the Bakri were wearing black or dark gray animal pelts.

They removed the orange wrap from the girl and helped her to lie down, naked, upon the hard platform. Her short brown hair and ruddy complexion spoke of her Lebeshan heritage despite her silence. Light-colored eyes twinkled, slightly glazed with more than just excitement, and her chest heaved as she waited for the ritual to begin.

Ravenhurst knew the most dangerous step was the first. Only the nelamite choker, its light blue metal in contrast with the redness of her neck, remained on the girl. The Bakri leader reached into a slit in his vest and removed the small pouch Adal had given him earlier in the library. The short man loosened the drawstring and held the package out to the prone girl. Adal reached for his saca, keeping the power ready to be unleashed.

Eager fingers probed inside the purse while her other hand rose to the necklace. The metal latch came loose with an audible click, the sound harsh and sharp against the singsong words. The young woman sighed in ecstasy as the warmth of her power leaped through her body. Shudders marched down her limbs in rhythm to the chant.

Adal heard Bacba draw a short breath, his nervousness apparent in his fidgeting feet. With the block removed, the student could call upon her saca and lash out in any number of deadly ways. Everyone in the room realized their danger if she had only been pretending to be eager to serve the master. The two Bakri standing beyond her head and out of sight, unsheathed the double-bladed knives their kind used in close quarters fighting. The responsibility to kill the girl, if she changed her mind, remained theirs to carry out.

But the student was true. She settled against the pedestal and awaited Ravenhurst. The Bakri leader backed to the edge of the light, pouch still in his hand, while his two companions held their positions.

Adal and Bacba walked to the side of the obsidian and stared down at the willing woman. Now that he stood so close to being refilled with life, Ravenhurst's muscles quivered in the moment. Every hair, every pore, every tiniest bit of his being screamed for the life he sensed surging through the girl's body.

*I must have her.*

His soul yearned to feel her vitality in every possible way. Visions swam through his mind as their eyes found each other and locked in an eternal stare. He imagined their bodies, slick with sweat, writhing in bliss. Her will yielded to his every whim, every desire. Different settings, different times, different circumstances—they all flashed through his thoughts, spinning faster and faster, until he barely felt Bacba sliding the black robe from his shoulders to reveal his bony nakedness to everyone in the cave.

Bacba reached beneath his cloak and withdrew a dagger as the red-robed students increased the pace of the chant. Halting, shaking hands raised the weapon, pausing for a moment as if he fought an internal battle to keep the blade for himself, then slipped the hilt into Ravenhurst's hand.

From the first touch of the blue-black dagger, Adal's focus

changed. It was not the woman's body he lusted, but the saca racing beneath her skin. He felt his own power leap to new heights as his thoughts cleared. His eyes turned black, mirroring the desire ravaging his face. All that stood between him and life was the piece of flesh laying on the pedestal.

Ravenhurst trailed the tip of the blade up the red-tinged skin of a slim thigh, past the sprouting hair of her blossoming womanhood, and across the youthful flatness of her stomach. The girl shivered at the blade's touch. It rested for a moment between the mounds of her breasts, her chest heaving with gasps for air as she stared, trance-like, into the master's eyes. With one breath, the chanters stopped, the last words echoing off unseen walls.

Ravenhurst leaned his weight over her body, lips pursed to kiss her, and shoved the blade deep into the woman's heart.

Two screams rang out. The woman's noise was a shout of pain and betrayal while Adal's was filled with joy. He held tight to the bloody hilt, the metal sliding in his palm, as he pressed his body close.

The student, realizing too late her real duty in the ritual, thrashed wildly on the stone top. Her saca fled from her grasp, flitting away in her mind every time she tried to grab it again. Strength bled from her body. Her flailing arms slowed, lessening until only an occasional twitch of her hands whispered of her clinging life.

Ravenhurst watched a haze seep from her body and pool above her head and heart. The fog glowed in his eyes as it flowed together into a vague animal form. The beastly vision hovered for a moment before flinging itself onto the dagger and Adal's hand. The creature leaped up his arm, cavorted across his chest, and then slid down his body until his entire frame convulsed in the colored light. He threw his head back and laughed, the cackle echoing as if a hundred madmen joined with him.

*Alive! This is alive!*

Ravenhurst gasped as the thought left him. Just as suddenly as it began, the glow died. Only the light of the five braziers continued to shine in the cave. Ravenhurst glanced down at the dead sagia as Bacba joined him. Her body no longer appeared human. Skin stretched taut over bones with the consistency of worn leather. The girl appeared as if she had been dead for many years, preserved by the heat and lack of moisture in the deep desert.

Ravenhurst, on the other hand, displayed the youth and vitality of a man just entering his prime. He slowly bent down and retrieved his robe, exhibiting his fresh form for as long as possible before covering up. After donning his black garb, he reverently cleaned the sacrificial dagger on the woman's garment before handing it to Bacba to replace in the sheath.

A Bakri appeared out of the darkness with a spit and hung it over the fire at the foot of the pedestal. Adal used the offered butcher knife to cut seventeen strips of flesh from the human offering and strung them on the metal rod. While they waited for the meat to cook, a Bakri slowly turning the skewer, Ravenhurst returned to stand beside Bacba. Hungry, devouring fire leaped from their fingertips and touched the corpse. The remains burst into a burning inferno that soon forced them back to the ring of braziers while the expanding light revealed the smoky ceiling above their heads.

Some of the red-robed pupils walked into the shadowed areas of the cave and returned with bottles of wine. Most drank to soothe aching throats caused by hours of chanting while others drank to forget what the ritual dictated they eat. Nervous giggles and whispers rose from the released tension now that the formal part of the ceremony was completed.

"It was almost too much," Ravenhurst said, his voice a soft whisper. Shock made his eyes widen at admitting any weakness to the man beside him.

"How so?" Bacba asked. "I've seen the glow of saca burn much brighter than hers. Why, Melse's last one..."

"No, you fool!" Adal hissed. "Not her saca. It was nearly impossible to fight my way through the physical desires of the replenishment." He paused, licking his lips with a mixture of nerves and exhilaration at the memory. "He's growing much stronger."

Bacba stared at the man he hated with a driving passion, but still considered almost an equal in saca. Almost.

"Perhaps the one your lackey went to retrieve is truly the Matra. It would not be the first time the Emperor knew far more than the rest of us could even guess at. I, for one, will be glad when this part of our task is complete. It's been a long time since I..."

"A long time," Adal interrupted. "You were only reawakened some sixty odd summers ago. It's been a thousand summers since I've lain with a woman. It wouldn't surprise me to find out I've forgotten how."

Bacba's deep, rumbling laugh echoed in the cave. It shocked the talking students into gaping-mouthed silence.

"You'd better remember, or all of this will have been for nothing," he said, the smirk still sitting on his lips.

Anger seethed beneath the hot flush of embarrassment on Ravenhurst's face. What had come over him? Why was he admitting anything to the man he would one day need to battle to the death?

"Come," Adal said, breaking into his companion's revelry. "Let's go eat some of the flesh and return to the Institute. If the Matra has been found, we've much work to do." He glanced down and noticed a pale white gleam shining from the corpse's face. "We must remember to harvest her eyes once the flames have died down. We'll need as many wizard's eyes as we can have before this is over." He walked away.

Bacba's laughter stopped as abruptly as it began. The haughty stare returned, sitting more naturally on his face than the previous grin.

"Someday it will be you on the obsidian, black bird," he whispered. "And I'll be the one with the knife."

eneral Bacba stood in the middle of the deck, as he had for two days, his hands clasped behind his back, and his feet spread wide to maintain his balance. He shifted his weight with the pitch and roll of the sloop, leaning when it struggled from one white-capped swell to the next. The craft had not been designed for this type of travel, and it showed on the ocean waves. The shallow keel remained better suited to racing along shore routes or in rivers. Even the experienced sailors who kept the vessel upright refused to look each other in the eyes for fear of seeing the reflections of their own clenched jaws and pallid skin.

Through it all, the tall figure in black appeared fastened to the foredeck as firmly as the mast. Neither the salty spray crashing over the bow onto his clothes, nor the dance of harried sailors around him, tore his gaze away from the horizon. As the most seasoned old tars eventually lost the fight to hold onto their breakfasts, admiration replaced their fear of the watching passenger. Though they sailed through the rainless squall on their own efforts and captain's skill, the superstitious men began to believe Bacba's vigil and saca piloted them safely through harm.

The general could not have cared less what they believed. In truth, behind the piercing gaze, the man who had made entire kingdoms tremble at his feet was too terrified to move. No one alive, most especially his fellow generals, knew even the flat calm of a pond sent shivers of terror down his spine. Perhaps even Ravenhurst would have admitted some grudging respect for the man if he realized the anguish Bacba endured each time his service to the Emperor called for him to travel on water.

From daybreak to early afternoon, the boat sailed valiantly on its course. As the sun reached its peak, the winds dropped from the ear-splitting howl to a steady breeze. The waves shortened with each roll until they only slapped the bow on the way past. The tension in the crew floated off with the last of the gusts and left the barbs the sailors threw at each other drifting in the warm sunshine. A rollicking, raunchy song rang out as they returned to their routine shipboard duties.

"Land!" shouted the lookout from where he stood on the main mast's boom. "Starboard bow!"

The bustle on the ship's deck turned more frenetic when the captain ordered a course change toward the sighting. A rocky mass rose from the desolate sameness of the Windward Sea as they approached. The clamor of thousands of birds wafted toward the ship like an invitation on the wind, beckoning the crew to land.

The island was small. Formed from the lava of the dormant volcano at its center, a man could walk from one end to the other in two days' time. When Movilian sailors had discovered it thirty summers earlier, Bacba had been the general sent to check for its feasibility as a staging area against the northern kingdoms. The Bakri he had taken with him, the short men turning almost as green in the face as he had been, searched the volcano's caverns and tunnels for inhabitants before declaring it safe for use. He had referred to the rocky outcropping as the "bastion" in his reports and conversations, since no record could be found of the island. The seamen who overheard his references twisted the name until they simply called it Bastard Isle. The general thought it a fitting title.

Dark specks in the water around the island took shape and grew larger until the stick figures of sail-less masts rose against the setting sun like the fingers of skeletons clawing out of their watery graves. Nearly one hundred ships swayed at the end of their anchor chains. The captain steered the sloop through the unintended maze towards the small cove and its wooden dock jutting out into the protected water.

For the first time since ordering the captain to cast off from the Sacara port three days earlier, Bacba relaxed. A hint of a smile played on the corners of his mouth, and his eyes twinkled at the sounds of troops practicing with weapons on the nearby decks of the taller warships. Even those crafts would feel as solid as land after this boat.

His smirk turned to a frown, however, when they sailed beneath the bow of General Melse's command ship. Illuminated by the orange glow of the day's last sunlight, the bloody corpse of a Movilian soldier swayed at the end of a rope. At least, he thought the body had once belonged to a trooper. A rope around both ankles snaked up and over the boom and held the naked body out of the ocean. Only from the stomach to the feet remained, however. Everything else up, or in this case down, had disappeared. Skin, skull, bones—nothing else was visible to tell who the man had been in life.

Crew mutterings floated to Bacba's ears. He turned on his heels, eyebrows pulled together and forehead creased. All the whispers froze on paralyzed tongues as the sailors quickly became fascinated with the most mundane task at hand.

"A commendable job of sailing, Captain," he said, a sigh escaping between words. "You must tell the men they did well despite the fact we're overdue."

Captain Regil's eyes flew open. Praise, even backhanded praise such as this, seldom came from one of the revered leaders. Every Movilian understood the generals' importance to Emperor Abaddon, so each word spoken, even one in anger or rebuke, held its special place in their memories.

"Thank you, Lord General. It's been an honor to serve. I'll have your bags taken directly to your ship." The captain bowed his head and kept it lowered until Bacba walked away.

The general's thoughts were already paces in front of his body. Thumps from his footsteps mixed with the calls of the birds as he strode down the pier. Shore boats stood moored on both sides and spoke of the number of men on the island. An honor guard snapped to attention when he reached the end and fell into step as he continued toward the few wooden structures erected on Bastard Isle. Bacba did not dare speak to the sergeant following a step behind for fear his relief at walking on solid ground again would ring in his words. He walked directly to the largest of the one-story structures in the middle of the compound and returned the salutes of the posted sentries. The door creaked open at his touch.

Only two people were in the room. General Melse glanced up in response to the noise while the other figure, a woman, held her head low as if she was asleep. Melse narrowed his small, close-set eyes before returning his concentration to the sword he was honing. A grin played across his thin face.

"You took a big chance, crossing in that kind of weather," he said over the screeching whetstone as it drew down the blade. "Zerene thought you'd probably be too...anxious...to wait until the storm passed before leaving Ravenhurst's kiddie school."

Bacba spared a glance at the older, entranced woman, before turning back to Melse. He smiled when he noticed the other man had tilted his head slightly so he could hear the reply in his right ear. Strangers might assume the long black hair pulled over and tied into a flowing tail on the left side of Melse's head to be simply a stylistic affectation. Nothing could be farther from the truth. Instead, the hair covered the charred hole where his ear had sat before the battle with the dragonlord many years earlier. The hand holding the sword steady also missed the last two fingers as further consequence of the lost fight. Not even a replenishment ceremony could regrow ears and fingers.

"I noticed your handiwork in the bay on the way to the dock," Bacba said by way of controlling the verbal sparring match. "Discipline problems?"

Melse's eyes gleamed, and he sat straight in his chair.

"Nothing to worry about, old friend. Zerene just helped to point out that the men weren't showing enough zeal while practicing their arm's play. The soldier was merely a motivational tool for the rest of the troops." He leaned forward, voice trembling with excitement. The sword leaned against his shoulder, the sharpening long forgotten. "You should've been here to see it, Bacba. I cut him first and let his blood pour into the water to call the sharks in for dinner. Then we started to dunk him—up and down, up and down—for longer and longer times. Ha, ha! I'm surprised you couldn't hear his screams across the water when the little sharks came swimming in for a taste. They started taking bites out of him. He fought with gusto then, let me tell you. Anyway, before too long, this big, dark shape swims underneath all of them like a drifting shadow, and all the little nibblers scattered. I ordered the trooper back down again and bam! I don't know if this new shark, if that's what it was, either didn't want to let go or his teeth snagged in the man's ribs, but when I ordered the men to hoist away, it was partially reeled in, too. The trooper's body wasn't strong enough to support that much weight so the fish slipped off the hook with half my bait." Melse leaned back and let out a low whistle. "If we've got time, you can help me go fishing again tomorrow. I really do miss the little things in life." He ended his tale with a raspy laugh.

Bacba forced himself to sip the wine he had poured during the recount of the afternoon's activities. What he really wanted to do was scream at the man for wasting a trained soldier on sadistic sport. Hopefully, they could complete their tasks before Melse's pleasures became too much of a detriment to morale.

"Has our dear comrade, Ravenhurst, convinced you we should wait even longer before we attack, Bacba?" Zerene asked as she woke from her meditation. She ran her fingers through shoulder length hair, black and silver streaked, while she waited for a reply.

It was not the first time Bacba wondered about the age of the woman. Even with replenishments, she appeared old, shoulders beginning to hunch and spidery veins decorating the back of her hands. He watched as she allowed her fingers to dance in a caress across her left cheek. Pockmarks marred the skin like an acne-cursed child. The marking from her part in the battle against the dragons would grow worse each day until her vanity would finally force her to wear a mask covering half her face. But until then, she would flaunt the scars, reminding the other generals of their own wounds.

Bacba glanced down and noticed he had clawed his red-tinged hands until blood appeared. He cursed himself silently before looking up again. Although she did not return the stare, Zerene smiled at the far wall.

"No," Bacba answered, returning his attention to the wine in the center of the table. "We sail at first light to begin our task." A smile bloomed on his face as well, when he noticed Zerene's head snap around to stare at him. "There's more urgency attached to the completion of our plan now."

Melse continued to examine his blade without comment, but Zerene guessed the significance of the statement immediately.

"So, you and Ravenhurst took it upon yourselves to test for the Matra alone," she said, before throwing a glance at their oblivious member.

"Wait, you did what?" Melse asked, his face turning red as his voice grew. "That's forbidden! The ceremony must have..."

"I know what the ceremony must have!" Bacba grabbed hold of his emotions and raised a calming hand. "And so does the old black bird. She hasn't been fully tested yet. As a matter of fact, I didn't even see her because she hadn't arrived at Ravenhurst's little school before I left."

Zerene snorted.

"Well, then. You don't know if someone suitable to be the Matra has been discovered or not."

"Yes, it's true Ravenhurst wasn't certain she was the one we've been searching for, but the report said she cracked the wizard's eye in two pieces," Bacba said. "That's not a sign that can be easily misunderstood. She'll be with him by the time our other companions arrive from the homeland. They'll be able to perform the testing ceremony at that time. I'll leave word with Captain Regil that they should all be taken to the mainland as soon as they arrive. We just need to make sure we have control of the cave by the time they sail to Xenalia with the Matra."

"That'll be no problem," Melse said with a rough laugh. "Have you forgotten that we swatted them like flies the last time?"

"And have you forgotten that we were defeated when the cursed dragons stuck their beaks into the fight?" Zerene asked. The two men winced at the comment, and Bacba fought the urge to scratch the skin on his hands and arms again. "But none of that may not matter. If Ravenhurst's reports are correct," she said, each word emphasized to let them know what she thought of that possibility, "there haven't been any dragon sightings in the kingdoms since a half-grown slug was killed almost two hundred summers ago."

"One hundred and eighty-seven summers, on the Balame side of the Teeth with all those blasted horse lovers," Bacba said, nodding his head in agreement. "I checked the records before I left Sacara." He caught himself rubbing his skin as he continued. "Let's make our final preparations so we can sail at first light tomorrow. And Melse, please try to have enough of your troops still alive when we reach the battle to carry out your part of the plan."

Melse grinned in reply.

◆ ◆ ◆

Gera sighed as he stepped down from the gelding's saddle and stretched his aching muscles. He glanced around the inn's dooryard and frowned before walking stiffly to the front door. The thought of a meal and a bed had brightened his thoughts for a while, even if it meant leaving Nava alone for the night. By the light of the setting sun, he noticed several wagons parked in the yard and a rope corral erected outside the fenced pasture. A pair of boys had spread out bedrolls by the pen. He could hear them arguing over who would sleep first.

*Still a full day's ride south of Greenville, and every inn is filled to overflowing with guards posted.*

Gera shook his head at the thought. The rumors of an imminent war between Crandor and Palamor had increased with every step north. Each day, he passed more and more people fleeing from the potential hostilities.

The questions deserted Gera's thoughts when an enormous din assaulted him from the meeting room. Every table and chair stood full with half again as many people milling around, waiting for an opening to sit. He turned to leave, giving up hope of finding a room at this inn as well, when a stocky man dressed in green hustled up to the young man. His brown hair lay damp with sweat against his forehead, and his clothing hung in a rumpled mess. Gera guessed him to be the most frazzled person he had ever met.

"May your ground bring you happiness until the harvest, good traveler," he blurted out, the words rushing together. "Welcome to the Farmer's Pride. I'm Innkeeper Till."

"Until the next planting, Master Till," Gera said with a smile. "My name is Gera Staghorn. I had hoped to find a hot meal and a soft bed for the night, but you appear to have a year's worth of business already. It won't be the first night I've slept under the stars, but I wonder if the meal might still be arranged?"

"Always plenty to eat at the Farmer's Pride. If you can find a place to sit, I'll bring a plate from the kitchen and a mug of ale as soon as I can manage." With a quick turn on his heels, the innkeeper slid back into the throng and moved at an astonishing pace despite his bulk and the press of people.

Gera began sweating in the stifling heat before he made three steps into the crowd. Throwing his cloak back over his shoulders, he worked his way farther into the room. Luckily, he appeared to be the tallest person present, something he was not accustomed to, which made it easier to see an open seat wedged back into a far corner.

After settling himself on the hard-backed chair, he turned to face the room again. An idea winked at the back of his thoughts of something unusual with the other guests in the inn, but the answer eluded his thoughts. Suddenly, like a hard slap across his face, the explanation hit him. Nearly every person in the room was a woman.

Gera's attention snapped back to the situation when he noticed the only men in sight gathering in the middle of the room. Most of them took turns glancing in his direction. After a few moments, two of the men broke away and went to stand in the doorway where he had entered. The other four began working their way through the women toward his corner.

Gera wiped his palms on his pants, drying away the sweat, while he glanced around, trying to act as if he had not noticed their approach. With his left hand, he slowly unclasped his cloak so it fell back from his shoulders while he inched his right across his lap and close to his sword hilt. At least he was seated in a decent spot in the room. With his back to the corner, it lessened the advantage the other men had in numbers and would stop someone trying to flank him. But even if he outlasted the six-against-one odds, the women were crowded in so close he would never be able to sprint to safety. If the men wanted a fight, Gera's only chance to survive would be to hold his ground.

He turned to the men as the women closest to him parted to allow the men to pass. The roar subsided to whispers, even softer after the previous clamor, as the men stopped on the other side of the table. Gera glanced them over and quickly realized they were not army regulars, or even sellswords, even though they each wore a sword. In fact, he wondered how much fighting experience they had when they did not fan out like the Crandori soldiers a few days earlier to confront him, remaining almost single file. He did not know if their lack of experience would make them more likely to attack, or less.

The Crandori leader looked Gera over in silence for several moments before opening his mouth.

"Where are you from, stranger?" he asked. "What's your business around here?"

Gera was surprised by the lack of the traditional greeting and did not answer.

Innkeeper Till, apparently blessed with the sixth sense all hostelers appeared to have that warned them when trouble was about to erupt in their businesses, burst through the edge of the crowd with his hands upraised.

"Hold, gentlemen, please!" he exclaimed. "Surely no insult was great enough to warrant bloodshed. Where do you think we are, a Galadon Royal Court? Can't this be settled without steel?"

Gera remained silent, determined to let the other men make

the first move. In his mind, he tested the door holding his saca, and felt it bend to his touch, a thin crack of light forming at the edge. Announcing himself as a sagia would cause a whole new host of problems, but he was no use to Dax or Keely if he was dead.

After several more breaths, the leader broke eye contact and half-turned to the innkeeper.

"Master Till, you know the duty that has brought me here," he said, the words just as rough edged as with Gera. "I wanted to make sure the stranger's business was not to interfere with those of us from Bushmill. He doesn't have the look of us, and he's refused to answer." With that said, he placed his hand on his sword hilt and turned back to Gera.

"Master Staghorn, please," the innkeeper said, his lips touched by a frown. "Master Greens and the other men are responsible for seeing the women and children safely to Bagdon. They're escaping the war on the border with Palamor. I beg your indulgence. Are you from Palamor?"

"No," Gera answered, his eyes remaining locked with the leader. "I was born in Moramet."

"You don't have the look of a Morametan, either," Greens said with a snort.

"How would you know, Tom?" asked a smiling older woman with gray hair. "As far as I know, you've never been more than two days ride from the house you were born in until now. Where did you acquire all this wisdom of the world that you're basing your judgment on?" The last question drew several giggles and a couple of laughs from the crowd of women.

"He's right, though," Gera said, while trying not to let loose with his own smile. Greens might think himself the leader escorting the women and children to safety, but Gera had a good idea who really made all the decisions. "I favor my mother who was not from Moramet." He continued after turning to Greens. "I'm traveling to Greenville on business and just learned of your troubles when I crossed the river from Bagdon."

The snort that erupted from the Crandori farmer told everyone what he thought of Gera's explanation. He opened his mouth again, but the woman silenced him before he could put his distrust into words, however.

"Tom, you and I might find it hard to believe, but the rest of the kingdoms may not consider a war between Crandor and Palamor news. Now, he's answered your questions with what appears to be the truth. Let him be."

A grunt escaped the man, but Master Greens bowed his head slightly.

"No offense meant, traveler," he said, the words spoken through a clenched jaw. "Until the next planting." With that, he and his men retreated to the table where they had been seated before and took turns casting sour looks in Gera's direction.

"Never mind him, lad," the gray-haired lady said. "He really hasn't been this far from his fields in his life, and I can tell it's gnawing away at him like a dog with a bone. Even though the men drew lots for the honor of guiding us to safety, I suspect those six consider themselves the losers for not being able to defend their own ground." Glancing around, she noticed Master Till approaching with Gera's supper.

"I'm Mrs. Sheaf. I'd be honored if you'd sit at my table while you eat. Perhaps you can share a little of what passes for news while you sup. All we hear at home is tidings of war."

"I don't know if I've anything to say that's worthy of being heard, Mrs. Sheaf. But I'll tell you what I've picked up on the road." He smiled and nodded. "And I'd be grateful for the company."

◆ ◆ ◆

Gera now understood what it felt like to be placed on a spit and roasted. Two bells had passed with only the innkeeper interrupting to say the stable boys would rub the gelding down and turn him out in the rope corral to graze with the other horses. Beyond that one break in the conversation, the questions from the women at Mrs. Sheaf's table started at his first bite and lasted long after his plate was empty. Although the queries ranged from ridiculous—What were the fashions for women in Willshire?—to the personal—Did he have a wife or was he betrothed?—the most probing questions came from the subtle old lady. From the look in her brown eyes, he suspected she did not buy one word of his cover story of a business trip to Greenville, but she let it pass without comment.

News of his mastersmith status elicited a few congratulations, however, once he answered that, yes, his family owned their own ground in Moramet, many more of the middle-aged women began to speak. Most of these women's daughters suddenly appeared at the edge of the crowd to be introduced to the traveler, including some that were still in pigtails and one girl only a couple of summers younger that sat down so close on the bench that Gera felt she was almost sitting in his lap. The inner circle of his audience closed in on him like a noose. For a while, he almost wished he had chosen to sleep underneath the stars instead of stopping at the Farmer's Pride.

"The tallow is burning low," Mrs. Sheaf finally said, "and even the cows have been put to bed. Let's allow the young man to get some rest so he won't fall asleep in the saddle tomorrow."

A couple of the mothers who had been extolling their daughters' virtues the loudest mumbled under their breaths at the announcement, but the crowd soon dispersed.

"Thank you," Gera said softly as the last of them moved out of earshot. "I was beginning to think they were going to start pinching me to see if I was plump enough for the feast."

The gray-haired woman bobbed her head as she let loose with a heartfelt laugh.

"You were probably closer than you know to wearing a green and brown coat with that crowd," she said. "They wouldn't normally have been that forward, but if open war breaks out, a lot of our young men will die. Babies need to be born. Life must go on." Mrs. Sheaf stared him in the eye. "Some of them would've turned away if they realized how much you were lying to them about going to Greenville."

Gera let his gaze drop to the floor.

"It brings me no pleasure, and I mean you no disrespect or harm by lying. I just don't think tonight would have gone as well if you knew the duty that lay on me."

He raised his head up and looked into her eyes. He had noticed the rich brown color earlier, but not how deep and drawing they appeared. After a few moments of study, she slowly nodded her head.

"True men sometimes have reasons to perform acts that would otherwise cause harm. No offense taken. You're welcome at my table anytime, young Staghorn." The mischievous grin sprouted on her face again. "Of course, I do have a granddaughter at home..."

A look of horror crossed Gera's face, and he threw up his hands in protest until he could not hold back his laughter any longer.

✦ ✦ ✦

Only glowing ashes remained in the meeting room hearth to remind anyone of the earlier blaze. Gera slept beneath his blanket on a bench to keep the spring chill from creeping into his body from the floor. Across the room, Greens and his men continuously shattered the silence with their snoring.

The front door of the inn flew open and banged against the stop. Shoes thumping on the floor announced the arrival of one of the stable boys as he ran into the room. Gera sat up, his sword in his hand, as the boy woke Greens.

"Sir! Sir!" the boy cried. "The horses are raising a ruckus. They're running around in the corral and actin' like they're scared."

Gera wiped the remnants of his already forgotten dream from his eyes. He suspected Nava caused the alarm in the horses. The dyr had probably crept close enough to be smelled. Leaving this early in the morning would raise some suspicions, but not nearly the alarm that an appearance by his companion would create.

"What're you talking about, boy?" Greens said through a fog of drowsiness. "If you woke me for a wolf or a wild dog, I'll..."

He froze in the middle of his threat as the other stable boy tumbled into the room and rolled to a stop beside his friend. Four Crimson Guards stomped through the door after him.

"Innkeeper! Innkeeper!" the sergeant shouted while his men spread into a perfect fighting formation.

Till stumbled through the entrance to the kitchen and his

quarters. Tousled hair and unfastened pants, held up by only one suspender, showed the man had been dragged from a sound sleep like the others. He had not even taken the time to put on shoes.

*He'll be no help. I can't count on the farmers fighting, either.*

Gera surveyed his position from a downcast face. Greens and the other men from Bushmill stood in open-mouthed shock on the other side of the room. He had caught a small break, however. His bench sat on the far right flank of the guardsmen and left him under only the partial attention of one soldier.

"Innkeeper," the sergeant said. "Our detachment was attacked this night. Have you taken any guests since nightfall?"

Till gulped as a horse neighed in terror outside.

"No, sir," he answered once his voice returned. "Master Staghorn was the last guest to arrive, and he was here well before dusk."

All the heads in the room swiveled to face Gera. That meant he was the only one left to see what was about to happen.

Nava padded silently through the open doorway. His coat remained the ebony color of pre-dawn night, except for the glistening crimson on his snout. Even as Gera's hand flew up with his sword, the dyr was already a blur of motion. The animal leaped at the back of the nearest guardsman and closed his jaws around the doomed man's neck, bones snapping under the pressure. Nava shook violently from side to side as they fell forward, the man collapsing like a child's rag doll.

The closest soldier whirled at the sounds and, despite the terror tattooed across his face, jumped to help his shieldmate. Nava tossed his dead prey aside and met the man face to face, bringing his hind claws up to rake his chest and stomach as he snapped at the trooper's throat.

Gera used the opportunity to vault the bench and land in a defensive position between the Crimson Guards and the farmers. The sergeant charged at once, a wordless roar springing from his throat as he advanced.

The guardsman overestimated the effect the yell and raised sword had on the young man in front of him, assuming he was frozen with fear. Gera waited until the last possible moment and then raised his short sword above his head, the tip trailing down at an angle. It was the first defensive stance Ham had taught him.

The soldier's sword struck Gera's weapon with a clang before skipping down the length of the nicked blade like a stone across a river until it dove on toward the floor. The guardsman stumbled forward a step to stop his momentum.

Gera used the moment as he remembered the lessons at the Greenwards, the hours spent with Bacon in the barn practicing with wooden sticks. He pivoted on the balls of his feet, his whole body behind the counterstrike. The swing looped over and down, striking home where the sergeant's mail tunic stopped. The man fell to the inn floor, screaming in agony over his severed hamstring.

The young man ignored the cursing and stepped towards the remaining Blood. This guardsman had watched and learned from his leader's fatal mistake and met him as an equal. Slash, thrust, batter with shield—he threw all these tactics at Gera with a practiced hand. Every parry and counterattack taught the veteran soldier more about his opponent. Despite Gera's mobility and teachings, his inexperience began to show. Training and armor would eventually prevail.

Consecutive slashes opened a nick on Gera's neck. A block, followed immediately by a thrust, caused an instant bloom of fire and red in one shoulder. A smile played over the Blood's face at the yelp of pain. Gera attacked, but the guardsman caught the strike on his sword and shoved his shield into Gera's chin, driving the young man back.

Gera feigned fatigue with his right arm and switched his sword to his left before fishing for his belt knife with the free hand. Inside his mind, he beat at the door, trying to unleash his saca. The more he tried, however, the stronger the barrier stood against his fear.

As Gera circled away from his enemy, his heel caught on the boot of the now silent sergeant. He stumbled backwards, out of control, dropping his sword so he could use his hand to stay on his feet. Light flooded through his mind the instant he abandoned attempting to force his saca into the open. Power and fire surged through his body.

The guardsman did not notice the change in his foe and thrust his sword forward. Gera twisted to one side, receiving an even deeper cut on his chest despite the move, and reached out to touch the Blood. His left palm pressed flat against the man's armor and the air throbbed, convulsing with the power of one hundred thunders. The soldier flew across the room like a discarded toy. While the man was still in the air, Gera finally gripped his knife. The weapon leaped from his fingers.

The thump of the guardsman striking the wall was followed in a blink by the wet crack of the blade burying itself in his forehead. The Crimson Guard collapsed on the inn floor.

Gera reached down for his sword before whirling to take in the rest of the room, saca surging through his body. Till jumped and sucked in his breath as the young man's gaze fell onto him. Gera glanced down at the hamstrung sergeant at the innkeeper's feet and noticed he now had a slit in his throat to match the one in his leg.

"He was going to strike at your back when you were fighting the other one," the hosteler said in response to the unasked question. "It didn't seem fair." He replaced the knife beneath the shirttail that had appeared so innocently untucked earlier.

As Gera turned to Nava, dizziness swept through his body, making his head swirl. The fourth soldier lay at the dyr's feet with one hand and most of his face ripped away. The body also had multiple claw marks through its armor and across the torso. At least the dyr showed the good grace to yawn widely, revealing blood and bits of flesh hanging from his fangs. His coat now appeared the same pale green as the walls of the meeting room.

A whimper from the corner where Greens and the other farmers cowered, reminded Gera of their presence. Some of them, no doubt, remembered they had attempted to run him out of the Farmer's Pride earlier in the evening. White-rimmed eyes darted back and forth from Gera to Nava, trying to make paralyzed minds decide which was more dangerous.

"Nava and I are going to go outside and see if there are anymore troops," Gera said to Master Till. "I don't want to be surprised by another patrol while we clean up this mess."

The sound of a sack of potatoes tossed on the floor was followed by a muffled scream. All the men turned to the staircase landing. An ashen-faced Mrs. Sheaf stood locked in a gaze with Nava. At her feet lay the slumped figures of two other women, passed out in dead faints.

"It's all right, Mrs. Sheaf," Gera said. The dyr must have risen to face the women as they descended from their rooms on the second floor. "Nava is my traveling companion and friend.

Perhaps it would be best if you stayed in your room until we've straightened up the unpleasantness."

The sound of someone speaking to her shook the woman out of her trance.

"No, no. I came down to see if Tom or any of the others had been injured in the racket that woke us. Are you all right in there, Tom?"

The question about his health from one of the people he was supposed to be protecting stirred the farmer into action.

"We're unharmed, Mrs. Sheaf." The words shook as he spoke, but gained in strength as he continued. "We weren't in the fight ourselves. But some of what we saw..." His voice trailed off as he abruptly realized he might be saying more than Gera wished.

Gera had no objections, however, crossing the room to where the final guardsman lay in a growing pool of his own blood. He tried unsuccessfully to free his knife from the victim. Finally, with an embarrassed glance over his shoulder, he placed his foot on the dead man's jaw for leverage and yanked the weapon clear. He wiped the blood and gray matter on the red cloak before sheathing it.

"Nava and I are going to make that quick round to see if there are anymore Crimson Guards outside." He cocked his head to one side and listened to the patter of little feet on the second floor landing of the stairway. "Mrs. Sheaf," he continued, "some of those feet sound like they're barefoot. I don't think we want any children coming down here."

As he and Nava walked out into the night, Gera heard the older lady muttering to herself about "bossy boys with barely enough dirt under their feet to be on their own" and "addle-brained old women." It did not take much imagination to decipher who she was talking about.

Outside, very little could be seen in the faint light. An orange glow from the east revealed a black pool close to the porch. Gera strode over and found another dead guardsman, partially covered by his cloak. The telltale signs of the dyr's attack stood out on the corpse's neck, but it appeared a horse had stepped on him as well. The two companions circled around the inn, searching for signs of more Crimson Guards. By the time they reached the front door again, enough light shined over the horizon to give Gera an idea of what had happened outside.

Nava had probably found the guardsmen camp and did some hunting on his own. The five soldiers had ridden in from the south in search of what attacked them. At that point, the dyr must have circled the men and came at the inn from the west, taking him past the edge of the corral. That explained why the horses had been so agitated. When the four guardsmen entered the building, they left one on rearguard to watch their mounts and sound an alarm if anyone else approached. The smell of Nava must have spooked the soldiers' horses, the sentry being trampled in the process. The dyr had merely finished off the wounded man before entering the inn through the open door.

"You don't get credit for this one," Gera said to the green eyes floating in the dim light. "He would've died even if you hadn't attacked him." He scratched the dyr behind the ears as he endured a foul-smelling yawn.

Gera decided to gather his gear and leave at once. He had no intentions of bringing danger to innocent people who were already fleeing a war.

The scene inside the Farmer's Pride had changed dramatically since he left for his scouting excursion. From the doorway,

Gera surveyed a full-scale cleaning operation under way. Mrs. Sheaf stood in the center of the room, directing the activity of a half-score of women and men. Master Till and two more mothers entered from the kitchen carrying buckets of steaming water and mops. None of the women fainted this time when they noticed the two fighters enter, but several stopped in their tracks for a few moments to stare. Gera decided he did not want to know which of them they stared at the most.

Mrs. Sheaf, Till, and Greens approached the twosome as soon as they became aware of their presence. Gera sensed no danger from the group, and Nava must have agreed, choosing that moment to take one look at Mrs. Sheaf before padding to the hearth. Once there, the dyr lay down and began cleaning himself.

"May we speak with you, Master Staghorn?" Master Till asked, a warble making his voice rise and fall. After Gera nodded, he continued with more confidence. "We mean no disrespect, and we don't wish to pry into matters that are only your own but..."

"Ugh, damn the droughts!" Mrs. Sheaf cursed, shocking the man into silence. "We'll be here the rest of the cycle if you keep tripping over your tongue. Going by what you and Tom already told me about what happened here, he could've killed us all long before now if he wanted to do so." She softened her voice and lowered it to a more conversational tone only the four of them could hear. "I knew you were keeping a secret, lad, but ashes, this was one for campfire tales. Did you mean what you said earlier about meaning us no harm?"

"Yes, ma'am," Gera replied at once. "If I'd known what was going to happen here by my staying for the night, I would've never walked in the door." He turned and faced the innkeeper. "I'll pay for any repairs you say are necessary, Master Till. I don't have much coin with me, but I vow to make good on any charges I can't pay for today."

"Leave that alone for now, son," Mrs. Sheaf said, drawing his attention back to her. "Will you tell us why the Crimson Guards are after you in the first place? After what they told me, I'd guess you to be an escaped student from Sacara, but Tom says the sergeant reported being attacked."

Gera glanced at all three of his questioners, trying to decide how much he could safely reveal of his mission. After a few moments, he dropped his gaze to the floor with a sigh.

"My sister was captured recently and taken away by the Crimson Guards. My brother and I tracked them to Willshire where they split into two groups. We had to split up and try on our own to rescue her. The one who followed the group she wasn't in, swore to harass and kill as many Bloods as possible so no other families would need to feel the pain we have. That duty has fallen to me."

Greens looked at Mrs. Sheaf before staring down at his boot tops. The elderly woman struggled to speak, obviously wanting to talk, but having problems with what needed to be said. The innkeeper responded first.

"Ten harvests ago, my sister's eldest was taken away. They took her even though she didn't light the stone in the test." His voice cracked. "The guardsmen said she was going to 'do some good works for the Institute.' My sis never heard from her again." He paused as he gripped Gera's forearm in a firm squeeze, his eyes glistening. "I'd better get back to the cleaning."

"You go, too, Tom," Mrs. Sheaf said, once she found her voice again. "Why don't you and the others drag the dead outside and check the livestock while I finish talking with Master Staghorn."

The two men walked away to their duties, leaving Gera and the older woman in the corner by the door. After a brief silence, she spoke in an even quieter tone.

"Bushmill is a small village close to the border with Palamor. We're not near any major roads, and all we do is raise crops and our families, so we escape special notice from outsiders. For as long as anyone can remember, we've had healers who have *special* abilities." She paused and stared Gera in the eyes to make sure he understood what she meant. "Some have been strong enough to almost work miracles, while others can barely deaden the pain of a headache. It runs in cycles a little bit, sometimes more, sometimes fewer—but we always have some who can heal.

"When the institute was opened, we sent our children to learn the ways of saca. But over time, the village elders lost faith in what was being taught there. When the drafts started with the testing stones, I was hidden because I'd already proved to possess saca. In order to save ourselves, the villagers have all taken oaths of silence to never speak of the healers or the hidden children. Son, I could be sentenced to death for telling you this. The silence is partly self-serving because without us, some of the villagers would surely die from the ills we can save them from now. Once the children are too old to be tested anymore, they move back into the village from the farms where we hide them. Oh, we've lost a few over the years, children who hadn't revealed their gifts before they were tested. But we've been able to save most." She took a long breath before continuing again, her face lighting up with a smile. "My granddaughter stayed behind when we left to help tend the men who remained to fight for our land. She appears to be stronger than any healers we've had in a long, long time.

"My point is that I can imagine what you're going through right now. It's obvious you should've had dealings with the Institute yourself. And traveling with a dyr isn't exactly a great disguise." Mrs. Sheaf winked and nodded her head. "But, no matter. Let's take a look at your wounds before I ramble on and let you bleed to death."

She led Gera to a bench along the wall and made him sit. After ordering one of the nearby women to bring her some hot water and a clean rag, she told him to remove his shirt. Mrs. Sheaf took the blood-soaked clothing and motioned to a young woman only a couple of years older than Gera. She had been standing nearby and staring at the half-naked fighter.

"Cindi," Mrs. Sheaf said. "Rinse the blood out of this shirt before it sets up. Then run upstairs and have Mrs. Haylin mend the rips." The girl scurried to obey, deep crimson settling in her cheeks at being caught staring.

Turning back to her patient, the healer examined his wounds.

"The cut on your neck is of no importance. It isn't any worse than a shaving cut, if shaving is what you do to that fuzz on your cheeks. I can heal that one without any hint of a scar. The one on your chest, though, is a goodly bit deeper." Looking up, she noticed the concern on Gera's face. "Relax, my boy. I can fix it so you'll never feel where the steel bit you. There'll just be a mark is all. My Gini could do it proper, but I'm thinking she might like your chest even better with the story a sword scar will give it. Cindi didn't seem to mind."

Mrs. Sheaf laughed and Gera noticed several of the other women closest to them were also trying hard not to smile. Memories of the night before, when he had felt like the prize steer at the butcher shop, flooded back into his thoughts.

"Do whatever you can," he said.

"Now, I suppose you've never had this done to you before?" she asked. Not waiting on an answer, she continued. "With the cut on your neck, you'll only feel a little tingling, like when your arm falls asleep. Your chest is going to be different, I'm afraid. The muscle is going to feel like it's being stretched and tightened. Then it'll burn like fire as it heals together. That's just the way it is, and there isn't anything I can do about it. I'll start with that one when you're ready."

Nagging fear gripped Gera with the unknown. He watched Mrs. Sheaf raise her hand, palm out, and reach for his chest. Instantly the heat of his saca filled his body with a boiling torrent. In the corner of his mind, he felt something moving at great speed.

The healer's fingers never reached his skin. They stopped about two hands from touching him, held in place by an unyielding barrier. At the same time, Mrs. Sheaf's hair moved from Nava's hot breath on the side of her face. Gera was so shocked at the dyr's sudden appearance, his saca fled from his thoughts. He shivered as the heat left his body, leaving him feeling like he had jumped in a mountain lake in the spring.

"Nava, hold!"

The dyr slowly settled back onto his haunches. Although the big animal had backed off a little, his gaze never left the woman's throat. The silence in the room weighed heavy against the shoulders of all present. Everyone waited to breathe, wondering what had just happened. Inch by inch, the gray-haired lady lowered her hand to her lap.

"That's twice this morning your beast has scared me out of ten harvests of my life. I'm surprised you don't bury me right now because I've used up my allotment." Her voice remained calm and soothing although her eyes flashed with anger. "And what's the idea of grabbing your saca? I can't heal you when you're holding it." A puzzled expression fell over her face, and her voice softened. "I still should've been able to touch him, though," she mumbled.

"I don't have a lot of control over it," Gera said. "None at all, if the truth be known." He leaned forward. "Can you teach me?"

"I could teach you how to hold and feel your power. I could also teach you some healing, but that's the extent of my wisdom. Healing is the only knowledge that's passed down in our village. Yes, we've had the occasional lass who had a special little trick. Some could light fires. Others worked with water. I can remember one who could hear any conversation from a long ways off. Nosy little...anyway. There's also a story about a woman who could tell you what kind of harvest we were going to have in three autumns. But those girls are few and far between. Besides, I've a feeling we aren't going to be together long enough for me to beat anything like that into that thick skull of yours.

"Now," she said as she wiped her sweaty palms on her skirt, "If you and your protector will let me, I'll try again to heal you."

"Nava," Gera said as he scratched behind the dyr's ear, "it's all right. She's not going to hurt me."

He was wrong. This time the healer's hand made it all the way to his chest. Gera fought the urge not to scream when the pain quivered his muscles. Waves of hellish fire rippled across his body, and the air in his lungs turned to flames. He was certain if he glanced down at his body, only charred ashes of skin and bones remained. The pain lasted an eternity, and was over in an instant. The moment Mrs. Sheaf removed her hand, the agony melted. He blinked in surprise, feeling like he had just awoken from a peaceful night's sleep.

The elderly woman, on the other hand, appeared as if she had sprinted in front of hell hounds for days. Sweat poured down her forehead. Her chest heaved with gasps for air. She even appeared older, as if several summers had been added to her tally.

"You're as strong a pair of prize-winning plow horses, lad," she said between breaths. "You're going to need to do with a bandage for your neck. I don't believe I've enough left in me to heal you again, and none of the others with me are strong enough to survive you."

Greens walked into the meeting room and stopped near the seated pair.

"Master Staghorn," he said with a nod, "if you're finished with Mrs. Sheaf, I've an idea of how to handle the bodies of the Crimson Guards. But we'll need your pet's help."

"Yes, sir. Let me grab a shirt, and I'll be right with you." He glanced down at his chest and saw what appeared to be a long-healed scar, its white path running about a hand's breadth across his skin. He moved his arm back and forth and found it was pain free. "Thank you," he said, placing his hand on Mrs. Sheaf's shoulder. "Can I do anything for you?"

"No. You go on and take care of your business, lad. I'll just sit here and rest for a few moments."

Nava followed Gera out the inn door and into the rosy light of dawn. Tom and his men stood over a line of dead guardsmen on the ground.

"What I was thinking was that three of them only show signs of bite marks," Tom said when the pair joined the group of farmers. "If your friend was to bite this one in the head and that one in the leg and throat..."

"The troops who come looking for them won't have any reason to blame anyone here for their deaths," Gera finished, a grin crossing his face. "That's a great idea. Nava, could you bite here and here?"

Several of the farmers turned away in revulsion as the dyr attacked his new duty with a zeal that said he did not mind at all. After he had finished mutilating the corpses, Nava trotted over to the horse trough and washed down his morning meal.

"I'd better be leaving before the rest of their friends arrive," Gera said to the other men. "I'll get my bedroll and be on my way."

"We can saddle your horse," said one of the farmers, and a couple of them walked to the rope corral to see it was done.

Gera shook his head, thinking of the night before when these men were ready to fight because he did not look like them.

*They probably just want me to be gone as soon as possible.*

Gera walked back into the inn. By the time he retrieved his blanket and packed it into his bedroll, Mrs. Haylin had his mended shirt ready, although it was still damp from washing out the blood. Several of the Crandoris gathered with Innkeeper Till to see him on his journey.

"Master Staghorn, if you ever want to sit and relax from your duty for a while," the hosteler said as he forced a small bag of bread and cheese into Gera's hands, "you're always welcome at the Farmer's Pride."

Greens and the other men all apologized again about the previous evening. It quickly became apparent from some of their comments that Tom must have relayed at least part of his reason of why the Bloods had been searching for him.

After everyone else finished, Mrs. Sheaf stared at him for a moment. Suddenly, she stooped over, grabbed a handful of loose dirt, and threw it on Gera. His mouth flew open in shock, but then he noticed several of the other women, most of them the loudest at praising their daughters the night before, dropping clumps of dirt to the ground, frowns and outright anger spreading over their faces.

"I claim the right for my Gini," Mrs. Sheaf said loudly enough for all to hear, "since her mother has returned to the land and cannot perform the duty."

Stepping closer to Gera, she let her voice fall to a normal volume.

"I won't hold you to the betrothal, lad. But this way, you can visit Bushmill without someone laying a claim that might be considered binding. If we haven't returned yet, just ask for my granddaughter." Her eyes twinkled. "Be sure to tell her about the dirt."

She stepped back.

"May your ground bring you happiness until the harvest."

"Until the next planting," Gera replied. He glanced around as he swung into the saddle, nodding to the Crandori refugees. With one last look, he heeled his gelding up the northern road with Nava trotting beside them.

ommander Gregol rode into the camp, ragged nerves clinging to rage beneath his face. Only his eyes spoke of the emotions. He did not trust himself to speak after he dismounted in front of Captain Ursel's command tent. Instead, he dismissed Captain Randel and the rest of the trailing patrol with a wave of his hand. They left quickly, sensing they did not want to be nearby when the cork finally exploded out of the bottle holding him in check.

Gregol and his men had left the Sacara Institute before sunrise the morning after Ursel's message reached Lord Ravenhurst. They rode their horses to the point of exhaustion in their rush to reach the Wall of Purley before Ursel, but then waited for another day and a half, the commander's mood growing darker and more foreboding with each passing bell the expected company did not arrive.

Randel watched his commander raise the tent flap. He had remained with Gregol that last night on the wall. They stood together, staring into the night while the moon rose high above their heads, and then began its descent. When his body could no longer deny sleep, the captain lay down on top of the battlement. His last sight, as his eyes closed for the final time, was of Gregol standing still, while the wavering torchlight cast shadows on his face. Randel's first sight in the morning as the warm glow of morning peeked over the horizon was of his leader, still in the same spot, as if he had been replaced by a lifelike statue.

By noon, the commander could not bear waiting any longer. The patrol rode out to discover what had befallen the missing company. They found the guardsmen here, less than a day's ride from the Wall of Purley. Randel shook his head and led his mount away.

Gregol stepped into the dark tent, the blackness of his mood following him like the shadow of an eclipse sweeping across the countryside. His voice, however, did not contain any heat when he spoke.

"So, Captain," he said over creaking leather as his thumb rubbed his scarred palm, "have you encountered problems on your journey to the Institute?"

Ursel snapped his head up, eyes narrowed in anger. Before he could curse, however, recognition spread over his face and terror replaced his rage. He did not look his best in any case. Gregol could not decide if a sleepless night caused the captain's disheveled uniform, or a night spent in a saddle, or both. His short-cropped black hair stood out at odd angles, giving the impression he was still in motion, even as he remained still. The stubble on the man's chin spoke of a few days without a razor as well.

"Lord High Commander," Ursel said, after attempting unsuccessfully to straighten his uniform blouse and saluting. His palms left dark streaks of sweat across the material, adding to the rumpled appearance. "I regret to inform you that the Chosen suspected of being the Matra escaped two nights ago. Four men were killed in the process of her flight." He hesitated only briefly before continuing. "I still do not know how, or how many people, affected her release. I've split the men into squads, scouring the countryside, searching for her as we speak. They were ordered to only stop to rest their horses. So far, we've found no sign of them." This last admission released a nervous twitch in the captain's left eye.

Gregol stood in silence in the middle of the tent. He had expected this report but, somehow, hearing it made the news harder to handle. The possible Matra was gone, and his men had no idea where. A terrifying thought flashed across his mind.

"You say you've found absolutely no sign of her since the escape?" He asked the question more calmly than he thought possible. "What about her escape? Tell me how it happened."

Ursel answered quickly, explaining the sentry rotations, and how the dead guardsmen were found. Gregol continued rubbing his palm as he listened, picturing in his mind what had happened on that night. The tent fell silent after the captain finished.

"There are three possibilities, Captain Ursel," he said after a few moments of staring at the far tent panel. "First, she had help to escape from guardsmen under your command." He raised his hand to stop the officer's objection before it started. "I know. Captain Randel pulled your roster, and you've had these men at the Willshire garrison for a while. Besides, I'd wager a month filled with whore mongering against guard duty that no men are missing from their posts, or you would've mentioned it in your report." He continued without waiting for confirmation. "Second, two men killed the sentries, crept through the guard line, butchered the guard at the tent without raising an alarm, and then overpowered the trooper inside. They then could have waited until the discovery of the sentries' bodies. Once the uproar started, it would've been easy to slip back through the lines, probably disguised as troops." He paused. "The last option is that she somehow removed the collar by herself and used her saca to escape on her own. But a child..."

"She was no child, Commander. She was a young woman, nearly of age."

Ursel's words hung in the air between them. Gregol felt his heart skip a beat.

"You did not mention her age in the message," he said.

"I didn't know it was important, Commander."

Gregol looked away.

"A mature sagia, never tested...on the loose..."

"Commander, the first option is easily ruled out. The second, on its face, is by far the most likely, and the rescuers were probably family members. But, if it's the third..."

Gregol nodded.

"I know, Captain. If it's the third choice, then your entire command is lucky to be alive, and we have no one here who can deal with the situation. How many men do you have in camp?"

"Two squads, minus the four dead. All the rest are out searching."

"Good, Well then, Captain. There's only one more thing left to be handled."

Ursel never saw the backhand that sent him sprawling, half-in and half-out, of the tent opening. Gregol pushed back the flap as he stepped over the fallen officer and out into the sunlight.

"Captain Randel!" His shout shattered the unnatural quiet of the camp.

His aide ran from the direction of the corral. As he stopped in front of the commander, he was not surprised to see Ursel on the ground. He was stunned to see him still breathing, however.

"Captain, assemble everyone still remaining in camp. We've work to do, and enough time has already been wasted." Gregol turned and started to walk away before stopping. "Oh, and find the captain's aide. He needs to be woke from his nap."

◆ ◆ ◆

Gregol studied the map on the table while his thumb worried his left palm. The man ignored the shuffling feet of Ursel's officers standing beside the still woozy captain. A colorful display of purples and yellows had already blossomed on the officer's cheek, and the top of his scarlet tunic remained a darker burgundy and his hair damp from the bucket of water his aide had used to revive him for the meeting. The men all straightened when the commander glanced up.

"This afternoon, you'll split your men into pairs and send them out to look for other nearby patrols," he said, his voice terse and clipped. "Any that are found are to be sent back here to camp immediately. In the morning, we'll split whatever troops have arrived into two patrols. I'll take one north into Crandor, and Captain Ursel will take the other south into Spirache.

"We'll drive this Chosen, and whoever aided her in her escape, straight toward the Pennick River. Captain Randel, you'll split the company we brought into squads and dispatch them to different garrisons along the water. They're to warn the captains that the prey is being herded towards them. Give each group a letter of authorization, with my seal, to act in whatever way they deem necessary to beat the runaway to the border."

He paced along the tent wall, his thoughts bending in another direction.

"What do we know of the Chosen's family?" Gregol turned toward Ursel. "Where are they?"

"We don't know where her family is, my Lord. Our ears in the village reported she has two brothers, one that lived outside of Milston, and another that was an apprentice in Willshire. Her father and another brother were killed in the Bakri War, and the mother died a few years ago. As I reported in the message to Lord Ravenhurst, the patrol sent to their home did not return. I left orders at the Willshire garrison to bring the younger brother in for questioning and testing. However, I left for Sacara before that was completed."

Gregol nodded and returned to pacing.

"Instruct all the troops to tell everyone they meet that the Chosen is a runaway from the Institute that has gone mad. No one else is to attempt to catch her because she's too dangerous for a commoner to handle. She is old enough for that story to stick. People will be afraid of what they don't understand, so it should keep her from receiving outside help. Captain Randel, make sure our men receive an accurate description of her from Ursel's troops before they leave. When you finish with that task, return and see me. I've other orders for you to carry out personally."

Captain Randel saluted and left the tent.

"Captain Ursel," Gregol grimaced as he said the name. "I've a bit of a problem with what to do with you. My heart screams at me one thing, while my head tells me another." He moved uncomfortably close to the nervous officer.

"I should tear your body apart with my hands and personally feed your flesh to the carrion eaters," he said, a vein throbbing on one side of his neck. "That's what my heart tells me to do. But, I need a captain to lead the southern search, so I must follow my head."

The commander backed away from the sweating guardsmen leader.

"Captain Ursel," Gregol said loudly enough for everyone in the tent to hear, "you'll report this evening at sundown, at which time you'll receive fifteen lashes for your failure in command. Dismissed."

The captain and his wide-eyed officers saluted before racing toward the tent flap. When Gregol spoke again, they all stopped short.

"And, Captain," he said, a smile on his lips, "you won't die on me."

The men resumed the dash to the exit, pushing each other in their haste to leave the tent and escape the commander.

"Yet," Gregol whispered so that only he could hear the words. "You won't die on me yet."

◆ ◆ ◆

By the time Captain Randel returned to the command tent, the day had almost lost its battle with the coming dark. He paused outside the closed flap for a moment and watched the blue give way to a vivid array of orange and reds. How many more sunsets would he need to endure before he could return to his home in Movil? No answer echoed in his thoughts. His short time of reflection at an end, he rapped on the wooden tent pole before entering.

"Captain Randel reporting as ordered, my Lord Commander."

Gregol sat at the wobbly field table, attempting to write clearly with a quill dwarfed by his hand. Several pieces of wadded and torn paper lay around his chair in physical testament to the difficulty involved in composing the message. Some of his long hair had worked its way out of the clasp at his neck. It appeared as if a nest of snakes tried to escape from the constant rubbing by the officer's callused hand. He glanced up at his aide, a sigh of relief escaping.

"Report, Captain," he ordered in his usual brusque manner. "Did you send all the men off to the garrisons?"

No amount of unexpected gratitude would allow the man to treat his subordinate in a more familiar tone. To do so would be to invite the same kind of response in return, and Randel suspected his commander did not want, or know how, to let that occur.

"Yes, my Lord. The last of them just left a few moments ago. I ordered them to ride deep into the night before stopping to rest their horses. Did you wish for me to finish writing your message while you told me what you wanted to say, my Lord?"

"No, Captain. This is one message that needs to be written in my own hand when Master Ravenhurst reads it, no matter how hard it is to write." He swiveled on the groaning, overburdened chair, and faced his aide.

"Lord Ravenhurst is not going to like this letter in the least, but you must deliver it directly to his hand. His hand only, Captain Randel. Even though I'm outlining my plan to retrieve the Chosen, he's likely to question you about what I'm doing. Tell him everything you know. Don't try to hold back or lie because he'll know immediately and, in which case, I might as well kill you now and keep your horse here as an extra mount.

"If he sees a flaw in the plan, he has ways of reaching me to correct my errors. If you survive meeting with him," Captain Randel felt a breath catch in his throat at the commander's offhand statement, "I've more orders for you to see to. You're to ensure the Cleansing Trees are completed immediately at the Institute compound. When they're done, each ten-man squad will draw lots and the loser will be sacrificed. Also, the first hundred men from Ursel's command to arrive back at Sacara without the Matra are to be placed on the cruciforms as well. If Lord Ravenhurst orders you to bring more guardsmen to me to help with the search, and I suspect he will, then you're to pass these orders to Captain Trana. Do you understand?"

"Yes, my Lord. Your orders will be carried out exactly." Randel saluted even while wondering what would happen to the troops' morale if one out of every ten were killed. He knew his leader played a dangerous game, but he had never known Gregol to lose in the past.

"Good. Don't take the time to rest your horse on the way back, Captain. Ride him until he drops dead underneath you and steal another, if you must. I want this message in Sacara as soon as possible." The commander rose from the wooden folding chair and stretched his back before walking with long strides to the tent flap. Randel could not help but notice the smile on the man's face as he walked past.

"Now, perhaps a little relaxation will help me write this

message. It's time to take care of Captain Ursel," he said to the growing darkness.

✦ ✦ ✦

The Crimson Guards stood around the bonfire in formation. The popping and crackling of sap in the burning logs remained the only sounds besides the occasional hoof stamp or horse neighing. The troopers did not even whisper, respecting the fear hanging heavy in the air.

Commander Gregol and Captain Randel walked out of the darkness and into the ring of light, flames causing shadows to dance across their faces like living masks. Gregol's stare promised pain.

"Bring out the accused," he said through clenched teeth.

Captain Ursel marched into sight between two of his junior officers. Stripped to the waist, his sweating skin appeared shiny and pale next to the fire.

Randel stepped forward until he stood face to face with the other officer.

"Captain Ursel," he intoned loudly enough to be heard by all the soldiers present. "You're accused of dereliction of duty by failing to deliver an affirmed sagia to the Sacara Institute. How do you plead?"

"Guilty."

Randel breathed a sigh of relief. He did not want to think about what would happen with Gregol's temper if Ursel fought the charges.

"The punishment for the crime is a stripping of rank to lieutenant and fifteen lashes. Sentence is to be carried out immediately." Randel returned to his place behind Gregol.

"Present the guilty for execution of sentence," the commander ordered. His eyes shined bright in the firelight.

Ursel walked to a nearby tree. Ropes, tied to his wrists, were looped up and over a stake driven into the trunk. His limbs quivered while he listened to Gregol unfurl the whip behind him. The officer leaned forward, placing his forehead against the rough bark.

Randel watched Gregol glance down at the little metal bits woven into the whip's thongs. At least the commander had been true about wanting the captain to live through the ordeal. The metal chunks would bruise and tear Ursel's skin, but would not rip out great chunks of flesh and muscle with every blow like a barbed whip would have done.

The commander growled like an animal as his arm flashed forward. Ursel's grunt of pain drowned out the sigh of delight as the first blow landed. Again and again the scourge flew, its straps glistening black in the firelight. Splatters of blood sprayed from their tips and showered down on the uniforms of the nearby guardsmen. Gregol grinned through a red-dotted face as the crimson on the officer's back grew until it appeared he wore a coat the same color of his pants. His arm moved even faster.

"Thirteen," Randel said, waiting in between for each strike. "Fourteen. Fifteen." He stared at the commander.

Gregol stopped. He gulped the cool night air and blinked, keeping his attention on the man tied to the tree. For his part, Ursel moved weakly, the rope helping to keep him on his feet. But he had not cried out in pain, and the area fell into silence. Randel wanted to step forward, remind his commander the punishment was over, that he needed this man for further duty, but he remained quiet.

The arm dropped to one side, whip ends trailing in the dirt by Gregol's feet. He turned and walked away, nodding to Randel as he passed.

"The sentence has been delivered," Captain Randel said in his command voice. "The guilty will resume his rank of captain. Dismissed."

## CHAPTER 21

Gera felt a change in his spirits as he and Nava traveled the road to Greenville. Up until his meeting with the Crandori refugees at the Farmer's Pride, his thoughts had grown increasingly dark and depressing since the news of Keely's abduction. Every day was filled with life and death decisions. His dreams were haunted by concern of his sister and brother. Just a few weeks earlier, his biggest worry was how he would handle meeting Dax again after years apart. Now he threw himself into sword fights with Bloods without a second thought.

But his chance meeting with Mrs. Sheaf and the others had brightened his outlook. The stories they told about the girls from Bushmill and Till's niece reminded him he was helping other families in the same situation. Even his own abilities with saca were coming more into focus. He had actively ignored the power for all his years at the Greenwards, only letting it escape a couple of times during his apprenticeship with Ham. It had frightened him, partly because of what it meant for his being sent to the Sacara Institute, but also because he had no idea how to use it. But now, after seeing what the old healer could do with saca, he wondered if it was something he could learn to develop for other uses besides killing.

Now he saw hope. He had hope the Bloods deserved the punishment he meted out. He had hope other families might join into the battle against the Institute. Hope that, with enough help, all the lost sons and daughters may one day go home again. He also had hope he could use his saca for good.

The revelation explained why he rode the gelding with a more determined look in his eye and a song in his heart, despite the danger still surrounding him.

The day passed uneventfully as he pressed to the north. Nava disappeared for longer and longer periods of time as the flow of refugees increased. Bushmill was not the only village moving its people to safer ground in the south. Gera caught bits and pieces of news from the war when he stopped to water his horse in the early afternoon.

"Burning the seeds and stores for no good reason," complained one grizzled old grandfather, echoing a common lament. "Even when a village has surrendered, those damn Palamorans put everything to fire."

"How are we supposed to feed ourselves this winter when there won't be a harvest?" asked one young mother with tears in her eyes and small children clinging to her dress.

The tales continued at each stop until Gera reached the south edge of Greenville at dusk. It was a thriving city on the shores of the Pennick River and gave him his first real glimpse of the fanatical reverence the Crandori showed toward the land. He had ridden through Bagdon after dark, so he had not witnessed it there, but the last rays of this day's dying sun revealed a beautiful sight. Row upon sectioned row of farming and gardening plots surrounded the city for as far as he could see in the fading light.

Some bits of ground were large while others barely covered ten paces by ten paces. All were tilled, planted, and neatly groomed. A dizzying variety of colors from flowers bloomed next to sprouting rows of beans or corn. Gera began to believe the tales he had only thought to be travelers' exaggerations. He had not been prepared to see enough plots for everyone in a city to own and work. Perhaps the rumors—that only Crandori who owned land could have legal rights in the kingdom—also might be true.

Gera entered Greenville as the city watch prepared to shut the gates for the night. He did not know if this was common practice before the hostilities with Palamor but, judging by the stares he received as he rode by the sentries, he would have had trouble trying to talk his way inside once locked out for the night. It remained to be seen if his foreign appearance would cause the same problems they had at first in the Farmer's Pride.

Finding an empty bed in Greenville soon proved to be an impossible task because of all the refugees fleeing the countryside. He finally settled for sleeping in the hay loft of an inn close to the northern gate. An overpriced meal gobbled down in the meeting room served as his supper before he spent some time on the porch in the cool night air. It had not taken him long to become comfortable away from city crowds again. Despite the years spent at the Greenwards in Willshire, the noise and crush of people never quite felt right to him. He watched the city denizens scurry back and forth under the street lamps, noise and smells swirling around them, appearing to be the human equivalent of an ant colony filled with constant activity. A yawn finally split his face, and he turned in for the night, his last thoughts of Nava outside the city gates by himself.

Oddly enough, Gera slept well despite the itchy hay poking through his shirt, and the man beside him snoring loudly enough to rattle the rafters. Before he knew it, the sun peeked its fiery head above the horizon, and a rooster heralded in the new day. The sounds of commotion at the nearby gate caught his attention, and Gera decided to have a look at the cause. He pulled on his boots and stepped over the dark lumps of the other sleeping travelers and climbed down from the loft. Mumbled threats and blankets drawn over heads were the only signs the other men knew he stirred.

As Gera and several groggy-eyed locals wandered into the streets, it did not take long to decide what led to all the noise. A Crimson Guard platoon had entered the city with a rolling cage, two stunned and silent girls riding inside. A fresh platoon from the city garrison prepared to leave Greenville at the same time. Confusion reigned as both sets of troops tried to go through the gateway simultaneously.

Gera jumped at the light touch on his wrist. He whirled and gazed into the kind, but pained, eyes of an elderly man standing beside him. The stranger tilted his head downward. Gera looked and noticed he had grasped his sword hilt so tightly, his knuckles were white. He let go and smiled a thank you to the old man before walking back to the inn. His emotions bubbled like thick stew over the fire while he packed his bedroll and saddled the gelding, fingers still trembling. It had been too easy to imagine Keely looking like one of those frightened girls in the cage.

He went inside the inn and ate a breakfast of tasteless porridge before he returned to the yard to start his journey for the day. Gera purposely moved at a slow, almost leisurely pace. His work against the just departed guardsmen could not take place until after nightfall anyway. He would track them all day, and then he and Nava would make them fear the night.

As he checked the gelding's girth, he listened to the stable boys discussing the large Crandori forces moving through Greenville the past few days. He shook his head when he realized it would not have been long ago that he and Bacon would have done the same things, talking about armor and weapons in a wistful light, and discussing killing Palamorans as if it would be some kind of adventure.

*Wait until they find out what war will mean to their beloved ground, and the dead are brought back to the city. See if they think it's an adventure then.*

The city watch stopped him at the gate to ask questions about his business before they would let him pass. For a few moments, he thought he would need to ride out the south gate and then waste time riding around Greenville before heading north again. The queries struck Gera as too inquisitive, even if he did not look like a Crandori, until he realized he was the only person leaving to the north. Finally, his amended story of business in Wapak passed. He suspected any attempts to re-enter the city from this direction later would bear even more scrutiny.

CHAPTER 22

eely could not stop her stomach from flopping as they rode along. When the dark figure exploded into her tent, spreading death as it entered, she still felt her heart skip a beat when she realized the man was Dax. As each day passed since the test in the Milston square, her hope of ever being free again had died a little more until it was a shriveled dream. No one would be fool enough to attack the Crimson Guards. But then Dax had appeared, and the hope bloomed once more.

She did not want to admit her hope was fading again.

Dax had led her past the sentries and to two horses. He surprised her when he did not head for the road to the east, but instead struck out across country, toward Crandor. They pressed the horses hard, trusting their safety to luck with ground-eating trots.

At dawn, Dax called for a halt on the edge of a clearing. Keely groaned as she dismounted, stumbling around in a circle to stretch her legs.

"Where are we going, Dax?" she asked, trying to take her thoughts off the pains shooting through her muscles. "Shouldn't we start heading east toward Moramet?"

"The first place the Bloods will look for you is in Milston," he said while continuing to search the area behind them for pursuit. "You might as well get it through your head that it'll never be safe for you there again." He turned to her. "We're going to Nason. Gera will meet us there."

Keely leaned against a tree, the world spinning beneath her feet. She never considered they would be heading to any place but home. Her only thoughts had been of finding a way out of that rolling cage before it arrived at the Sacara Institute. She shook her head, eyes closed tight against the world.

The sound of Dax moving past her made her glance up and watch him walk to his mount. He grabbed his waterskin and took a long drink, a sigh escaping when he was done. He rummaged through his saddlebags and found her some bread and dried meat, handing it to her with a smile. She flinched when the gesture appeared more like a grimace than a grin.

"Why is Gera in Nason?" Keely asked when she realized no further explanation was coming. "I would've expected him to be here with you, too."

"He'd have been here if he could!" Dax growled, anger rising in his voice. He whirled to face his sister. "He'd have been here, even though he would've been in the same danger as you if he'd been captured. But don't worry. I'm sure he didn't trust me to find you anymore than anyone else did. I had to trick him to keep him away from the Bloods."

Silence settled over the siblings like a fog separating two islands. The sun finally climbed the rest of the way above the tree line, and Keely received the first clear view of her brother since his appearance in the tent the night before. Sweat glistened on his pale skin despite the cool morning air. Black bags hung under his eyes, and his hands shook when he brushed damp hair away from his face. She quickly walked to his side and placed a hand on his arm.

"Dax, are you all right? Are you sick?" she asked.

"No illness but the self-inflicted," he replied with a smile that appeared forced. "I'm going to backtrack a little way to see if anyone is on our trail. There should be some clothes in my saddlebags that you can wear. It'll be best if you appear to be a man from a distance while we escape. Pack away the Bloods' cloaks, too. You never know when they might come in handy again."

Dax turned and walked a few paces before he stopped and spoke over his shoulder.

"If I don't come back, or someone else comes by while I'm gone, go find Gera in Nason. That's a town in Moramet on the northern Pennick River. Ask for a man named Legin Barlow. He was a friend of father's and should be able to help you." He hesitated for a moment before continuing. "Gera was trailing another group of Bloods that I told him you might be in. He's headstrong, so he might do something stupid and get caught. If he doesn't make it to Barlow's, you'll be on your own. You both have the power to control saca, just like Mother did. If you end up on your own, change your name and find a way to blend in. But you'll need to watch your children for signs as they grow up." His shoulders slumped as she watched. "I'm sorry I didn't tell you about Mother and Gera before. I should've taken you back to the cabin to protect you long ago. It's just that the Bloods hadn't been to Milston for so long I...I'm sorry, Keely. This is my fault."

"Gera can use saca, too?" she asked, the words barely strong enough to reach her brother.

Dax nodded and then loped into the trees. After a few strides, he disappeared among the trunks, no flashes of movement in the gaps to reveal his progress.

Keely walked to the horses, her emotions racing in all directions at once. The news about Gera both excited her and made her fear for his safety. She dug through her brother's sparse belongings and found the clothes he had mentioned. After changing, she ate the last of the dried meat her brother left for her and watched for his return. The salty taste left her thirsty, so she pulled down the waterskin and took a long pull.

She gagged as fire scorched her tongue and blazed a trail down her throat. Black spots and wraith-like visions danced in her eyes while the world tilted beneath her feet. Keely knew she had collapsed on the ground, but the ache was distant and remote, as if she had watched the fall happen to someone else.

The chest formed in her mind again, the first time it had appeared since the guardsmen handed her the stone in Milston. It surged and threatened to buckle beneath the weight of the light attempting to escape its prison. Her saca was almost within her grasp, but the barrier held.

Her senses slowly settled. Keely wondered how Dax could have possibly taken a drink of the same liquid and act as if it was water. She rose to her feet and staggered to the other horse. Careful sniffs told her nothing unusual was in the other skin. She took a sip and was relieved when cool water poured into her mouth, dousing the last of the fire in her body. After she was full, she stared in the direction Dax had disappeared.

era ate an apple and some cheese while he sat in the shade of an oak tree by the road. After a morning riding on the trail of the Crimson Guard patrol, he had decided to rest the gelding and eat lunch.

He felt like the whole kingdom of Crandor lay at his feet to do with as he wished. The farmhouses he rode past appeared to be deserted. He had not met a single traveler moving south the entire time. Enough warning and time had passed through the countryside that all the farming folks who were going to seek safety had already fled the area.

A feeling of being watched fell over the young man. Eyes crept across his body and left the hairs on his head standing like fur on a cat's back. Taking a chance, he suddenly flipped the last bite of cheese back over his shoulder. Powerful jaws snapped shut, and the click of teeth rang into the silence.

"It's about time you showed up, Nava," Gera said with a laugh. "I was afraid some farmer's litter of puppies had tracked you down."

He turned to see if his comment elicited some sort of reaction. The grin froze on his face, however, when he saw the dyr had stalked to within a pace before he felt the animal's presence. A self-satisfied yawn cracked Nava's impressive set of teeth.

Gera laughed again while he reached back to scratch the grass-colored coat on the dyr's chest.

"Another round to you, my friend," he said between chuckles. "But one of these days, it'll be my turn to surprise you."

Nava chose that moment to sneeze.

The companions resumed their journey to the north. Gera thought the time passed more quickly now that Nava traveled on the road with him and the gelding. For the first time since he left the Greenwards' on his Liberty Day, he had fun enjoying his surroundings.

But the day could not last forever. As the sun flamed on the distant horizon, Gera found himself wriggling on his stomach up a slight rise. A careful peek over the lip revealed a shallow valley beyond. He watched as the Crimson Guard patrol pitched their camp with military precision in the depression.

Horses were turned out on a picket line to feed on the grass and tents were pitched in quick succession. Sentries walked in pairs to their postings as cooking fires blazed brightly in the gathering gloom. Light and shadows danced on the tents while the smell of cooking meat drifted up to the hungry observers.

"Knowing where the guards are posted is a nice change of pace," Gera mumbled as he reviewed in his mind where they had taken up their spots. He backed away from the incline until he could safely stand, then started to walk back to where he had left his horse tied to a tree. He abruptly stopped in his tracks.

Had he missed it? Had the trail turned off the road somewhere, and he did not notice the tracks? Had there even been one present this morning at the gates?

Gera frantically searched his memory, trying to remember if this platoon had taken a cage with them out of Greenville this morning. Several long moments passed while he reconstructed in his mind the chaotic scene at the gates this morning. Slowly, he concluded that, no, the outbound guardsmen had not brought along one of the rolling boxes.

"But what are they doing out here then?" he asked Nava and the winking stars. "If they're not out on a testing patrol, why would they head into an area that's ready to explode into open war at any moment?"

No answer came from his companion, not that he really expected one. Gera sat down to chew a cold supper and pondered his own questions. The moon rode high in the sky when more questions slid into his thoughts. What if the encounter at the gate had not been by chance? Could the chaos have been a diversion to hide the fact these guardsmen were not on a testing trip?

Each successive question led closer to the reason for Gera's trip in the first place. His mind turned to more personal thoughts. Had Dax caught up to Keely yet? Had he found an opportunity to help her escape?

Gera let his thoughts remain on his sister. Dax said she looked exactly like their mother. That made him happy. But Gera had the feeling, however, his brother had made the observations from afar. Dax never mentioned talking to her, and his description never ventured beyond the physical.

"I wonder what she's like, Nava?" he asked. "Does her laugh make everyone else want to join in, like Mother's did? Does she enjoy the woods and outdoors, or did she become a village girl after growing up in Milston? Was she happy with the Gassems?" He let his imagination answer the questions while he swallowed the last of the hard biscuit in his hand. In his mind, he decided she grew up tall, strong, and happy. He hoped he and Dax could still provide that ending for her.

"We can't kill any of the Crimson Guards until we figure out what they're doing," Gera said to the black shadows hiding Nava. "I need to understand their plans better, so I can decide how to ruin them. I'm sorry, friend. Tonight, you must feast on other flesh."

## CHAPTER 24

The afternoon sun beat down on the seacoast of Tralain, glaring off the stone walls of the Sacara Institute, and creating shimmering visions in the air. Ocean breezes kept the air cool enough to be outside, but even light activity quickly left workers drenched with sweat. It was the pleasant sort of late spring day that convinced lovers to sneak away for a picnic in the shade or children to find water for a swim. Hearts sang and the mood floated light everywhere at the school, everywhere except atop the western escarpment where a black knot of tension consumed the mind of Master Ravenhurst.

A hand and a half had passed since his replenishment ceremony, but still he had not received any word from Commander Gregol or Captain Ursel about the suspected Matra. At times, Ravenhurst paced back and forth like a restless animal searching to escape a cage that held him. More often, he stood with his hands atop the stone wall and stared out between the merlins at the ocean. His mind raced between a thousand different answers for the silent delay. He liked none of the choices.

The whisper of a soft slipper against the walkway made it to his ears, breaking his study of the waves. He turned to the student, Chara, waiting patiently with her head bowed.

"Yes, child, what is it?" His voice revealed none of the storms raging beneath his calm face.

"I'm sorry to break your solitude, my Lord," she said. "Captain Trana is waiting with a report he says you requested. He also has a message from the bird loft that he calls important."

Ravenhurst's heart leaped into his throat at the mention of the messenger birds, wondering if this was the letter he had been waiting on for so long. Common sense quickly grabbed hold of his thoughts, however. Any letter from Gregol would have been sent with a black seal and delivered immediately to him and no one else, including Trana.

"Show him out here and bring us some iced wine, Chara. While we talk, I don't want to be disturbed."

The rustling of the sagia's orange robe told of her departure and soon signaled her return with the captain. Adal turned and noticed Chara had enlisted the help of a fellow student, this one a male dressed in yellow, to carry a small table to the parapet. She placed a tray containing a serving set on it before both sagias, bowed, and left.

Ravenhurst turned his attention to the saluting officer. Though Trana led the garrison of guardsmen at Sacara, making him third in the chain of command behind only Gregol and Randel, the man had only reported directly to the master a handful of times in the two summers since his promotion. Trana's eyes never wavered from the distant horizon, and his body remained still in its stance. If he was nervous, the man did a good job of hiding its signs.

"Yes, Captain Trana," Ravenhurst said. "What's your report?"

"My Lord, the deception between Spirache and Lebesh has been started. Four battleships, all carrying both kingdoms' flags, have been dispatched to create havoc upon the vessels of each other. I sailed with two ships that met a convoy of Spirachi merchanters. We struck the Lebesh colors and attacked."

"How did the battle go?" Adal interrupted, his curiosity getting the better of him. "Were they able to put up much of a fight?"

"No, my Lord. Their guards were no match for our sea troops. We captured two of the ships, killed the crews, and sailed the vessels back here to unload the goods. We allowed the third ship to escape with some minor damage so they could spread the word about the attack." Trana paused briefly before venturing a question. "My Lord, I've not given any orders to the sailors I left unloading the ships. Should I have them put back out to sea and scuttle the boats when they're done?"

"No, when the men are done taking off the supplies, leave a skeleton crew behind, but have them anchor in the bay. Remove any markings that would give away the ships." Ravenhurst felt a shiver run through his body when he thought about how the ships would be used. "I understand you received a message as well."

"Yes, my Lord. A bird arrived in the loft this morning with a report for Commander Gregol from the garrison at Greenville. Since it was marked as official, I opened it. Captain Sinnell was rotating a company of troops with Willshire. These men were attacked on the road over the course of several nights. They lost a squad and a half before they reached their new post."

Adal's mind worked quickly to calculate the time it had taken for the message to reach Sacara. Icy fingers ran over his emotions as he meshed the new information with what he suspected about the possible Matra. But why would someone attack the guardsmen if they had already freed the girl?

"Captain Trana, I want you to take a company of men and travel to Galadon in search of Commander Gregol. His report is overdue, and I fear it has something to do with this incident. Once you..."

He stopped talking as Chara's shouts rang out and then came closer. Trana ran to a position between Ravenhurst and the door to the landing, his sword in hand. The sagia ignored the man. Instead, he drew on his saca and held the power, ready to unleash its fury at whoever walked into view.

The door flew open, and Captain Randel limped out onto the rampart. A wounded knee, bruised temple, and bleeding cheek all told of the hardships he had withstood on his journey. Even so, he made his way across the stone floor despite the best efforts of Chara to stop him.

"My Lord," he said, "I've an urgent message from Commander Gregol that he ordered me to deliver at once to only your hand." The student continued to press against his chest with both hands, but she might as well have tried to move the Wall of Purley.

"Chara!" Ravenhurst snapped after he recovered from the absurdity of the scene. "Go get some chairs and another goblet. Gather any help you need, but bring them at once before the captain falls over."

Chara shot one last withering look at Randel, which he ignored, before she bowed to Ravenhurst. The sudden thought she had not been able to carry out a direct order from the master caused her dark skin to pale as she ran from the landing.

Randel reached into his carrying case and retrieved the message Gregol had labored to write. He brought it forward at the wave from Ravenhurst's eager hand. As he walked to the master, the officer passed uncomfortably close to Trana, who had not backed away at his approach, their shoulders brushing.

*A little competition between officers can be a good thing when used for motivation. I'll speak to the commander about these two later.*

The thought flew across Adal's mind and was gone just as quickly. His gaze darted over the message, whipping across the page like the tail on a puppy. He devoured its story once, twice, and a third time while his face echoed a mixture of disappointment, sorrow, and anger. When he could not read it again, Ravenhurst paced silently in front of the low parapet.

While the master walked, Chara returned with a handful of students and three chairs. She also carried a refill for the carafe and a third goblet. The orange-robed sagia directed the others where to place the furniture and, with everything in its place, she turned to leave. At the last moment, she shook her head and hesitated, as if remembering an unpleasant dream. Chara walked to Randel and reached inside her robe, removing a plain handkerchief and handing it to the officer. He stared at her, furrowing his forehead. She gestured at his bleeding cheek in answer to his silent question and then left the landing.

"Captain Randel," Ravenhurst said, his quiet words sounding loud over the distant pounding of surf. The officer jumped after the distraction of the young woman. "You had trouble delivering this message?"

"Yes, my Lord. Commander Gregol ordered me to ride through the nights to get the letter to you as quickly as possible.

Two nights past, my horse stepped into a hole in the darkness, and I was knocked unconscious in the fall. A farmer found me and brought me back to my senses. When he refused to let me have his mount to continue, I was forced to kill him and take the horse."

"If the accident was more than two days ago, why are you still bleeding?"

Randel raised the handkerchief to his face and stared in amazement at the red stain on the cloth. His neck changed to scarlet, but he answered at once.

"The student gave me the mark when she tried to keep me from seeing you, my Lord." His eyes narrowed, however, his expression never changed when a muffled laugh rose from Trana.

"Captain Trana," Ravenhurst's words contained steel, but not an ounce of warmth. "Go see to the preparation for warnings about what happened in Greenville for every garrison west of the Teeth. Tell the officers to take whatever steps they deem necessary to stop further losses. I want the birds to be on the wing tonight. Also, have the original message delivered to Captain Randel's quarters so he can read it once we've finished here."

"Yes, my Lord," Trana said, dropping his gaze to the floor. He saluted and left without glancing up again, leaving Ravenhurst to wonder if the action was out of embarrassment or anger.

He cleared his thoughts before he waved Randel toward the wine. The delay gave him a chance to walk to the closest chair, each step dragging, and slumped onto the cushioned seat. Ravenhurst rubbed a hand across his face, imagining the feel of lines etched into his skin. Despite the recent replenishment, he suddenly felt every one of his vast number of summers.

Adal glanced up and watched Randel gulp down half a glass of wine.

"You know you're going to need to kill Captain Trana someday, don't you, Captain?"

"Yes, my Lord." Randel answered without hesitation. "I've known that for quite some time."

Ravenhurst bobbed his head. He believed the officer was willing to tell him the truth, no matter what the imagined consequences.

"Let's make sure we get through the current situation before that happens." He sat straighter in the chair. "Now, tell me. What do you think of the commander's plans to recapture this escaped Chosen?"

Randel opened his mouth immediately. He had ridden for several lonely days with a lot of time to think as he traveled back to the Institute.

"My Lord, I believe Commander Gregol was correct in his assessment of the situation. Captain Ursel's troops would most certainly have found the Chosen if she had run straight to the east and her home village. She, and whoever helped her, must've either traveled north or south close to the coast. The story about her being insane will help gain the favor of the country folk, and she'll eventually need to turn east. The problem," he paused to swallow, "is that the commander does not have enough men to ensure he'll sweep her to the river. If she finds a way to slip through a gap in the lines, she'll be able to disappear, and we may never find her again. And the longer the hunt goes on, the more likely it is that will happen."

Ravenhurst returned to his position at the wall and let his hands rest on the warm stones of the Institute's defenses. His sleeves rippled in the breeze that circled the building, carrying the tang of ocean air. Slowly, deep breaths helped to calm his tumbling emotions. Even assuming the Chosen's escape earlier had not prepared him for the blow of knowing it for fact.

"Captain Randel," he asked without taking his gaze from the horizon, "how bad are your injuries?"

"I can ride as soon as I saddle a fresh horse, my Lord."

Ravenhurst turned back to the officer and shook his head.

"No need for that just yet. We'll leave at dawn with two companies plus an honor guard. Have the men equip with solitary rations and pack horses. No wagons. Once we reach the Wall of Purley, they'll be dividing down to squad strength. Half will go north, half south, to help herd the Chosen toward the Pennick. Send birds to our garrisons in northern Crandor and southern Spirache and order them to send out all the troops they can spare to help squeeze the trap shut. That will give the commander some immediate help."

Ravenhurst paused while his eyes took on a blank, unfocused stare.

"I have something else in mind for even more aid," he continued. "But first, you, I, and the honor guard will go to the site where she escaped. I'll have work to do there."

Randel saluted and, with only a small grimace of pain, turned on his heel to carry out the orders. He had only taken a couple of steps, however, when he was brought up short by the sound of a man's voice behind him.

"Did the guardsmen say what she was like?" The voice was deep, filling the air with a rich bass.

The officer whirled, hand dropping to his sword. He expected to find someone had scaled the outer wall in secret, sneaking onto Lord Ravenhurst's private sanctuary. The breath left him when he realized they were still alone.

"How did she act with the troopers, Captain?"

Sweat dotted Randel's lip. If he had not seen the master's lips move, he would never have believed it was his voice.

"They said she was very beautiful, with long black hair, my Lord," he stammered. "She never cried out or pleaded after her capture. Captain Ursel described her as brave and steady."

A long sigh erupted from Adal, and his muscles relaxed. Eyelids closed in long blinks and then snapped open, as if trying to shake off a night's sleep. He gave the impression of a man who had been wandering in a drunken stupor only to sober up in an instant and not realize where he stood.

"Thank you, Captain," Ravenhurst said, his voice returned to normal. "You may see to your duties."

Randel saluted again and quickly left the rampart. Adal never saw him leave, however. His attention was already back on Gregol's message.

*She is a young woman of age.*

His chest rumbled with a sigh that was not his own.

eely wondered how much longer she and Dax could continue to attempt to escape. She glanced sideways at the silent figure of her brother in his saddle. His gaunt frame hunched over the pommel, and he clutched his stomach with one trembling claw of a hand. Dax alternately went through periods of heavy sweating followed by terrible bouts with chills. His pallid skin stretched tight over his cheekbones, giving him the look of a man who had not eaten well for weeks.

Yet, every day, he rode onward. Even in his weakened condition, he managed to keep them from detection as they rode north into Crandor. They skirted around towns, big and small, and had only seen people at a distance. At the beginning of the journey, Dax had talked to Keely as they traveled, even making the occasional small joke. For a while, it felt as if she was eight summers old again, and she was out riding with her older brother without a care in the world.

Those times were gone.

The situation changed after the first few days. At first, Keely only noticed Dax growing more quiet and testy as they rode. The banter quickly turned into one-word answers, snapped in her direction. The jokes changed into sullen silence. That was when she noticed he ate less and less when they stopped for meals. Afraid he was holding back because they were running out of food, she searched the saddlebags and found plenty to eat. Finally, her brother stopped eating altogether, only cooking for her, and then watching as she ate her own meals, sometimes leaving to retch nearby where she could still hear him.

His condition worsened, matching the bleakness of their situation. Three days into Crandor, a Crimson Guard patrol nearly rode into their camp, missing them by about as far as Keely could throw a rock. The soldiers were riding slow, searching the trail as they went. Dax waited until they were out of hearing range and then led them in a looping circle, eventually turning back to the north. A day later he repeated the maneuver, this time spotting the guardsmen in the distance, well before they were close enough to be in danger.

But the patrols kept appearing. Dax circled and dodged until they could no longer travel north towards Palamor at all. The only roads that appeared to be free of Crimson Guards led to the east, but Dax swore softly, even as he turned toward that direction.

"We can't be too far from Bagdon," Dax said one evening when he showed a little of his old life. "Maybe we should go into town and hire passage to Nason on a riverboat. You ever been on a riverboat, Keely?"

She shook her head.

"Why don't we just take the ferry into Moramet?" she asked.

But it was too late, the old Dax was gone again. He lapsed into a mumbling, delusional conversation with himself that always appeared to end with him losing an argument. Eventually, he rolled over, curling up on himself and falling to sleep.

+ + +

Keely woke with a jerk, not sure what had dragged her out of her dreams. She jumped when Dax spoke again, his words slurring together until they ran into one.

"All gone, all gone. Leave me alone. Please, leave me alone. I did what was best. All gone. How can I forget, if it's all gone?"

His rambling continued, the words repeating themselves until Keely finally crawled to her brother and cradled him in her arms. Dax quieted down for a while, with only an occasional moan, before his eyes suddenly flew open, filled with terrors only he could see.

"No! No, Mother, not you, too. I tried to do what was right, what was best for everyone. Can't you see that? I was just trying to do it right. Why don't you all just leave me alone? All gone. But now it's all gone."

Dax sobbed himself to sleep again in Keely's arms. She held him and watched the night until she could not keep her eyes open any longer, finally nodding off herself.

In the morning, when she shook him awake, he did not mention his dreams from the night before and neither did she. He simply pushed himself to his feet with a groan, and then inched his way into the saddle, heeling his horse toward Bagdon without a glance back to see if she followed.

Keely turned her head away, squeezing her eyes shut against

the tears filling the corners. She did not cry for Dax. The tears came because of the shame she felt for wanting to ride in the opposite direction while he was not looking. Deep down, she wondered if her best chance of escaping the Crimson Guard was to get away from her brother. Whatever physical ills he was fighting were only compounded by the personal demons he battled, and lost to, in his own mind. She stared at him curled over in the saddle, nose nearly touching his horse's mane, as his mount walked away.

Keely pulled on the rein and followed.

The sun bloomed full in the sky and promised a beautiful day. Dax appeared to rally under its warm glow, and he straightened. After a while, he turned his head and noticed her riding alongside.

"When did women's fashion become so plain?" he asked, gesturing toward the choker around her neck. "I don't think I've ever seen one that was only metal with no jewels."

Keely's fingers wandered across the necklace. She tried to remember the exact shade of blue as she thought about the matching piece around Jen's neck after their capture in Milston.

"It's not jewelry, Dax. The guardsman put it around my neck as soon as the stone shined in my hand during the test. They put one on Jen Markem, too."

They rode in silence a while before Dax shifted in his saddle.

"Tell me about it," he said. "Tell me everything. Give me every detail, no matter how small. It might make a difference if we run into some Bloods."

Keely talked for a long time. She described the uneasiness of all the villagers as the Crimson Guard gathered the children on the green and began the testing. Her excitement grew with each word as the memories crept through her mind, each one playing over and over as they flew by. Sweat beaded on her forehead when she began talking about the emotions racing through her as the guardsman walked through the crowd and pulled her into the ring with the children. She described the look on Mr. Gassem when he glanced away, unable to stare her in the eye, the guilt written all over his face. For the first time, she wondered aloud if Martha knew what had happened, if she knew her husband had turned her over to the Crimson Guard. But mostly, Keely talked about how she could not believe any of it was happening.

"I watched them put the necklace on Jen," she said. "I'd seen her around but...I don't remember anything about her that suggested she could handle saca. I mean, they lived outside of town, and she was a few years younger, but still, Milston wasn't that big. I should have at least heard a rumor."

Keely rode in silence for a while, and Dax did not prod her to continue. When she spoke again, her voice quivered.

"When they put the jewel into my hands, it was like I'd just walked through a door into a different world and taken the first breath of my life. The colors were sharper. The air smelled sweet. I felt my heart pumping and the blood flowing through my body. I heard the pounding of the guardsmen's hearts, saw the fear explode in their eyes. My heart sang a song of joy as the light poured out of the stone like water from the well of life and was matched by the light and power in me. Dax, I was alive! I may have been breathing and walking around before, eating and talking, but I wasn't alive until that moment."

She paused, glancing at her brother while he stared into the distance.

"The leader of the Crimson Guards jerked the stone from my hands, and the light disappeared, throwing my mind into darkness. Then they shoved this," she touched the metal, "around my neck. The box in my mind closed again, and the other world was gone. The power was gone. The difference was that now I knew my saca was hiding there. I could still feel it, just out of my touch behind a wall. A wall that was built from something I could not break down, no matter what I tried. Dax, I can barely believe it, but part of me would do anything to go back to that other world just to touch my saca for a moment, for half a breath. The gods help me, even if that means going to the Sacara Institute." Keely turned to see the reaction in her brother from her confession.

Dax slumped over the saddle again, soft snores climbing into the air.

eely pulled the blanket tighter over her head and let it trail down her back and shoulders. The rain sloughed over the wool and pooled at her feet, making it appear as if she floated on mud. At least the wind had died. Wet was one thing to endure, but wet and cold would lead to her becoming sick.

She glanced out into the late afternoon gloom, the sky a swirling gray of clouds, and searched the area for Dax. Her brother had left shortly after waking this morning, turning down any food as had become his custom, and walked off. Bagdon was less than half a day's ride away, just past this stand of trees and over a few hills. But they had remained in the same spot for two days now. Even in his diminished state, Dax realized something was wrong, hesitant to move on until he understood the danger.

Keely felt it, too.

The pair had dodged Crimson Guard patrols for days after turning north and crossing out of Galadon into Crandor, turning to the side if the patrols were far enough in the distance or hiding if they were too close. But in the past hand, fewer and fewer of the red-clothed soldiers were around. It was almost as if Dax and Keely had outridden them, even though they had not pushed the horses.

Two days ago, the guardsmen patrols disappeared altogether. That was even more worrisome than seeing them on the horizon.

Dax had called a halt to their travel, sticking her into this clump of trees and warning her not to light a fire or be seen by anyone. He returned last night after sundown, earning a little squeal out of her when he suddenly stepped out from behind the tree beside her, then abruptly lay down and went to sleep after saying he had found nothing. That must not have satisfied her brother, however, because they had not continued on yet.

Keely leaned back on the stump and used the trunk behind her for a rest. She was more exposed to the rain this way, but her legs were cramped from sitting in the same position for too long. She glanced back at where the horses were tied between some trees. They stood head to back, using each other to weather the storm together.

"At least you've got each other to keep warm," she muttered.

Keely wondered if Dax had walked into Bagdon. They were approaching from the north and hoped the effort would help fool anyone who might be searching for them. During one of his lucid times in the saddle as they escaped, he had told her they would ride into town and head straight for the docks. There they would purchase passage on a riverboat for Nason.

She listened to one of the horses nicker and thought about riding on a boat. Keely remembered seeing some of the masts sticking into the sky when the guardsmen took her through

Willshire, great canvas sails rolled around wooden booms. A few quick glimpses were all she could glean while at the Crimson Guard garrison. At least that was better than riding in and out of town in the rolling cage, sides pulled down, cutting off her sight and the touch of any breeze.

A horse stamped its hoof, turning her thoughts to Gera and the metalsmith shop where he had been apprenticed. Keely imagined him having the time to examine the docks, maybe even catch a ride on one of the sailboats up and down the coast. Some of the traveling merchants Mr. Gassem dealt with in Milston would sometimes share stories about the big cities they visited. One even talked about sailing all the way down the Pennick River to where it dumped into the Windward Sea where the waves towered over the side of the ship, splashing everyone on board with water that was too salty to drink. She thought she would like to ride upon the sea one day, feel the spray in her face, and go to places where they had never heard about the Sacara Institute or saca.

The horse stomped its hoof again, and Keely turned to hush it, but the words stuck in her throat. Both horses were staring into the woods behind her. She stood and whirled around.

A dark figure stood a few paces away. A hood was pulled low over its head, rainwater dripping off the edge.

Keely did not move. The stranger was obviously not a Crimson Guard, his clothes a mixture of browns and blues, and a dark gray cloak that had been repaired in more than one spot. Her relief lasted only long enough to let her gaze drop to the man's waist where a sword was strapped. After several moments, the other person slowly raised their hands and threw back the hood, revealing a brown-haired young man who appeared to be a couple of years older than Gera.

"May your ground bring you happiness until the harvest," the young man said. He wore a small smile, but he did not move any closer.

Keely nodded, but kept the blanket up, hiding some of her face.

"Hello," she said.

His eyebrows shot up at her voice.

"Are you lost, good lady? You're a long way from any town, and there's danger afoot in Crandor these days."

"No, I'm just passing through."

He nodded, the smile still holding.

"I'll help you move along if you like. The nearest road to Bagdon and Dubin is just over the next rise. But you can't stay here. This is my land."

"I need to wait on my traveling companion," Keely said. "We didn't realize the land belonged to anyone."

"Yes. It's mine." He blushed. "Not just anyone can own ground like this at my age. I know it doesn't look like much yet, but give me a couple of summers to clear these trees and till the ground, and this dirt will put out some of the best crops in Crandor. I guarantee it!" He finished with a laugh, his grin growing wider.

Keely was fascinated by how proud the young man was of owning the land. She let the blanket fall to her shoulders so she could see him better.

The smile melted from his lips in sections, turning into a wide-mouthed stare.

"You...you're..."

Keely glanced down at her clothes to see if something was out of place.

"I'm what?" she asked when she looked up again.

"Hair as black as coal," he muttered. "Face as pale as the moon. Traveling alone or," he glanced at the horses before whirling back to face her again, "with one or two others." He took a step backward, caught his heel on a tree root, and fell hard on his back. He stretched out a hand as if to hold her off. "I won't tell anybody..."

"What are you talking about?" Keely asked as she stepped toward him and reached out to help him up.

"I see your necklace. Don't kill me!" he screamed. "Crazy! Don't use your saca on me, crazy witch!" The man scrambled to his feet and ran.

Keely blinked, heart racing as she stared after the young man. A moment later she jumped sideways.

"Who was that?" Dax demanded, running to her side. "Did he hurt you?"

"No, he didn't touch me," she said. "But what he..."

"Not now," Dax said, leaping after the man. "Stay there."

✦ ✦ ✦

*He fell here. Slipped on those wet leaves, rolled down into the gully.*

Dax followed the path. He did not even need to slow down to find the signs, the panicked young man leaving a trail a city dweller could see at midnight. The trees thinned in front of him and a flash of movement caught his attention. He slowed, swinging in an arc to his left.

A few moments later, he stared around a tree, watching a small cabin and barn for any sign of life besides the chickens pecking in the yard. The barn door flew back, and the stranger walked into view, a saddle slung over his arm and bridle on his shoulder. In his left hand, the man carried a short spear.

Dax watched as he walked to the corral, placing the saddle on the top rail before climbing inside and catching the horse who had been calmly munching on grass. Fingers curled into fists, making the woodsman wish he had his bow. There would have been less chance for something to go wrong. He slipped his hand into the game bag slung over his shoulders.

Within a few moments, the saddle was cinched tight and bridle looped up and over the horse's head. The man turned for the gate. Now was the time to act.

Dax stumbled into the open, hunched over, his hands gripping his stomach.

"Help me!" he yelled, making his voice tremble at the end.

The man whirled and reached for the spear.

"Help!" Dax said again, stumbling toward the corral and nearly falling. "A woman..." He let his voice trail away.

The man grabbed the spear and slipped through the corral rails, approaching slowly.

"What's wrong?" he said.

Dax held out his right hand, palm stained red with blood. "There was a woman in the trees..."

The man closed the gap between them.

"Come on," he said as he gripped Dax's other arm. "I'll get you inside the cabin before I ride into Bagdon for help. It's that blood and ashes crazy witch that escaped from Sacara. She tried to catch me, too. The Crimson Guard..."

Dax spun, arm flashing up, and drove his knife straight through the man's throat. Blood sprayed into the air as the man tried to stop the bleeding and bring his weapon up at the same time. He managed to wave the spear a couple of times before he fell to one knee, gurgles replacing the gasps. The movements weakened, and the man fell over, flopping like a fish on the bank, then stopped. Dax retrieved his knife and ran into the woods.

◆ ◆ ◆

Keely was not surprised by her brother this time. She watched as he moved through the trees, flowing in and out of view, until he was closer than she thought possible in such a short period of time.

"Help me saddle the horses," he said. "We're going into Bagdon now." He walked toward the mounts.

Keely did not move. She stared in the direction he had come from, searching for more movement.

"Where is he, Dax? Where's the man who ran away from me?"

She watched the cinch slip through her brother's fingers. He bent over and grabbed the end again, feeding it through to tighten down the saddle. Finally, he turned and faced her.

"I couldn't let him tell anybody he saw you."

Keely's skin went cold. Her trembling fingers touched her chin, and she took a step backward, needing to ask the question, but not wanting to hear the answer.

"What did you do?"

"I tracked him to his cabin. Talked to him right in front of his barn and convinced him not to tell anybody about you. He's going to stay right there." Dax turned back to the horse. "It'll be all right. He won't tell anyone."

Keely let out the breath she had been holding and grabbed her saddle.

♦ ♦ ♦

The horses plodded by the creek banks as the sun flared orange on the horizon. When they reached the top of the next low crest, Keely saw the lights of Bagdon twinkling in the distance. She glanced over at Dax, and he was also staring at the city. Her brother had appeared to draw strength from an untapped reserve in the past few hours, sitting straighter in the saddle than he had since he first rescued her. He still doubled over occasionally, body almost leaning on the pommel, but usually fought off whatever pain he felt with a shake of his head and a grimace. Keely remained silent but kept track of him out of the corner of her eye. Part of her wondered what he would have been capable of if he had not tossed away his life and tried to destroy himself for so many years.

They entered Bagdon and rode straight to the docks. The first few rivermen Dax talked to were all trading to the south, away from the approaching war. She hid underneath her cloak hood as he went from boat to boat, most of the time just being told to go away, but once he was shoved down the plank, stumbling to keep his feet on the dock. He finally found a Crandori flat boat headed north, but so many supplies for the troops in Elarton lined its deck, the captain had no room for passengers. Keely wondered if they would need to chance using the ferry and ride into Moramet.

After trying at least a score of possibilities, Dax finally convinced the captain of a large riverboat to sell them passage. The man was from Halon and had been traveling north when news of the hostilities between Crandor and Palamor reached this far south. Now the Crandori crown blocked the rest of his journey to Birse, along with any other boat with supplies for Palamor.

"It's just as well they won't let me go." He spit as he talked, a sullen look settling comfortably on his face. "There won't be any Stonacre weapons to trade for in Birse anyway, with all the fightin' goin' on. The Palamorans'll be keepin' them all for themselves."

He went on to say the crown had contracted him to take military replacements and supplies to Elarton, but his deck remained only three quarters full for the next voyage. Since the kingdom paid him by the man, he said he could use the extra money from the fare for Dax and Keely to help him offset his losses.

In a short while, Keely settled into the small cabin she and her brother were going to share on the journey north. While Dax disappeared down the dock to sell their horses for their passage, she stared around the sparse accommodations and questioned how much longer the nightmare would continue.

eely draped her cloak across a chair so it could dry, the rain dripping off and forming a pool on the worn deck. She thought about lying down on the narrow berth, but her clothes would have the bed wet, too, if she did not change first. All the dry clothes were in the saddlebags with her brother, however. She was still trying to decide what to do when tapping on the door broke the quiet. Remembering how the man in the forest reacted when he saw the blue necklace, she flung the cloak around her shoulders again and grabbed the knife Dax had left behind for her.

"Come in," she said, trying to sound confident but the words wavered and ended like the squeak of a mouse.

The door opened, and the ship's first mate stepped forward. He removed his brimless cloth cap and bowed his head.

"Excuse me for the breakin' in, mum," he said. "The captain's about to take a late supper and wanted to know if you'd wish to eat with him. Your man's welcome to join when he gets back."

Keely thought about Dax's warning to stay out of sight, but the thought of a hot meal almost made her throw caution to the gods.

"Please thank the good captain for his offer, but I'm tired from the traveling and wish to turn in early." She forced a smile to her lips.

"As you wish, mum." The man replaced his cap and started to shut the cabin door when he abruptly froze. He only stared at her for a couple of heartbeats, the time stretching to eternity for Keely, before he finished closing the door.

She took a deep breath and removed the cloak after the latch clicked behind the first mate. The choker would have made him stop, but she was certain it had been covered. She sat on the edge of the bed, ignoring her wet clothes, and tried to reason out the mystery. After a while, she gave up. Her falling eyelids said the lie about being tired was closer to the truth than she wanted to admit and besides, a night in a bed, no matter how hard and narrow, would be a dream come true.

Keely ate a cold meal of traveler's bread and dried venison while she attempted to forget about what the captain was eating in his cabin. After she finished her paltry supper, she washed up the best she could with the water remaining in the old cracked vase and basin. Finally, full and ready to lie down, she thought about some warm dry clothes again and realized that was not going to happen.

Grief and self-pity wracked the young woman, the one last disappointment proving too much to bear. She realized the damp shirt and pants were not the real reason tears rolled down her cheeks, but still her body shook with sobs. After the death of her parents and brother, her life had been relatively calm and stable while she was living with the Gassems. But from the moment Mr. Gassem had turned her in to the Crimson Guard, and the light had shined from the testing stone, everything had fallen apart. Even her rescue was topsy-turvy, with her spending more time taking care of Dax the past few days than he of her. The wet clothes were just the straw that broke the dragon's back.

Keely lie on the narrow berth, curled into a ball beneath the musty blanket, and cried until her sides ached. Slowly, physical and mental exhaustion took over, and she drifted off to sleep.

✦ ✦ ✦

Keely woke with a jerk. For a moment, her mind searched for what had roused her until she recognized the rocking of the boat had increased. She leaped from the bed and checked the top bunk, hoping to find her brother.

Dax was nowhere to be found.

Worried the captain had double-crossed them and left Bagdon before her brother returned, she grabbed her cloak and rushed into the dark passageway. A hulking, dark figure in the shadows caught her eye before she turned and rushed in the opposite direction, hand gripping the knife at her belt. She leaped up the stairs and reached the landing for the main deck. Laughter reached her ears as she threw open the door and stepped into the bright morning sunshine. Silence fell while her eyes adjusted to the light, and she shaded them with one raised hand. After a moment, she saw what had been so entertaining.

Dax stood on a plank, about a pace and a half long, balanced on a barrel turned onto its side. His hands were tied behind his back, and a noose cinched his neck before looping up and over the boom. Gentle swells in the Pennick River caused the barrel to roll back and forth, forcing Dax to constantly shift his weight on the moving base. This would normally have been an easy trick, but her brother was faced with two complications.

He had been savagely beaten during some part of the fun. His shirt hung from his shoulders, a blood-soaked, tattered rag. Both eyes were swollen shut, and dried blood had caked on his face where his nose bled after being broken. Even this abuse had not been enough for the tormentors. A large man had been lashing his legs with a multi-thonged whip when she arrived on deck. Now, even he was standing still, watching her in the sunlight.

Keely had no idea how long this game had been going on, but she saw her brother could not play much longer and remain alive. Rage she did not know existed within her screamed for vengeance. In her mind, the box formed, and her saca attempted to burst free, the sides bending, but the power remained locked away. Her fury fading, she turned her attention to Dax's torturers.

Doubt, and then despair, drowned the rest of the heat in her emotions when she recognized the red uniforms of the Crimson Guard. Her loyalty to her brother won over her fear, however, and she yanked out her knife and prepared to leap at the nearest guardsmen.

Suddenly, only her toes touched the deck. One muscular arm circled around her and raised her up while another hand grabbed her wrist. A growl of pain resonated in her abductor's chest, but he did not lessen his hold. Keely squirmed in his grasp, but several other nearby soldiers came to his aid, and soon she stood, disarmed with her hands bound.

Two guardsmen held her in front of Dax for a few moments

before leading her past her brother to the bow of the ship. Her captor stood in front of the trooper who had used the whip on her sibling.

"It just surprised me, Lord Commander," the soldier said as she moved into earshot. "I've used that same hold countless times to subdue Chosen without hurting them, and I've never had that happen before now. It's not a bad burn. It's just that...I've never even heard of a sagia who could make the collar warm, let alone hot enough to scald."

"You're dismissed, trooper." The leader returned the salute and then spun on his heels to face Keely. She barely noticed. She was too busy watching the guardsman walk by her with a look of fear on his face.

"Leave us," the leader commanded, and her guards walked away. He glared down at her, his dark eyes narrowing, staring as if he meant to search her for whatever answers he wanted. Keely felt his gaze was as heavy as if his hands pawed her body.

"I'm Lord Commander Gregol, leader of the Crimson Guard. Would you tell me your name, please?"

"Keely Staghorn." Her words were clipped through clenched teeth. "Release my brother! I'm the one you want not..." She stopped when Gregol raised one gloved hand.

"So, he *is* your brother. I must say I agree with the captain when he said you two don't even look like the same kindred. Same mother and father?"

Keely nodded in silent reply.

"I'll make a deal with you, Lady Staghorn," the commander continued. "I'll have your brother cut down and let you tend to his wounds on one condition. You'll not try to escape or harm anymore of my men between here and the Sacara Institute. Otherwise, I'll let the troopers continue to play with him until he dies. Then you'll be bound, hand and foot, placed under constant guard, and you'll still go to the Institute." He took one long step forward and loomed over the young woman. "Are my terms acceptable?"

Keely's heart sank as she realized her fate had not changed, despite Dax's efforts. She nodded.

"If you want my oath, I'll give it."

Gregol stared at her for a few moments. Finally, he nodded and glanced over her head.

"Sergeant, cut him down and place him under guard in their cabin." Gregol's voice boomed in her ears and made her jump. She listened to the sounds of boots thumping across the deck to carry out orders, but she did not remove her gaze from the commander.

"You'll have the run of the boat, but you must stay inside when we're near the various ports," he continued, his voice dropping to a normal volume. "You'll be watched, but none of my men will touch you or harm you in any way unless you attempt to break our agreement. Do we understand each other?"

Keely's gaze dropped to the deck again.

"Yes." She barely recognized her own voice.

Commander Gregol pulled his knife and slit the rope binding her hands together.

"You may go, Lady Staghorn."

Keely turned and had taken a couple of steps towards her cabin before he spoke again, halting her in her tracks.

"Are there anymore family members I should be worried about?" Gregol asked.

Keely had already prepared for the question during the

nightmarish escape attempt.

"No. My father and other brother were killed while fighting in the Bakri War, and my mother died from the grief of the news. Dax and I were the last of the family." With any luck, the Sacara Institute would never find out about Gera.

She did not notice Commander Gregol rubbing his palm with a wide thumb as she walked away.

CHAPTER 28

For several days, Gera and Nava passed their time in so much the same way, even trailing the Bloods became tedious work as they neared the border between Crandor and Palamor. On this morning, however, the companions left the roadway to skirt around the village of Elarton. After all the questions and distrust when he was headed north out of Greenville, he did not want to risk being held up on his journey at this point.

Calling Elarton a village exaggerated its standing. Normally, only an inn, a general store, and a handful of houses comprised the city limits. It was no wonder the city watch in Greenville had been so disbelieving about him having business in the town. If it had not been for the ferry across the Pennick River to the large Morametan city of Wapak, the burg would not even have warranted a name on a map.

But Gera did not approach the village in normal times. The population had swelled by twenty-fold to include about twenty-five hundred Crandori troops in tents around its borders. Everywhere he looked, the gold sheaf of wheat and the scythe danced across green banners in the breeze. Rows of archery targets decorated one area and resounded with the steady thumps of arrows striking home. The clackity-clack echoes of swords with practice guards in place rang into the air as well. Even an inexperienced novice like Gera could tell these were not just drills. These soldiers were readying themselves to go to war.

Into this beehive of activity rode the Crimson Guard patrol. Part of the Sacara Institute's long held agreements with the kingdoms consisted of a promise of neutrality. In exchange, the guardsmen observed safe passage from all sides. This meant they could continue to test and recruit even during times of war.

Gera sat on the gelding and tried to decide how best to follow the patrol. The Bloods might be riding for the ferry crossing to Wapak. If that was the case, he doubted the Crandori troops would stop him from going over the Pennick River as well. After all, he was a Morametan.

But what if they were not headed for the river? Would they let him ride into Elarton, ask some questions, and then travel out to the north in pursuit? In the end, Gera decided his first reaction was the safest choice. He would circle the army encampment and try to pick up the patrol trail on the northern side of the village. If they had not ridden through, he could always double back and then head for the ferry landing.

By late afternoon, Gera found the northern road and heeled his horse into a ground-eating trot, moving faster to make up the lost time for the route he had chosen. Avoiding two Crandori patrols had not been hard, but it cost him even more ground. His heart leaped for joy, however, when he found signs of the

Bloods' horses on the road before long.

While he rode in pursuit of his prey, the ground rolled in gentle swells that, compared to the rest of Crandor he had seen, appeared almost hilly. Gera pressed on through the ups and downs until well after full night had fallen. He was beginning to wonder how long he would need to continue when Nava's black shape stopped in the roadway in front of the gelding, the moon giving him just enough light to see the dyr's dark hide.

Gera hopped down from the saddle and followed Nava to the crest of the next swell, a score of paces up the road. From other travelers' talk, he knew he must be close to the Palamor border. He might even have passed over it for all that he knew. Even so, he had to know what was happening with the patrol.

He raised his head above the ridge and stared at the Crimson Guard encampment. His breath caught in his throat when he noticed the amount of activity among the tents, much more than he had observed on other nights. Reaching over, he scratched Nava behind his ears, making sure the dyr remained close. There was too much happening, so he decided to wait for a while longer before making his own camp for the night.

After a while, the dyr crept away into the darkness. Nava had been going off on his own the last few nights, once it became apparent he would not be allowed to eat Blood meat. Gera envied his companion. With no time to hunt and no villages to stop in and have a meal, his steady diet of dried meat and travel biscuits had gone well beyond boring and bland.

A small group of guardsmen parted in the camp, and he noticed they were readying to leave with several loaded pack horses. He had never noticed this happening before tonight. Gera crawled back from the crest and quickly returned to the gelding. He did not know how close he would need to be to the Bloods to learn about their plans, so he rechecked the cloth on the mount's bridle. This was no time for a stray sound to give him away.

For the first time since his initial fight with a Crimson Guard patrol, Gera was nervous. A glance around at the night did not reveal Nava, although only the dyr's green eyes would have given him away in the black. But he could not wait. Hopefully, his friend would not be hunting long and return soon.

The small group of Bloods led their horses off the road to the east and Gera walked on a parallel course to them. The troopers were easy to keep pace with since the ten pack horses did not move quickly with their bundles. Also, the guardsmen did not attempt to hide their presence, either. Their voices and laughter carried to him on the cool air, although he could not make out the words.

Gera's head swiveled from side to side as he moved, searching for dangers and Nava. His suspicions about being in Palamor increased the longer he traveled in concert with the guardsmen. The trees stood closer together here, and even the open meadows remained untilled, something he had not seen in the farm-loving countryside to the south. Eventually, a large grove came into view like an ebony sea against the night. The moon threw its pale light down from directly overhead as they all walked into the shadows.

The tracker breathed a sigh of relief when the Bloods lit torches to guide their way through the trees. As the stand grew thicker, this allowed him to angle his path closer. The men had either stopped talking, or the trees had cut off the flow of their voices. Either way, if he wanted to learn about their plans, he had to hear what the guardsmen said.

Gera abruptly froze in mid-step. Light floated in the corner of his eye, and he slowly turned his head in that direction. A twinkling glow answered the troopers' torches, and the two groups moved toward each other. He tied his horse to a tree and stepped forward, his mind racing at the thought of finally gaining some answers to all his questions.

His father's voice sang in his ears as he moved from trunk to trunk like a puff of air, every lesson, every talk about fieldcraft, replaying in his thoughts. Only the forest animals sensed his presence, retreating silently from his path. He wondered if Nava had returned and picked up his trail, but quickly squelched the idea, concentrating on the task at hand.

*Land on the ball of your foot. Rotate your weight to the outside. Shift your weight forward for another stride.*

*Never look directly at a light at night or keep one eye closed. It will take too long for your eyes to adjust back to seeing in the dark. Stay blind for too long, and you'll be dead.*

*Use the tree trunks as a shield, not a wall. If you get too close to them, you can be reached by someone hiding on the other side.*

Tyre's lessons poured through Gera's memory as if his father still lived and whispered in his ear. Blood pounded through his veins with excitement. The air felt thick, and his lungs begged for more than he drew in slowly through his nose. Danger called to him like a forbidden lover, screaming to come closer. He blinked. A small clearing was only a few paces away, and no one in a red uniform was facing his way.

The torch light pooled with that from a campfire. The commanding officers exchanged salutes and welcomes while the troopers bandied their greetings in a more raucous manner. Calls questioning heritage and sexual practices mingled with laughter as the troopers performed what appeared to be a familiar routine of trading pack horses. Gera saw "his" guardsmen now controlled bundles not nearly as loaded as the ones they had brought to the meeting.

The officers continued to talk in low voices in the center of the clearing. Gera strained to hear the odd word about supplies, gems, and "the damned dragon brood." Nothing made much sense, however, until the leader he trailed became excited and spoke in a louder voice.

"Yes, Commander Gregol was at the Greenville garrison a cycle ago. He ordered double the raiding parties and wanted the burnings to increase, too. I heard him ask what it would take for them to grow spines and fight for their bloody precious land." The man laughed before he continued. "Those idiot dirt eaters are so mad now they can't see the barn door from inside the barn."

Gera's attention abruptly flew from the conversation as two things ripped it away.

"Beware right," the now familiar voice whispered in the back of his mind.

But even the warning felt pale to the power of a compulsion that suddenly grabbed Gera and tried to jerk him forward. His feet felt the urge to run to the other side of the assembled soldiers and into the shadows opposite the clearing. The call pleaded—no, ordered—him to answer its summons while a glimmer of his saca's light shined around the closed doorway in his mind. He felt like the harness attached to competing oxen at a village fair, stretched in opposite directions. Only a tremendous effort kept him rooted to the spot. Instead, ever so slowly, he turned his head to the right. His eyes searched the black pools for enemies while his arm eased the sword from its scabbard.

There!

Three shadows skulked from tree to tree in movement toward him. But a moment later, confusion clouded his thoughts. The trio's line of direction would miss his hiding spot by a few paces, as if they only knew roughly where he stood. Or, were there more shadows he had not noticed yet?

The call rang in his mind again, stronger and with an infinite amount more urgency. Gera's head whipped back to face the clearing, and his foot took a halting step forward.

A metal clatter rang from the far side of the open area and cursing echoed in its wake. A guardsman rolled into view on the ground in the dingle, blood pouring out of his stomach around clutching fingers. Fearing the noise was a distraction to help catch him unaware, Gera did the first thing that came to mind.

He attacked.

The nearest Bloods had turned to stare in shock at their fallen comrade and left their backs to Gera's assault. The first fell to a crushing swipe at his neck. His blood had barely started to spray into the night when the second dropped from a thrust to the spine. The training and instincts of the other nearby soldiers took hold, and they backed into an inverted wedge to face the enraged Gera. The maneuver forced him to fight a battle on three sides, with the unknown shadows still to his rear.

The counterattack fell apart immediately. A midnight tornado collapsed one side of the formation and threatened the other guardsmen with panic. Nava trampled two men before stopping at the third and ripping out his throat with a stomach-churning growl.

His enemies' attentions diverted again, Gera killed a third trooper with no resistance. He whirled like a child's top to face another Blood who regained his composure after the dyr's attack and tried to catch him from the rear. The world danced to his whim as he reacted on blind instinct. As he fought the attacker, the sounds of other battles echoed around him.

Block, parry, thrust. Gera settled into a rhythm as he confronted the Blood in front of him in the dimming fire light. The torches had been dropped at the first scream, and now only the campfire lit the clearing. His pace quickened as another trooper joined the fray against him. The young man jumped gracefully around the already fallen soldiers as he tried to stay out of the middle of the two men.

Nagging, fleeting questions worried his thoughts and threatened to destroy his concentration. Why weren't the other soldiers ripping him to shreds from behind? Why had Nava stopped that terrorizing snarl after the first kill? If Nava was dead, who else attacked the Bloods? Most perplexing of all: What caused the irresistible call from the far side of the clearing?

A guardsman blade nipped his arm, and Gera slammed the door shut on his stray thoughts. He leaped wildly to one side and scored a minor hit upon his first attacker, but the second remained untouched. That soldier moved in a mirrored dance with Gera in the fight.

The call suddenly pulled at him again, his head turning toward it, even as he blocked a thrust from his wounded opponent. The glance was all the distraction the unharmed Blood needed to unleash a ferocious swing at Gera's sword arm.

The blade whistled downward. He flinched back, saving his forearm from being cleaved in two, but the same could not be said of his borrowed weapon. With the tip of Ham's sword still on the blocked soldier's steel, not even the thick blade could withstand the force that crashed onto its flat side. Gera stumbled backward, only the hilt and a hand's breadth of sword remaining in his hand.

He hopped and skittered sideways from the follow up slash at his stomach. But as he moved, his heels caught on the leg of a fallen guardsman. Arms waving, he tumbled to the ground, twisting to break his fall, even as the memory of his father's voice told him to never turn his back on an opponent.

Gera bounced on the ground with a gasp. His gaze frantically swept the area for a shield or weapon, expecting his enemy's steel to bite through his back at any moment. After a lifetime in his mind, he noticed he had fallen in a circle of five or six dead Bloods. In the middle lay a powerfully built man dressed all in black. A sword had punctured his stomach and exited through his back, remaining in the wound. Despite the growing pool of blood around the fighter, he was clinging to life. His lips moved wordlessly, while his chestnut-colored eyes pleaded with Gera below his battered helm. The dying man's arm spasmed, and a sword flopped from his hand.

The door exploded in Gera's mind, and his saca leaped through his body, spreading light and heat wherever it touched. He stretched his hand towards the weapon and cried out in his thoughts to feel the leather-wrapped handle in his palm. The light shot toward the sword.

The long hilt slammed into his hand. The raging inferno Gera had felt from his saca a moment earlier exploded, making the previous heat a firefly compared to a volcano. His skin crisped and fell away while his bones turned to ash. He screamed into the night with the agony of a man tortured in one of the gods' hell. Gera's eyes flew open, as if for the first time in his life, and he saw...

*He flew in high over the mountain peaks, the early morning sun shimmering off his red-gold scales. The sounds of men fighting drifted lazily to his ears from below, interrupting the beauty of the day. As he glanced down, anger simmered beneath the surface of his emotions and threatened to boil out of control, even while he marveled at the foolish courage of the soldiers with which he had sided. From these heights, he could see they charged headlong into a three-pronged trap meant to crush them before they came close to where the main fight lay. Observing the overwhelming odds they faced, he did not doubt the snare would succeed. But their deaths were not his concern. Those men who would die were merely the distraction he needed to get close for the real fight.*

*He and his clutch flew to the east of the battle. His leathery wings folded back, and his heart raced with the same sweeping exhilaration as the air rushing against his body when he went into the dive. His fifty companions followed and plunged alongside, arriving out of the blazing sun on the main encampment of the enemy.*

*He released his anger, and it boiled free when he spotted the rear guard of the force, the soldiers finally glancing upward and releasing a flight of arrows as he and the clutch pulled out of the dive in a swooping arc. Most of the missiles bounced harmlessly off his mature scales, but a few managed to cause cuts to his massive wings.*

*"Yiaeeee!" Battle fury bred screams that poured into the morning from his maw. He was no longer a material being in this world. His rage had transformed him into a breathing flame of retribution, sent to deliver the death song to his enemies.*

*Part of his blazing hatred leaped from his mouth, engulfing tents and men in devouring flames. Somewhere in the shadows of his thoughts, he heard one of his own clan scream, not in anger, but in pain* and surprise. The realization fanned his passion higher.

An invisible wall slammed into his body and threatened to drive him sideways into a stand of trees. He lashed out with his saca, searching for a weakness in the air barrier. A younger, green-black dragon streaked by overhead and released a withering stream of flame toward the side of the mountain where eight figures stood on a rocky outcropping. The pressure on his flight stopped, and he climbed into the sky again.

The other dragon's fire stopped short of its target, exploding against another unseen barrier. The attack had been a close call, however, as evidenced by the smoking clothes on the two figures on the far right.

No doubt remained in Lord Modig's mind that these were the sagias he and his followers had been sent to destroy. They were also the reason why a thousand foolhardy men had volunteered to be destroyed in an obvious ambush, to buy time for the dragons to kill the leaders of their shared enemy.

A blue and silver-streaked dragon attacked on the other side of the formation with what appeared at first to be only a low, wordless droning. But soon the air vibrated in sync with the singsong chant. Two of the sagias became so disoriented, they fell to the ground in a stupor while a third threw his hands over his ears and screamed in pain. Modig aimed a short, concentrated line of fire at the fallen foes and managed to catch one's clothes on fire. Another of the sagias helped them to extinguish the flames and then stagger into an opening at the back of their ledge.

The battle settled down to probing and testing the other side's defenses, searching for a weakness they could use to destroy. Time after time, the dragons found small deficiencies and, one by one, wounded the sagias. Sometimes the saca users continued to fight, but when they became too injured to continue, they were always led back through the entrance into the mountain.

The dragons were not the only ones to cause damage, however. The right wing on the blue and silver female was mutilated by a fireball to the point that Lord Modig doubted she would ever fly again. Other dragons were riddled with arrows. Even he had been surprised by a volley of spears thrown by invisible hands. One lance still quivered in a scale on his breast with his every move. On one sweeping turn, he glanced toward the battlefield of men and noticed several of his clutch that he had sent to bolster the attackers were on the ground and no longer moving.

His anger turned white hot with the thought of so many of his loyal subjects dead or dying because of these invaders. Another ear-piercing scream left his mouth before he directed a blast of heat and flame at the only two remaining sagias. But his rage turned to joy as he watched one of the men turn and flee to the supposed safety of the mountain, his hair and clothing smoldering.

The invisible wall dwindled with every attack. On each pass by the last three dragons, the defense drew closer to the last sagia until it was barely a pace away from his body. Suddenly, loose rock on the mountainside shifted and began to slide. Lord Modig prepared to help the avalanche, changing his focus, and never saw his opponent's real attack.

Puzzlement fed pain and anger in Modig's ancient mind as the spear point drove through his scale and buried itself in his heart. With the last beat, the dying king watched his subjects release a wall of fire that incinerated the sagia and melted the wall behind him into molten slag.

Even as his essence flew from his body, the dragonlord's final thoughts turned to the battle of the men...

...his attacker's blade streaking downward in an overhead, two-handed strike. Gera threw up the new sword in front of his body without thinking. The blow slid down the blocking weapon until it struck the ground beside his shoulder, kicking dirt into the air. Perhaps a remnant from his vision when he was sure he was about to die, ignited his own rage. He lashed out with his foot to the inside of the Blood's knee and felt it give beneath his heel. A pop sounded as the joint dislocated, and the leg buckled beneath the guardsman. Gera cut the soldier's scream short when he slashed the sword across the man's throat.

He rolled to his feet to meet the charge of the other injured Blood. The man had apparently been content to let his shield-mate finish off the fallen young man himself. But when he saw Gera turn the tables, he waded back into the fight with a curse.

Gera only had a moment to marvel at the balance and feel of the weapon in his hands. He gripped the hilt with both hands and waited for the guardsman to strike. The trooper started with a looping, diagonal slash and then reversed into a level, back-handed cut. Gera sidestepped the first attempt easily and then caught his opponent's blade on the backside of his sword. He slashed downward from the block and straight through, feeling no resistance from flesh or armor. He cursed, thinking he had missed the mark.

Agony-filled screams tumbled from the soldier's mouth. Glancing down again, Gera saw he had almost severed the man's right arm below the elbow. The useless limb dangled, attached by some tendons and skin as blood gushed from the wound. Gera ended the noise, and the man's torment, by slashing across his neck.

The victorious young fighter whirled at a howl of pain from Nava. The dyr and a tall, long-haired warrior stood surrounded by three Bloods. Most of the other guardsmen lay dead, but several other men still walked about in the carnage.

Even as he moved to aid his friend, Gera watched in horror as a fourth trooper, only lying on the ground pretending to be dead, rose up behind the dyr and raised his sword to strike. The memory of the powerful anger in his dreams bubbled to the surface and reverberated across his thoughts. His saca gathered in his fingertips as he lifted his empty left hand.

"No!"

A solitary bar of flame, no more than the width of his hand, shout out of his fingers toward the fight. It entered the back of the nearest Blood and exited his chest with a wet popping sound before slamming into the body of the ambushing trooper and then continuing on to another. All three men collapsed to the ground, dead, with smoldering holes left in their bodies. The aroma of burned meat drifted through the air in the clearing.

The ground shifted, and Gera collapsed when the heat and anger flew from his body. The light of his saca dimmed in his mind and exhaustion washed over his frame in waves. Just as a black fog settled over his eyes, he watched Nava and the other warrior battling the final Blood on even terms.

## CHAPTER 29

The man paced back and forth in the dancing light of the bonfire, his impatience revealed in every stomp of his boots. Pony-tailed blond hair swung back and forth across his back like a lion's tail, waiting to pounce on his prey, while his breath escaped in rumbling sighs. Every few moments, he muttered at the impenetrable darkness, as if arguing with someone standing just outside the ring of light. He occasionally stopped in front of the flames long enough to place his hands over the logs before his restless nature drove him to wander again. The placement of his fists was an unconscious act. No heat rolled off this fire. But the habit learned while growing up in the frozen wastelands in Faarene was too deeply ingrained into his manners to accept a change.

His head snapped around and turned the ponytail into a yellow whip. Light blue eyes stared for an icy heartbeat as another man entered the circle of light. They softened, however, and a wide grin creased his face at the recognition of his friend.

"I was beginning to think I was the only one coming," he said as he clasped the other's arm in greeting. Just as quickly as his demeanor had turned joyful, a moment later it returned to its somber mood. "Truth be told, I was really hoping I'd misunderstood what I felt last night."

"No, Kegan," the newcomer said with a touch of sadness that felt out of place with the smile curling the corners of his mouth. "You felt the passing of one of our brothers, the same as the rest of us. But I'd forgotten until now that you were the last to join our group. It's no wonder you were confused since you've never felt the death of a fellow D'Alikar before now. Come, lad, let's stand before the flames and pay our respects to the fates that brought us here. We'll discover soon enough which of our brothers has fallen."

"Yes, Sanchere."

The two men would have been an odd sight for a stranger to encounter as they wandered into view. Kegan towered over the smaller man, carrying almost five stone more in his heavily muscled frame and appearing ready to step into a fighting pit to earn riches by killing his opponents. With his pale skin, light eyes, and blond hair, he was easy to name as a man of his country north of the Skriemount range.

But Sanchere was just as much a product of his country of Spirache. Olive-skinned and black haired, he moved with the speed and grace of someone born to walk the decks and climb the riggings of the best sailing ships. Although he was the opposite in nearly every physical aspect, they had meant it when they named each other brother.

Both men stared silently into the flames, thinking their own thoughts of the paths that had led them to this day. Kegan managed to stop fidgeting now that he had the calming influence of the older D'Alikar beside him. For his part, Sanchere also remained still except for occasionally stroking the goatee on his chin.

After a short while, although time was hard to keep track of in this meeting place, two other men appeared on the edge of the circle and broke their quiet meditation. One stood only slightly taller than Sanchere, but somehow appeared to stare down his nose at even Kegan. His companion wore the forest greens and browns of a woodsman and was by far the shortest and lightest of the group.

"I would've guessed our fallen to be you, Kegan," the taller newcomer said, breaking the silence with only a hint of humor. "I imagined you challenging all the Bakri in the Teeth to a battle, swinging that bastard sword of yours until your arms fell off." He dropped his gaze when his smaller companion tapped his elbow.

"That might yet come to pass, Latham," Kegan said, his words calm and even despite the barb. "But my day wasn't today."

"It appears that Balew is our fallen member," Sanchere said softly. "Let's remember why we're here and honor our beloved brother." He glanced at the shortest D'Alikar. "Tagre, you look even more concerned than usual. We don't want to look worried when Ennis arrives."

The woodsman raised his gaze and stared each member in the eye. His brow knit together, and he nibbled at his lower lip, his mind obviously turning over what he wanted to say.

"How long's Ennis been in training with Balew? Six cycles? I can remember how much Ahanu still needed to learn when he'd only been with me for that short amount of time. What if he's not fully trained yet? I was the last to enter the D'Alikar and not be fully taught, but I had Latham to help me as another new member. We learned together. Is Ennis ready to take the sword and become a D'Alikar?"

Silence settled over the brooding group as they each pondered Tagre's questions. The fact he delivered them in what was for him a long-winded speech, only added weight to their seriousness.

"Ready or not, his time has come," Sanchere said after a while. "We must take comfort in the fact that six cycles with Balew was like six summers with any of the rest of us." Even Latham nodded his head in agreement with the compliment to their dead comrade. "The sword was only claimed once and was never falsely taken. We all would have felt that as well. Ennis must have survived whatever trouble they ran into, or we would've known differently by now."

The others mumbled agreements, and the quiet fell again.

"How're you and Aquil getting along these days?" Kegan asked after the silence lengthened for an awkward time.

Sanchere let the rudeness of the question go unchallenged. D'Alikars rarely discussed the relationships with their seconds to the individual swords. The binding was too personal, melding together two fighters who might never have acknowledged each other under different circumstances. He understood the big man's unease, however, realizing the attempt to break the tension with talk.

Latham, however, refused to let a socially impolite remark go by without a stinging rebuke. He opened his mouth to chastise Kegan, but Tagre silenced him with another tap on his elbow before the comment flew. Sanchere realized he needed to keep this conversation moving before they began quarreling amongst themselves. He suddenly realized one of the traits he would miss most about Balew. As the oldest D'Alikar, and the one holding a sword the longest, his most important function might have been as the calming peacekeeper in the diverse group. He wondered if that role had suddenly fallen to him.

"We've had our moments since the hostilities between our two countries has grown worse," Sanchere said. "But I suppose it could be much graver. We could be from Crandor and Palamor."

This comment broke free the other D'Alikars' tongues. News about the war and other current events floated between the members accompanied by either disgusted shakes of the head, chin rubbing contemplation, or laughter. Information passed on everything from the possibility of purchasing remounts from the Balami (not likely), to the rumors of the Bakri once again attacking villages on the western slopes of the Teeth (too many stories to not hold at least some truth). At long last, the conversations died, and the feeling of apprehension covered the area again.

"Ennis isn't coming," Sanchere said, stating what the others were already thinking. "I believe Tagre has raised legitimate concerns about his readiness. I also think we should send someone to discover what has happened with Balew."

"My clutch and I are the closest," Kegan said at once. "We're already halfway up the east trail to the Gap and could cross into Palamor in two days with good travel. The trick will be finding them once we're there. I'll start in Truro."

"Tagre and I will send a messenger to Placado Island, also," Latham said. "Balew's family should be informed of his death, and Navis needs to know for the obvious reasons. Besides, the old man might have an even better idea than any of us if Ennis is ready or not for his responsibilities."

All the men nodded in agreement at the plans and vowed to meet every night until the mystery of Balew's successor had been solved. Kegan left first after the farewells had been said. His hand reached up to his neck and then pulled away. His body became less and less visible, fading like a fog in sunshine, until he disappeared from view. Sanchere soon followed.

Tagre reached for his neck as well before he noticed his companion once again stared silently into the flames. He waited, voicing no objections, while Latham finished saying his farewells to Balew's memory. When he was ready at last, he turned to Tagre with a smile and glistening eyes. Together, they left the meeting area.

era stood in the middle of a room so large and dark, he could not see the walls or ceiling. A sense of vastness swept over his emotions and left him feeling small and insignificant. His gaze darted blindly about the ebony curtain while he wondered why, and how, he had been brought to this place.

A chill ran down his spine when the feeling of being alone disappeared. Movement he could sense, but not see or hear, circled and danced around his body in wild gyrations. But after his initial shock, his fear subsided and left behind only curiosity about whatever whipped through the room. He wanted to touch them, hear them. He opened his mouth to ask if they held the answers to all the questions flooding his mind, but no sound escaped over his dry and swollen tongue.

Two areas of light appeared on opposite sides of the expanse. Gera thought at first that someone had thrown open two doors leading out to a bright day. Shadows moved into one opening, and he recognized Dax and a young woman who looked so much like his memories of his mother, he knew she must be Keely. He strained to make out every feature on his sister's face. Frustration shook his body as the opening expanded and contracted around his siblings, sometimes leaving only Keely visible, occasionally just Dax.

Gera felt a pull, and he looked at the other doorway. He gazed into the searing light pouring into the room. No figures or shapes broke up the white. Yet, he sensed a presence, an authority, hovering just beyond his sight. The being called to him, urged him, and he fought the desire to run through the door and learn everything it wanted to teach him.

He alternated back and forth, staring first in one direction, and then the other while the unseen beasts continued to swoop and dive around him in the black. Both openings now beckoned to him, calling like a mother to her child at dinner time. Which should he choose?

Dax and Keely, when they could be seen, waved their arms in an invitation to join them. Their mouths moved with silent pleadings, and Gera's heart ached with the desire to bring his family together again. Visions of a happy life, with all of them at the family cabin, swam through his thoughts.

But the untouched light remained just as persistent. Kindness and hope swirled through its call, mixed with unbearable suffering and despair. The opposite emotions played off each other like mirror images, revealing no day existed without night, no pleasure without pain. Power intertwined through the promise and bound the combination together, enough power to cure the whole world of its ills if used wisely.

Time was forgotten as Gera wrestled with the decision.

The responsibility tied to his answer threatened to crush him, flattening his body and spirit beneath the weight. Now, not just the huge room made him feel small, but also the choice. This was a choice he lived within.

He stared at Dax and Keely and saw a lifetime of joy, the vow of no pain or hardship. It was a life everyone would want. But it was also a life no one could have, nor be happy living.

In the end, he knew he had no option. Gera turned to his brother and sister again. Only part of Keely showed now, the frame obscuring a section of her face. As he watched, her outline turned into wisps of shadow, and she was gone. Dax was still standing there, but even he was less than he had been, a ghost with some of the light shining through his body. He smiled at his brother, raising his hand in a half-wave.

Gera turned and walked toward the unbroken light, the unseen creatures lining up to follow him through the doorway.

◆ ◆ ◆

Gera cracked open an eyelid and winced at the sunlight pouring over him, brighter even than the light from his dream. He attempted to roll into a sitting position, but before he made it halfway up, he collapsed back to the ground with a groan. His head pounded like the ra-ta-ta-ta-tat of a good hammer on metal. Unfortunately, the drumming gave no sign of letting up anytime soon. Soft laughter floated around him, and it slowly registered the chuckle was not from him. Ego made him grit his teeth against the pain he anticipated and tried again. Ready this time, Gera opened his eyes and glanced around.

He guessed it was late afternoon by the sun's position, but

his muscles felt like they had not been used for years, so what day was it? Nava must have been lying beside him from the looks of the flattened grass, but now the dyr sat on his haunches, partially blocking the sun from Gera's face. He risked further self-inflicted pain by propping himself up on one elbow.

A few paces away, two figures sat on a log watching his progress. Both wore black pants and short-sleeved, chain mail shirts. Gray tabards, trimmed in black and showing plenty of wear, partially covered the armor. His gaze was pulled to the left breast of each uniform where an embroidered dragon rose in flight. Now that he was able to focus, he turned his attention to the people.

The man on the left glared at him with an intensity that made Gera want to grip his sword. Despite the ease with which he wore the armor and weapons, he appeared to be only a couple of years older than Gera. The other fighter quickly grabbed his attention, however. Long-limbed and blonde, the woman wore a mischievous twinkle in her light blue eyes. He guessed immediately where the laughter had started.

Gera opened his mouth to speak, but his parched throat and tongue only let a squeak come out. After swallowing a few times, he tried again.

"How long?" The words sounded more like a croak than speech.

The woman turned to the man. When he made no move to answer, she turned back.

"It was three nights ago tonight that we battled the Crimson Guards," she said. "You've been asleep since then. I would've poured some water down your throat, but your pet wouldn't let any of us near you. We couldn't see any open wounds, and you seemed to be breathing, so we just let you lay. If you hadn't awakened by tomorrow morning, we were going to drive off the dyr so we could tend to you." From the grimace on her face, Gera could tell the decision had not been a popular one. She took the time to toss him a waterskin before she continued. "How much do you remember?"

"I remember," Gera began as he tried to rebuild the memory in his mind. "I remember trailing the guardsmen to the clearing. The fight began on the other side, away from me, while I listened to the officers. Someone approached me from behind, so I leaped into the clearing so I had room to fight. After fighting with a few of the Bloods, my sword broke, and I scrambled across the ground..." He stopped, deciding not to describe his terror at holding only the hilt of Ham's sword in his hand, to not tell them about the surety he was about to die. It also seemed best not to mention the hallucination about the dragons. "Then I remember seeing Nava and another warrior fighting side by side. There was a growl..."

All thoughts of the previous events flew from his mind as he scrambled to his knees beside the dyr. The throbbing in his temples might as well have been in someone else's head for all the attention he paid to it while he examined the animal. Out of the corner of his eye, he noticed several other men in the gray and black uniforms approach the seated fighters as he continued to run his hands over Nava's body. His search produced only one wound of any size, a hand's breadth gash on the animal's right rear haunch. It had stopped bleeding and appeared to have been licked clean.

"Toss me your helmet and see if you have any avoa leaves in your supplies," Gera ordered without thinking. A few moments later, one of the new soldiers threw him an open-faced helm with a few stems inside. He poured most of the rest of the waterskin inside and let the dyr lap at it while he broke open the leaves and forced the sap into the wound. The plant's secretion would help a scab to grow and keep out dirt while the injury healed. After he finished, he stood on shaking legs and faced the seven fighters.

"Thank you for allowing me to treat my companion. If I'm to be your prisoner now, it'd be best if you let me send him away." A rumbling growl escaped Nava at the suggestion.

Most of the men broke into smiles, and the woman laughed out loud at the statement. They all grew silent, however, when the somber young warrior spoke.

"How did Balew D'Alikar happen to die in battle and you, someone barely old enough to be on his own, manage to survive?"

"Who's Balew D'Alikar? Gera asked, his head tilting in confusion.

A murmur swept through the group while the leader visibly strained to keep his emotions in check, cheeks turning scarlet. Nava rose to all four feet and bared his teeth, tail sweeping back and forth.

"Balew D'Alikar was the man whose sword you now wield!"

Glancing downward, Gera looked with surprise at the weapon lying beside where he had fallen. Its slightly curved blade shimmered black in the sunlight by his feet. He picked it up by the long hilt and felt the balance of the sword again. Memories of the fight, and how it had felt in his hands as he attacked, flooded back. A sigh escaped his lips before he offered it handle first to the leader.

"My blade was broken during the fighting with the Crimson Guards. This, Balew, had already been run through and lay on the ground bleeding. With the amount of blood that lay around his body, I was shocked to see he was still alive. His dying act was to push the sword toward me so I could use it to defend myself.

"It was a blade borrowed in defense of my life and returned with thanks. Your friend died with courage and honor, if the amount of fallen enemies surrounding him was any sign. His final, unselfish act gave me a chance to live. For that, I owe him and his family a debt."

None of the soldiers moved to accept the sword. The leader's hands twitched, and a pained expression fell over his face. Gera saw in his eyes that the man wanted to grasp the weapon and never let go until he breathed his last breath. After a few moments, the fighter slumped, his gaze falling to the ground near his feet. The woman spoke instead.

"Sheath the sword, stranger," she said. "It's yours to keep until the day you also move to meet your gods. None of us may touch the blade. Only the D'Alikars can touch the gifts and continue to live." The last remark drew a sharp breath from the leader. She glanced at him before continuing. "I'm Dilane Amathon. What may we call you?"

"Gera Staghorn."

"Bestill your beast." She stood and walked toward him. Gera's puzzlement turned to astonishment when she knelt before him and bowed her head.

"Gera D'Alikar, guide and protect me under your wing. Accept my service, my life for yours, 'til the fires take our ashes to the nest."

Gera stood paralyzed, not knowing what to do or say. Dilane's head suddenly snapped back, and she stared him in the face. He held himself from stepping back as her anger flashed across her eyes like bolts of lightning.

"Is it me you don't accept or the fact I'm a woman?" She spit the words at him between clenched teeth.

"I don't know what to do!" Gera's whisper carried as much of a question as statement.

A smile formed at the corners of Dilane's lips, the realization of what he said settling over her.

"You've no idea who we are or what you've become," she said, more to herself than to him. She shook her head as if waking from a dream. "Take your branded hand and place it on my head while you hold the sword with the other. Then if you accept me, tell me to 'rise and fly with the dragons.'"

Gera opened his mouth to tell her he did not have a brand on his hand when he glanced down at his right palm. There, looking as if he had carried it for years, a single flame of fire was etched into his skin. A flash of half-recalled memory skittered across the corner of his mind before receding into darkness again.

"Rise and fly with the dragons," he said. His voice trembled as he touched the woman's head. Heat, similar to what his saca felt like, but wilder and more uncontrolled, started in the sword in his left hand, engulfed his body, and then poured down his right arm onto Dilane's head. She gasped, and her eyes opened wide, for the first time her amusement replaced by questions. The light of his saca glowed dimly in his thoughts while he watched her stand up and join the other men.

One by one, the other fighters followed her lead. They even rotated a man out to sentry duty so the one on watch could pledge his fealty. Finally, only the young man who Gera thought of as the leader, remained to give his oath. A long time passed and still he did not remove his gaze from the ground.

"Ennis, you fool!" Dilane stamped her foot in anger to match her voice. "You saw he was able to handle the blade and live. The sword has chosen!" Her voice softened. "You know more about what the D'Alikar must do than the rest of us combined. Swallow your damnable pride and continue to serve."

Ennis shook his head and remained seated.

"Please," Dilane continued, placing a hand on his shoulder. "I can only imagine the disappointment you must be feeling right now. But the sword chose another. You'll have your turn at a different time."

"You don't understand!" Ennis shoved her hand away as he rose, red-rimmed eyes speaking volumes of his torment. "I haven't felt the call of the sword since before the fight with the Bloods. That's why I gasped while watching the meeting. That's why I gave away our position. I'm the reason Balew is dead!" He whirled on Gera. "It was like a part of my spirit was ripped away and left a bloodied stump of myself, raw, bleeding to the world. For the first time since I met Balew and the sword, I'm no longer its second." He turned and ran into the nearby tree line.

Gera looked away, not wanting his embarrassment for Ennis to show on his face. But even as he stood motionless, his mind raced around one question.

What had he gotten himself into now?

eely woke from her nap to the sound of gentle knocking at the cabin door. She continued to lay on the upper berth while Dax rose from his bed with a groan.

*At least that's an improvement. Maybe he'll finally start acting like himself again.*

Dax took a tray of food from an unseen seaman without a word. Keely's fragile hope for her brother's health evaporated as soon as he turned to place the meal on the small table fastened to the floor in the center of the room. His eyes still held the vacant stare they had reflected since the moment the Crimson Guards cut him down from the boom. Each day he continued this way worried her more that he may never return to normal.

The rest of his physical condition continued to deteriorate as well. Although the swelling from the beating around his nose and eyes had subsided, and the whip cuts on his legs were healing, he appeared even closer to death now than he had on their journey through Crandor. Never a big man, he had always leaned toward a slight build. Now, however, he had lost enough weight to look like an under-stuffed scarecrow. His pale skin was almost always covered in a thin sheen of sweat, hot one moment, and then chilled the next. His hands trembled constantly, and his strides, when he chose to walk at all, were short and faltering.

But it was Dax's eyes that concerned Keely the most. They contained no spark, no fire, no hope. That scared her. The fact her brother had just shut down and given up on life ate away at her own confidence. She wondered if there might be something she could do for him with her saca, somehow heal his broken mind. But that thought remained hopeless, as well, as long as she wore the Institute necklace, and she had not gathered the courage to ask Commander Gregol for the chance to try.

Keely lamented the loss of her visions as well. She still had normal dreams like everyone else, but ever since she had been collared in the Milston square, they were not the same vivid, painfully real images she longed to see again. She wanted to stare at them, listen to them, and live with them. She ached for them like a drunk for his next drink, wanting them more than what life had handed her.

The siblings sat in silence at the table while Keely ate, and Dax rearranged the food on his plate. Watching him not even attempt to keep up his strength proved the last straw for the young woman. Her heart raced as her anger rose, causing her lips to contort into a sneer.

"What's wrong with you, Dax?" she asked. "If you've given up on living, why did I take the time to tend to your wounds?" Keely leaned back on her shaky chair and crossed her arms in front of her chest.

"I can remember a time when the only man better than you, west of the Teeth, was Father. Now look at you! I've played with stick dolls that were filled out more than you. You used to have fire in your belly. What was it Mother always used to say? 'When Dax sets his mind to something, his backbone's as stiff as an old ironwood tree.' You drove her crazy with your stubbornness. Now you'd sway in the wind like a weeping willow."

"I'm sorry," Dax said. His face remained pointed down at his plate.

"For what?" Keely's words were spit in his direction, each one holding an edge that tried to cut her brother's skin. "For not taking care of yourself? For failing to get me free? For trying at all? What are you apologizing for now?" Her voice rose with each question until she was screaming by the end of her tirade.

"I'm sorry," Dax answered, his voice all the softer after her yelling. "I'm sorry that I didn't have the courage to kill you while you slept to save you from whatever the Bloods have planned for you."

Keely felt the air rush from her body. Her mouth opened and closed, gasping like a fish on the bank. Black spots danced in her eyes, and she sat her chair back down on all four legs before she fell over backwards. She stared at the top of her brother's head until she had control of herself again.

"Dax, what did you do to the young man who found me in the woods outside Bagdon?"

"I killed him," he said. His voice remained level during the confession, no emotion, no inflection in the words. "I tracked him back to his cabin and killed him so he couldn't tell anyone he had seen you." He finally glanced up, tears on his cheeks. "The Bloods spread your description everywhere and told the people that you were an escaped Sacara student. They told everyone that..." He paused. "They told everyone that you were insane and had already killed some men who tried to help you." His gaze dropped to her neck, and his face went blank.

Horror turned Keely's blood to ice. She stared into his eyes and did not see a man. She saw an animal that killed without thinking, killed because he believed it was best for her. Now he said it would be best for her if she died.

Keely did not remember climbing the passageway of the stairs. When she blinked, she realized she was standing on the deck, her hands gripping the gunwale so tight her fingers ached. Her mind swirled in a tornado of questions and accusations. Inch by agonizing inch, she crawled out of the trance she felt trapped within until she found herself staring at the Pennick River and the far shoreline. Her mind searched for some small crumb of comfort to cling to, some small bit of hope for her while her life spun out of control. Again and again, she ran over what had occurred in the past few days on the trail, on the boat, looking for some clue into Dax's state of mind. When nothing helped, she dug further into the past.

Dax's infrequent visits to the Gassem's house, his avoidance of the other townspeople as much as possible, his fall into his own physical hell—the clues pointed back to the time of her father and brother's deaths. The deep depression he had displayed so prevalently in the past few days must have lurked somewhere below the surface of his emotions for a long time. It had only waited for a big enough disappointment to provide the trigger for its release, bubbling to the front like a festering infection.

"What happened when Father and Ryne died?" Keely whispered to the flowing water.

Dax's melancholy dived way beyond the normal sadness of loved ones' deaths. She had, of course, heard the half-whispered conversations in Milston after she moved in with the Gassems. Dax had abandoned their father, brother, and the other men when the Bakri attacked. Dax had been drunk on sentry duty, and the Bakri crept right past him to attack the militia. There had even been one absurd rumor that said Dax had been the one to kill Tyre and Ryne. Keely heard all the tales and the variations so many times, she had walled them off inside her mind until it felt like her friends talked about characters in a story. Now, all those rumors rushed back to her, each one slamming into her like a fist in the stomach.

She did not remember which particular memory caused the tears to start, but she realized her body shook with quiet sobs. Keely was so caught up in the remembrances, she did not hear the heavy footsteps behind her until they stomped to a stop.

"Lady Staghorn," Commander Gregol said, "I believe we made a deal for your brother's life. As you can see, we're clearly approaching the port of Ponte, yet, here you stand on the deck. If you've changed your mind and wish to be bound for the rest of the journey, I can arrange it."

He stopped in mid-threat as Keely gained enough control over her emotions that she stopped crying and turned to face the Crimson Guard officer. She watched a look cross his face, some mixture between awe, terror, and rage.

"I'm sorry, Commander," Keely said, as she wiped the tears from her cheeks. "My mind was on other things, and I wasn't paying attention to the shore. I'll return to the cabin immediately."

Gregol held up his hand.

"Did one of my men hurt you, Matra?" The commander

barely managed to gurgle out the question, his anger winning his emotional battle. "Did they touch you?"

"Hurt me?" Keely asked. Despite the worst tales of gossip she had been told growing up, the guardsmen had been respectful, some almost kind, since her bargain had been struck with their leader. "Commander, your men have behaved exactly as you promised they would."

She watched his face contort with conflict. He was obviously battling something within himself, but she had no idea what. Keely actually felt a pang of sympathy for the soldier.

"Sentry!" Gregol yelled with the roar of a waterfall. "Bring me the sot!" A flurry of activity rose from the soldiers on deck. Those not rushing to retrieve Dax drew their weapons, believing only an enemy attack could force so powerful a bellow from the commander.

"Oh, please, my Lord," Keely pleaded, tears rising into her eyes again. "I'll go back to our room right now. There's no need to kill my brother!" Despite his insane threats and instability, she could not bear to think of Dax dead with her the cause.

"Matra, has your brother harmed you?" The gentleness in Gregol's voice sounded odd based upon everything she had seen from the man. "What has he done to upset you so much?"

Keely lowered her head in embarrassment. Had the sentry outside their cabin door heard their argument and reported it? She shook her head in disbelief. No, no one could have heard Dax's whispered revelation at the table.

As her chin moved back and forth, she noticed it rubbing against something rough. She reached up, letting her fingers probe along her neckline. When she raised them to look, black soot remained on the tips. She glanced up at the commander, her eyebrows arched in surprise.

"Your blouse has been burned away wherever it touched the collar," Gregol said. "I've heard stories that can sometimes happen if the sagia feels strong enough emotions. That's why I asked if your brother had hurt you. If you were frightened enough..."

A light went on in Keely's mind. She had not been conscious of it at the time because of her anger, but the locked chest in her thoughts had become more distinct during the argument with her brother. In hindsight, she felt her saca had been close to bursting free.

"Dax and I were arguing. I was mad," she said, hesitating on each word, "really mad. But then he apologized to me for not being able...being able to kill me in my sleep. He thinks my death would be better than whatever you've planned for me. He's sick, Commander. Don't punish him for being sick. Please."

Keely halted her confession to Gregol when they both turned at the sounds of a commotion. Three guardsmen appeared with two of them supporting the limp body of Dax between them. The third soldier ran over in a breathless rush and stopped in front of his leader.

"My Lord," he said between gasps for air. "The prisoner was swinging from the roof timber when I entered the cabin. I cut the rope around his neck as quickly as I could." The man hesitated, not knowing what the commander had in store for the captive. "I believe he'll live, my Lord."

Gregol stared across the deck at Dax, his brow furrowed in concentration.

"Take him back to his quarters and tie him to the bed so he can't hurt himself again." He paused to glance at Keely, who returned the glance with a quick nod of thanks, before he turned back to the trooper. "If the Matra's brother dies, so do you."

Keely felt her mouth drop open in shock at the ease by which Gregol had given the order. She was almost as disturbed by the apparent calm with which the guardsman accepted the announcement.

"Sergeant." Gregol turned to another nearby soldier. "Find a cloak that'll fit the Matra and bring it to her. Then you're to accompany her around the boat." He looked back at Keely and dipped his head. "Matra, I'll not hold you to our bargain when we're in port, but you must remain on board. It's no longer safe for you in your quarters, so I will find another room for you. In the meantime, my only requests in exchange are that you don't try to leave the boat, and you keep your collar covered. Now, I must be off to decide what to do with your brother."

Keely watched the commander walk away, rubbing his palm furiously with his thumb as he went.

◆ ◆ ◆

Keely stood in the bow of the riverboat in the deepening twilight and watched the lights on the far side of the Pennick River wink in and out of sight. The sergeant had answered her question earlier by explaining they shone from the Lebeshan city of Picase. When she turned in the opposite direction, she watched the well-lit sky over Ponte in Spirache. She decided she could be enjoying herself if not for the reason for her trip and the events of earlier in the day. That memory still sent a chill down her spine and caused her to wrap her borrowed cloak around her even tighter.

At least the thought of the cape brought a small smile to her face. It must have been taken from the smallest guardsmen on board but, even so, a full hand's breadth of cloth scraped the rough planks of the vessel's deck.

Those boards began their distinct rumbling to announce the approach of Commander Gregol. He had disappeared on shore as soon as the gangplank thumped on the dock and only returned a short while ago.

"Sergeant," he said, "see that the Matra's things are brought out on deck." He waited until the man left before continuing. "I've arranged for your brother to be taken to one of our worker colonies. His life will be hard, but he will be alive for as long as he wishes. It's the best I can do for him, Matra. Where we're going, he'd be killed for just the thought of harming you, despite our agreement."

Keely turned back to the rail and glanced across the water toward the dancing lights. How strange it felt to know she was safer with the guardsmen than she was with her own brother.

"Thank you. How soon will he be taken away?"

"Tomorrow morning. We'll be transferring to a different ship and leaving tonight for the Institute by the sea route, however. If you have any goodbyes to say, now would be the time, Matra."

Keely nodded and walked toward the door to the cabins. The little bit of levity she had allowed herself flew into the night like a black bird disappearing into the darkness, close and then gone in a blink. She heard boots behind her and realized Gregol must have assigned a trooper to follow her below.

Each step she took as she moved down the short passageway seemed to take her farther from her previous life and toward the murky mystery of her future. Her stomach churned when she walked into the cabin and looked at her brother. She forced a smile as she walked to the berth where he was tied, hoping good cheer would help raise his spirits. Her grin froze to her face, however, when she stared down at the human shell that had once been Dax.

He was even worse than before. Sweat poured from his body in the pleasant night air, his shirt a soaked cloth stretched over his emaciated frame. His breaths came in short, quick gasps, and his glistening skin accentuated the raw wound around his neck from where the noose had marked it. Most horrifying of all, a stench like rotting meat escaped his skin. Keely had never smelled anything so awful in her life.

Trying not to gag, she stepped closer to her brother. Keely searched for the words to comfort him, realizing she probably would never see him again.

"Dax, I came to say goodbye. The guardsmen are splitting us up…"

She stopped talking when her brother's eyelids snapped open. He stared at her with frightening intensity, the whites showing completely around the colored portion. Where before they had been devoid of emotion, now his eyes roiled with lunacy.

"I wanted to thank you for trying to rescue me from the Institute," she continued. "I don't blame you for what's happened. It's not your fault. It…"

"Look what you've done to me," he snarled, foamy spittle flying from his mouth as he spoke. "You must've contacted the Bloods and set a trap for me on the boat that night. You want to stay with them. Yes, I see it now. I see it. How else could they have found us so quick and be waiting for me? Was there someone else besides the man in the woods? Did you have other help? It had to be you. You did this to me!"

"No, Dax, please." Keely reached out a comforting hand as

she pleaded with her brother. She jerked back, however, when he contorted his lips and snapped at her like an animal, his teeth clicking when he missed.

The escorting soldier quickly stepped between the two siblings. He gently, but firmly, moved Keely farther away from the berth. Dax thrashed wildly at the ropes binding him, trying to break loose, growling the entire time.

"Matra, the person you knew as your brother is gone," the guardsman said. "His brain has been rotted away, and he'll never be the same man you knew before. Maybe we should just leave so you can remember him like he used to be."

"No, no!" Dax cried. Drool flowed down his chin. "I can still forgive you, sister. Come closer, and I'll release you from their bonds. Yes, I'll kill you. Yes, yes."

Keely ran blindly from the cabin and toward the fresh air of the deck. She could not see through the tears pouring from her eyes, but she wished she had lost her hearing instead. His final screams echoed in her ears as she fled.

"I WILL KILL YOU, KEELY! COME TO ME, AND I'LL KILL YOU!"

alf the sun lay buried beyond the far horizon when Gera sat down on a log to rest. He had busied himself, after Ennis ran away, by eating and checking on his gelding. The scouts had found the horse while searching for stray guardsmen who escaped the battle and brought him back to camp. The mount neighed at the sight of his master and playfully pushed his head into Gera's chest. He had obviously adapted to his situation better than his owner.

Gera watched the everyday life of a soldier continue at a busy pace around him. He did not observe uninterrupted, however. Every few moments, another fighter approached to ask for advice or to report an already completed task. Gera answered the simple questions with what seemed to him to be only common sense, but the men appeared pleased when they left to continue their duties.

Off to one side of the clearing, two men practiced weapons

drills, while a third worked on a piece of mail. Gera had just decided to walk over and see if he could help with the repairs—it also felt like the best way to get everyone to leave him alone—when Dilane approached. She appeared hesitant as she stood before him, despite the smile playing at her lips.

"Lord D'Alikar," she said while she saluted, "I wish to make a report."

"Oh, bloody hells!" Gera said before he even realized his mouth had opened. "My name's Gera. Just plain Gera. If you want to talk with me, just sit down here beside me."

The hint of a smile blossomed into a grin.

"I thought I might try to explain to you, as best as I can since we can't seem to find Ennis, what I know about the D'Alikars. He'll know a great deal more about the details, and probably a lot of things I know nothing about, but at least I can give you a general history." She sat down on the log. "But where do we begin? First, what do you know about the D'Alikars?"

Gera shrugged after a few moments.

"From what I can remember from bedtime stories, they're supposed to be some kind of half-man, half-dragon warriors. Something out of legends and myths."

Dilane shook her head, the grin fading.

"That's the kind of answer I'd expect from someone who grew up on the western side of the Teeth. Don't they teach you anything about your history and tradition?" She settled herself more comfortably and then continued.

"Over a thousand winters ago, the western and eastern kingdoms were invaded by men from across the Windward Sea. Why they came was either never known or lost to time. Anyway, they captured the lands at will. After many years of fighting, all the eastern kingdoms had fallen except for the horsemen in Balame and the tree dwellers in Faramor. In the west, only Moramet and Crandor still stood. But they were both so bloated with refugees that they probably would've been starved into surrendering in a short time. My own people in Faarene were refugees who escaped over the Skriemount when the invaders took Abdalain and Salche."

"I can remember Father sitting in front of the fireplace, when the battles with the Bakri started, and telling tales he'd heard about the Apocal War," Gera said. "I guess I was too young to understand how much it affected all the kingdoms. I was probably more interested in the swords and fighting. It just seemed like a children's tale because it all happened so long ago."

"It may be exactly that shortsightedness that leads to our downfall in the end," Dilane said. "Anyway, when all hope was about lost, and it looked as if the few people who did survive the battles were going to spend the rest of their lives as slaves, the dragons entered the fight on our side."

"The dragons? Why?"

Dilane shrugged.

"Who can know what a dragon thinks?" She laughed and leaned forward, lowering her voice to a loud whisper. "There are some people who think the D'Alikars know what dragons think. You might want to keep that idea going." She winked as she sat straight again. "With their help, we began to win battles and take back lands. Eventually, the kingdoms became strong enough again to challenge the invaders in one heroic battle in Xenalia. Dragons and men fought and died, side by side, and defeated the Emperor and his generals. The Dragonlord Modig allowed himself to be defeated and killed by the Emperor in the final fight, sacrificing himself so the other dragons could destroy him and the generals."

Gera whistled low and long, Dilane stopping her history lesson at the sound. He had so many questions, he did not know where to begin. But first, he thought of his vision when he grabbed the sword and wondered why it did not match the legend. He never had the chance to ask.

"Yes," Ennis said. The two of them turned at the sound of his voice behind them. "That's what you saw when you first claimed the sword." He threw a glance at Dilane, but did not tell her to leave. "Somehow, the memory of that final battle, from Dragonlord Modig's point of view, is trapped inside the sword and transferred to the new holder the first time they touch it."

He walked around and stood in front of them so they did not need to look over their shoulders to see him.

"When the battle was over, only twelve dragons and five men remained alive from the original army. A pact was made between the two groups, binding them together for all time as allies. To seal the deal, the dragons fashioned gifts from the body of the dead dragonlord.

"The sword you hold now is made from a bone. If anyone besides its rightful owner touches it, they'll die a horrible and immediate death. A dagger was formed from a tooth. These can be handled by anyone," Ennis glanced at Dilane again before continuing, "but we don't let everyone know that information. That's why I haven't removed yours from Balew's body. You'll need to do that yourself.

"Lastly, there's a choker made from a scale. You'll need to remove that from Balew as well, because only the owner can see how it latches. It has a special use, but I'll show you that later after Balew D'Alikar's funeral pyre.

"Over the centuries, the swords have chosen the successors to the original five. Somehow, for some reason, the sword has now picked you to become the latest in a long line of brave and courageous warriors who are known as the Draig D'Alikar. I just hope you're ready for the responsibilities that come with the honor."

"Ennis was chosen as Balew's second by the sword," Dilane said, watching the other man as she spoke. "It should have gone to him when Balew fell in battle."

"And that's why you're so upset with me," Gera said, glancing away when he saw Ennis flinch at the words.

They sat in silence after Ennis finished, Gera's head swimming with the memories of everything that had happened to him in the last few hands. Not very long ago, in time anyway, he had believed his biggest decision was whether or not to go into business with Master Greenward. The memories of being chased in his dreams since childhood had not prepared him for this path in his life. Was this the answer he had sought?

"What's the purpose of the D'Alikars now?" Gera asked Ennis.

"Hundreds of summers ago, the D'Alikars discovered the remaining dragons were being hunted and killed. They traced almost all the deaths to the Bakri. Since then, the D'Alikars and their rangers have been trying to fulfill our end of the pact by hunting the cave dwellers down. One of the reasons why we aren't as known in the western kingdoms is because almost all the fighting has taken place in the east. I heard you mention a Bakri War as I walked up. The D'Alikars had been in the fight for more than five hundred summers before that skirmish took

place. Balew fought the battle himself for seventy-five of them."
Ennis finished with a sneer on his face.

Gera rose slowly and walked over to stand face to face with
Ennis. His face remained devoid of emotion, but his eyes burned
bright with anger. Every muscle in his body was coiled like a
tight spring, waiting to be released. Nava suddenly appeared at
the edge of the tree line and bared his teeth.

"My father and brother were killed in that skirmish, as you
call it," Gera said. "And my mother died from the heartbreak
of losing them."

Silence settled over the area. The sounds of the practice
swords' clatter flew away, and the daily activities ground to a
halt. Gera felt the soldiers staring at them, only a bare breath
of light separating their bodies. Nava shattered the quiet with
a rumbling growl.

Ennis appeared to wake up at the sound. He had stood his
ground at Gera's approach, but now, his cheeks bloomed red at
the unintended insult. He broke his gaze with the angry D'Alikar
and backed away.

"I'm sorry," Ennis said. "I meant no disrespect for the dead
and their sacrifice. Though I haven't given you my oath, I'll stand
for whatever punishment your family's honor demands."

Gera's posture softened, but his gaze never lessened in its
intensity.

"Then I demand your help."

Ennis' head jerked up, and his eyes opened wide. Gera heard
Dilane muffle a snort behind him. He thought the noise sounded
relieved.

"Look," Gera said, dropping his voice so only the two of
them could hear it. "It's obvious I need the knowledge Balew

D'Alikar was able to pass on to you. I'll need your guidance if I'm to fulfill my new responsibilities. You were right earlier. We here in the western kingdoms don't know what's going on in other places. I want you to be my guide until the sword chooses another to be the next in line. It could be you. It's already chosen you once before. But stay with me for now and teach me. If you want to leave after that, then so be it."

Ennis half-turned, staring into the distance as the sun settled below the horizon. With the shadows reaching out to them from the trees, he finally answered.

"I'll stay and teach you," he said. "But you may not like the lessons."

## CHAPTER 33

Full dark had fallen before Gera stood over the body of Balew D'Alikar. The rangers had cleaned off the dried blood and dirt and dressed the corpse in a pair of black pants, shirt, and old weather-worn cloak. On the left breast of the garment was an embroidered dragon of faded gold thread. Ennis choked when he told him the covering was one of Balew's favorites.

The dead man appeared to be taking a nap as the firelight glistened on his ebony skin and gray-streaked hair. After watching how Ennis and the others treated Balew in death, Gera found himself wishing he had known the man in life, and not just to ask the D'Alikar some of the multitude of questions tumbling through his mind. He reached down and gently tugged the choker around the man's throat, the clasp snapping free with a click. A beautiful piece of jewelry, the necklace appeared to change colors, from red to gold and now black, as the light hit it from different angles. He reached up and fastened it around his own neck.

Gera wondered if he looked half as ridiculous as he felt. In addition to the choker, the dragon dagger hung from his waist on a black leather belt while the sword rode in its scabbard along his left hip.

But the weapons worried him the least. He had grown accustomed to wearing Ham's sword over the past several hands. It was the rest of his clothing that made him feel like a child playing at dress up. Over black pants and a short-sleeved shirt, he wore a sleeveless vest of mail consisting of a leather jerkin covered with small, overlapping pieces of metal that looked like the scales of a fish. Though its weight hung from his body as a reminder, the armor was surprisingly supple and caused little loss in movement. When Balew had worn it, the mail also had sleeves down to the elbow. Unfortunately, the previous D'Alikar had been quite a bit broader across his chest and the ranger who altered the armor to fit Gera only had enough time to mend the body. Black metal bracers gave some protection to his forearms and over all of this, he wore a hooded black cape with a gold dragon on the breast. The only pieces of his own clothing he still wore were his soft woodsman's boots. He had flatly refused to wear the hard, knee high boots the rangers wore because he could not imagine trying to walk quietly through the forest with them on his feet.

He might not feel like a D'Alikar, but he certainly looked the part.

Ennis stepped forward from the assembled rangers and handed him a lit torch. Gera glanced once more at Balew and the other two men who had died in the fight with the Crimson Guards. They had also been stripped of their armor and weapons. Gera found it disconcerting that despite the respect for their fallen comrades, nothing went to waste while they were on a campaign. The rangers had packed the weapons and armor away to be brought out when needed.

Gera lowered the flame to the wood and stepped back once the oil-soaked logs caught hold. The fire built slowly until it engulfed all three bodies. One by one, the rangers drifted away in silence until only Gera, Ennis, and Nava remained to watch over the pyre. They stood in a speechless vigil until the blaze started to abate.

"Now it's time you learned the collar's power," Ennis said. "Remove it from your neck and toss it into the flames."

Gera stared at his new lieutenant for a moment before deciding to trust him. Sparks flew up as the choker settled.

"In a few moments, you must remove the scale and place it back on your neck," Ennis continued. He laughed when he noticed the expression on Gera's face. "Don't worry. A fire this small can't heat up a dragon's scale enough to harm you. But, it'll allow you to enter a place where you can meet with the other D'Alikars. The problem is that you were supposed to do this the first night after you received the sword. They would've all been waiting for you then. But that was two nights ago, so I don't know if there'll be anyone there for you to talk to."

Gera glanced at the ground and shuffled his feet. A battle raged within his thoughts as he struggled with a question. Twice he opened his mouth to speak and then closed it without speaking.

"You might as well ask me," Ennis said. "I'm still acting as your second, though I'm still not sure how that happened. What can you say to change that?"

Gera sighed. He felt relieved to have the burden of the choice lifted from his shoulders.

"No one has spoken about what I did the night of the fight with the Bloods. It's almost as if they're used to seeing fire spring from a man's hand."

"I'd venture to say that none of us have ever seen anything like that in person." Ennis wore an expression somewhere between a grimace and a grin. "It was like one of your children's tales brought to life. But, you're the D'Alikar, and no one will speak of it, if that's your wish."

"Can any of the other D'Alikars use saca?" Hope hung on every word of Gera's question.

Ennis cupped his chin in his hand and drew his eyebrows together. After a few moments, he shook his head.

"None of the current ones as far as I've been told. And I can't remember Balew ever mentioning one from the past, either. Beyond that, your best hope for an answer would come from Master Navis the next time we're at Netros Keep."

Ennis smiled and gestured with his hands toward the fire.

"Now, you've put off your duty long enough. I'm assuming that Sanchere D'Alikar has taken leadership since he's held the sword longer than anyone else after Balew. I'd suggest you address yourself to him. Balew was never very clear about the structure of the Draig D'Alikar, but it appeared he always took the lead whenever we were together with another clutch. But, I don't know what that'll mean with the others."

Gera grabbed a branch from the ground and fished the collar out of the smoldering ashes. Trusting blindly to Ennis' words, he grabbed the scale and sat on the ground. Only the barest hint of warmth, as if the choker had only sat for a few moments in the sunlight, touched his fingertips when he strapped it around his throat.

The forest around Gera fell into a dense fog. As he watched the trees disappear, visions of his life with his parents and siblings rolled across his mind. Happy times and the long-forgotten pains of scraped knees and bruises paraded by in a kaleidoscope of his memories. Like his dreams at the Greenwards' house, he felt as if he could step out of himself and return to live in those times forever. On and on, different events replayed from his past and called out for him to join them. Suddenly, an image of Balew flew across the corner of his sight. The man hustled by without stopping, moving as if he was late for an important destination.

Gera turned his head when he sensed another presence and stared at a nearby dark spot growing larger in his sight. The area appeared to be a deep pit, absent of any light. The void beckoned to him or, rather, the choker. His emotions flared as he moved toward the black, leaving his happy memories behind. He wanted to stay! His breathing grew shallow, and his heart stopped beating as he walked away from the shadows of his mother and father. The visions changed once more, Kellin's body being lowered into the ground at her funeral the last image he saw before the soulless black enveloped him.

A fire's glow became visible a short distance away. As he approached, Gera saw three men talking together though no sounds of their conversation reached his ears, despite the closeness. When he walked into the ring of light, the youngest looking of the trio stopped speaking. He had obviously been agitated about their discussion from the way he had been trying to drive home his point with arm waving and finger pointing.

*Latham, Tagre, and Sanchere.*

Ennis had taken the time while they built the funeral pyre to describe the other D'Alikars. His lieutenant had not gone farther than their descriptions, however. Gera was glad. He wanted to make up his own mind about their personalities.

An awkward silence stretched until almost snapping before Sanchere finally stepped forward, his hand outstretched.

"Welcome, my brother," he said with a warm smile as he clasped Gera's forearm in greeting. "You must forgive us for being rude, but we'd expected another to come. Although, as the days passed, we suspected that events might have happened differently than we first thought."

"Thank you, Sanchere D'Alikar." Gera noted the surprised expression that leaped to the man's face at the mention of his name. "I must admit, I'm still a bit overwhelmed myself at what's happened."

"Damn you to a night in Faarene without a fire, Ennis!" exclaimed a voice from behind Gera. "We've damn near rode our horses to death trying to get to you." Kegan froze, his cheeks turning rosy in embarrassment when Gera turned to face the big warrior.

"Kegan D'Alikar, I'm sorry you've been searching for me." Gera extended his hand in greeting. "I'm Gera Staghorn."

Both men stopped in mid-handshake at the gasp from Tagre. The small woodsman approached the newest D'Alikar and stared at him with unblinking eyes.

"I once rode with a man with the name Staghorn before the sword found me," he said. Raising his voice a little and half-glancing over his shoulder at Latham, he continued. "Brother, do you remember me speaking of a man who could walk through the forest and not even the trees would notice? I watched him track Bakri across bare stone and, with half a chance, sent their blood flowing through their beards before they even knew he was around."

"Fagri," Latham said, hesitating over the word. "Fagri Na... something."

"Nava," Gera finished. He was not sure this meeting place understood hot or cold, but he felt a chill run down his back.

"Fagri Nava," Latham said, a smile spreading on his face. "Forest Wind. His name is still a legend among the Xenalian Mountain troops. He was in charge of the scouts who hunted the Bakri."

"That was just the name the Xenalians gave to him behind his back," Tagre said, his attention still on Gera. "He was also born of my people but shunned the life in Faramor and took the name of a wanderer, Staghorn. I never knew his real name. But I must admit, you don't look anything like the man I'm talking about."

"I don't know who that person was," Gera said. "But your description sounds like my father and brothers, and the way they moved through the forest. But I was born and raised in Moramet and have only heard travelers' tales about Faramor." Gera decided to take a chance. "My father's name was Tyre Staghorn."

Tagre nodded.

"That's the name I knew for Fagri Nava." He paused. "But I notice you speak of him in the past."

"Yes. He died in the Bakri War with my brother, Ryne, nearly ten summers ago." Gera took a deep breath before he continued. "I've never had a chance to talk with someone who knew him besides the villagers in Milston. I'd be grateful to hear some tales when you've the time to tell them."

"No, it's I who would be honored to sit and talk with the son of Tyre. But that won't be now. Welcome, my brother." Tagre grabbed Gera by the arm.

Latham greeted Gera with a handshake and a few words of encouragement as well. The new D'Alikar was surprised at the warmth of the welcome from the man. He had appeared aloof at first, never quite making eye contact. But his smile now was genuine. Gera locked away the information about how much Latham respected Tagre's opinion.

"Why'd it take you so long to meet us? Did you have problems making the collar work?" Sanchere asked once the greetings were finished.

Gera glanced at the other D'Alikars before dropping his gaze and answering.

"I was unconscious after the battle where Balew died. It wasn't until this afternoon that I woke up. Ennis told me what I had to do to meet with you tonight."

"Ennis is still alive?" Kegan's voice boomed across the open area and echoed against the black curtain.

"It's happened before, my friend," Sanchere said. He flashed a smile and clapped the other man on the back. "Navis has shared stories of a couple of seconds who were passed over for a newly chosen. Although, I must say those aren't tales I've told to Aquil. I'd suggest the same caution with you and Ivar."

"How did Ennis take the change?" Latham asked. "I'd have thought there would be some trouble with him, considering his age and breeding."

Tagre tapped his elbow, and Latham looked away.

"He...he's been helpful," Gera said. He hoped the shock did not show on his face. "He was more hurt than angry about not feeling the sword any longer than it passing to me first."

Sanchere gasped, but the other D'Alikars stood in stunned silence, all their attention on Gera. He took a step back from the expressions on their faces.

"He'd be the only other one, besides Navis," Sanchere said. His voice trailed away, letting the statement hang in the silence between them for a moment. "Kegan, how far have you traveled?"

"I'll make the western base of the Teeth by tomorrow at midday, not far from Truro. Where are you now, Gera?"

The newest D'Alikar smiled at the small sign of acceptance by the use of only his first name.

"We're a day's ride north and east of the Crandori town of Elarton, just inside the Palamor border. But we won't be here for long. Tomorrow morning we'll be riding toward you and the town of Nason, on the northeastern border of Moramet."

"I know it," Kegan said. "What's there?"

"I've business with a man by the name of Legin Barlow. I must see him before I can fully accept the title of a D'Alikar. Besides, my adventure seems to have had a connection with Balew's past."

"How do you mean?" Latham's head tilted back slightly, and he appeared to be looking at Gera over the bridge of his nose. "What could your personal affairs have to do with the battles of a D'Alikar?"

"I was trailing a patrol of Crimson Guards which met another patrol followed by Balew and his rangers. That was the night he was killed. It was simple bad luck that started the fight. Ennis reacted when he lost the connection to the sword. A guardsman went into the forest to investigate the noise, and the battle started."

"Were you able to capture any prisoners?" Sanchere asked. "Were you able to discover why the two groups met?"

"Forget that," Kegan said. "Did any of the Bloods escape?"

"None got away, but we weren't able to keep any of them alive, either," Gera answered. "My traveling companion killed the last two before he could be stopped. I'm afraid he's a little bloodthirsty once the fighting starts."

"I need to raise a mug with this warrior," Kegan said with a smile.

"Yes," Latham said, "he sounds just like your kind of brawler. Kill them all first, then ask questions. Perhaps he'll transfer to that barbaric clutch you call rangers."

Sanchere cut into the conversation before the big D'Alikar could be goaded into losing his temper.

"Gera, could you hear what was said before the fighting started? What brought them together?"

"It looked like a supply run of some sort, but nothing very exciting. The group I followed was transporting weapons, picks, and shovels. Balew's patrol had a few packs of uncut jewels, a little gold, and some kind of light blue ore that no one here knows anything about."

"I told you! You can't trust anyone involved with saca or that blizzards-be-damned Institute. It's nelamite." Kegan clenched his hands as he spoke. "Those damn Bloods are involved with the cursed Bakri! That must have been the group of men Balew trailed from the mountains."

Gera tilted his head to the side, trying to follow the course of the conversation. Tagre caught his eye.

"Balew was in position to make a raid on a Bakri patrol when he saw a group of men meet with the cave dwellers. He decided to track them to find out who would be dealing with Bakri."

Latham nodded his head.

"It appears the barbarian is correct," he said. "They must be tied together somehow, but the Crimson Guard has only been formed in the last eighty summers. The D'Alikars have been battling the Bakri for more than five hundred. What possible motive could the guardsmen have for dealing with our enemies? What's the connection?"

"Why do they need a reason? They're blood and ashes sagias after all!" Kegan's face was red, even in the firelight.

Tagre turned to Gera.

"It was Balew's men who were discovered and started the fighting. I'll wager Tyre Staghorn's son was close enough to hear what was being said."

Gera bowed his head at the compliment.

"I heard a little before all hells broke loose."

He relayed the snippets of conversation he had been able to catch. The comments about "wanting a war" drew surprised glances between Tagre and Latham. They stepped to one side where they began a whispered conversation.

Gera almost laughed out loud every time Tagre opened his mouth. Latham did most of the talking, using hand gestures to drive home his points. But the moment the smaller D'Alikar began to speak, Latham instantly closed his mouth and leaned over to listen. For his part, Kegan spent the next few moments pacing back and forth in front of the flames, everything about his manner saying he was done talking and ready for action. Every few strides, his hand wandered toward the sword strapped across his back, but then he would jerk it away without grabbing the hilt.

Gera glanced sideways at Sanchere and noticed that, once again, the carefree smile rested on the man's face. The man noticed the movement and turned away from the discussion between the two D'Alikars. His grin grew wider, as if he and Gera were in on a joke that no one else had heard.

"They're good men," he said, leaning his head toward the pair. "They were brothers, you know. Identical twins, actually."

Gera blinked twice and shook his head before staring at the pair again. He turned his attention back to Sanchere when he heard the man chuckle.

"Ha, not them. The first two men to hold those swords were twin brothers from Galadon. Tagre and Latham work together better than any two people I've ever seen. According to Navis, it's always been that way for the holders of those weapons. The bones remember, and they bind the pair. But those two, put them together, and they'll devise a plan or figure out a riddle better than any kingdom of wise men combined. Even the pair before them weren't as good as they are as a team. That's why they and their clutches always travel together. Of course," he turned back to the men, "I don't know if we could separate them if we tried."

Tagre and Latham walked to the fire again.

"The Bakri and the Sacara Institute have an agreement," Latham said, his normal voice signifying the end of the discussion. "They're trading weapons and equipment for the money needed to finance starting a war between Palamor and Crandor. I, we, also think they're behind the rising tensions between Spirache and Lebesh."

"If that's true, you won't like what I've heard in the past few days," Sanchere said. "There's been talk of fighting between Salche and Abdalain."

"Damn the bloody diggers and sagias," Kegan said. "Why would they want war everywhere at once?"

The answer to Kegan's question had obviously not been agreed upon by Tagre and Latham. They glanced away from each other as silence surrounded the group, each man searching for a reason behind the madness.

After a few moments, Gera cleared his throat.

"I once watched three dogs fight over the same bone," he said, hesitating over the words. He ignored Latham opening his mouth, only to be stopped by Tagre. "The smallest of the three stayed on the outside, nipping at the two bigger dogs' heels, remaining out of the trouble, while they fought. Once the winner was decided between the two larger dogs, he jumped in and took down the tired and injured mutt. It was easy for him, despite his lack of size." Gera glanced around the other four men. "How strong is the Crimson Guard? Could they be a threat to some kingdoms if their armies were already beaten and bloodied by war?"

Latham snorted.

"Not even then," he said. "Not by themselves."

"Not just with men and arms. But what could a school full of trained sagias do to help them in a war?" Sanchere asked.

The group stood in stunned silence at the prospect of that much devastation and killing. It remained hard to imagine anyone being so devoid of human emotion that they could devise such an evil plan.

"This isn't something we can solve this night," Sanchere continued after a while. "I'll leave in the morning for Placado Island to see what Navis thinks about what's happening. If I can find a ship right away, I can be there in three hands. I might even try to find out more about Salche and Abdalain while I'm in Xenon. Kegan, you go ahead and meet with Gera in Nason." He paused for a breath and rubbed his eyes. "All of you, if you can find new recruits, go ahead and take on as many as will say the oath to join your rangers. I've a terrible feeling we're going to need a lot of help if the Bakri and Sacara have formed an alliance."

Farewells passed between the D'Alikars, along with vows to meet again in four nights. Gera quickly relayed to Kegan the amount and types of weapons they had taken from the Crimson Guard patrols so the big D'Alikar could plan for more rangers on the road to Nason.

Gera did as Ennis had instructed and imagined removing the choker from his neck. He felt his mind drifting along the path, floating in the shadows and dark, but this time no visions haunted his passing. Something began to pull at his mind, guiding him, and he felt his body again. His chest rose and blood flowed through his veins. The cold metal of the collar weighed down his right hand, and he was whole.

Gera opened his eyes and found Ennis seated on the ground beside him under a starlit sky. A shadow, darker than the surrounding night, moved by his feet and Nava's green eyes stared at him from the black. The flames of the funeral fire had died to just glowing embers, telling him he had been in the meeting place with the other D'Alikars for quite a while.

Turning back to his lieutenant, Gera spoke with as much confidence as he could muster. Even so, he heard the waver in his voice.

"Get some sleep, Ennis. It might be the last good night's rest you have for a long time."

wirling, gray nothingness roiled and heaved against itself. A haze hung in the air, permeating the void and leaving its essence everywhere in the boundless area. No fire existed to produce smoke, no moisture to make fog. Instead, the gray only spoke of how it could be, would be, somewhere else in existence.

Creatures, lacking solid forms, floated in the veil. They searched for prey to stalk, to devour, to suckle until their life was stolen away. Raw, uncensored emotions trailed in the wake of the beasts, hunting for someone to cling to, desperate for a way to survive.

In the eye of this activity sat a black mass. The formless fliers dove into, around, and through the object with complete freedom. It radiated no emotions itself—no fear, no comfort, no loathing, no love—it simply existed. Only power flowed from the body in darkness.

A darker gray manifestation appeared in the void and moved

toward the black center. Fast or slow, near or far—they were inadequate descriptions of how it moved. Time and distance meant nothing in a place of thoughts, dreams, and terrors.

"Yes, my beloved master." A powerful thought erupted from the gray newcomer. "Your servant is here for your bidding."

The answer returned in as great a magnitude as a campfire's heat compared to the molten inferno of a forge, with the promise of even more power still hidden beneath its surface.

"The one who can end our battle has been found."

"Can, my master? Not will?"

"The first step has been taken, but there are forces at work who still oppose our goals, perhaps even among us. They will try to stop our champion, and I cannot yet see if they will succeed. The pin has only now been removed from the scales, and we may need to wait for some time to find which way they will tip. The enemy has gained an advantage."

"Shall I go to aid our champion, my master?"

"No. Everything that can be done, has been done. At the right time, in the right way, the helper will come to you to ask for your help. You must only prepare and wait for the call. For right or wrong, the end is coming."

"And if the summons never arrives, my master?"

"Then we will lose this battle, and I fear for all that we have accomplished, my servant."

The void convulsed at the thought.

ABOUT THE AUTHOR

Kirk Dougal is an award-winning author who grew up with a book in one hand and a bat or ball in the other. He lives in Ohio with his wife and four children.

*To learn more about upcoming releases, cover reveals, or where Kirk will be appearing, please go to his website at kirkdougal.com.*

Printed in Great Britain
by Amazon